Marie Antoinette

Marie Antoinette

A NOVEL

by

F. W. KENYON

THOMAS Y. CROWELL COMPANY
New York

Manufactured in the United States of America
by the Vail-Ballou Press, Inc., Binghamton, New York

LIBRARY OF CONGRESS CATALOG CARD NO. 56-5696

Marie Antoinette

Part I

ONE

THE GIRL LOOKED IN MILD SURPRISE AT THE TWITTERING LADIES-IN-waiting who surrounded her.

"I am expected to undress?"

Yes, they assured her, with little giggles, she was expected to undress.

"I am to take off *all* my clothes?"

Yes, yes, most certainly all of them.

"But—*why?*" she demanded.

One of her ladies gave a pouting explanation. "They are Austrian clothes. It has been decreed by the French court that the wife of the Dauphin cannot enter France in any but French clothes. Married to the Dauphin, she must, in all things, be French."

Marie Antoinette laughed scornfully. "The silly conceit of these French courtiers! Still, I expect it will be fun." She struck a haughty attitude in front of her ladies. "Very well, undress me."

It was a pity, the fourteen-year-old girl reflected, that Mama, while hinting darkly about the wedding night, had failed to give her warning of this earlier ceremonial undressing. Mama, of course, especially during those last days in Vienna, had not been quite herself. There had been a surprising agitation, an unbelievable casting aside of the dignity and imperiousness which she, Empress of Austria, almost always wore. Funny to think of Mama bending over you with tears in her eyes, asking God to forgive her if this marriage which she had wanted with all her heart brought her youngest daughter, her little Toinette, even one moment of unhappiness.

1

Her Austrian ladies, serving her for the last time, had all but completed their task. Kicking off her shoes, she stood first on one foot, then on the other while they removed her stockings with respectful fingers. All that now remained was the fine linen shift. She clung to it for a moment, feeling for the first time a little pang of fear.

"This Louis Augustus, is he handsome or ugly?" she begged. "Am I going to love him or hate him?"

"He is the Dauphin," came the prompt reply. "Some day he will be King of France. Nothing else matters."

Nothing else matters . . . That was what Mama, in her saner, matchmaking moments, had said. That, when you came to think of it, was what you yourself had echoed. And with enthusiasm, so much enthusiasm! You had known, from your earliest conscious thought, who and what you were, and what your destiny was likely to be. Of royal birth yourself, you married one of royal birth and, for reasons of state, bore royal children. In you rested the balance of power between Austria and France and the hope of a lasting peace. If love and happiness were the result of this political marriage, so much the better; if hate and unhappiness, so much the worse. You, as an individual, counted for nothing. Yet Mama had wept and prayed, and you— What had you thought? Queen of France some day and the fun of it all. A fig for weighty conjecture, a fig for political expediency! Versailles, though some spoke of it as a den of iniquity, a cesspool of intrigue, was a marvellous fairy palace in which, when the old king died, you would rule undisputed, the fairy queen.

Laughing gaily now, Marie Antoinette straightened her shoulders and threw back her hair.

"Come! Remove the shift!"

Naked, she was no longer a girl, not fully a woman. Her fair hair, shot with red-gold lights, hung loosely about her slender shoulders, a halo which cast a warm glow over her flawless limbs, her young small breasts. She rose on her toes and stretched her arms in delight. Her eyes, never serious for long, sparkled merrily.

"Well, let me see my fine French clothes."

The new clothes were brought for her inspection. She fingered the French silk, the French lace, the French linen. With a shrug she nodded her approval.

"Dress me at once. I find it chilly on this island."

This island in the middle of the Rhine was an isolated piece

2

of land lying between French and Austrian territory. On it stood this hastily built but quite magnificent pavilion containing two sets of anterooms separated by a large hall. What a pleasant little game the ambassadors of France and Austria had invented for themselves! Here, changing her clothes in an Austrian anteroom, she was, officially, on Austrian territory. Presently, on entering the hall and reaching the center of it, she would be on French territory. Such a game might well have been invented in the nursery by her sisters and her brothers.

"Your Highness is satisfied?"

She realized that she was fully dressed again. With tapering slim fingers she touched the feathery folds of the white dress. The smoothness of the purest of silk delighted her. She wriggled her toes in the shoes which had been fashioned for her by the royal shoemaker in Paris. The softness of the fine leather was sheer luxury.

"More than satisfied. Now you may dress my hair."

Her ladies chattered excitedly as they arranged the abundant tresses in the still-prevalent Pompadour fashion. One of them remarked with a well-bred sneer that little was now remembered of the King of France's late mistress but an attractive hair style. Doubtless the King, with Madame la Comtesse Dubarry at his side, gave not a thought to the dead Marquise de Pompadour.

"Is it true," Marie Antoinette asked, frowning, "that Madame Dubarry was born in the gutter?"

Yes, it was true, they told her.

"And was once a serving wench in a tavern?"

"That, and *worse*," one of the ladies giggled.

"What a disgusting man the King must be! Shall I be expected to meet this creature at Versailles?"

Nothing was more certain, they told her.

"Then I shall cut her," Marie Antoinette said firmly.

When her hair was dressed to her satisfaction and she had examined her reflection approvingly in the mirrors held before her, Count Starhemberg was summoned. He, the best man who had accompanied her from Vienna, entered the room with so solemn an expression on his angular face that Marie Antoinette burst into a fit of laughter.

"Gracious, how very grave you look!"

The count clicked his heels together. "It is a very grave moment, your Highness."

Ceremoniously he led her from the anteroom. In the hall, a

long lofty room hung with costly tapestries, her ladies and all the other members of her Austrian suite formed themselves into a solid group behind her. A long table had been placed down the center of the hall. At the other side of it, waiting in silence, stood her French suite, elegant ladies and gentlemen of King Louis the Fifteenth's court.

As Count Starhemberg began to lead her round the table she felt another little pang of fear. She thought with longing of her mother's court in faraway Vienna where she had always been the center of interest, the spoiled darling of the whole family, the whole court. She thought too of the triumphant journey from Vienna to the French border: at every halt—and with so large a train there had been many halts—crowds had gathered to cheer her, admire her, bow before her. It had all been so gay, whereas now, in this frightening, silent room . . . !

As she drew back, the pressure of the count's hand warned her to remember who she was. Her lower lip, that Habsburg lip which people said was the only flaw in her beauty, quivered noticeably. Biting it, she stepped forward hesitantly. Round the table now, she was on French territory at last, and glancing over her shoulder she saw, with tears stinging her eyes, that her Austrian attendants were backing from the hall, disappearing, forever it seemed, from sight.

From her new attendants, shattering the silence, came a rising babble of voices, French voices. It swamped her utterly, this French atmosphere, foreign and frightening. In a moment she was surrounded. There were faces everywhere, faces in a waking nightmare. One in particular, that of an elderly lady, heavily painted, heavily powdered, loomed closer than the rest. She choked back a little cry of dismay. Her knowledge of the French language, gained so painfully, entirely deserted her.

The count made a stiff-sounding presentation.

"Your Highness's chief lady-in-waiting. Madame la Comtesse de Noailles."

Madame de Noailles curtsied. Her painted face broke into a brief smile and from her scarlet lips came a few quick words of welcome, not in French, but in the girl's native tongue. This, an unexpected kindness when the world seemed so cold, was too much for Marie Antoinette. With a little sob she threw her arms round the comtesse's neck.

"Ah, come, come, your Highness."

4

Madame de Noailles still spoke in German. Her tone was kindly enough, yet faintly impatient, faintly reproving. She sounded just like Mama, Mama who would have been shocked at this lamentable lack of dignity. Marie Antoinette stood back and tilted up her chin, though the too-full Habsburg lip still quivered.

"I am ready to proceed," she stammered.

"We must of course speak French," Madame de Noailles murmured pleasantly.

With a tremendous effort Marie Antoinette repeated herself in French, whereupon Madame de Noailles flinched visibly. Oh, it was a perfectly well-bred flinch but there was in her eyes an unmistakable French mockery. Having been prepared to love her, the girl now hated her. Hated her quite violently. Let them like it or not, the French court *and* Madame de Noailles would have to put up as best they could with her German accent.

The Abbé Vermond was now at her side.

She was prepared now to hate him too, this abbé who, months ago, had been sent to Vienna by the King of France to superintend her education. This would never have happened except for the fact that the French ambassador, having conversed with her several times, had found her distressingly ignorant. The Abbé Vermond, on arrival, had also found her distressingly ignorant. She knew nothing of history, at least of French history, which from the French point of view amounted to the same thing. Worse, the little French she knew was well nigh unintelligible, to French ears. She could of course dance, the abbé was willing to admit that. She was very light on her feet, quite prettily graceful, and she even had a slight appreciation of music, but name of a name the appreciation, like the music itself, was unhappily German.

She glanced quickly from the abbé to the comtesse, and addressing them jointly, her accent deliberately exaggerated, she said loudly:

"It must be remembered that I have only one master in France, the Dauphin my husband."

The look of surprise on their faces filled her with a wicked delight. She clapped her hands and laughed merrily, and her small feet kicked into a little dance.

"How good it is to be in France! What fun it's going to be, what delicious fun!"

5

TWO

Madame la comtesse de Noailles, jolted by the sudden stopping of the coach, woke from a fitful slumber and looked vaguely about her. She began to brush from the shoulders of her velvet travelling coat the powder which had fallen from her hair. As she did so she glanced out of the window.

"Merciful heavens!" she cried, fully awake and vastly agitated, "his Majesty the King!"

The Abbé Vermond, waking too, yawned widely.

"Well, well, we must stir ourselves."

The journey from the French border, where merrymaking had reached a feverish pitch, had been yet another triumphal progress. They were in the forest of Compiègne now, and here, Marie Antoinette had been warned, she would come face to face with the King and his grandson the Dauphin.

Though the warmth of the welcome in town and village had excited her, the scolding little lectures of the abbé on the one hand, the comtesse on the other, had first angered then bored her. The abbé had pestered her with silly questions about French history, the comtesse had spoken incessantly of court etiquette, while both, quite remorselessly, had corrected her grammar and tried, as they put it, to iron out her German accent. Ah well, all that was at an end now; the King and her husband the Dauphin awaited her.

She looked out of the window herself. There, in the near distance, the King's grand coach had drawn to a halt and magnificently arrayed ladies and gentlemen from the many coaches of the royal cavalcade were crowding about it. There were soldiers too in gleaming armor, and drummers and trumpeters by the dozen. In the warm spring sunshine it was an inspiring, exciting picture. And for me, she thought, all of it for me! Beside herself with excitement she was ready to leap down from the coach.

"Wait!" Madame de Noailles commanded.

Even as she spoke, the royal fanfare echoed and re-echoed

through the forest. A special sort of music ringing on the clear air, it almost seemed as if the great trees were bowing and curtsying before it.

Unable to hold back longer Marie Antoinette flung open the door. Horrified, Madame de Noailles still restrained her. His Majesty, she said, must make the first move. Etiquette decreed it.

"Etiquette, etiquette!" the girl shrilled, and pointed a slim quivering finger. "Madame, I have a new name for you. Now and forever I shall always call you Madame Etiquette!"

With that she slipped beneath the restraining hand, jumped lightly to the ground and ran to greet the King. His Majesty had now descended from his own coach and was watching her with his head on one side. Something in the stillness of his figure made her cease to run. She remembered that a princess, especially a princess who was also a future queen, must walk not only in beauty but with elegance. "And dignity too," she could hear Mama's voice reproving her. A moment later she was standing before the King. Mama had told her what to do. She fell on her knees at his feet, aware as she did so that he was standing on a thick soft carpet.

Slowly she looked up at him. She was curious and just a little nervous. So this was the fabulous Louis, about whom the whole of Europe, shocked and fascinated by his dissolute habits, had gossiped for years. How many mistresses had he set up at Versailles? Scores of them, if gossip spoke truly. And what of the inmates of that shameful Parc aux Cerfs, the brazen girls, taken for a night or two, then carelessly set aside? She had wondered many times about this, not quite understanding what 'taken' really meant.

She was looking closely at his face as he gazed down on her. What a dreadful disappointment! How old was he? Sixty? Sixty, but at one glance you would say eighty. Eighty and disgustingly dissipated, cheeks deeply lined, heavy jowls quivering as he moved his head. Horrible, horrible! And yet the eyes, bloodshot as they were, had a kindly, friendly look. They were twinkling too, disarmingly, quite boyishly.

"Delightful," he murmured, "delightful."

She lowered her eyes. "Your Majesty . . ."

He sighed dramatically. "If only I were young again, standing in my grandson's place!" He raised her to her feet and kissed her moistly on the brow. "Welcome to France, my sweet child."

7

"Thank you, Sire," she said dutifully, and longed to wipe her brow with the back of her hand.

He turned abruptly. "Louis, my boy!"

Thus commanded, the Dauphin came tumbling down from the royal coach and joined his grandfather. Marie Antoinette looked at him shyly. Her first impression was that his silken clothes sat oddly on his plump ungainly figure. He might well have been a stable boy dressed up for some special fete. Handsome or ugly? she had asked. He was neither, and certainly he was clumsy. And the way he stared, stared without any appearance of *seeing*. She hid her disappointment. He was not quite sixteen. Perhaps in a year or so he would begin to show a necessary improvement. He is the Dauphin of France, she reminded herself, nothing else matters.

"Closer, closer!" the King urged, and to Marie Antoinette he explained, "My grandson is distressingly short-sighted."

The Dauphin took a nervous step towards her and then, for one brief moment, his eyes came to life and a wavering smile lit his solemn fat face.

"You see? All they said, and more," the King enthused.

The Dauphin, apparently speechless, merely nodded.

"Embrace her, my boy. Come, come, embrace her!"

Dutifully the boy placed his arms lightly round her shoulders and brushed her cheek with his lips. This done he stood back, blinking.

"Ah me," the King said dreamily, "this takes me back so many years." Ridiculous tears filled his eyes. Then he recollected himself and coughed. "Time moves relentlessly and drags us with it." He offered Marie Antoinette his arm. "Come, child."

He helped her into the royal coach, signalled to the Dauphin to follow and gruntingly climbed up himself. The final stage of the journey to Versailles had begun.

THREE

IT HAD ALL SEEMED SO UNREAL.

Every single incident, from the meeting in the forest to this last, the solemn blessing of the nuptial bed, was invested with a dreamlike quality.

She tried to assemble things in their correct order. Yesterday, after a drive through the crowded streets of Versailles, the arrival at the palace. Strange to have discovered that there was a town by that name as well as a palace, but she had been careful not to remark on this in case they spoke again of her ignorance. Many of the people who had crowded the streets of the town had later pushed their way into the palace and followed her, cheering madly, right up the grand marble staircase. After that she had been sent early to bed, with Madame Etiquette scolding her slightly, but the Abbé Vermond, kinder than usual, patting her encouragingly on the shoulder. She remembered the restless, excited night, the sudden waking in the strange room, not knowing where you were, Vienna or Versailles, not caring, yet caring dreadfully. Missing Mama too, hating and loving it all; thinking of the wicked old King and doubting, in one clear moment, that he really did remember his own bride of so many years ago; thinking of her husband the Dauphin, who had addressed not half-a-dozen words to her, and resolving that if, like his grandfather, he set up mistress after mistress, she would loathe him and make him suffer.

She remembered the formal wedding ceremony in the King's chapel, the lords and ladies in their brocades and silks, the archbishop blessing the wedding ring, the Dauphin placing it on her finger, then kneeling with her at the altar. Long and tiring, boring and exciting, followed by the signing of the marriage contract, her own signature written jerkily with a trembling hand, *Marie Antoinette Josepha Jeanne,* once of Austria, now of France. The old King watching, stiff-kneed and querulous from having knelt so long at his prayer desk. The Dauphin watching too, fat and

9

uncomfortable, actually sweating, in his heavy robe of the Order of the Holy Ghost.

More clearly she remembered her first real public appearance on the balcony, the vast wings of the palace extending to right and to left. It seemed as if the whole of Paris had flocked into the courtyard beneath to catch a glimpse of her, to hear the King cry, "My children, I give you your future Queen." What a pity that heavy rain had scattered these cheering people, ruined the fountain display and left the gardens desolate.

But later, within the palace, all had been gay and happy as the elite of France had laughed, danced and paid her homage, had gathered round, breathless with admiration, while on the arm of her shy and silent husband she had withdrawn from the feast to prepare herself for what Mama had called her Duty, ordeal though it might be.

She had thought of Mama's enigmatic words while they were undressing her. She thought of them again now as, in her night-gown, she stood with the old King, watching the archbishop sprinkling the nuptial bed with holy water. Her Duty, ordeal though it might be . . . You were married with pomp and cere-mony, you were put to bed with pomp and ceremony, and in the course of time, with pomp and ceremony also, you bore your husband a child. That, and very little else, was all she knew. She looked timidly round the King's bulky figure at the Dauphin, standing there in his long pleated nightshirt. He caught her eye, blushed and looked hurriedly away. A duty for him too, and perhaps an ordeal also. An ordeal the *first* time, she had heard someone giggle, then the greatest fun. Well, that was what she wanted from life, fun, and as much as possible.

The archbishop drew back from the bed and, more majestic than any king, stalked from the room, causing the courtiers who crowded about the door to fall back in confusion.

The King made a great show of clearing his throat.

"Dear innocent children," he murmured emotionally. "Ah me, how well I remember my own wedding night. How sweet my wife was and how I adored her."

Marie Antoinette almost laughed. And treated her shamefully in later years, by all accounts!

"Nevertheless," he added, patting her shoulder, "you remind me more of your namesake, Toinette."

"Toinette, Sire?"

10

"Madame la Marquise de Pompadour, God rest her soul."

To be likened to a royal mistress! Intolerable, quite intolerable!

"You must be kind to each other," he went on. "Kind and understanding. And you, Louis—" his voice grew stern—"you must be gentle always, and faithful till the day you die."

"Yes," the boy whispered, his eyes downcast.

The King gave each a little push forward.

"Now into bed with you!"

The courtiers surged forward but he spread out his arms to hold them back. When they persisted he turned on them and with lusty panting cries drove them from the bedchamber. He came back for a moment to draw the bed curtains across, to say, "God bless you, my children, God grant you a fruitful union." When he had gone and all seemed unnaturally quiet, the boy stirred heavily in the bed.

"The day I was born," he said, his voice muffled in the tent-like darkness, "a courier fell from his horse and broke his neck." He was speaking nervously, phrasing his sentences in little jerks. "The courier was taking the news of my birth to the King. Everybody said it was a bad omen."

Marie Antoinette wriggled. "I think it's silly to take any notice of omens."

He left her comment unanswered. "Afterwards, when my mother and father were driving to Notre Dame, there was a demonstration. The people were hungry and wanted bread. That wasn't good, either."

"I don't care much for bread, Louis."

"The day you were born there was a tragedy too."

"There was?"

"November 2nd, 1755. A dreadful earthquake in Portugal, at Lisbon."

"How nice to know you have memorized my birthday."

Not accusingly, merely stating a fact, he said, "You dropped ink on the contract when you were signing your name."

"Did I? I don't remember. Do you think that a bad omen too?"

He laughed shakily. "No, Toinette. Everybody says I'm clumsy. It made me happy to know you could be clumsy too."

Angrily she cried, "I prefer not to be known at Versailles as Toinette."

11

She knew he was frowning over this. "They call you Toinette. Your family and your friends, I mean."

"A baby name, and now I'm a married woman. And besides, that was Pompadour's name. I refuse to answer to the same name as the King's late mistress. That is understood, Louis?"

"That is understood—Marie. And—and I do admire you for it."

"You do?"

"Very much indeed."

"Then I forgive you."

"For what, Marie?"

"For telling me about my clumsiness with the ink."

After that there seemed no more to be said, and the silence which had fallen between them lengthened painfully. She knew from his breathing that Louis had moved away from her, was sitting near the edge of the great wide bed.

"Louis . . ."

"Yes, Marie?"

"I thought you had fallen asleep."

"I thought *you* had done the same."

"Are you nervous?"

"I was never so frightened in my life."

She too had never been so frightened in her life, but she would rather have died than admit it.

"I wish someone had told me what to do," he blurted out.

"You have never done it before, Louis?" She was shocked to find that her teeth were chattering. "Never?"

"Never."

"Nor have I."

He yawned loudly. "Perhaps we should just go to sleep."

Impulsively she reached out for his hand and took it in hers. He edged closer and she placed his hand against her breast. The palm was rough, there were callouses at the base of the fingers. Not the palm, surely, of a prince! Yet the roughness and the growing warmth on her cool firm flesh sent a tingling through her whole body. She twisted quickly and lay against his broad muscular chest. Very slowly his arms went round her. She could hear as she lay there the deep quickened beating of his heart.

"Funny, isn't it, Louis. We only met each other yesterday."

"I think you are very pretty."

"You can't see me in the dark."

"I remember what you looked like in the forest, with the sun

12

on your hair. And today at the ceremony. I have never liked girls, but now, because of you, something queer has happened to me." He sounded lost and bewildered. "Something *here*," and he placed her hand against his heart. "It— Oh, Marie, it *stifles* me."

"It stifles me too, Louis," she whispered.

FOUR

SHE WOKE AND LOUIS WAS NOT AT HER SIDE. SHE PARTED THE BED-curtains. He was nowhere to be seen. It was a bright fine morning with yellow sunshine streaming through the windows. She let the curtains fall back into place, clasped her arms round her legs and sat immovable with her chin on her knees. Duty . . . ordeal . . . she pondered. Ordeal? There had been no ordeal in it. Pain? No pain at all, though Louis had mumbled something about pain. A woman felt pain, she had once been told, a man no pain at all. Very odd, that. Gradually her own tension had lessened, leaving in its place a feeling of bewilderment, disappointment, a great nothingness. Presently she had fallen asleep . . . *That* sort of thing, it seemed, was neither as exciting nor as important as her imagination last night had led her to believe.

She reached suddenly for the bell-cord and tugged it vigorously. A waiting woman came hurrying into the room.

"Where is the Dauphin?" Marie Antoinette demanded.

The waiting woman peered inside the curtains and threw up her hands in dismay. Louis, obviously, was not where she expected him to be, where, of a certainty, he ought to be.

"Search for him," Marie Antoinette said imperiously. "Acquaint him with the fact that her royal Highness the Dauphine is now awake."

The waiting woman fled, to be replaced a few moments later by Madame Etiquette, bleary-eyed, her dressing-gown rumpled, her silly pointed nightcap still on her head.

"Name of a name, what has happened to him?"

Marie Antoinette was on the point of tears now. "I believe he likes riding. Perhaps he has gone for an early morning ride."

A message was sent to the royal stables. Back came the reply that the Dauphin had not gone riding. At this point three stern, middle-aged ladies, all wearing nightcaps, filed silently into the room. Vaguely, Marie Antoinette remembered their aristocratic faces. They were the three spinster daughters of the King, Louis' maiden aunts, who were now *her* maiden aunts. The haughtiest

14

took a pace forward. She stepped out like a soldier on parade, or else a horse. Yes, that was it, more like a horse than a soldier.

"Well, did you quarrel, child?"

"No indeed!" Marie Antoinette said indignantly.

"He has gone for a walk," suggested the second maiden aunt.

"With the dogs," added the third.

"You are sure there was no quarrel?" the first demanded. "I, since no doubt you have forgotten our names, am Madame Adelaide. Behind me is Sophie. The one who is giggling is Victoire. There are really four of us, but Louise lives at the Convent of Saint-Denis. She, heaven help her, is a Carmelite nun. You are sure there was no quarrel?"

"Quite sure, Madame Adelaide."

A message came back from the kennels. The Dauphin had not been seen there. His dogs were still on the chain.

Marie Antoinette buried her head in the pillow and burst into tears.

"There, there," Madame Adelaide said soothingly, "the truth of the matter is this: Berri has gone to see the King."

Marie Antoinette turned and sat up. "Berri?"

"On state occasions, Louis. In private, among the family, we call him Berri. Always have done."

Marie Antoinette remembered that Louis Augustus, apart from being the Dauphin, was also the Duc de Berri.

"He has gone to see my father," Madame Adelaide went on heartily, "to tell him how happy you made him last night. My father, being the sort of man he is, would expect it and enjoy it. You did make poor Berri happy?"

"Of course," Marie Antoinette said quickly, but she very much doubted it.

"That's what Berri has done, I'll gladly wager my finest horse on it," Madame Adelaide cried.

Marie Antoinette, having been taught that all forms of gambling were wicked, shrank back from this.

"My finest horse against one gold livre, you can surely afford that, child. You hesitate? Oh come, you live at Versailles now!"

Marie Antoinette brushed the tears from her cheeks. What an odd amusing creature she was, this maiden aunt.

"Very well," she agreed.

A page was sent to the King's apartments, not to burst in on his Majesty, of course, but to make discreet inquiries in the royal ante-

15

room. Back he came, a bright-eyed cherub of a boy, who seemed for the moment to have nothing to say for himself.

"Well?" Madame Adelaide rasped.

He bowed deeply. "His Majesty is still in the apartments of Madame Dubarry."

Madame Adelaide's eyes flashed dangerously. "Pah!" The single ejaculation gave Marie Antoinette a complete understanding of the hatred felt by Madame Adelaide for the royal mistress. "And his Highness the Dauphin?"

The page bowed deeply again. "No one has seen him, Madame."

For two hours the palace was in an uproar, with pages, *valets de chambre* and ushers dashing hither and thither, and every guard alerted. In the end, during a hasty breakfast, it was Madame Adelaide herself who solved the mystery.

"The roofs, of course. He does it often. His favorite occupation."

"Favorite occupation?" Marie Antoinette echoed.

"Chasing cats across the roofs. Highly diverting, I imagine."

Induced to come down, Louis presently entered Madame Adelaide's drawing-room with a large ginger cat under his arm. He had a sheepish expression on his face, which was smeared with dirt, and his clothes were in shreds. He thrust the cat at Marie Antoinette.

"One of my favorites. I wanted to catch him for you."

The girl tossed her head. "I hate cats."

Her displeasure, she was quick to note, left him shamefaced and tongue-tied.

"Most inconsiderate of you, Berri, to frighten us all like that," Madame Adelaide said sternly.

Marie Antoinette gave him a scathing look. "He could have broken his neck for all *I* cared!"

"Fine language, this, for a bride on her first morning," said a breezy voice.

The King was standing at the door, glancing lazily round the room. All rose to their feet and stood in silence, awaiting his Majesty's pleasure. He wore a fine cherry-colored coat, pink hose and black shoes with jeweled buckles, all of which, Marie Antoinette noticed as he sauntered forward, gave his lined face an older, more weary look.

"I have unpleasant news from Paris," he said gravely. "Last night, as you remember, the weather cleared and the people celebrated with a fireworks display. There was an explosion, and a

16

fire. The Rue Royale became jammed with frightened people. A hundred or more were crushed to death."

"A bad omen at his birth, another at his marriage!" Madame Adelaide gasped.

"A fig for bad omens!" Marie Antoinette cried impatiently.

"Really, child—"

"I care nothing for them, nothing at all." And to change the boring subject she impishly reminded Madame Adelaide of her wager. "You lost, Madame. You owe me a horse. Your finest, remember?"

"What's this, what's this?" the King inquired. "Gambling already?"

Marie Antoinette remembered Mama's stern face.

"Gambling is wicked," she said hurriedly. "I shall never engage in it again."

"But you will take the horse?" Madame Adelaide asked anxiously.

"Of a certainty she will," the King laughed.

"Of a certainty," Marie Antoinette echoed.

"And ride it at once?" he suggested.

Marie Antoinette clapped her hands. She liked sudden decisions where something new in the way of pleasure was concerned.

After she had changed into a riding costume, cherry-colored like the King's coat, she went with Louis to the stables. He had changed into riding clothes too, and had actually washed his face. Walking through the corridors of Versailles with him she became more aware than ever of his clumsiness. With none of the elegance of the courtier, he seemed to move by pushing his legs awkwardly forward from the knees. Oh well, she would have to put up with it. He was, whatever his shortcomings, heir to the throne.

As she tripped along at his side she chattered gaily about life in Vienna at her mother's court. There she had been permitted to do almost anything but ride a horse, and that had made her want a horse now more than anything else.

"A donkey, I was allowed a donkey. But a groom had to lead it. Sedate, but ridiculous, don't you think?"

She ran on gaily, talking of this and that, while Louis, a slow-moving lump of flesh and muscle at her side, answered with either a brief yes or no. At the stables, however, a complete change took place in him. He laughed and joked with the stable boys, he slapped his thighs, he stamped his feet. He was quite at home while she, conscious of her dignity, her high station, stood aloof and impatient.

Presently, when Louis had recollected himself enough to realize that his wife was with him, two horses were brought. In a kindly manner he drew her attention to Madame Adelaide's horse, the finest of her own stables, a sleek handsome chestnut.

"Gentle but keenly responsive," he said. "Not in the least likely to throw you."

His face beamed good-naturedly, his eyes were alight with pleasure. He was the happiest boy in the world.

"Let me help you mount."

She hesitated for one startled moment. "But it isn't a side-saddle!"

Louis chuckled. "Madame Adelaide and lots of ladies at Versailles scorn side-saddles. They ride astride, like men."

Marie Antoinette could see Mama's face. That frightening look of frozen horror! Recklessly she declared that if the ladies of Versailles rode astride, so would she. With a full-throated chuckle she pulled up the tight skirt of the riding costume and placed her foot in Louis' hands. Once mounted she seemed much too far from the ground, but it was a heady, thrilling feeling.

Looking up at her, Louis said seriously, "Those poor people who died in Paris last night. Ever since Papa King told us I've been wondering what to do. Now I know. I shall give all the money I possess to the relatives."

She looked at him in surprise. "That is very generous. How much do you possess?"

"Almost two thousand livres."

"Is that a lot of money?"

He frowned. "I suppose so. What do you think?"

She frowned too. Having no understanding of the cost of things it was hard to say. She remembered her dowry, the 200,000 florins mentioned in the marriage contract. But what was a florin, what was a livre?

Still frowning, Louis said, "I know my grandfather spends millions on Madame Dubarry, so two thousand can't be that much."

She shrugged, no longer interested. "I suppose you can do what you like with your own money."

Unaware of her lack of interest, he went on seriously, "I want the people to know that when I follow my grandfather on the

18

throne I'll be a good king. A father to my people. I do so want to be pious and just and good. And firm too, of course. A father must be firm with his people."

He was running on now, like a river in flood. "I have studied kingship. My best subject, you know, is history. Not that my tutors think me clever. They don't. My brothers are much cleverer. People think it a pity I am the eldest. Nobody really cares for me much. Only for my rank."

Marie Antoinette yawned pointedly, but there was no stopping him now.

"I find study very hard. They say my brain is half asleep, but I do try to wake it up. Indeed, Marie, I do. I am best with my hands. I like to work at the forge, and I can make clocks. Once I even made a printing press."

Marie Antoinette blinked down at him. "Gracious, what an occupation for a prince!"

"A lot of people say that, but I think my father would have understood. He was a good man, just and kind. Kind to my mother. He never hurt her by taking a mistress. At least, I don't think he did. He once told me to remember that all men are equal."

Marie Antoinette was amazed. "All men? Princes and peasants, for instance?"

"Yes."

"What awful nonsense, Louis! When you are king it will be by divine right. God will have given you absolute power."

"Yes," he said doubtfully, "and that frightens me. My father said the monarchy might fall unless we began to see that all men are equal. Grandfather laughed at him, of course. That was why I made the printing press."

Her interest was flagging again but he was still eager to confide in her.

"You see, Marie, I had written an essay on political morals. The next thing to do was to print it. My brothers helped me with the typesetting. They weren't keen, but they obliged me. I took the first copy straight to grandfather. He was amused at first, then very angry."

She could feel the horse moving nervously beneath her, as impatient to start off as she was.

"Why was he angry?"

"I said a king was just a man, in spite of his rank. He didn't seem to like that. He went purple in the face when he also read that a king needed to be an example of virtue and piety and religious zeal. Do you know what he did? He forbade me to print any more copies and he made me break the plates."

"I should think so!" she cried.

Louis flushed and grew silent. The hurt look on his face affected her surprisingly.

"I didn't mean to hurt your feelings," she said impulsively.

"I only did what I thought was right, Marie."

"No one can do more than that," she said wisely.

He took a deep breath. She could see that he was about to burst out again. She told him quickly that they had years and years in which to discuss *that* sort of thing, and reminded him that they were supposed to be going for a ride. He nodded disconsolately and mounted his own horse.

"How much better you look, sitting a horse than standing on the ground," she said. "Quite a commanding figure, Louis."

He smiled gratefully. "I am always happy on horseback. Are you nervous, Marie?"

She tossed her head.

"I mean," he amended, "not having ridden astride before."

"It is surely safer astride than side-saddle," she said haughtily.

"We'll take it quietly then, to begin with."

But she leaned towards him and, snatching the whip from his hand, gave her mount a sharp cut across the flanks. For the next five minutes she feared that the world was coming to an end, but somehow she managed to cling on and by accident more than anything else wisely gave the horse his head. After that, with the wind in her face, the trees rushing by, the burst of sunshine as clearing after clearing was passed, she began to enjoy herself. And Louis' shout as he galloped at her side, "What a fine seat you have—for a girl!" added to her enjoyment.

An hour later, when they were cantering back to Versailles, they were met and surrounded by a detachment of Royal Horse. In their midst was the Abbé Vermond, his face both anxious and angry. Behind rolled one of the royal coaches.

"The moment I was informed," the abbé cried, "I came in pursuit. Your Highness will dismount—" he threw up his arms. "Merciful heavens, and riding astride too! Your Highness will dismount and return to the palace in the coach."

"What nonsense is this?" she asked angrily.

"It has been expressly stated in the instructions from Vienna that your Highness will not, *at any time,* take more than a quiet ride on a donkey, the donkey led by a groom."

"Then you, Monsieur, would make an excellent mount," she said icily.

The abbé flushed, Louis giggled. Both the flush and the giggle made her feel happier. She dismounted and entered the coach, but then indignation got the better of her again. Mama had not the right to spoil her pleasures. It was insufferable!

Back at the palace she found a solemn group of people waiting for her. Madame Etiquette was there, and the three maiden aunts, as well as the Austrian Ambassador, Count Mercy-Argenteau. Even the King himself was there. Almost a state gathering, or an important council meeting. You would have thought that the peace of Europe was in the balance.

She looked only at Madame Adelaide. "A splendid horse, Madame. I enjoyed myself enormously."

"But astride!" the Abbé Vermond wailed.

The King laughed softly. "It must have been a most diverting sight."

"Her Highness will be stiff and sore tomorrow," Madame Etiquette commented.

Count Mercy-Argenteau stepped forward. He gave her his deferential little bow and his usual fatherly smile. He spoke gravely but his eyes twinkled.

"My dear, you have committed a very big sin."

"By riding astride?"

"By riding at all. We will do our best to keep it from your imperial mother, but it must not happen again."

The twinkling of his eyes forced her to smile at him. She had always liked Count Mercy, as most people called him, though she knew that in sending him as ambassador to Versailles Mama's chief intention was that he should keep a watch on her and make reports to Vienna. He was not an Austrian—he had been born in the Low Countries—but he was a good and faithful servant of his adopted country. She had heard him spoken of as shrewd and farsighted. He was wealthy, a man of independent means, and a bachelor. He would never be seduced, Mama had said, by the intrigues of the Court of Versailles. His clothes were expensive but plain. His habits, apart from the fact that he kept a mistress,

21

the same one for years and years, were austere. She had been urged by Mama to confide in him, listen to his advice, and trust him.

"If I may be permitted to ask a question," the King was drawling, "why this amazing prohibition?"

Mercy looked down his nose. "It is not considered ladylike, your Majesty. There is also the danger of horseback riding ruining her Highness's figure."

The King looked critically at Marie Antoinette. She felt herself reddening under the concentration of his lingering gaze, but she held her head high and stared right back at him.

"The child is slim," he remarked at length, "almost thin. She could do with a little widening of the hips. Still, the purpose for which she was born, and brought to France, will no doubt see to that, in time."

Her color deepened. She knew he was thinking of last night. So were all of them, everybody in the room. Their eyes were boring into her. Each was asking himself the same question. She wanted to run from their presence and hide in shame. She wanted to, but there was such a thing as dignity, and pride too. She resolved that when she knew she was pregnant—though just how she would know was more than she could say—she would keep the fact to herself, let them remain curious and anxious.

"Your Highness may of course ride a donkey, side-saddle," Mercy murmured. "The donkey—"

"Yes, yes! Led by a groom. I am not a child any more!"

The King yawned noisily, and that made her smile to herself. He and she had at least one thing in common, they were quickly bored by the stupidity of silly people. He made a lazy gesture, just a slight movement of the hand but clearly a royal dismissal. The others bowed, curtsied and backed from the room. He chuckled loudly and tweaked her ear.

"A donkey only, remember," he whispered.

"I hate them all!" she raged.

"Ah, a girl of spirit. Such spirit that even now she must be planning a little subterfuge. What, for instance, is wrong with a gentle, genteel donkey ride from the palace to a clearing in the woods where a horse is waiting? Eh, my dear?"

"What indeed!" she cried, and began to feel that she was growing to like this dreadful old man.

22

When he had ambled from the room Madame Adelaide returned to say that the excitement of the morning, the roof climbing, the prohibited horseback riding, had disturbed the routine of the new Dauphine's day. She uttered the word 'routine' in capital letters, making it sound like a depressing act of strict discipline.

"We shall begin afresh tomorrow. You will rise at nine, not later than ten. Berri, who always rises early, will have left your bed by then. You will immediately say your prayers, then begin your toilette. Did you say your prayers this morning?"

"No, I quite forgot."

"Tut, tut! The hairdresser will come at eleven, immediately after breakfast. At midday you will go to Mass. It is past midday now. Never again, on any account, must Mass be missed."

"Will the King be there?"

"That depends on his state of health. If ill he will fear he is dying and will go to Mass like a lamb. After Mass you will dine with Berri, always providing he hasn't run from you to make a lock or a clock or something equally ridiculous. After dining you will sit with poor Berri in his apartments. If he is reading history or writing a treatise meant to put the world in order you will sit in your own apartments, read, write and sew."

"Sew?" Marie Antoinette was appalled.

"I imagine that in *that* respect your pretty fingers are quite useless."

"Quite!"

"Practice, practice. In time you will be able to make *and* embroider a coat for the King."

"Never!"

Madame Adelaide smiled. "I hate sewing myself. However, to continue . . ."

"*Must* we?"

"In the late afternoon you will visit me and my two old-maid sisters. I, you understand, am a spinster, but *not* an old maid. There is, child, a nice distinction."

Marie Antoinette laughed politely. Obviously it was meant to be a subtle kind of joke.

"Ah, a sense of humor. Splendid! The Abbé Vermond will talk to you at, say, five o'clock, and your music teacher will instruct you for an hour. Between seven and eight, a brisk walk. Dinner or supper, or whatever you like to call it, at nine. The King is always expected but rarely comes. At eleven, or earlier, bed. Is all that perfectly clear?"

"Perfectly."

So for this, the ROUTINE, she had come to Versailles. Where was the delicious fun she had expected? What a dreadful mistake! There were more restrictions at Versailles than at home in Vienna under Mama's stern and watchful eye.

There was only one thing to do when you were in so dismal a frame of mind and that was sulk. Sulking meant not speaking. She began at once—oh, she was polite, frigidly polite—and kept it up for the rest of the day. The trouble was no one seemed to notice, which made it doubly difficult for a girl who was by nature friendly, gay and talkative. She kept it up until she and Louis were alone for the second time in the great curtained bed. She felt lost and lonely. The foreign atmosphere had engulfed her and the rapid colloquial French of her attendants had bewildered her. More sorry for herself than ever before she was ready to burst into tears of self-pity.

Louis touched her gently, inquiringly. "Poor little Marie . . ."

His touch, the unexpected kindness of his voice, brought a lump to her throat. Instinctively she flung herself into his arms and clung to him in the darkness.

Later, lying sleepless at his side, she felt a strange frustration. She felt cheated of an exciting something which she found herself desiring . . . not quite knowing what it was she desired, but still desiring it.

"Are you awake, Louis?" she whispered.

"Yes."

"It isn't what I expected."

"It isn't what I expected either."

"Getting married is disappointing."

"Yes."

"Goodnight, Louis."

"Goodnight, Marie."

FIVE

DINNER HAD BEEN OVER AN HOUR OR MORE AND MARIE ANTOINETTE
was growing fretful. She had been induced at last to begin work on
a coat for the King. This, and the fact that Louis had gone immediately after dinner to his workroom, had not improved her
temper. With a dramatic sigh she dropped her needle and glanced
at the aunts, one by one, at Madame Adelaide and her two shadows, Madame Victoire and Madame Sophie. Madame Adelaide sat
with a brooding, bad-tempered look on her face; the other two,
busy at their everlasting needlework, looked like two gray, down-
trodden seamstresses.

Seated on a stool by the fire was Louis' sister, Madame Elizabeth, a pretty, rather serious child of seven, while lying on the carpet at her feet were his two brothers, the Comte de Provence and
the Comte d'Artois. Provence was her own age, plump like Louis,
but with an engaging manner and a ready if spiteful wit. He was
much admired at court, spoken of as clever, highly intelligent. He
often paid her pretty compliments but she felt that it would never
be wise to trust him. Artois, two years younger, was slim and
quite graceful. He, following Provence's lead, was ready, she suspected, to resent her marriage which, if she bore a child, would
give neither of them much hope of some day mounting the throne.

Madame Adelaide rose abruptly. "That wretched woman!"

Marie Antoinette hid a smile. The 'wretched woman' was of
course Madame Dubarry.

"Her extravagance is rapidly bringing us all to the point of beg-
gary. What an old fool he is, that father of mine!"

Marie Antoinette drew her chair closer to the fire. It was the
end of December and bitterly cold. Forgetting the King's coat she
stretched out her hands to the warmth of the blazing logs. How
long now since she had come to France? Not more than seven
months, yet it seemed like seven years. Madame Adelaide's routine was well-established, but fortunately the monotony had been
relieved by a number of court balls and the Christmas festivities,

25

during which Versailles had resembled the fairy palace of her dreams. Madame Adelaide, in spite of her severity and rough manners, had of late shown a surprising kindness. Marie Antoinette smiled as she thought of the reason for this: all you had to do to please the old-maid aunt was sneer at Madame Dubarry behind her back and, when you chanced to meet her, cut her haughtily.

The door was flung open and Louis came shuffling into the room.

"What a disgusting sight!" Madame Adelaide exclaimed.

He was in shirt sleeves. Both sleeves were torn, the shirt was filthy and his brow was smeared with grime and sweat.

"I've been making a new kind of lock," he announced.

Provence scrambled to his feet. "Are we expected to congratulate you, Berri?"

"Poor Berri," Artois tittered, "should have been apprenticed to a blacksmith."

Madame Adelaide stamped her foot. "You forget yourselves, boys. Try and remember, Provence, you also, Artois, that Berri is the Dauphin, next in importance to the King. You owe him respect and obedience. Come! Apologize at once!"

The younger brothers obeyed with a poor grace. Insolently they begged his forgiveness and vowed eternal obedience. Louis accepted all this with a brief nod and an uncertain grin. Furious with him, Marie Antoinette suggested that he should go and wash before the King paid them a visit. Confused and tongue-tied he shuffled from the room without a backward glance. This infuriated her more than ever. First he should have boxed his brothers' ears, then he should have told her to mind her own business. Had he behaved like that she might have felt respect for him, even admiration.

"And you, child," Madame Adelaide said sharply, "hasten or that coat will never be finished in the King's lifetime."

Laboriously Marie Antoinette began to ply her needle. Louis, she thought, what a disappointment he is! It was hardly flattering that he preferred his workshop and his hunting to his wife's company. She appreciated his kindliness and in a way loved him for it but she was constantly irritated by his ineffectualness in things that mattered, such as making gay conversation, and dancing. Tongue-tied, always tongue-tied, except when he felt an urge to lecture her about the state of France and Europe in general. Just now he was full of the disgrace and dismissal of the minister,

Choiseul, as was Madame Adelaide, for Choiseul had been dismissed at the whim of Madame Dubarry. Choiseul had played a big part in bringing about her marriage, and for this she had liked and hated him, turn by turn. A determined little Miss, the King had once called her. Either she loved or she hated. Well, what was wrong with that? She and the King were quite good friends now. I have only one complaint, he had said, only yesterday; you show no sign yet of giving your husband, and France, a child.

They were all the same where that subject was concerned. The aunts, Madame Etiquette, the Abbé Vermond, Mercy, all of them. And Mama too, in all her letters, asking over and over again if she was pregnant yet. The biggest disgrace a wife could suffer was to be barren. Mama wondered now whose fault it was, hers or her young husband's. It was hard to know what to say in reply. Was Louis a normal attentive husband, Mama kept asking. Marie Antoinette supposed he was, though his attentions still left them both full of disappointment and, as far as she was concerned, anger too. And the anger, while it lasted, made her hate him and want to hurt him, made her criticize his boorish habits and jeer at his lack of elegance.

"Marie, my dear . . ."

It was Madame Adelaide, and standing at her side was Count Mercy-Argenteau. He bowed and smiled his most diplomatic smile, but she knew he had come to scold her. Perhaps he had discovered the duplicity of her sedate donkey rides, but what did it matter if he had?

"I must compliment your Highness on the success of the visit to Paris," he said.

"It was very pleasing," she admitted.

She would long remember how the people of the capital had received her with demonstrations of joy. Louis said that the enthusiasm might not have been so great except that the price of bread had unaccountably fallen, but she refused to believe him. The people, entranced by her beauty, grace and charm, had taken her to their hearts. She resolved now to wait with patience for the death of the old King. Her own mistress then, adored by the people, she would please herself in all things, be held back by nothing.

"Your Imperial mother will be very pleased."

27

She smiled. Mercy was cautiously approaching his subject, a complaint of some sort, she was sure, from Mama in Vienna.

"Her Imperial Majesty is not always pleased," he went on smoothly, turning to Madame Adelaide. "If I may suggest . . ."

Madame Adelaide nodded and the three sisters left the room.

"Her Imperial Majesty is disturbed by the undoubted fact that her royal Highness, the Dauphine, persists in practicing one distressing form of rudeness."

"Rudeness?"

"It is not desired in Vienna that your Highness should hurt the feelings of Madame Dubarry."

The girl tossed her head. "How can I possibly hurt the feelings of a person who, as far as I am concerned, does not exist?"

"By cutting her, child."

"I have never seen her."

Mercy permitted himself a chuckle. "An understandable blindness. Nevertheless . . ." He drew out the word, repeated it, "Nevertheless . . ."

Marie Antoinette thought of Mama's face and felt a little frightened. All the same, Mama was becoming a distant figure these days and Vienna was far, far away.

"A nod of the head, a few kind words," Mercy murmured. "That is all that is asked."

"Never!"

"In that case . . ." Mercy bowed and strolled to the door. Over his shoulder he said, "Her Imperial Majesty will no doubt write to your Highness . . ."

From then on Marie Antoinette took a delight in aggravating the royal mistress beyond normal endurance. Prevented by etiquette from speaking first to the Dauphine, Madame Dubarry nevertheless was ever close at hand when the girl appeared in public.

"Oh, I see her game," Madame Adelaide fumed. "She knows the King can't live forever. Through you she seeks a way of remaining at court, after. A way of retaining some of her power."

"No one at court shall have power, except Louis and myself, no one!"

Madame Adelaide's eyes clouded. "Of course not," she said stiffly.

When Mercy urged her to reconsider her attitude, Marie Antoinette laughed in his face. Vienna had made no move, Mama had not written. Besides, it was great fun, this baiting of the be-jeweled, over-painted, over-dressed favorite. It was in fact a first taste of court intrigue and she was enjoying it immensely.

The next move was made by the King, but made in a round-about way. He sent for Madame Etiquette who, returning red-faced from the royal presence, scolded Marie Antoinette soundly, say-ing among other things that it was ill-bred to be so rude.

"The time will come, Madame," the girl said haughtily, "when I shall have the right to dispense with your services."

With no one to confide in but the Abbé Vermond, she told him indignantly what the King had done. Too late, she realized her mistake. The abbé, always the tool of Count Mercy, made his report, and Mercy sent a courier hotfoot to Vienna.

He spoke gravely of this to Marie Antoinette, adding, "It is necessary to respect the wishes of the King of France. It is neces-sary to be polite to his friends. The situation, my dear young lady, is fast becoming desperate. Because of the power Madame Dubarry wields the alliance between France and Austria is badly shaken."

"You mean that unless I speak to Dubarry France and Austria might go to war?"

"I mean precisely that."

"But how ridiculous!"

"The world we live and move in is a ridiculous place."

"Childish too!"

"The people in our world *are* childish."

Suddenly she grew bored with it all. If this was a sample of court intrigue she wanted none of it. And yet to give in now, at this stage . . . She set her mouth stubbornly.

"You must try and think of your own future," Mercy went on. "The success of your coming reign will depend, largely, on peace between Austria and France." He smiled charmingly. "War would limit expenditure at Versailles, might even leave you with an empty purse."

She smiled back just as charmingly. "Really?"

"You will spare the poor woman a kind word in passing? Just one kind word?"

"If the King himself asks me, not otherwise," she said daringly.

A week later the King commanded her to take supper with him, alone. She chose a gown of gold-embroidered white brocade to make her look completely grown up and went gaily to the royal apartments. In the anteroom she glided past Madame Dubarry, in a gown cut far too low, and smothered in diamonds. She paused for a moment and looked right through her. So much for the royal mistress, now for the royal rake!

The King received her with a silly smile on his face. Encouraged, she listened attentively while he asked her if life at Versailles was to her liking and went on, the smile growing fixed, to say how much pleasure it gave him to know that a beautiful woman would some day be Queen of France. The silly fixed smile grew more appalling as he spoke of the Polish question. She had never heard of the Polish question and pointedly smothered a yawn.

He yawned himself. "All international problems affect me the same way, my dear, but they have to be faced, sooner or later."

He said something then about the partition of Poland, but she scarcely listened until he mentioned her mother's name.

"If I express an active disapproval the whole scheme will be wrecked. Your Imperial mother would grow angry, my dear, with me and, more important, with you." He looked at her vacantly. "Terrifying when angry, I believe."

She said faintly, "Yes, very, but—"

"But Vienna is many miles away? Quite, quite, but how would you like to go back there?"

"There is no reason for me to go back to Vienna," she said uneasily.

He sighed. "Marriages that have not borne fruit are sometimes dissolved."

She began to play with a wineglass, twisting it round, staring intently at the flashing lights of the cut crystal. How easily she had been deceived by that silly fixed smile! She had not been very happy at Versailles, but the future lay temptingly before her.

As if changing the subject he said, "A king never begs a favor of one of inferior rank." He let the words sink in. "Come, my dear child, you must try the stewed oysters. Desecration to stew oysters, but I invented the special sauce myself."

Shaken as she was she still remained stubborn, and then came Mama's letter, brought to her by Mercy. It was short and sharp. Mama might well have been in the room at Mercy's side, her stern eyes holding yours till in confusion you had to drop your gaze. It made you a little girl again, a very little girl. It reminded you that though by rank you were the first lady of France you still remained the King's subject. Without mentioning Madame Adelaide it hinted that you were under her thumb and being used in the pursuit of a dangerous political intrigue.

Marie let the letter fall to the floor.

"Well?" Mercy asked.

"*Well?*" she challenged.

"Willynilly you are being used by a certain faction at court. It is hardly dignified for the first lady of France to be used as an instrument of somebody else's intrigue."

"No," she agreed.

"And so, my dear . . . ?"

She thought it out carefully, this necessary compromise with herself.

"The position of official mistress to the King," she said coldly, "is considered by many as one of complete respectability. I see now that I can with dignity show recognition of the *position,* whatever I n ght think of the woman who holds it."

Mercy chuckled. "What a pompous little speech!"

She chuckled too, though had Louis made the remark, or one of the aunts, she would have flared up in anger and still refused to speak to Madame Dubarry.

He uttered one more word. "When?"

She shrugged. "At the first opportunity."

The first opportunity proved to be a reception in the long Hall of Mirrors. She had chosen a simple pale blue gown and was deliberately wearing very little jewelry, tiny plain gold earrings and a string of pearls. At her side stood the Princesse de Lamballe, the young widow of a grandson of the fourteenth Louis. Marie Antoinette had met her recently and though she thought her a little too quiet and gentle, quite liked her and had asked her to come to court more often. A gay companion would have been better, but at least the princess was young, and that was a change from the society of the elderly ladies favored by Madame Adelaide and old Madame Etiquette.

One by one the foreign ambassadors came and bowed before her. They were followed, in twos and threes, by the ladies and gentlemen of the court. There were smiles, laughter, compliments, but underneath it all a growing tension, an atmosphere of excited anticipation.

There was a little stir. The King had entered, accompanied by a pink, indignant-looking Madame Adelaide. Marie Antoinette felt happier. He had had the good sense, thank heaven, not to enter with Madame Dubarry. There was another little stir, followed by complete silence. Madame Dubarry had entered with the Duchesse d'Aiguillon. It was annoying to see that in spite of her vulgarity she was strikingly attractive, yet gratifying to know that, over-dressed and weighted down with jewels, the contrast with her own simple appearance would be complete.

Madame Dubarry approached with her companion and paused. Again came the silence. All were watching, standing on tip-toe, pushing each other aside. Marie Antoinette threw back her head, conscious of her lovely unblemished throat, her blue eyes framed in enchanting dark lashes, conscious that thus she had succeeded in making the royal mistress look exactly what she was, the tavern wench who had had the good fortune to snare a senile king.

"Goodness," Marie Antoinette said, gazing directly at Madame Dubarry, "what a crowd of people here tonight."

Madame Dubarry's eyes snapped with triumph. "Yes indeed, your Highness."

It seemed then as if everybody was talking and laughing at the same time, but Marie Antoinette, a little pain in her heart, was swamped with a feeling of misery and defeat, a feeling which persisted, even when the King, beaming on her ridiculously, came and kissed her on both cheeks.

Presently Louis joined her.

"You saw?" she said bitterly. "You heard?"

He nodded gravely. "Poor little Poland."

"Poland? What do you mean, Louis?"

"My grandfather will hold his hand. No intervention now from France. Poland will be torn to pieces. Oh, shameful!"

"Louis—"

"You have no understanding of the Polish question, have you?" he said gently.

"None whatever."

"I have often talked about it, Marie."

"I admit I have scarcely listened."

"It is quite simple. Frederick of Prussia and Catherine of Russia want to increase their power by dividing up Poland. They feel the need of your mother's approval. To gain this they are willing to give Austria a share of Poland. But all three countries are afraid of what France might do. They needn't be, now. Madame Dubarry's vanity has been satisfied. France will do nothing." His

32

young voice was bitter. "I am not a war-minded person, but if I were king I'd say better war than dishonor. Poland," he repeated vehemently, "will be torn to pieces."

"Because of me!"

He shook his head. "You had no real choice in the matter."

SIX

"THERE, MOST GRACIOUS HIGHNESS! EVEN THOUGH I SAY IT MYSELF IT is a masterpiece of ingenuity. Never yet have I created so perfect a gown. Never, never, never!"

The plump little dressmaker, down on her knees at Marie Antoinette's feet, sat back on her substantial haunches and quivered all over in vast excitement. Her mouth was full of pins. She glanced up expectantly at the little gathering of ladies in the Dauphine's dressing-room.

"I find it most delightful," said the Princesse de Lamballe, in her quiet, unexcited voice.

"Too daring," said Madame Etiquette.

"A very feminine creation," Madame Adelaide barked.

Mademoiselle Bertin laughed archly. "What else would one create for the most feminine creature in the world?"

Madame Etiquette frowned on her. "You are much too free with your tongue, Bertin. You forget your place. The unwarranted liberty permitted you, low-born woman that you are, of entering the Dauphine's apartments has quite gone to your head."

Mademoiselle Bertin gave Marie Antoinette a sly smile and remained silent. Marie Antoinette smiled down on her. The little dressmaker, recommended by the Princesse de Lamballe, was rapidly becoming her favorite dress designer. She had already decided that when she was Queen Bertin should enjoy exclusive royal patronage.

"I have one criticism," Madame Adelaide remarked dryly. "The whole effect is far too virginal. A married woman should at least look like a married woman."

Mademoiselle Bertin leaped to her feet. "Ah, but the virginal look, in one who is not a virgin, is an unsurpassed art. It is to enhance such a look that this creation of mine has been, oh, so *cunningly* designed."

"It is cut too low," Madame Etiquette declared.

Marie Antoinette stamped her foot. "I like the gown. It has my full approval. Do please let us have no more argument."

34

Mademoiselle Bertin clasped her hands over her breast. "I am overwhelmed, your Highness, utterly overwhelmed."

Marie Antoinette dismissed her, and presently, having dismissed the others also, she sat down to wait for Louis. Today was her eighteenth birthday and tonight she and Louis were to attend a dinner party given by the King for the members of the royal family. Afterwards there would be a ball with all the courtiers present. There were two new members of the royal family now, for Provence and Artois had recently been married at the wish of the King. So odious it was, watching them strut about as if they were grown men, and hearing them speak, with sly giggles, of the pleasures of the marriage bed.

It had been the same just now with Madame Adelaide. Her acid remark about the effect of the gown being too virginal had somehow rankled. Her eyes had held an accusing look, especially when she had added that a married woman should at least look like one. What precisely had she meant? Madame Adelaide, soured by the triumph of Madame Dubarry, was never really friendly these days.

"As if it was my fault!" Marie Antoinette cried to the empty room.

One should continue the fight against the Dubarry dominance, Madame Adelaide was always urging, but Marie Antoinette would have none of it. Never again would she become involved in court intrigue. A fruitless, stupid occupation, at the best of times. Her own particular task was to wait with patience for the old King's death, to wait and to enjoy herself as best she could. Yes, and to assert herself too! She chuckled as she remembered how she had dismissed Madame Adelaide just now, how the old-maid aunt, scowling certainly, had stamped out without a murmur.

The Princesse de Lamballe came quietly into the room and stood at a slight distance, waiting for permission to speak. At Marie Antoinette's insistence the princess now had a small apartment at Versailles and acted in the capacity of an unofficial lady-in-waiting.

"Yes, Louise, what is it?"

"His royal Highness the Dauphin sends his apologies," the princess said, with a slight smile. "He was so engrossed with the new clock he is finishing for your birthday that he quite forgot the time. I thought it odd that a clockmaker should have no knowledge of the time."

35

Marie Antoinette felt her quick temper rising. "Perhaps I did marry the wrong brother after all!"

"You can scarcely mean that," the princess chided. "The Dauphin is devoted to you."

"So devoted that he spends his life hunting and clock-making, and goodness knows what other menial occupation!"

"His Highness will be especially attentive tonight after seeing you in the new gown."

"Because it is too daring, or because it is too virginal?"

"Perhaps because of both," the princess smiled.

Afterwards, during the family dinner party, Louise's words rankled. *His Highness will be especially attentive tonight* . . . She had grown to dread that sort of attentiveness, to dread and to loathe it. Often she had escaped it by going late to bed. Many times when Louis, poor dancer that he was, had grown tired of the balls she had stayed up till three and four in the morning, dancing. She had even been able, during the last few months, to forget Mama's accusing face and spend long hours at the gaming table.

The words still rankled when the King opened the ball. They came between her and the gay scene which usually delighted her heart. It seemed to her that the immaculate gentlemen and the extravagantly dressed ladies had a dowdy look, while the music lacked its former fire and spirit. She danced first with Louis, as etiquette required, then she danced with Provence, an excellent dancer. He remarked at once on her quietness.

"Pensive, but maddeningly beautiful," he said.

She disliked the pressure of his hand. "One cannot always be talkative."

The pressure increased. "Dearest Marie, how I envy Berri this night. I have never seen you more provocative. It is being said that by nature you are cold. To test you and give the story the lie would be mightily stimulating."

She broke away from him. "The musicians are out of tune. Or do I mean you are? In any case, I have had enough. Escort me back to my ladies, please."

Provence bowed. "Perhaps it is true that your beauty masks a cold heart, but as I say . . ."

"You have a wife, Monsieur. Go back to her."

"What, you have no love for me at all? Not even a passing fancy? I assure you I am much better in every way than poor Berri."

"How you flatter yourself!"

36

"You have seemed at times to encourage me."

"Never!"

"Is it just a game you play? Encouragement, then haughty rejection? A sideways glance, a slight suggestive tilt of the head, then nothing further! What a fraud you are! A coquette, no more! And what a dangerous game you indulge in. No man enjoys being driven to extremes, then rejected."

"A man!" she retorted. "You may be married but you are still a callow youth."

Approaching, bowing at the sight of her, was the Prince de Rohan. She smiled on him quickly, and to teach Provence a lesson asked him to escort her to the gallery.

"With pleasure, your Highness," the Prince said eagerly.

It was a relief to know, as they made their way to the gallery, that she would not have the same distressing trouble with this priest that she had just experienced with her brother-in-law. Glancing at his purple vestments she thought how strange it was that a member of so powerful a family, a prince no less, should have chosen a career in the church.

On the gallery, seated at her side, he began to talk about Vienna, her mother and her brother Joseph who, as Emperor, shared the Austrian throne equally with Mama. She remembered now that he was more than just a priest. The King had sent him as ambassador to Vienna. He was now making a brief visit at Versailles before returning to his duties at Vienna. She remembered also that, on behalf of his uncle, Bishop of Strasbourg, he had made her a touching speech of welcome during her journey to Versailles.

"My mother is well?" she asked politely.

"Your Imperial mother is well," he said softly, "but deeply troubled on your Highness's behalf."

"Goodness, why?"

"Troubled," he added, "by the unsatisfactoriness of your marriage."

She had no reply to this and felt herself growing hot with embarrassment. He reached out casually and covered her hand with his. The long slim fingers were cool and hard, like bands of iron.

"It is felt," he murmured, "that the Dauphin's inadequacy stands between you and complete happiness. It is also felt that natural instinct might force you to take a lover."

She freed her hand quickly. "I cannot believe that my mother would ask you to talk to me like this."

He smiled and slowly shook his head.

"Then you have not the right, Monsieur—"

"It would be difficult," he went on dreamily, "under the ever-watchful eyes of the court, for your Highness to engage in a secret love affair. But if one is clever enough . . ." He paused, chuckled softly. "I myself have always been clever in such matters. I think I make my meaning clear?"

She rose indignantly. "Most clear!"

"I shock you?" he asked in surprise.

"You fill me with horror. You make me despise you."

"You would never despise me if you really knew me."

She thought of the things Provence had said. "Monsieur, can you say truthfully that I have ever encouraged you?"

"It has seemed so whenever you have talked to me. Other men —and men discuss you continually among themselves—have felt the same. Even at Strasbourg, that first time—"

"But this is horrible!" she cried. "Never have I intended, never!"

"I can see," he smiled, "that you lack a full understanding of yourself."

She turned from him quickly.

"Wait, your Highness!"

"You fill me with shame, Monsieur. Let me go or I shall tell the King."

"That lecherous old donkey? He would roar with laughter."

"Perhaps he would, Versailles being what it is."

He looked at her wonderingly. "As pure and virginal, I do believe, as that artful gown suggests."

She stayed to hear no more. Hurrying back to the ballroom below she came face to face again with Provence. He was grinning openly.

"So you spurned him! How hurt and amazed he must feel."

"Provence," she said beseechingly, "is the church in France as corrupt as all that?"

"Probably not. De Rohan is an exception. But he, like many others of his class—" for all his youth Provence spoke with pompous authority—"seeks advancement in the church as a means of gaining power in the state." He laughed admiringly. "A gay dog, and a cunning one. When he travels he always takes a young abbé with him. Or so people think. The abbé, you know, is a slim boyish girl."

"Disgusting," she said, and fled.

She was not sorry when the King, anxious no doubt to join Madame Dubarry, announced that for once Versailles would go early to bed, but her heart sank when he added gaily that he would see his dear grandchildren to bed.

When they were in bed he returned for a moment and poked his debauched face through the curtains.

"I do believe," he chuckled, "that I should have married you myself. You would have been queen immediately then." He chuckled again. "Sleep well, *mes enfants.*"

The moment he was gone Marie Antoinette turned her back on Louis. The words of the Princesse de Lamballe came back to her, she saw again the eyes of Provence and the Prince de Rohan. As if trying to escape from it all she sprang out of bed and ran to the window. It was a bright clear night; the twinkling stars seemed to mock her. She heard Louis padding across the room to her side, felt his hand on her shoulder. It seemed more like Provence's hand, or the Prince de Rohan's, or the disgusting old King's.

"Marie . . ."

His voice was gentle, as always. She forced herself to turn.

"Marie, what have I done to displease you?"

"Nothing," she said irritably.

He bent his head to kiss her. She turned quickly away.

"I am what I am," he said nervously. "No use trying to make me behave like a fancy fop of a courtier."

"No use at all," she agreed.

"I was never any good at making pretty speeches, paying insincere compliments. Nothing of the poet about me, Marie." His voice in the darkness grew very earnest. "I wish, tonight, I was a poet. I have never seen you look so desirable as you did at the ball. You have grown up completely. My grandfather noticed it, though I can't say I liked the lewd smile on his face when he looked at you. Just a glance at you is enough to drive a man crazy."

It was the longest speech he had ever made, apart from his political discourses which were interminable.

"Marie, I want you tonight more than ever before."

His hands, large and warm and rough, tightened on her shoulders. He drew her against his barrel-like chest and held her there in a grip that left her powerless. For a moment she listened to the beating of his heart, then the repugnance was on her again. Never before had she felt so trapped and helpless; never before so strong a desire to escape. She remembered one of her mother's recent letters. *It is your duty to be obedient to your husband in all things.* Duty, duty! She had rebelled many times against Mama's instructions, but never so urgently as now. In the letter Mama had also said that true happiness in this life was contained in one thing only: a happy marriage. The mockery of it, the sheer mockery! She tried to turn in his arms but he tightened them about her all the more.

"Louis, let me go!"

His grip slackened. "Marie . . ."

"A clumsy oaf and I hate you!"

His arms dropped to his side. The room seemed full of star-light. She could see that his face was working strangely; that his eyes, squinting at her, were full of tears. She hated herself for having hurt him like this; she felt the weight of his humiliation as if it were her own; but the repugnance had become too strong for her, had passed beyond control. She laughed hysterically, turned, and ran from the room. In her dressing-room she paused only long enough to snatch up a wrap. Drawing it hurriedly about her she rushed headlong from her apartments, vaguely conscious of the blank staring faces of the waiting-women and the guards outside. Not quite knowing where she was going she found herself in the apartment of the Princesse de Lamballe. Her whole body was quivering, her teeth were chattering.

"Oh Louise, Louise!" she sobbed.

The princess, who had been sitting in a chair reading, threw her book aside and took Marie Antoinette in her arms. She held her calmly for a few moments and tried, with soft phrases of endearment, to soothe her. Presently, with tear-stained cheeks and large pitiful eyes, Marie Antoinette looked into the princess's untrammelled face.

"I'm so unhappy, Louise."

"Well, then, confide in me if you wish, if you think it might help."

Marie Antoinette hung her head. "It isn't easy, Louise."

The princess embraced her warmly. "How touched I am by your innocence and modesty! For a girl to remain pure and untouched in this place is an achievement beyond my comprehension."

"I hate him, Louise, I loathe him."

"The Dauphin's demands are too great?" the princess suggested.

Marie Antoinette looked hesitantly at her friend. She liked the long blonde curls and the dark thoughtful eyes which showed none of the malicious curiosity that abounded at Versailles.

"Or is it true," the princess added, very gently, "that in that respect he is not quite a man?"

"Oh Louise, I don't know, I don't know!"

Impulsively Marie Antoinette hid her hot face in the elder girl's breast and confided in her as fully as she could. It was altogether an experience full of shame.

After a little silence the princess stroked her shoulder gently and spoke in barely a whisper.

"It would seem, Marie, that whatever the cause you are still a virgin."

"But not barren?" Marie Antoinette begged. "Mama thinks I am, I know she does."

The princess smiled. "Your childlessness is a worry to everybody, except the younger brothers, but the fault is clearly not yours. The King, of course, must be told."

"That nauseating old man? Oh Louise, how could I!"

"As if I meant that you should speak to him yourself! The utmost discretion is necessary. A word from me to the wife of the minister of state, a word from her to her husband. It is after all a very grave matter of state. A word from the minister to the King, and there you are!"

"And then the whole thing will be debated at the council table. I shall die of shame!"

"If there is any shame at all it will reflect on the Dauphin, not on you. I do insist that the King be told. It is indeed a matter for the council table. Its implications are serious and rise above the feelings of the individual."

"You sound just like Mama! Worse, you sound like old Madame Etiquette."

The princess apologized quickly. "But even from a personal point of view this unfortunate situation concerns your own happiness. If the trouble can be set right—and from what you have tried to tell me I think it can—it will make an immense difference

41

to you. You and your husband will be able to start life again on a normal satisfactory footing. You would want that, surely."

"I don't know. I—I suppose so."

"And once the King knows the truth the gossip as far as you are concerned will be silenced. No one will then be able to blame you for your childlessness."

"Oh, very well. Let the King be told."

"A wise decision. Do you feel calm enough now to return to your apartments?"

"Oh no, I—I couldn't. Truly I couldn't. Let me spend the night with you, Louise. *Please!*"

"I can hardly refuse, but it is against my better judgment."

"What do you mean by that?"

"Still, it may not matter. The story will have started to spread already."

The next morning the gossip was well-established. Marie Antoinette knew this by the sly expressions on the faces of all the people she met when she returned to her own apartments. The corridors, usually deserted at that time of the morning, were crowded. All these people, she felt certain, had gathered together to watch for her.

Madame Etiquette was waiting in the dressing-room. Her face was long and stern, her darting eyes alive with curiosity.

"The King will be most displeased."

"Let him be!"

"Your Imperial mother will be even more displeased."

"Why? Because I refused, just once, to spend the night with my husband?"

Madame Etiquette pursed her lips. "It was a wicked thing to do."

The next protest came from Madame Adelaide, who entered the dressing-room while the toilette was in progress and waited impatiently for the dismissal of the ladies and the waiting-women.

"A pretty state of affairs," she burst out, the moment they were alone together. "Poor Berri is quite distracted."

Marie Antoinette felt a stab of guilt. "Where *is* Louis?"

"In his workshop."

"I—I'm sorry if I hurt his feelings."

"Well, that is something. What made you do it, child?"

"Because . . ." Marie Antoinette bit her lip.

42

"Because?"

"Just because."

Madame Adelaide's eyes were searching her face.

"You quarrelled, of course."

"What if we did!"

"According to one story he thrashed you quite unmercifully."

"As if Louis would ever do a thing like that."

"According to *another* story—"

Marie Antoinette stopped her with a little scream of rage.

Madame Adelaide shrugged. "I wonder what will happen when your mother hears about this."

"She will write me a sharp letter reminding me of my duty. Has a special courier been sent to Vienna already?"

Madame Adelaide smiled maliciously. "Probably. I hear from the Austrian embassy that Count Mercy is most disturbed."

"The whole palace must be seething with gossip."

"It is," Madame Adelaide chuckled, "indeed it is."

Recovered from the hysteria of last night, Marie Antoinette felt now nothing but a cold and bitter anger, which remained with her, sustaining her, during the formal routine of a normal day at Versailles. After Mass, at which neither Louis nor the King was present, but at which every other member of the court appeared, as if attending an exciting play, she dined alone, for Louis was still shut up in his workshop.

During the afternoon, while she was as usual in Madame Adelaide's drawing-room, pretending to work on the coat she had not yet finished for the King, the Abbé Vermond came to see her. A look passed between him and Madame Adelaide, upon which Madame Adelaide, reluctant to do so, withdrew. The abbé, always more forthright than Count Mercy, came to the point at once.

"Tell me, child, why you did this dreadful thing."

She shook her head stubbornly. She had confided in the Princesse de Lamballe; she would confide in nobody else. Besides, it was unthinkable, even though the abbé was her confessor, that she should speak of such a thing to a man.

"It is your duty to tell me; mine to help you."

"Have you been sent by the King?"

"Well—no."

"Then you have come because of the gossip. Shame on you, Monsieur l'Abbé, to listen to gossip."

43

"Your Highness did without doubt desert the Dauphin last night."

With a flash of insight she said angrily, "The waiting-women are paid by you to spy on me. You are paid by Mercy. Mercy is paid by my mother."

He shrugged easily. "As far as Count Mercy and I are concerned it is a labor of love."

"Love! Having assisted at a political marriage, you and Mercy, yes and my mother too, are now concerned with one thing only, my bearing of a child."

"It is of paramount importance."

"And when I do have a child, he too will be sacrificed on the altar of political expediency."

The Abbé Vermond smiled delightedly. "I am proud of the French you now speak so fluently, even though the German accent still persists. I think I can say that you have grown up and are developing an understanding of state affairs."

"You are making a grave mistake," she said tartly. "Serious subjects bore me. You always knew that and made your report accordingly."

"Ah, but you have a certain intelligence, and it is salted by a rare imagination. Whereas the Dauphin, good fellow that he is, has no imagination and his mind moves sluggishly. When the time comes you will rule, if you want to, not your husband."

"I came to France to enjoy myself."

"Yet enjoyment, in one direction, seems to have been denied you. Was that why you spent the night in the Princesse de Lamballe's apartment with the Comte de Provence?"

"Monsieur l'Abbé!"

"He was seen following you when you left your own apartments. He too was in a state of undress."

Anger rendered her all but speechless.

"It is a vile lie," she whispered.

"Possibly it is. I was not a witness myself. It is just one of the stories that is being circulated and the Comte de Provence has made no denial."

"Please leave me, Monsieur."

"If your Imperial mother were to know the full facts, from your own point of view . . ."

"I have nothing to tell you, nothing!"

And with that he had to be satisfied.

44

The routine of the day continued. The music master came and, after she had practiced for an hour at the clavichord, departed. She walked in the gardens with the aunts, a solemn little procession, up and down, up and down. Madame Adelaide told her that Louis had asked for dinner to be served in his workshop. He was still very busy there; the hammering, Madame Adelaide said, was quite frantic.

On returning to her apartments she found the Prince de Rohan waiting for her. He bowed and told her that he was starting out in an hour for Vienna.

"Taking a young abbé with you, perhaps?"

He smiled slyly. "I see we are beginning to understand each other very well."

"I understand you; you refuse to understand me."

"Oh come, I know you better than you know yourself."

"Then you know just why I hate and despise you and always will."

He hesitated for a moment. "Perhaps your Highness has a personal message for your Imperial mother."

"None that I care to send by you."

"Not even after last night's pitiful fiasco?"

Fury shook her voice. "Please go, Monsieur, and remember that I never want to see you again. Present yourself if you must next time you return to Versailles, but I shall refuse to receive you."

The prince flushed. "I see you really mean that. How very unwise of you."

He bowed stiffly and withdrew.

When she went, as usual, to dine in Madame Adelaide's apartments she found, not surprisingly, a guest at the table. After the Abbé Vermond, Count Mercy, the superior, more subtle intelligence. Much to her amazement, however, Mercy made no comment on the events of last night and the subsequent gossip. Not once did he utter a phrase containing even a hint of a gradual coming to the point. He seemed, in fact, to be in the best of spirits. He told a few good, if long-winded stories, and he teased her about her needlework.

"It is being said," he laughed, "that the King's coat, begun so long ago, might not be finished in time for his Majesty to wear it in his coffin."

"Nor might it," she agreed.

When at last he rose to go he made the only significant remark of the evening.

"The Dauphin has been summoned to the King's apartments. They are dining together, alone."

The evening dragged on. Marie Antoinette's anger was beginning to abate now. Thinking of Louis, face to face with his lewd old grandfather, she remembered the shame and confusion she herself had experienced while confiding as best she could in the Princesse de Lamballe. How much more difficult it would be for Louis, *compelled* to confide in the King! She could imagine him sitting there, tongue-tied, miserable, answering or trying to answer the questions which without doubt would be jocular and crude.

Presently, one of the King's valets entered the room and with a too grave face engaged in a whispered conversation with Madame Adelaide. Horrible to think that even the valets of the palace would be whispering and sniggering now. After he had gone Madame Adelaide, avidly curious as ever, issued what sounded like a tremendous ultimatum.

"There will be no repetition of last night's foolishness."

"I have no intention of running from Louis a second time!"

Dignity, that was the right attitude. One must cling at all costs to one's dignity. She clung to it when Provence paid her a brief visit and insisted on speaking his mind, even in front of Madame Adelaide.

"I understand, dear little sister-in-law, that we spent a merry night together last night."

"I rely on you to deny the ridiculous story," she said coldly.

"Why should I? It adds to my prestige."

"Everyone knows you were not seen following me."

"Ah, but I was there in one of the corridors at the same time. I was on my way to another rendezvous. I almost changed my mind. Some other time, perhaps?"

She still clung to her dignity during the punctilious nightly undressing. If the eyes of her ladies and the waiting-women held a piquant curiosity she refused to see it.

Louis, when he came to her from his own apartments, was distressingly silent. He climbed into bed and without even a glance turned on his side away from her. She lay back waiting. He made no move whatever.

"Louis . . ." she said at last.

"Yes, Marie . . ."

"I'm sorry, darling."

She couldn't remember having called him darling before. She wondered why she had done so now. Perhaps it was because she felt sorry for him, unaccountably tender toward him.

"I'm sorry too," he mumbled.

"For last night?"

"And all the other nights."

He still lay on his side with his broad back squarely against her. She touched his shoulder lightly and felt his instant quivering response, but he made no move to turn and face her.

"It must have been embarrassing, Louis, the interview with the King."

"It was. He made me tell him everything. So many things I didn't really understand."

"Was he angry?"

"No. He said it was a tragedy. He said he was sorry for me. He said he thanked heaven it had never been like that with him. After that . . . Well, he sent for his chief physician. The examination didn't take long but it sickened me. I—I am very tired, Marie. Goodnight."

"But Louis . . ."

"The physician said an operation would set things right."

"When will it be performed?"

"Never. Please understand that, Marie, never!"

"You are afraid?" she said, in wonderment.

"The thought of the knife is more than I can bear."

"But *Louis*—"

"Goodnight," he said, with a finality that silenced her completely.

She lay awake for some time, brooding. The tenderness she had felt disappeared and the bitter anger returned. Hot tears filled her eyes and rolled down her cheeks. This, then, was what fate had had in store for her. Marriage with a weakling. A husband who would never be a real husband because he was afraid. Not a coward in anything else, but clearly a coward in this.

"Louis!" She raised herself on one elbow. "Please understand that you will force me to take a lover."

"Of course."

She sank back on the pillow in disgust. It would have been better if he had turned and struck her. She repeated the words

47

to herself. *You will force me to take a lover.* Well, who, for instance? Provence? De Rohan? What a cold-blooded thing to contemplate. A lover, but no love involved. Deep in her heart, angering her beyond all reason, was the firm belief that never, whatever happened, would she be unfaithful to this husband who was only half a man.

"What a miserable creature I am," she sobbed.

SEVEN

Count mercy had been chatting for at least half an hour about nothing in particular. Normally she could listen with pleasure to the music of his well-bred accents, but this afternoon there was a monotony in his voice that made her drowsy. She yawned unashamedly; in another moment she would fall asleep over her needlework.

"The King's new coat, I see, is not yet finished," he laughed, and repeated once again the time-worn joke.

She laughed politely.

"Being a man of strange fancies," he went on musingly, "I sometimes wonder if the King's life lies entirely in your slim and beautiful hands."

"Whatever do you mean, Monsieur?"

"Each stitch you make, for all we know, brings him one step closer to the end."

"But I don't hate the King."

All the same it was an amusing thought, a thought not entirely free of superstition. If by finishing the coat quickly she could bring about the death of the King, finish it quickly she would. To become queen with as little waste of time as possible, that was all she wanted now. There could be no other compensation in this strange frustrating life she led at Versailles.

"Nor, for that matter, do you hate the Dauphin," Mercy said.

Dryly she said, "You speak of my husband, and that means you are coming at last to the point."

"At last," he agreed, and chuckled.

"You have received another letter from my mother."

"Yes. Her Imperial Majesty is distressed by the fact that we at Versailles have failed with him. Our only hope now lies in you."

"I have failed with him too, Mercy."

He rose from his chair and looked down on her benevolently. "May I speak to you like a father?"

"If you wish."

"It has occurred to me that sympathy and understanding,

gentleness and compassion, might move the Dauphin where impatience and sneering have failed."

"I have tried, believe me I have! Is this your own suggestion or my mother's?"

"My own. Her Majesty has another suggestion. She feels that the time has come for you to issue an ultimatum."

"And that?"

"The Dauphin adores you," Mercy went on. "It might move him if you threatened him with a dissolution of the marriage."

Dissolution! The King had hinted at that when forcing her to recognize Madame Dubarry. If the marriage were dissolved she would never be queen. Better to be a virgin queen than never queen at all. Angrily she took up the unfinished coat and stabbed at it viciously with the needle.

Mercy laughed softly. "Nothing is further from our minds, but an ultimatum *could* be issued. Are you clever enough to issue it convincingly?"

Her blue eyes hardened. "Yes, I think so."

"When?"

"It is months since I could bear to dine with him alone, but I shall do so tonight."

"Splendid!"

"But remember, Mercy, there is no need to pay servants to eavesdrop. I shall give you a true account of what happens."

He bowed. "Your Highness will make a splendid, haughty queen."

Louis showed a pathetic pleasure when he found that the table in their private dining hall had been laid only for two. He said how grateful he was, but as she looked at him candidly he quickly grew confused and began nervously to talk about the latest court intrigue.

"Madame Adelaide," he blurted out, "has made up her mind that my grandfather is not too old to marry again."

"Are you joking, Louis?"

"Indeed no. It all arises from her hatred of Madame Dubarry. She feels sure that a young wife would never stomach the official mistress and would send her packing. Her own words, not mine."

Marie Antoinette felt her heart racing with alarm. "If the King marries again and his wife bears him a son, court intrigue could make that son the future king instead of you."

50

"I had thought of that, Marie, but kingship is something I don't always look forward to. Marriage for my grandfather might give me the way of escape I sometimes crave."

"Even at *my* expense?"

His shortsighted eyes searched her face. "*Your* expense?"

"I want to be queen. I shall never be fully a woman but I must be a queen."

He blushed, lowered his eyes to his plate and began to eat with the utmost rapidity. No more talk was possible until the next course was served and the servants had withdrawn.

"However," Marie Antoinette continued then, "even if the King never marries again it looks as if I shall remain a princess, no more, no less."

Louis looked puzzled. "Why?"

"No doubt the dissolution of our marriage would cause a great scandal, but what else have I to look forward to but that?"

"Dissolution!" he gasped.

"My mother is of the opinion that his Holiness the Pope would grant a special dispensation."

Louis threw back his chair and jumped to his feet. His face was suffused with sudden unexpected anger. It was an amazing, unbelievable transformation. Never before had she seen this gentle, mild-mannered Louis in such a state.

"No!" he shouted, "by heaven no!"

Quickly she remembered the part she had been given to play.

"My mother has made up her mind. Your grandfather has made up his. The Pope will be acquainted with the full facts. A dissolution, my poor Louis, is inevitable."

Louis' anger subsided as suddenly as it had risen. He turned and carefully picked up the chair. He replaced it and sat down. He leaned over the table with his head in his hands. For an intolerably long moment he remained like that, a figure or ridiculous tragedy. Finally he looked up.

"But I love and adore you," he said simply.

Her heart went out to him. What had Mercy said? Sympathy and understanding, gentleness and compassion. She felt them all but she steeled herself to complete the task she had been given.

"It is either dissolution or . . ."

His face went white and tense, yet as though not knowing what he was doing he started eating again, stuffing the food into

51

his mouth with a frantic haste. "I am a weakling, I know that. I keep arguing with myself. I dream about it. I have horrible nightmares. Really, Marie, I wish I had never been born."

Marie Antoinette rose and ran round the table to him. She flung her arms round his neck, pillowed her head against his breast.

"I love you with all my heart, Louis. I want you, I need you. I care nothing for the throne, nothing for state affairs. All I want or care for is my husband and the children he should give me."

She was shaken and amazed at this uprush of emotion. Half-sobbing she added, "I would gladly resign the throne and live contentedly forever with my husband, the little clockmaker."

He laughed happily. "I do make better clocks than anybody else in France, don't I!"

She drew back from him. This was going a little too far.

"When?" she demanded.

"Tomorrow." He cleared his throat. "Tomorrow without fail."

"Why not see the chief physician tonight, make the arrangements at once?"

"Why not!" he cried.

He jumped to his feet, said "Why not!" again and rushed headlong to the door.

"Louis!"

He turned. "Marie?"

"Make the arrangements, then take me to Paris."

"Paris?"

"There is a masked ball at the Opera. You know how I love masked balls, but usually you leave me to go with your brothers and their wives."

He hung his head. "You know what a poor dancer I am."

"Nonsense! My husband, soon to be my lover, is the best dancer in the world."

"By heaven yes!" he shouted, and ran from the room.

Leaving her dinner unfinished she went with light steps to her dressing-room, called her ladies about her and began to dress for the masked ball. During the last few months, stretching her wings and insisting on her freedom, defying even the strict routine set by Madame Adelaide, she had gone many times to the Opera balls. Mercy had at first objected but in the end had agreed that it was a harmless enough occupation, providing she went always in the company of the Dauphin or other members of the royal household, and providing she was careful to preserve her anonymity by retaining her mask throughout the evening. These masked balls, a piquant addition to the more formal balls at Versailles and the Palais Royal, had given her an escape from boredom.

Ready at last in a pale yellow ball-gown, but shrouded entirely by the long black domino which, with the mask, was the fashion at the Opera, she sent a message to Louis, telling him that the coach was waiting. She began to suspect that something was wrong when the servant returned to say that his royal Highness the Dauphin was closeted with the King. An hour passed. Word came that Provence and Artois had already set out with their wives for Paris. She then learned that Louis had now retired to his workshop.

"Intolerable," she stormed, "intolerable!"

Carrying her mask, the black domino billowing about her, she hurried in a rage to Louis' workshop. He had changed into rough clothes. The shirt he wore was old and torn, the sleeves rolled up. He was bending over the vice, busily occupied with a long slender file.

"Louis!" she all but screamed.

He looked up uneasily. There were beads of perspiration on his brow.

"You were to take me to the Opera!" she stormed.

"Dear me, it had quite slipped my memory."

"Did you see the chief physician?"

"No." He resumed his work at the vice. "I changed my mind."

"Fear got the better of you again!"

He glanced at her reproachfully. "You tried to play a trick on me."

"A trick?" she echoed.

He put down the file and looked at her squarely. "I am slow-witted. I admit it. But left to myself I sometimes work things out. I did in this instance. I went to see the King. He isn't in very good health, by the way. And do you know, Marie—" his look was owlish now—"he knows nothing of the suggested dissolution. You said he had made up his mind but it was the first he had heard of it."

"I see I should have confided in him first!"

"Yes. One must be very precise when practicing intrigue. I also gave your mother some considerable thought. For many years she worked for this marriage of ours and the Austrian alliance. It was silly of me to believe that she would allow all her plans to be set aside by dissolution. Very silly."

"Coward, coward, coward!" she cried.

He flinched. "I don't like to be coerced."

"You said you loved and adored me."

"I do," he said earnestly. "With all my heart and soul. With all my mind too, even if it isn't a very good mind."

He bent over the vice again and began to file a piece of metal. "Louis!"

He pushed and pulled at the file more vigorously. The noise made all conversation impossible. Seeing that further argument was useless she flung herself violently from the workshop. Back in her own apartments her eyes fell on the King's coat. Such a silly-looking thing, with one sleeve yet to be sewn in. All the same, it had a grotesquely human appearance. She picked it up and stabbed at it furiously with the needle.

"Die, die, die!" she raged.

She dropped it after a moment, thoroughly ashamed of herself.

"But I shall still go to the Opera ball," she said, her voice shrill in the empty room, "and I shall be the last to leave, even if I stay there till five in the morning."

EIGHT

"This," the princesse de lamballe protested mildly, "is the fifth time that you have started out for the Opera unaccompanied by the Dauphin."

Marie Antoinette and the princess were making their way down the marble Versailles staircase. Marie Antoinette paused for a moment and twirled the mask in her hand defiantly.

"What of it, Louise?"

"It is scarcely in good taste."

"I have never yet been recognized at the Opera."

"But Versailles knows. And there is much gossip."

Marie Antoinette glanced at her coldly. "I love you dearly, Louise, but there are times when you begin to bore me. Come, we are wasting precious time."

Before they reached the coach they were met by Madame Adelaide.

"Ah," that lady said scathingly, "on your way again to a night of frivolous enjoyment. Well, it scarcely matters now *what* you do."

"No," Marie Antoinette agreed, thinking of the cowardly Louis.

Madame Adelaide was grinning wickedly. "You have, of course, heard the latest gossip."

"That the King is thinking of marrying again? I heard it ages ago. You started it, didn't you?"

"I did more than that. I suggested it, and he was most interested."

"He may marry again for all *I* care."

It was almost midnight when they reached the Opera. With the princess close on her heels, Marie Antoinette went at once to the box which was always reserved for Provence. She glanced about her with pleasure. Never before had she seen so many people at a masked ball. These Opera balls, as people said, were fast becoming the most popular diversion in Paris.

For a lady of high birth, especially if she came unattended, as many did, the masked ball was an excuse for a little quiet dalliance. Wearing domino and mask she moved about freely and if a man—the men wore no masks—attracted her sufficiently she graciously permitted herself to be monopolized. A gay conversation, sprinkled with innuendo, quickly followed, while flirtatious advances, by word of mouth only, became the order of the day. All very innocent, unless you removed your mask, which was an established sign that you were ready to follow dalliance with a serious assignation. Nothing vulgar in that, surely! The only pity was that to the Dauphine of France such things were prohibited.

Artois and his wife were already in the box, and with them was the Duc de Chartres, son of the Duc d'Orleans, surrounded by a group of insolent young bloods. Provence took her aside. There was a hint of amused mockery in his eyes.

"Masked you are, your charms hidden by that ridiculous domino, but your light springing step gives you away every time."

"The rule of the Opera," she said tartly, "should be that men are masked also. Then I might find your attentions less odious."

"Always the haughty Austrian. Has poor Berri completely given up dancing?"

"Apparently. He has a regular appointment these nights with a vice and a file."

"Ah, a vice and a file, but not the surgeon's knife. Poor frightened Berri. How easy it is to fill the simple fellow with fear. And how it amuses me to see him quake when I explain the details of the operation. Supposing the surgeon is drunk, I chide him, or nervous, or over-awed by the high station of his patient. Imagine what might happen if the knife should slip."

"You sound as if you hate him."

"No, no, I merely hate the fact that he was born first. That, nothing more." He offered his arm. "Come, stroll with me among the crowd. We can flirt and dally. I might even persuade you to unmask for me, with the usual implications." He threaded his arm through hers. "Well?"

She freed herself quickly. "I loathe the sight of you."

He flushed. "How easy you find it to make enemies. Take the Prince de Rohan, for instance. He is gossiping about you in Vienna. Why make an enemy of me also, little spitfire?"

With a sob she hurried from him and leaving the box was soon engulfed in the crowd. The Princesse de Lamballe, anxiously following her, was soon lost. All about her were masked and dominoed ladies, flutteringly pretending to run from the pursuing gallants but eager, she knew, to be caught. Her heart beat high. This was the first time she had ventured forth alone. She felt a compelling need for reckless abandonment, and resolved that the first man to approach her should win her for the night. The first man was the younger brother, Artois. She evaded him by giving her arm to a tall young man who, standing a few paces away, was staring at her fixedly. She moved with him to a quiet corner.

"Thank you, Monsieur."

He bowed. He was still staring at her.

"Forgive me," he said at last. "I cannot see your face. What held me spellbound was the way you walked. Your movements are sheer poetry."

He spoke with an accent which she found hard to place.

"Flattery," she said, addressing him in German, "is commonplace at the Opera."

"I spoke in all sincerity," he replied, in the same language.

She looked at him with increasing interest. "You speak German, as you speak French, with an accent. What is your nationality?"

He made a comical little face. "My German is poor, I admit, but I had flattered myself that I spoke French like a Frenchman. My homeland is Sweden. You, if I may say so, speak French with an accent, but German perfectly."

"German is my native tongue."

She was studying him carefully now. His clothes were elegant and obviously of French origin. He wore them with a grace that had in it a certain not unamusing air of gravity. She thought he was trying to assume a manner which would make him seem older than he was, more experienced.

"Have you been long in Paris?" she asked.

"A few weeks only, but I have been away from home two years, completing my education in Germany and Italy and Switzerland."

"Not really completing it," she laughed. "That can only be achieved in Paris."

"Paris, I admit, is the center of the civilized world."

"So the Parisians claim, Monsieur," and to tease him she added mischievously, "You must have been a mere babe in arms when you left Sweden."

His face broke into a charming boyish smile. "I was about to lie to you, but somehow I could never do that. I was sixteen."

57

She found herself liking him immensely. He was the most handsome young man she had ever met, tall and slim, with easy fluid movements. His blond hair was thick and glossy and set in natural waves, his skin was clear, as fine almost as her own, and his chin attractively pointed. A mere child, of course, very nearly girlish, except for the steady dark eyes—eyes, she thought fancifully, of a young man who weighed every problem deeply, who never acted impulsively, who could be trusted implicitly, who gave his word and, whatever the cost, kept it. She laughed aloud in surprise at these serious thoughts. What a strange effect he was having upon her, forcing her against her very nature to be serious.

"It's too ridiculous," she cried.

"I beg your pardon?"

"Tell me more about your travels," she evaded.

"There is little to tell. In Italy I studied music. In Germany I gave most of my time to military matters—I am, you see, intent on an army career. In Switzerland I observed the very curious habits of the Lutherans. From Geneva I went over the border to visit Monsieur de Voltaire at Ferney. It was he who advised me, perhaps mockingly, to spend some time in Paris where I might receive a final polish as far as manners are concerned."

"You are acquiring the polish rapidly."

"But not the affectation, I trust."

She laughed merrily. What a delightful young man he was, and how refreshing his company after that of Provence.

"Tell me what you have done in Paris, Monsieur."

"A great many things indeed. Yesterday, for instance, I went to that great school of learning, the Lycée; I took a drive in the boulevards; I went to the Ecole Militaire, and for more than an hour I watched the workmen who are building that new church, the Madeleine, I think it is."

"A very full day, and a dull one too!"

"But I learned something important about the French people."

"And that?"

"They drink far too much wine, especially the workers. Millions of gallons will be drunk before that church is completed."

"Have you been to the Théâtre Français?"

"Yes."

"And Versailles, have you been there?"

"Yes indeed. His Majesty was gracious enough to receive me

58

and ask me a few questions about my own country. Madame Dubarry also received me."

"*That* creature!" Marie Antoinette burst out.

"I found her very charming."

"What fools men are!"

"Forgive me if I have displeased you," he said mildly.

"Did the Dauphine also receive you?" she asked, smiling behind her mask.

"No, but I caught a glimpse of her. A very beautiful young lady but not, I think, a happy one."

"Really?"

"Frivolous, pleasure-seeking, yet discontented with the aimlessness of her life."

"You came to a very quick conclusion, after just a glimpse!"

"Yes," he admitted, "but I think I was right."

His smugness was intolerable. She turned away, ready now to seek diversion elsewhere. He was much too serious, that was obvious, for dalliance and light flirtation.

"One moment, please," he begged.

"Well, Monsieur?"

"I should like to think that we might meet again."

"That is impossible."

"May I see your face without the mask?"

She hesitated for a moment, but thinking happily of his consternation on recognizing her, she tore the mask from her face. He studied her carefully and earnestly, yet without the slightest flicker of recognition. She waited impatiently for him to speak, she waited for quite a long time.

"You find me beautiful?" she demanded.

His dark eyes lit up. "How self-satisfied you sound."

She stamped her foot. "The polish you came to Paris to find is not as pronounced as I thought."

"I promised myself long ago never to indulge in insincerities."

"Speak frankly then!"

"Yes, I find you beautiful."

"Ah!" she said, melting.

"The beauty of your face is quite flawless."

She tilted up her chin; her anger with him disappeared completely.

"Yet the flawlessness," he frowned, "disconcerts me by the suggestion of soullessness that accompanies it."

59

Soullessness! Nettled but not yet angry again, she said: "Surely my Habsburg lip is a serious flaw."

"Your Habsburg lip!" he exclaimed. "That, and the accent, as well as the haughtiness . . . ! Great heavens, now I know who you are!"

"You should have guessed earlier, Monsieur."

He bowed low before her. "Your Highness, my humble and sincere apologies."

"It must have been a very tiny glimpse you had of me at Versailles."

"Your Highness, I am speechless, quite speechless."

"You might at least find sufficient speech to take back your unjust words."

His jaw set stubbornly. "I have already apologized."

"Nevertheless—"

"What I said, I said in all sincerity."

She held his eyes steadily. "Then the sooner you return to Sweden the better. You will never acquire in Paris the polish you came to seek."

"I am beginning to believe that," he said humbly.

"Nor tactfulness, so necessary in civilized society."

He smiled. "Ah, but where does tactfulness end and insincerity begin?"

She replaced her mask. "Goodnight, Monsieur, and goodbye."

With all the dignity she could assume she walked slowly back to Provence's box. She found that she was trembling, that her lip was quivering, that she was stupidly on the point of bursting into tears. At the box an agitated Princesse de Lamballe sprang forward to greet her.

"Your Highness, where have you been!"

"Take me back to Versailles, Louise, take me back at once!"

In the carriage, driving back through the night, she was so silent and brooding that the princess looked at her anxiously.

"What has happened to upset you so, Marie?"

"I have been grossly insulted."

"My *dear!* By whom?"

"An odious young prig. A foreigner. If I knew his name I would have him flung into the Bastille, indeed I would!"

Inconsequently she wondered what his name was, what his friends called him, if he had any friends! She saw his face again, his dark earnest eyes. She felt that she had known him for many years, had met him before, if only in a dream. She knew that if she wished to she could place her faith and trust in him and call him friend for the rest of her life. It was the oddest of feelings, comforting, yet at the same time alarming.

"No," she contradicted herself softly, "not the Bastille, except perhaps for a few days, in one of the grand apartments, to teach him a lesson."

At Versailles she found Madame Adelaide waiting for her, a surprisingly agitated Madame Adelaide with tear-stained cheeks but angry eyes.

"If you propose to lecture me—" Marie Antoinette began defensively.

"No, child, no."

"Ah, then the King has *not* decided to marry again!"

"No marriage will be possible for my father now. He had indeed decided on marriage, but to my horror his choice was not a young innocent princess but Madame Dubarry."

"Oh nonsense, Madame Adelaide. He was teasing you."

"It is of no consequence now, though the thought of it still makes me furious." Madame Adelaide crossed herself unexpectedly. "It is wrong of me to feel anger against a dying man."

Marie Antoinette's heart almost stopped beating. "A . . . dying man?"

"He is ill. There are unmistakable signs of smallpox."

"Not everybody dies of smallpox," Marie Antoinette said faintly.

"The King is a physical wreck. He has no resistance. Very soon, child, you will be Queen of France."

Marie Antoinette, laughing hysterically, could think of only one thing.

"That coat! He will never wear it now. Not even in his coffin!"

In the days that followed the King grew steadily worse. On the seventh day he was told the nature of his illness, and for him that was the end. Madame Adelaide attended him constantly, and so, to everybody's surprise, did Madame Dubarry who, scorning the risk of infection, nursed him with a fanatical devotion.

"A brave woman," Marie Antoinette admitted.

"Brave!" Madame Adelaide scoffed. "She is frantic with fear. She knows that her days are numbered. You could if you wished have her sent away at once."

61

"If her presence gives him comfort, let her remain till the end."

A few hours later Louis came with the news that Madame Adelaide had had her way. In conjunction with the King's confessor she had issued an ultimatum. If the dying monarch wished to leave the world in a state of grace he must first send Madame Dubarry away.

"She has already gone," Louis said.

Marie Antoinette's eyes snapped. "I see we are going to have trouble with Madame Adelaide."

The days dragged on and still the King lingered, his body half-dead and rotting. The stench, Madame Adelaide said, was insufferable. Though many courtiers kept vigil in the royal anteroom, many others had fled from the infection, and as each day passed the palace grew more deserted. The future King and Queen remained isolated in their own apartments, waiting for the end. Marie Antoinette for her own part waited patiently, irritated only by Louis' air of gloom. How clear he made it that he had no real wish to be king, was even afraid to rule!

"I find it hard to understand you," she told him.

"The responsibility of the future appals me, Marie."

"A king must have an heir. Is that what makes you afraid?"

Louis blinked his shortsighted eyes and made no reply.

"You must agree," she added, "that the need for an heir is much more pressing now."

"I—I agree."

"You will waste no time in taking the necessary step?"

Again he made no reply, but he came closer, went down on his knees and took her hands in his. She stiffened at his touch and thought with loathing of last night when he had attempted again to make love to her. To be used like that was the same as being offered a meal when you were desperately hungry, only to have the meal snatched away from you at the last moment.

"All I want," he said, laying his cheek against her palm, "is to make you happy, give you everything in my power."

"Everything except one thing, Louis."

"Give me time, Marie," he pleaded. "I know my duty to my wife and the throne."

They were warned the next day that the end might come at any moment. With them as they waited was Count Mercy, talking softly about the main events of the reign that was drawing to a close. He touched lightly on the weaknesses of the fifteenth Louis but stressed quite heavily the fact that they had brought the country close to ruin. Marie Antoinette saw Louis nod wisely, heard him say "It is an example I shall try never to follow," but she was scarcely listening. Her mind was full of plans for the future. Freedom at last, complete freedom! Never again need she submit to the domineering Madame Adelaide, and as for Madame de Noailles, old Madame Etiquette, *she* would be the first to go. She would surround herself with young people, gay, lighthearted people. Versailles, when the necessary period of mourning was over, would be more splendid, more magnificent than ever before.

"And so," Mercy was saying, "his passing will go unmourned in Paris. The people, I fear, will rejoice, not mourn. To many it will be the lifting of a crippling yoke. Already the poor of the city are looking to the new reign with hope in their hearts. In the new King and the new Queen they are trying to see salvation." He paused, listening. "Ah, what was that!"

Marie Antoinette listened. At first she heard only a low murmur of voices, but rapidly, like a river in flood, the murmur rose to a sustained roar. The door was flung open and a surging crowd of courtiers, led by Madame de Noailles and carrying the two brothers in their midst, swept into the room. Madame de Noailles was the first in the crazy scramble to reach Marie Antoinette. She fell on her knees. Her face was working painfully.

"Your Majesty!" she cried.

For a long moment all was confusion.

"The King is dead, long live the King!" everybody was shouting.

"The fight is on," Mercy whispered.

"What fight?" Marie Antoinette whispered back.

"The fight for power." He bowed and kissed her hand. "Your Majesty."

She looked at Louis. Tears were rolling down his cheeks. His shoulders were heaving. To her surprise he fell on his knees and the crowd stood back, forming a circle about him.

"May God help and guide me," he said brokenly. "I am too young to reign."

It was the height of sentimentality. She saw little in it but a public admission of weakness, though it was obvious from the murmur of approval which arose that he had made a good impression. Promptly, with the utmost grace, she fell on her knees at his side and placed her hand in his.

"God help us both," she said piously.

63

Part II

ONE

"I EARNESTLY SUGGEST, SIRE, THAT YOU RECALL MAUREPAS."

Madame Adelaide's tone, rather than her words, made it clear to Marie Antoinette that the old-maid aunt was wasting no time in attempting to rule the new King. Well, Mercy had said that the fight was on, and on it certainly was! Louis, indulgent enough when she had dismissed old Madame Etiquette, was stubbornly set against sending the aunts into retirement.

"Who is Maurepas?" Marie Antoinette demanded.

Madame Adelaide laughed joyously. "Monsieur le Comte de Maurepas is a very astute old gentleman. My father sent him into exile because he wrote a number of witty, if dirty, verses about Madame de Pompadour."

The new court had been here at Choisy for nearly a week. The smallness of this royal hunting lodge, after the vastness of Versailles, was by no means to Marie Antoinette's liking. Unsafe as it was to return just yet to the disease-infected palace, she could only regard residence at Choisy as a form of banishment.

"Thank heaven," Madame Adelaide added, "royal mistresses are a thing of the past."

"I do promise you this," Louis said stoutly. "Women will never rule me as they ruled my poor misguided grandfather."

"I see I am being warned," Marie Antoinette flashed back. "Does this royal edict apply also to maiden aunts?"

Madame Adelaide bristled instantly. "I am a woman of considerable experience. My sole wish is to help the new King. That is why I suggest the recall of Maurepas."

64

Marie Antoinette shrugged. "Recall him if you must, Louis. He sounds amusing, at least."

Louis looked uneasily from his wife to his aunt. "I need you both. I want and need your help. I am working hard, studying every problem. I need everybody's help. France is in a dreadful state. The financial position is frightening. Strict economy will be necessary. We are close to ruin. Only economy can save us. Economy in every government department, economy at Versailles. I myself must set a personal example by reducing the cost of running the royal household." He sighed deeply. "I have decided to make a personal gesture by setting aside the *joyeux avénement.*"

"What is that, Louis?"

"An old tradition which gives a new King the right to impose a tax of 40,000 livres. I should like you to make a gesture too, Marie, by refusing your own traditional *droit de ceinture.*"

"Tell me what it is, first."

"The ceremony of the Queen's Girdle. In the old days a new Queen wore a girdle, and money raised by a special tax was placed in the purse that hung from it."

"She will refuse it gladly," Madame Adelaide said.

Marie Antoinette shook with anger. "So I, too, am expected to jump through the hoop held out by Madame Adelaide!"

"My dear . . ." Louis begged.

"Money means nothing to me, Louis, but I do prefer to make my own decisions."

"The people will love you for it."

"That will be nice. My chief concern is this: when can we return to Versailles?"

"How bored she is with Choisy," Madame Adelaide exclaimed. "Rather than miss one moment of pleasure she would gladly endanger all our lives."

Marie Antoinette looked at her with loathing, and as she looked a delightful idea occurred to her. Heaven knew, she had had her lesson as far as court intrigue was concerned, but challenged by Madame Adelaide's aggressiveness she was prepared, just once more, to indulge in it. And the woman did, after all, look flushed and out of sorts.

"Poor Aunt Adelaide," she said quietly, "I think you must be ill without knowing it."

"Ill?" Madame Adelaide's head shot up.

"You look quite feverish to me. Have you a headache?"

"Headache?" Madame Adelaide touched her brow experimentally.

"You have, of course, gone through a terrible ordeal. Small wonder you are irritable and out of temper. Your head really is aching intolerably, I can see that clearly."

"A little, but not intolerably!"

"You keep squirming in your chair. Have you a backache also?" Madame Adelaide's eyes began to betray alarm. "There *is* a faint pain in my back, but—"

"Have you ever had smallpox?"

"Smallpox?" Madame Adelaide leaped to her feet. "You are trying to frighten me, child!"

Marie Antoinette shook her head sadly. "Poor Aunt Adelaide, you nursed the late King with such disregard for your own welfare."

Madame Adelaide clapped her hand to her brow. "My God, the infection!" She was sweating now. Her face was flushed, her hands were trembling. "My God, my God!"

Louis rose and went heavily to her side.

"Keep your distance!" she shrieked. "As you value your life, don't touch me. I must be placed in complete isolation at once!"

"And so you shall be," Marie Antoinette murmured happily.

To her surprise, however, Madame Adelaide was indeed suffering from the dread disease, and the two other aunts immediately imagined that they were similarly afflicted. All three were hurried away to a house well removed from the hunting lodge, an event which Marie Antoinette viewed with considerable satisfaction. Hardy Madame Adelaide was in no real danger, but her absence from court would be lengthy, and when she returned she would be made to understand just who was mistress.

Meanwhile the chief physician tentatively suggested that the King and Queen should submit to the new preventative treatment.

"Inoculation?" Louis said, in alarm.

"I earnestly advise it," the physician said. "Already fifty people who were at Versailles during the late King's illness have been struck down and five have died."

"Most distressing," Louis wailed.

"Only the superstitious disapprove of inoculation, Sire."

"Yes, yes, but surely it is highly dangerous to have one's arm slashed in three or four places and serum taken from a smallpox victim forced into the wounds."

"We take our serum from only the mildest cases, Sire."

"And the result is a mild infection, accompanied by fever and—and spots on the face and body!"

"Four little knife cuts," Marie Antoinette said softly. "You would never feel it."

Louis shuddered. "No!"

"You have often hurt yourself in the workshop. Once you cut a great gash in your hand. It pained you for days but you never complained."

"That was an accident. Accidents happen . . . well, *accidentally*. But to deliberately expose yourself to the knife, to wait for it to plunge into your flesh . . . !" He swallowed painfully.

"Darling Louis," she said persuasively, "once you have this inoculation and realize how simple it is you will submit without a murmur to the other little ordeal."

"You—you actually think so, Marie?"

"I am sure of it."

"We-ell . . ."

"What are the people going to think of their King when they learn how much he fears inoculation?"

Louis began to plod about the room with heavy, dragging steps.

"My grandfather had no right to die, no right at all! I am much too young to rule. I—I feel as if the whole world has fallen on top of me. Aunt Adelaide was a real tower of strength, but now she can help me no longer."

Marie Antoinette kept her temper in check. "There is only one tower of strength in this life, Louis, and that is Almighty God. God has chosen you to rule France and God will guide you."

"You believe that, Marie?"

"Yes, Louis, of course I do."

"We-ell . . ."

"If you wish I shall be the first to have the inoculation."

He squared his shoulders. "No, no! I, the King, shall be the first victim."

Monsieur le Comte de Maurepas' arrival at Versailles coincided with Louis' inoculation. Marie Antoinette received the old gentleman while the 'operation' was in progress. She liked him instantly, this former minister who had dared to make fun of a royal mistress, and who as a result had suffered an exile from court of almost twenty-five years. In spite of his age—she had learned that Maurepas was seventy-three—he was as lively as a monkey and had the most mischievous eyes she had ever seen. After he had made his bow and kissed her hand he stood back, head on one side, studying her critically.

"You like the look of your Queen, Monsieur?"

He took out his snuff-box. "To gaze on your beauty makes me feel young again."

"Ah, we shall become good friends, you and I."

He took a pinch of snuff. "What a relief to return to a court free, at last, of royal mistresses." He sneezed delicately. "No longer shall I feel called upon to write derisive verses. Now I shall be a real poet and write odes to the most beautiful queen in the world."

"I may yet command you to write at least a few derisive verses, Maurepas."

"Old-maid aunts are now my speciality, Madame."

She laughed delightedly. "How well we understand each other!"

Louis came hurriedly into the room. Briefly he acknowledged Maurepas' bow and words of gratitude. His face was white and drawn; with his right hand he was clutching his left arm, but tenderly, below the shoulder.

"Horrible!" he cried. "Had I known I would never have faced it."

And as hurriedly as he had entered he took his departure.

Maurepas looked quizzically at Marie Antoinette. "The inoculation?"

"The inoculation!"

Maurepas shrugged. "We have a new King, yes; but more important, we have a new Queen." He bowed ceremoniously. "Madame, now and forever, your humble servant."

Mercy, to whom with glee she reported this incident, shook his head disapprovingly. Maurepas, he said, belonging as he did to the old order of courtiers, was not to be trusted. Like all the others of the last generation he sought power for its own sake. France itself was of only secondary consideration.

"Better Maurepas than Madame Adelaide!" she cried.

"Madame Adelaide brought him out of exile."

"And I, if necessary, will send him back to it."

Mercy looked most disturbed. "I wonder, your Majesty, if you realize how dangerous it is, this game you are trying to play? Dangerous for you, dangerous also for France." Since she remained silent, staring at him indignantly, he went on carefully:

"Your Imperial mother is most distressed by the death of the late King. She feels that you are much too young to become involved in court intrigue. In effect, she advises against it, wishes you to stand aloof until you are older and more experienced."

"In short, the Queen of France is to take her orders from Vienna!"

Mercy smiled faintly. "I see that I spoke hastily."

"You did indeed, Mercy."

"Yet it seems odd that a girl interested only in pleasure should show such a sudden interest in state affairs. Why, I wonder, are you doing it?"

She could think of two reasons. The interference of Madame Adelaide was certainly one. Then too, restricted as she was by the mourning period, real pleasure-seeking was impossible, so better an interest in state affairs than no interest at all. Unwittingly she thought of a third reason. That odious foreigner, the elderly young Swede—what had he said about her? Frivolous, pleasure-seeking, discontented with the aimlessness of her life. His words, really, had been a challenge, a challenge to which she was replying as best she could. She thought of his handsome figure, his steady dark eyes. Was he still in Paris? Would he, when the court returned, present himself at Versailles? Let him, let him! she raged. I shall treat him coldly, with complete disdain!

Mercy was still waiting for her answer.

She smiled brightly. "Why am I doing it? Because I realize the importance and seriousness of my new position."

"Most commendable."

"You don't believe me!"

"Tell me what is wrong with France in this, the year of your accession; tell me what should be done to put matters right. Then, your Majesty, I will be glad to believe you."

She was cornered and knew it.

"I have agreed to set aside my *droit de ceinture*," she said defensively.

"Poor little Toinette," Mercy sighed, "your ignorance of the true situation would be laughable were it not so tragic. Still, who can blame you? Having known nothing but luxury and privilege, you take both for granted. If there are people in the world who are penniless and hungry you are no doubt sorry for them, but you know nothing of what it means to be penniless and hungry. A King to you is a King by divine right. He is all-powerful, absolute. That there are people in the world, particularly in France, who are beginning to question the rights and privileges you take for granted, never occurs to you. Yet there are such people, and their numbers are growing. For years I have watched and listened. What amazes me is that the late King was allowed to reach the end of his life without being swept from his throne."

"What an extraordinary thing to say, Mercy!"

"No one can blame you for such an attitude."

"Tell me what you think should be done," she said, but her interest was flagging.

"The most pressing need is a big reduction in taxation. That would bring at least a little relief to the poor, though it is not from the poor that I expect active opposition, but from the well-to-do middle classes who more than any other group resent the privileges and prerogatives of the aristocracy."

"You must talk to Louis," she said, stifling a yawn. "You and he have a lot in common."

"His Majesty is badly handicapped. Maurepas and the ministers he appoints will see that the truth is kept from him."

"Then there's nothing I can do, except try and enjoy myself."

"Better to concentrate on enjoyment, my dear, than to meddle."

"Meddle? You call it meddling when I resent Madame Adelaide's interference?"

"In point of fact, all that worries you is the old-maid aunt's attempt to rule your husband, eh?"

"In point of fact, yes."

Mercy smiled comically. "How I must have bored you, talking as I did. What an old windbag you must have thought me."

"Yes indeed!" she laughed. "Now tell me, how soon will it be safe to return to Versailles?"

TWO

With the imperiousness of an orchestra leader the new hair-dresser, Léonard, held up his hands for silence. All chatter ceased. Her Majesty's ladies, fluttering and simpering, crowded together at a respectful distance while old Maurepas, who had been lounging at the door, strolled negligently forward. Léonard, nattily dressed, self-important as a cock-sparrow, fierce of eyebrow, glanced sharply at all the staring faces. Finally, his eyes came to rest once more on her Majesty's new headdress.

A tension began to grow as Marie Antoinette, saying not a word, intently examined her reflection in the mirror. Aware of the anxiety she was causing it amused her to prolong the silence. Léonard, dear little man that he was, was growing purple in the face, so severe was the strain of waiting. She looked at her ladies' faces in the mirror. Each was obviously ready to praise or condemn, once she herself had expressed an opinion. For a moment she held Maurepas' eyes in the mirror; his gaze alone remained impassive.

"Léonard," she said at last, "you have excelled yourself."

He fell on his knees; tears of gratitude sprang to his eyes.

"Your Majesty's humble servant," he gasped.

"Monsieur Léonard has excelled himself!" her ladies cried, and clapped their hands.

Marie Antoinette looked again at the reflection of this new, quite monstrous headdress. It resembled a tower— No, she decided, more correctly it resembled a pyramid but blunt at the top. Her own hair, luxuriant of growth, had not been sufficient to cover the frame over which it had been twined, and large quantities of false hair had been supplemented. The weight gave her rather a giddy feeling. It would be necessary to walk with the utmost circumspection.

"Monsieur de Maurepas," she said, "has not yet expressed an opinion."

Maurepas, snuff-box poised, said teasingly, "I never saw anything so ridiculous in my life."

71

Léonard made a chattering sound, half groan, half cry of indignation.

"Still," Maurepas went on, "the accent today is on the ridiculous. Without a doubt this new headdress will be the rage of Versailles tonight, the rage of Paris tomorrow, while the next day couriers will be speeding forth with the news to all the cities of Europe. A revolution, your Majesty, is about to take place."

Marie Antoinette laughed merrily.

"And furthermore," Maurepas added, "the builders and stonemasons will be kept busy at Versailles for months to come."

"Indeed?"

"Your Majesty will find it impossible to pass through any doorway without bending the knees."

Marie Antoinette rose immediately. "Open the door, Monsieur!"

Maurepas opened the door.

She moved towards it, stepping forward gingerly but holding her head erect with all the dignity the weighty headdress would permit.

"There!" Maurepas chuckled.

Marie Antoinette laughed gaily. "But what a joke, what a joke!"

Her ladies clapped their hands. "What a joke, what a joke!"

At that moment Mademoiselle Bertin, now enjoying the exclusive patronage Marie Antoinette had promised her, came bustling along the corridor. In her arms she carried, most lovingly, a roll of silk.

"A new discovery, your Majesty! A fine new color. A sort of puce, your Majesty."

"Show me," Marie Antoinette demanded.

The ladies gathered excitedly round Mademoiselle Bertin who, with many important flourishes, unwound a few yards of the silk.

"Delightful," Marie Antoinette pronounced. "Just the color of Madame Adelaide's face when in a temper."

Laughter rose immediately. Hands were clapped.

"Say rather," Maurepas commented, "the exact shade of a well-fed flea."

A gasp of horror rose, but Marie Antoinette, in a mood to be amused at anything, readily agreed.

"Nevertheless, we will call it *couleur d'Adelaide*. You will of course make me a new gown without a moment's delay, my dear Bertin."

72

"I have already in my head a design that will rock the whole world, your Majesty!"

When the little dressmaker, said now to be the most prosperous in Paris, had hurried importantly away, Marie Antoinette gave her arm to Maurepas.

"Take me to the King's apartments. I must show his Majesty the new headdress."

How delightful it was, she thought, as she walked with Maurepas through her inner anteroom, to be back at Versailles, to know that her early dreams had at last come true. It scarcely mattered that Madame Adelaide, fully recovered from her illness, was back at Versailles also, still intent on ruling Louis. Forming a Madame Adelaide party, she had gathered a little group of supporters about her. So amusing, it was, to watch the formation of these little groups, for each of the royal brothers had his own supporters too, as had the various ministers of the crown. Highly diverting, to see the shifting loyalties, the quarrelling, the splitting up, the grouping and re-grouping. It was like a new dance which began solemnly, grew hectic, disintegrated, and began all over again as something quite different.

"Have a care," Maurepas warned, as they approached the outer anteroom.

She chuckled, bent her knees and passed safely through the doorway.

Louis, she reflected, as they continued their slow and stately progress towards the Queen's Guard Room, was trying to remain aloof from the various factions. Taking his new position with a heavy seriousness, he spent hours and hours each day studying what he called the "situation." Mercy spoke well of his efforts, as did Maurepas, but then, Maurepas, as chief adviser to the King, had his own smooth ax to grind. She still liked Maurepas and found him more amusing every day. The fact that he owed his appointment to Madame Adelaide mattered not at all, for the moment the trouble with the Parlements arose he opposed that lady wholeheartedly.

Marie Antoinette frowned in an effort to recall just what it meant, the recent trouble with the Parlements. There were twelve Parlements in France, or so Louis had told her, chief of which was the Parlement of Paris. They were law courts, founded at one time and another by the kings of France. During the last reign the

Parlement of Paris had grown in power, grown to such an extent that its magistrates had seized a sort of right to approve or disapprove of royal edicts. Normally a king issued an edict and an obedient Parlement of Paris registered it without demur, but during the old Louis' reign there had been quarrels between king and Parlement and the old King, stirring himself, had replaced the Parlement with magistrates of his own choosing.

Marie Antoinette felt her head begin to whirl. "Maurepas, just how did the trouble with the Parlements begin?"

"One moment, your Majesty!"

She understood, laughed, bent her knees again and passed cautiously into the Queen's Guardroom.

"As your Majesty will recall," Maurepas said lightly, "no sooner did the wicked old King die than the people began to agitate for real Parlements again. I myself felt that to meet the demands of the people in that direction would be a wise move on your husband's part."

Marie Antoinette's eyes narrowed. "And Madame Adelaide, interfering as usual, was against it."

"She was indeed."

"And for that reason I allowed myself to be drawn into the argument."

Maurepas made a face. "For that reason only, I fear."

"Yes, and because the supporters of the wretched maiden aunt are such spoilsports, while the Parlement people, like yourself, are gay amusing companions."

"The motive was shockingly immoral, but the result praiseworthy."

She laughed happily. The means she had employed could be called "shockingly immoral" too. She had waited until Louis, swayed this way and that in the heated argument, had reached a state of pitiful indecision. She recalled the scene vividly. So easy to sympathize with him, to remark in honeyed tones on the worry the problem must be causing him, and then, with a rapier-like thrust, to attack him once again about his fear of the surgeon's knife. So much easier after that, while he was reduced to silent confusion, to say, "Maurepas is right; it is an injustice not to recall the Parlement of Paris." There was one sure way, she reflected now, of getting what she wanted, whether it be more money to spend, a pension for a friend, or his signature on a state document—a neat, scathing little gibe about the surgeon's knife.

"Yes, the result was praiseworthy," Maurepas repeated. "No King of France has ever been so popular with the people."

She was glad of that. A step in the right direction, Mercy had said, a sign that the throne might yet keep pace with the aims of the people to attain a fair and proper political status. Madame Adelaide, on the other hand, had declared bitterly that Louis had lost his first battle with the people. What a melodramatic thing to say! All that mattered was that she, the Queen, had won a most important battle with the old-maid aunt.

A sudden searing pain shot through her scalp.

"Maurepas," she cried, "you should have warned me!"

They had passed through the vestibule and on entering the Guardroom of the King her headdress had collided heavily with the top of the doorway.

"Is it ruined?" she asked.

"A trifle battered, your Majesty." He called one of the guards. "A chair, if you please."

A chair was brought, Maurepas climbed onto it and set to work to repair the damage.

"There," he chuckled, "even better than before. I shall be able soon to set up in competition with Léonard."

Without further incident they reached that holy of holies, the royal cabinet. It would have been quicker to have reached the cabinet by way of the little corridor which connected her bedchamber with Louis' apartments, but she still found pleasure in strolling through as many rooms as possible of her grand new apartments. Oh, childish, she admitted, but it was one sure way of reminding herself that she was indeed the Queen.

Louis, shortsighted as ever, did not immediately notice the new headdress, but Monsieur Turgot, who was with him, started visibly, after which he stared and stared, quite rudely. Marie Antoinette decided at once that what people were saying about Turgot—that he would never be a polished courtier—was true. Of all the ministers appointed at Maurepas' suggestion Turgot was the one she liked the least. Had he not said, soon after he became Comptroller of Finances, that he would permit interference from no one, not even the Queen? A man stupid enough to make such a remark, clever financier though he might be, could hardly expect to remain long at Versailles. Turgot, she decided, was Maurepas' one mistake.

"We were just about to send for you, Maurepas," Louis said.

"To discuss the coronation, no doubt?" Marie Antoinette asked eagerly.

"The coronation?" Louis echoed vaguely. "Yes, yes, plans are being made, but the coronation, I fear—" his voice sounded fretful—"will have to be postponed."

"Postponed? But why?"

It was Turgot who answered.

"Madame, there are riots in Paris. The news has just reached us." He continued to speak, as was his wont, in short sharp sentences. "Corn riots. A wave of discontent is sweeping through Paris. It must be checked before it sweeps through all of France. Coronation plans now? Impossible, your Majesty!"

"So this," she said indignantly, "is all your policy has achieved—riots!"

With Maurepas remaining silent and watchful, Louis came to Turgot's defense.

"Turgot had my full approval when he set up free trade in grain. There was a poor harvest. His aim was to avoid famine. No one can blame him because speculators have bought up large quantities and are releasing it slowly, at a high price."

"The riots," Turgot said tersely, "have been organized by the customs officers. I feel sure of that. They used to be a privileged class. I deprived them of personal revenue when I freed the grain trade. That is the position in a nutshell."

"Yet the fact remains," Louis said miserably, "that the price of bread has gone up and up. There is little enough of it even for those who can afford to buy it. The others, the poor, are going hungry." While speaking he had come closer to Marie Antoinette. He stared at her now in amazement. "Gracious heaven, what is *that* contraption?"

"A new headdress," she told him haughtily. "Whether or not you like it, it will be sweeping through Paris tomorrow."

Turgot laughed shortly. "On the one hand, corn riots, on the other, a new style in headdresses."

"You suggest, Monsieur Turgot, that there is a connection between the two?"

"No, Madame, but I do suggest that royal extravagance might provoke further riots."

"You speak with amazing frankness!"

"I pride myself on frankness, your Majesty."

"Some people would call it rudeness."

76

Turgot looked genuinely amazed. "Forgive me if I give that impression. Looking to the future I have but one desperate wish, to save the monarchy."

What an alarmist he was, what an idiotic thing to say!

"If the monarchy is in danger," she said brightly, "the sooner we have the coronation the better."

Since neither Turgot nor Louis laughed, she was glad to turn her back on them and return to her own apartments. There, to her delight, she found the Comtesse de Polignac waiting for her.

"Ah, so you came, my dear comtesse!"

"No one may lightly turn a deaf ear to a royal command," the young woman replied.

"It was anything but a command," Marie Antoinette said impulsively. "It was the request of a lonely young woman. Do please be seated, and remember, the last thing I want is formality."

The Comtesse de Polignac inclined her head and seated herself.

Marie Antoinette looked at her intently. She had received her last night at a private ball which, in spite of the period of mourning, Louis had indulgently permitted. Instantly she had been attracted to her and had decided without a moment's consideration to install her at Versailles.

"Why had I never seen you at court before?" she asked.

The comtesse smiled guilelessly. "I am able each year to spend only two or three months in the capital."

"Gracious, Madame, I imagined that everybody who was anybody spent as much time as possible in Paris."

"My husband is a very poor man," the comtesse said frankly. "And as for my lover, he is either very poor also, or very mean."

A lover as well as a husband! This was intriguing! She looked at the comtesse with great care. She wore a simple dress, just as last night she had worn a plain but quite becoming ball gown. Nor did she wear jewelry. Last night, a rose in her hair; this afternoon, a ribbon. It was beautiful hair, too, blonde and loose about her shoulders. There was a ribbon round her waist also, a dark rich blue which gave color to the folds of the pale blue gown. Her nose, slightly *retroussé*, made you want to laugh, and her mouth, turning up at the corners, was designed more for smiles than frowns. Her large eyes were dark and steady. Last night they had reminded Marie Antoinette of the eyes of the foreigner, the Swede. That, really, was why she had asked the comtesse to wait on her today.

77

"Tell me more about yourself, Madame."

"There's very little to tell, your Majesty. My husband is a member of an old family, a good family, even a most respectable family. A loyal family, that goes without saying, but also, alas, a poor one."

"What a dreadful bore *that* must be."

"To be poor? Not at all. I dress simply because I prefer simplicity."

"Where do you live when in Paris?"

"We have a modest house in the Rue des Bons Enfants. We also, I assure you, are the best of good children."

"Except that you have a lover."

"Fashionable, surely, though I care nothing for fashion. The truth is, I find a lover necessary."

Marie Antoinette all but clapped her hands. Such a delightful conversation!

"Does he live at the house in the Rue des Bons Enfants?"

"Naturally."

"But in the same house!"

The comtesse gave her a wide-eyed look. "Why not?"

"Your husband has no objection?"

"My husband is most accommodating—*and* civilized."

Marie Antoinette laughed merrily. "This is exactly like a play at the Théâtre Français. It would give me very great pleasure, Madame, if you would invite me, another very good child, to visit you at the Rue des Bons Enfants."

The comtesse looked at her placidly. "I can scarcely afford to entertain a Queen."

"Please invite the woman, not the Queen."

"The rule of my house is informality," the comtesse warned.

"I have already commanded informality."

"When do you wish to come?"

"Tonight, my dear comtesse, tonight!"

When the Comtesse de Polignac had gone Marie Antoinette frowned as she thought for a moment of Louise de Lamballe, now holding the official position of *surintendante* of her household. And how very seriously the poor Louise was taking that position. So irritating to find her going with such care through all the accounts, probing, questioning, even arguing. The friendship had outgrown itself, existed now on an uninspired level of monotony. She decided to take Louise with her tonight, Louise who would certainly disapprove of the irregular household in the Rue des Bons Enfants. The disapproval might well provide an excuse for dismissal, providing Louise could be induced to give expression to her disapproval. The trouble with Louise was that, ever since the old King's death, she had tried on every occasion to say the things she thought you wanted her to say, except, of course, in the matter of the household accounts. For the rest, no spirit, no independence. Her mind switched to Turgot. He, on the other hand, had too much spirit, too much independence.

She laughed aloud. "To the devil with Turgot!"

Léonard came again, just before the departure for the Rue des Bons Enfants, to reset the new headdress. He was bubbling over with excitement and as he worked he chattered gaily about the formidable future which lay immediately ahead for the Marie Antoinette headdress.

"Providing your Majesty has no objection to my choosing that name."

"None whatever, Léonard."

"It will make my fortune. Of that there is no doubt. Why, I shall be able to buy a neat little chariot and drive out to Versailles with a flourish."

"Four or six horses, Léonard?"

"What does your Majesty advise?"

"I insist on six horses, my friend."

"Then six it shall be, your Majesty. Ah, but the hired carriages I am now compelled to use! They are almost the death of me. They rattle, they all but fall to pieces, the horses are old and tired. To-night, for instance, I was shattered, completely shattered. And to add to my exasperation I was delayed for several precious minutes near the Hotel de Ville by some sort of vulgar demonstration. I feared that I might be late for your Majesty's appointment and tore out my hair in handfuls."

"Ah, but you were not late, my dear Léonard."

He laughed triumphantly. "Indeed no, your Majesty. Out of the wretched hired carriage I thrust my poor head and I cried, 'Make way, good people, or Léonard will be late at Versailles and the Queen will be angry.'"

"And they did make way?"

"Instantly, and with cries of 'Long live the Queen!'"

Marie Antoinette was most impressed. So much, then, for the fears of Turgot the alarmist. The monarchy in danger? What utter nonsense!

Her passage through her apartments and down the marble staircase was one of complete triumph. Little groups of courtiers had gathered everywhere, even round the coach in the courtyard, to gaze in awe and wildly applaud. She was used to the weight of the headdress now and could pass through doorways with ease and grace. Ascending into the coach, however, caused unexpected trouble.

"The headdress is much too high," Louise de Lamballe said.

"Then send for a higher coach," Léonard shrilled.

He was assured that there was no higher coach.

"An impasse!" he moaned, and beat his breast. "My creation will be ruined, ruined. I also will be ruined!"

"Wait!" Marie Antoinette commanded. "I have an idea. If I sit on the seat, ruination for the headdress, ruination for Léonard. But if I kneel on the floor—a cushion under my knees, of course— both will be saved."

And kneel on the floor she did, with grace and dignity.

"Bravo!" everybody cried.

Marie Antoinette glanced mischievously at the Princesse de Lamballe.

"My poor Louise, etiquette being what it is, you too will have to kneel."

"I know my duty," the princess said, with a thin smile.

The journey to Paris was made in anything but comfort.

"We must console ourselves," Marie Antoinette said bravely, "with the thought that the dictates of fashion brook no rebellion. Tomorrow every lady of fashion will be kneeling in her carriage. And if they complain, let them take a prayer book with them, especially those who never go to church."

The princess emitted a hollow groan.

"You are not amused, Louise?"

"I— Yes of course, your Majesty. A fine joke indeed."

And the hollow groan became a hollow laugh.

In the boulevards, which she always insisted on driving in, Marie Antoinette was thrilled as always by the gay crowds taking the evening promenade. Court etiquette frowned on a royal personage being seen too often here, but the Boulevard Saint-Denis was a sight never to be missed. Tonight the crowded cafés, the sweet stalls, the fascinating tawdry little theaters, had a gayer look than usual.

80

"There may be a shortage of bread," she remarked, "but the people still know how to enjoy themselves."

Near the Place des Victoires the coach was held up by the congestion of traffic. Suddenly she realized with a little stab of excitement that she was in the thick of a demonstration such as Léonard had mentioned. With the coach surrounded by an excited, gesticulating press of people Louise de Lamballe suggested uneasily that the curtains should be drawn.

"Nonsense! Let them see me. Let them see their Queen!"

She regretted that the height of the headdress made it impossible for her to put her head out of the window, but face after face was peering in and she was soon recognized.

"Long live the Queen!" a voice cried.

The cry was taken up, and while the whole street echoed with it a path was cleared for the royal coach.

"See how they love me!" she exclaimed happily. "Turgot is nothing but a fool."

The coach went on towards the Palais Royal through even thicker traffic—all Paris, it seemed, was abroad tonight—but always the way was made clear, and always, as she was recognized again and again, the cry of "Long live the Queen!" rang out.

"All they wanted was a glimpse of me," she said complacently. "There'll be no more demonstrations tonight, I'll warrant!"

Skirting the Palais Royal they at last reached the Rue des Bons Enfants, and there, except for the urchins who had run along behind the carriage, all was quiet.

Descending to the ground presented considerable difficulty. It was necessary to turn on one's knees, back out on them and bob one's head low. With stiff knees it was a tiresome business and took up much time, while the urchins gathered round and cheered shrilly.

The house was small, with neglected walls and an overgrown garden. The interior, Marie Antoinette noticed, as servants bowed her in, was shabby, the furnishings old-fashioned. The comtesse, slim and beautiful, but wearing the gown she had worn that afternoon, greeted her in a most off-hand manner.

"I invited the woman, not the Queen, but it seems as if the Queen, after all, has come."

Marie Antoinette glanced at the still-open door. Others beside the urchins had gathered outside and the cheering was deafening.

81

"I would gladly apologize for them," she said, "except that apparently I have quelled a riot. I do assure you, my dear comtesse, if it was the Queen who stepped from the coach, it is the woman who now stands in your house."

The Comtesse de Polignac's eyes were on the headdress.

"*Stepped* from the coach, Madame?"

Marie Antoinette laughed ruefully. "Ah, you should have seen the dreadful struggle!"

"I can well imagine it."

Marie Antoinette had almost forgotten Louise de Lamballe. Quickly she introduced the two young women. Madame de Polignac submitted the princess to a lazy scrutiny; the princess returned it with a look of fretful disapproval. Marie Antoinette, vastly amused, linked her arm through Madame de Polignac's.

"Introduce me at once to your husband. Note, please, I ask to be introduced. Not on any account must he be presented to me. The same applies also to your lover."

A warm excited feeling filled her breast. Never before had she dared such a flouting of etiquette. She glanced at Louise. The poor creature's nose seemed to have grown abnormally long as, glancing down it, she threw up her neat little aristocratic chin.

Negligently the comtesse was saying, "You shall be introduced to both of them, and to all my guests, a writer or two, an artist, and any amount of lazy gallants with whom I have at least one thing in common, informality."

"It sounds delightful!"

"My *salon* is full to the doors, but before entering it, remember the rules. No weighty conversation, just light gossip, the more scandalous the better. Are you an intellectual person? If so, though I doubt it, not a sign of intellect will be tolerated here."

"Your *salon*," Marie Antoinette gushed, "is a veritable oasis."

A moment later, with Louise de Lamballe dragging unhappily behind, she entered the crowded *salon*.

"First names only?" the comtesse suggested, before making the first introduction.

"First names only!" Marie Antoinette agreed eagerly.

As introduction followed introduction she grew quite confused. There was Jules, then André, Jacques, Pierre and a dozen more. It was not at all clear who was the husband, who the lover, who the dear friend. There was Victoire, then Sophie, Annette, Françoise, oh and countless others. She remembered Victoire because

82

the comtesse, making an easy gesture, warned that it was unsafe to play cards with her—"A cheat, my dear Marie, watch her."

No one, not a single man or woman, showed her the slightest deference. They treated her with a casualness which delighted her. Some, after a passing glance, completely ignored her. So novel, so very novel, to be just a nobody. She asked who the writers were. One of them was not really a writer, except of outrageous love letters. Jacques, the other, wrote light romances unfit for innocent eyes. "Pornographic, I think, is the word." Pornographic! Suddenly she remembered her mother's face, severe and disapproving. Pornographic! Actually Mama wouldn't know what the word meant!

Suddenly she remembered Louise, searched for her and found her alone in a corner, biting her under lip quite savagely.

"My poor Louise, you don't seem to be enjoying yourself."

"We-ell— But of course I am."

"What do you think of them all?"

"They are highly diverting," the princess said miserably.

Marie Antoinette began to lose her temper. "For heaven's sake say what you think, just for once, not what you imagine I want you to say."

The princess took a great gulp. "Very well, then. I think you have fallen into a trap, or are about to. I think the comtesse is cunning and scheming. I feel sure she plans, by treating you like this, to worm her way into Versailles, to gain for herself and her husband places of importance at court. And for her wretched lover too!"

Marie Antoinette smiled blandly. "I intend to set them all up at Versailles."

Louise de Lamballe's face whitened. "I—I apologize. I have nothing more to say."

"You have a lot more to say, Louise. Please say it."

"Very well! Their treatment of you tonight is much too casual. They have all been warned to ignore the fact that you are the Queen. Of course they have! In spite of the studied casualness they still hesitate to show real disrespect."

"*Real* disrespect?"

"I—I am still to say what I think?"

"Naturally!"

"Ah well, here it is. No one has dared to make one single remark about the headdress."

"The . . . headdress?"

"No one has dared to laugh at it."

"To . . . *laugh* at it?"

"They want to, and so they should, if they are honest! But no, not a smile, not a sneer, not one little joke."

"Obviously you have no love for the latest fashion, Louise!"

"I—I think it the height of folly. To have to bend the knees while passing through a doorway, to have to kneel in a carriage! I think it—yes indeed!—I think it an imbecility."

Furious, Marie Antoinette turned sharply on her heels, sought out Victoire and suggested an hour or so at the card table. The hour lengthened into three hours, by which time she was able to rise from the table with a neat little sum of four thousand livres.

"You see," Louise de Lamballe declared hotly, "not even a notorious cheat has the courage to rob the Queen. A plot, I warn you, a plot!"

"Presently, Louise, I shall be obliged to ask you to relinquish your official position in my household."

Louise bowed her head. "Your Majesty's will is law."

It was four o'clock in the morning when Marie Antoinette succeeded in tearing herself away from the Rue des Bons Enfants. With frigid politeness she commanded Louise to sit in the coach, not kneel, but Louise, still a slave of etiquette, refused.

"Oh, confound you!" Marie Antoinette cried. "I shall sit myself, and to the devil with the headdress!"

By the time they reached Versailles the headdress, jogged constantly against the roof, was a sorry spectacle, a spectacle which, when they were being lighted into the palace, was too much for Louise. She broke into great gulping laughter and pointed a derisive finger.

"How crazy it looks! As crazy as the world we live in. A world that will come toppling down some day, like the headdress."

In her own apartments Marie Antoinette found Louis and Maurepas waiting for her. Both looked amazingly harassed.

"Thank heaven!" Louis cried.

"Whatever is the matter, Louis?"

"You left Versailles without telling anyone where you were going. I have been crazy with anxiety."

"Goodness, why?"

"The riots, my dear."

She laughed contentedly. "I put an end to the riots hours ago."

84

Maurepas and Louis exchanged a quick glance.

"The people cheered me till they were hoarse," she said.

"After which they went on with their demonstrations," Louis told her.

Maurepas smiled for the first time. "One may at least take some consolation from the fact that her Majesty is still popular."

"Yes," Louis agreed, "but Marie, the situation is unchanged. Turgot is in Paris, doing what little he can to control the riots. He is sending me a report every hour."

"The streets were quiet when I drove through them on my way back."

"The demonstrations in the center of the city may have ceased, but the real trouble continues. Grain stores are being broken into everywhere. Many people have been seriously injured. Turgot is at his wits' end."

"And so he should be," she said indignantly. "The fault is surely his." She yawned and stretched. "I have had a delightful evening. Please don't spoil it for me." She yawned again. "How tired I am. I do believe I could sleep for a week. Certainly I shall not go to Mass tomorrow."

"Marie . . ." Louis said hesitantly.

"Well?"

"I entreat you never to go to Paris again without telling me."

"I realize," she said icily, "that though I am Queen I should first ask the King's permission."

"I realize that too, but I would never insist on it," he said earnestly. "But your personal safety is of paramount importance. Go to Paris as often as you wish, but tell me first, and take an armed escort with you. A detachment of your own bodyguard is usual, in any case."

"If I do that the people will change their good opinion of me," she said haughtily. "Goodnight, Louis! Goodnight, Maurepas!"

Maurepas withdrew but Louis lingered.

She looked at him apprehensively. "I really am very tired, Louis."

He smiled faintly. "I have no intention of . . . pestering you."

"Thank you!"

"I was thinking of the Little Trianon."

She wondered what was coming. "Yes, Louis?"

"I should like to give it to you. I know you find the formality of Versailles very irksome. The Little Trianon would make a pleasant retreat. You could escape there from time to time and live as you pleased."

"Why Louis, what a kind thought!"

He smiled happily. "You will take it?"

"Oh gladly, gladly! But Louis—" she looked at him teasingly— "your grandfather used it almost exclusively for the pursuit of love affairs. Are you inviting me to take my lovers there?"

THREE

THE FOUR OF THEM WERE TAKING SUPPER TOGETHER, LOUIS AND
Marie Antoinette, Maurepas and Madame Adelaide. Louis, pretending always to ignore the antagonism which existed between
his wife and his aunt, insisted, once every two or three weeks, on
inviting Madame Adelaide to what he called a quiet little supper
party. For Marie Antoinette this was never a happy arrangement, and tonight not even the presence of Maurepas lightened
the heavy atmosphere. He tried, however, and made just one
joke.

"If Léonard is allowed to continue his madness, it will soon
be impossible for a lady to ride in a closed carriage, even when
kneeling."

Nobody laughed.

"Turgot is still in Paris," Madame Adelaide said.

It was a statement rather than a question.

Louis looked up resentfully from his plate and grunted.

Marie Antoinette smiled contemptuously. How he hated to be
disturbed at his food! Apparently he was unable to eat and at
the same time think. Or perhaps it was that by concentrating on
eating he was able to escape from such tiresome problems as
Turgot. Still it was not displeasing to know that Louis, Turgot's
only real friend at court, was growing weary of the man who
had caused the riots.

"The situation has not improved."

Again from Madame Adelaide it was a statement rather than
a question, and this time Louis, scowling, refused even to look
up from his plate. It was Maurepas who spoke, Maurepas who
was just as distressed by the riots as Louis.

"Since Turgot called out the troops there have been no further
demonstrations in Paris but grain stores are still being pillaged
all over the country."

"The man is a fool," Madame Adelaide snapped. "The people
hate him more than ever now, and through him they are beginning to hate the King."

Louis, in one of his rare, ineffectual rages, crashed both fists on the table.

"Turgot is a man of the most liberal principles," he said, his mouth full of chicken, "but even to such a man comes a time when strong action is necessary."

"You were against calling out the troops yourself."

"I was. I deplore it. But it was necessary."

Marie Antoinette, thinking of the riots, was reminded again of the analogy of the dance, with a near-revolt taking place at court, more groupings and re-groupings, shifting loyalties, new intrigues. But all directed against Turgot, a lonely figure, aloof, harassed, yet strangely determined to do his duty as he saw it. And duty to him, at this stage, still included opposition to an immediate coronation, over which, fortunately, he was fighting a losing battle.

"Louis," she asked softly, "have you decided yet on the exact date of the coronation?"

"Sometime in June."

"But the exact date, Louis."

He made no answer. She looked at Maurepas, he lowered his eyes; she looked at Madame Adelaide, she shrugged and scowled. She looked again at Maurepas. How irritating when an easy-going, amusing old gentleman lost his head and tried to be serious. Why, he even talked now as Mercy did. Postponement would be wise . . . the riots were more than just riots, they were serious revolts . . . one must take the utmost care . . . the throne was in danger . . . What utter nonsense!

"How stupid to be intimidated by a handful of agitators," she said scathingly. "Where is the royal dignity, the royal pride? Postpone the coronation and the King of France, still uncrowned, will be the laughing stock of Europe."

Louis threw back his chair. "I have agreed *not* to postpone it."

"But the date, the exact date!"

He belched. "There! You have given me indigestion." He belched again and rubbed his stomach. "You shall have the exact date tomorrow."

And with that he stumped from the room.

"You get your way in all things," Madame Adelaide complained.

Mercy had said the same thing only that morning, and saying

88

it had implied so much more. The King was most indulgent towards her, denied her nothing except . . . There Mercy had paused and gently added that he sympathized with her unfortunate position, and hoped most sincerely that a solution might soon be found, not only for her own sake but for the sake of France and the peace of Europe. Confusing, that last bit. What in heaven's name did it matter to the peace of Europe whether or not she had a baby?

"Not in all things," she told Madame Adelaide. "Turgot is still with us."

"Yes," Madame Adelaide said slowly, "Turgot is still with us."

Marie Antoinette saw that she was looking at her speculatively. Was the old-maid aunt playing with the idea of a friendly gesture? Was she about to suggest a combining of their forces for the purpose of ridding the court of the wretched comptroller-general?

"My dear Aunt Adelaide," she said, "you dislike poor Turgot, not because he called out the troops, but because his attempts at economy are directed in the main against the privileged classes to which you belong."

"You dislike him for the same reason!"

"The Queen of France is above all classes," Marie Antoinette said cuttingly. "Her privileges are privileges set far apart." She rose, thus forcing Madame Adelaide and Maurepas to rise also. "I have an appointment in Paris. You may withdraw."

Madame Adelaide withdrew but Maurepas remained.

"What a shame," he murmured, "to force Madame Adelaide, who loves her food, to leave a meal unfinished." He grew quickly serious again. "Your Majesty, if I may give expression to a passing thought . . . ?"

"If you must, Maurepas."

"It occurs to me that you are cleverer than one might suspect. Your understanding, for instance, of the motive behind Madame Adelaide's dislike of Turgot—" He broke off and digressed for a moment. "I have been a waster all my life, but I do on occasion experience a flash of seriousness. And experiencing it now I wonder what in the world is going to happen to France when those at court are guided by one thing only, by personal acquisitiveness, the guarding and furthering of privilege."

"We were talking about my cleverness," she reminded him.

Maurepas bowed, not ironically, as one might have expected, but sincerely: "You could, Madame, if you wished, become a stateswoman as clever as your respected mother."

"And in the process die of boredom."

"The boredom arising out of feverish pleasure-seeking is also—death-like."

"Possibly, Monsieur, at *your* age."

"What I am trying to say is that your natural talents are being wasted. You have a weak husband. Kindly, thoughtful, sincere, but—forgive me—weak. A strong woman might save him, and doing so save France."

"Save France from what?"

"Revolution."

"Oh come, Monsieur!—"

He smiled compassionately. "I fear I have spoken too soon, before you are ready or able to understand. I trust you will be ready before it is too late."

She felt a faint stirring of apprehension, a groping toward understanding, but little more. Abruptly she dismissed Maurepas, ordered her coach and attended by her youngest lady went eagerly to Paris to call on the Comtesse de Polignac. In defiance she left without telling Louis and scorned the mounted escort he had tried to insist upon. She gave a moment's thought to Louise de Lamballe as, kneeling in the coach, she felt the intolerable weight of the headdress pressing down on her. Tendering her resignation, Louise had quietly vacated her apartment, but had promised to come often to court. "Do, please do," Marie Antoinette had urged, and felt a twinge of remorse.

At this, her second visit to the Rue des Bons Enfants, she found the house in darkness. Disappointment swamped her. One could hardly expect the comtesse to remain at home, waiting for unexpected visitors, but even so, the house in complete darkness, an air of desertion and gloom about it, no sign of servants . . .

"Knock, in any case," she told her lady.

While the girl was knocking a small carriage drew up and a cloaked female figure alighted. Marie Antoinette remembered the Comtesse de Polignac's first name.

"Gabrielle . . ." she called, uncertainly.

The figure came forward out of the gloom. She was indeed the comtesse.

"Your Majesty . . ."

90

"Something is the matter. I can see that at a glance."

The comtesse laughed easily. "Nothing of very great moment."

"Help me down, Gabrielle. My knees are paining me. It will do them good if I stretch my legs."

The comtesse helped her down.

"I, thank heaven, am not a slave to fashion," she laughed.

"I happen to be an innovator of fashion, not a slave," Marie Antoinette said, with some asperity.

"Call it what you like. It means the same thing. You must have special pads designed for the knees."

Marie Antoinette took her arm impulsively. "Walk up and down with me and tell me what the trouble is."

"The trouble is a not uncommon one. The creditors are at my heels again. My husband was the first to run. My current lover soon followed him. I closed the house this morning and went to stay with a friend. I returned tonight to get some books."

Marie Antoinette frowned. "I suppose it *is* dreadful, being hounded by creditors?"

"I have never found it so."

"Nevertheless, to have to *hide* from them . . ."

"In time it becomes a fascinating game."

"What an amusing creature you are! But surely, when they know the Queen is your friend they will cease to hound you."

"That is quite possible. They will also put up their prices."

"I know, Gabrielle, let me pay your debts!"

"You may if you wish," the comtesse said casually, "but the total amount is quite staggering."

"As if that mattered! Send the accounts to my secretary and forget all about them."

"I shall never be able to repay you," the comtesse warned.

"I am making a gift, not a loan."

"A loan, even if one can never repay it, is one thing, a gift quite another. A gift places one under an obligation and I should hate that."

"What a strange thing to say! Let us call it a loan, then. And better still, Gabrielle, let us agree that it shall be repaid—out of your salary."

"My *salary*, Marie?"

"I have an official position to offer you in my household, that of *surintendante*."

Gabrielle de Polignac's shoulders began to shake. "*Surinten-*

dante of the Queen's household! Can you see me holding such a position? Why, I'd feel a perfect fool!"

Nettled for a moment, Marie Antoinette was soon chuckling at the effrontery of the comtesse's attitude.

"Dear Gabrielle, how I love you!"

"What you need," Gabrielle said dryly, "is an old and dignified marquise."

"No, I need a young woman who can make me laugh and save me from boredom. I suggest a salary of 150,000 livres a year."

"That is certainly a lot of money."

"It is? Splendid! A suite of apartments shall be prepared for you. How soon can you come to Versailles?"

"I have not yet decided to accept the—er—honor."

Marie Antoinette very nearly lost her temper. "When a Queen commands—" she began haughtily.

Without a word the Comtesse de Polignac turned and walked away in the darkness of the street.

"Gabrielle!" Marie Antoinette called plaintively, "come back, I beg of you."

Gabrielle came back, slowly. "Your Majesty?"

"Forgive me, Gabrielle. I spoke hastily. I issue no command, only a request, the request of a friend."

Gabrielle smiled serenely. "And as a friend I promise to consider it."

"Where may I find you?"

"At Victoire's house."

"You will let me know soon?"

"Tomorrow, the next day. But *surintendante!* Ludicrous, grotesque!"

And Gabrielle's merry laughter faded away in the darkness.

During the drive back to Versailles Marie Antoinette grew aware of hoofbeats some little distance behind her coach, and on her arrival a detachment of cavalry thundered past on the cobbles of the courtyard. Angrily she went at once to Louis' apartments, where she found him busy at the desk in his cabinet.

"So you are spying on me now!" she accused.

"Spying on you, my dear?" He began to look uneasy. "If you mean the armed guard—"

"An armed guard if you insist, but you must have set spies on me or they would never have known I was leaving Versailles. Humiliating, Louis, humiliating!"

"You must have protection. I—I only did what I thought was right." Quickly he tried to change the subject. "You were anxious about the coronation. The date decided upon is June 11th."

Her anger with him melted at once. "Ah, then I can begin my preparations at once!"

"But only modest preparations," Louis warned. "We are of the opinion, Turgot and I, that it would make a bad impression if too much money was wasted on lavish display and elaborate celebrations. Certain moneys, which would normally be spent on a coronation, will be given to the poor of Paris."

Marie Antoinette laughed unpleasantly. "No doubt my crown will be made of imitation diamonds."

"Er—" Louis coughed.

"I knew it, I knew it!"

Louis avoided her eyes. "No crown will be required for you, my dear."

"How can I be crowned without one?"

"Such a pity," he wailed, "that your study of French history has been so restricted. You will not be crowned at all."

Anger was shaking her again. "Is Turgot responsible for this decision?"

"Dear me no! Poor fellow, must he be blamed for everything? The ceremony of crowning a Queen has fallen into disuse."

"Disuse!" she echoed indignantly.

"For generations now, no King has been married until after his coronation."

"*You* are married."

"Y-yes, but a precedent has been established."

"A husband in name only, I admit, but nevertheless—"

"That is scarcely kind, Marie."

"Turgot *is* at the bottom of this. I know it, I know it!"

"No, my dear. A matter of precedent and—and economy."

"Economy! There! Turgot, Turgot!"

"You do the poor fellow an injustice."

"I am to be no more than a spectator at the coronation? Is that your intention?"

"An honored spectator, Marie. The most important one."

He was quite immovable, she could see that. She attacked him again the next day, and the next. She argued, she jeered, she wept, but to no avail. Louis remained unmoved, unhappy and utterly miserable, but unmoved. She appealed to Mercy. He

93

shrugged; it was a pity, her mother would be most distressed, but there was nothing he, a foreign ambassador, could do. She appealed to Maurepas and he, half-heartedly, with no success at all, pleaded with Louis. Finally, and foolishly, she appealed to Madame Adelaide who, smiling triumphantly, declared that she preferred not to interfere.

Meanwhile, adding to her misery, Gabrielle de Polignac was delaying her decision.

"But what of my husband?" Gabrielle said, when Marie Antoinette at last insisted on yes or no. "How will the poor fellow feel, left out in the cold while I bask in royal favor at Versailles?"

"Goodness, Gabrielle, is that your only worry! A position shall be found for him, an important position."

Gabrielle's face broke into its serene smile. "And my lover? I have a new one now, by the way. How can the Queen's *surintendante* receive a lover at Versailles?"

"Since when," Marie Antoinette demanded, "was Versailles a nunnery? Receive a dozen lovers if you must, but do please make up your mind."

With an indifferent shrug Gabrielle capitulated. "But I warn you, Marie, I shall never be a fashionable court lady. I shall live at Versailles as I have already lived, without formality, and surrounded by the most disreputable friends."

Marie Antoinette embraced her warmly. "Why else did I ask you to come to Versailles!"

Before Gabrielle's apartments were ready the court travelled in state to Rheims for the coronation. On the night before the important celebration Marie Antoinette slept alone. She had slept alone for many months now, but this time, since the King, not the Queen, was to be crowned, she did so by royal decree, in full accordance with precedent and tradition. The next morning, while her ladies dressed her, Maurepas lounged in a chair and gave her a racy account of the preparatory ceremony which was taking place at that moment in the King's chamber.

"It goes by the name of 'bringing the King,'" he said, his features solemnly composed but his eyes twinkling. "Two or three venerable bishops, dressed in their pretty frocks, go in procession to his Majesty's room. The grand chamberlain, knowing very well what they want, asks them what they want 'We want the King,' they say. The grand chamberlain, knowing very well that the King is wide awake and waiting, says, 'His Majesty is asleep.'

This is repeated several times, and at last, quite coyly, I vow, the grand chamberlain admits the bishops to the King's august presence. Well, there he lies, flat on his back in bed but fully dressed —in fact, wearing all his coronation robes and trying to give the impression that he has slept in them. The bishops, very very solemn now, but enjoying themselves, bless him and sprinkle him with holy water, get him on his feet and lead him to the cathedral."

Marie Antoinette gave him a grateful look. "Thank you for making me laugh, Maurepas."

"Better to laugh and go forth an amused spectator, your Majesty, than to scowl and go forth resentfully."

"I quite appreciate the moral you are trying to point at me!" she said tartly.

Later, in the cathedral, from a gallery near the high altar she carried out the part of chief spectator assigned to her. Here, surrounded by her ladies, she watched Louis make his slow and nervous entry. He was dressed in heavy robes, gold and crimson in color, while round his shoulders hung a silver cloak. As he walked, his feet clumsy and uncertain, the plumes of his velvet cap bobbed grotesquely. She could see that he was sweating already, and she was prepared, with the old resentment nagging at her, to sneer at the unhappy, undignified figure he made. She was prepared to sneer, but to her surprise a lump rose in her throat and she began to feel for him an unwanted, unsought compassion. This grew and grew until, by the time he was lying before the altar, the tears were streaming down her cheeks. She managed to check them when the ancient crown was placed on his head, but they flowed again beyond control when, looking lost and bewildered, he walked in the procession to the cathedral doors.

Cheering rose then, even in the sacred precincts, while outside guns fired the royal salute and trumpets blared. As the procession continued the spectators, shouting crazily, fought with each other for a glimpse of the King, fought so frantically that the guards were scattered, Louis was surrounded and lifted off his feet.

On leaving the gallery Marie Antoinette came face to face with Louise de Lamballe. Her cheeks also were stained with tears. She made a touching, pretty sight and, impulsive as ever, Marie Antoinette embraced her warmly.

95

"Louise, my dear!"

"Your Majesty!"

"No, no, Louise! To you I am Marie, just Marie. It was a stupid quarrel. Shall we forget it? Please do say yes!"

"Oh gladly, Marie, gladly!"

"Your old apartment has not been used since you left Versailles. Return to it, I beg of you."

"Oh yes, if you wish it."

Marie Antoinette smiled faintly. "I have a new *surintendante*, but it really is a most boring position. Come, come, admit it!"

"I admit it," Louise laughed.

"With Gabrielle I shall find amusement when I need it; with you, when I need it, *if* I need it, a little quiet seriousness."

Louise gave a little sob. "I shall serve and love you till the day I die."

When at last Marie Antoinette was able to meet the King alone she fell into his arms.

"How wrong you all were, wanting to postpone the coronation!" she cried.

"I admit it, Marie, and yet . . ."

"Yes? And *yet* . . . ?"

"The people love a spectacle. They were carried away by an instinctive emotion."

"Even as I was," she said dryly. "I found myself weeping, heaven knows why."

A few days later, after Louis had touched for the King's Evil, the court returned to Versailles. It was an exciting journey, with people lining the streets of every town and village to cheer the newly crowned King.

"The riots are forgotten," Marie Antoinette said. "They might never have happened."

Everyone, with the exception of Turgot, echoed her words. He, speaking acidly, said he saw no difference between the instinctive emotion aroused by the corn riots and that aroused by the spectacle of the coronation. He added that a coronation came only once in a king's lifetime, while the poor on the other hand could go hungry countless times.

Having thus expressed himself he intensified his campaign of economy to such an extent that he became hated at Versailles more bitterly than ever. Time and again Marie Antoinette was approached by various groups. She and she alone, everybody said, could bring about his dismissal. Everyone else had tried, and failed. She listened but remained aloof. The groups, temporarily setting aside their differences of opinion, banded together and Madame Adelaide became their spokeswoman.

"For the sake of the country you must help us remove him," she told Marie Antoinette gruffly.

"For the sake of the privileged classes, you mean! We have argued about this before."

"Turgot prevented you from being crowned," Madame Adelaide reminded her.

"I am not a spiteful woman."

But it was spite in the end that moved her. Turgot, murmuring against the appointment of the Comtesse de Polignac, had protested vigorously at the extravagance of the 150,000 livres a year, and when Marie Antoinette signed an order for an additional 6,000 livres in the form of a life pension, the order came back to her with the word "rejected" written on it. The word was followed by Louis' usual signature.

She went to Louis in anger and made him, or tried to make him, the biggest scene of her life. He listened in complete silence. She stormed as she had never stormed before, yet the silence continued.

"This is maddening," she raged. "I doubt if you are even listening."

"Well, partly, my dear, partly." He made a helpless gesture. "Marie, I grow so weary of it all."

"Weary of Turgot too, I hope!"

"Yes, I admit it, but the man is no fool. His only fault is his complete lack of diplomacy. He has a harsh tongue and never hesitates to say what he thinks."

"He has everyone against him but you!"

"Yes. You see, even if I grow weary of him I am obliged to admire him."

"Admire him!"

Louis shrugged. "Give me the order, Marie."

She did so and watched him with interest as he scratched out the word "rejected" and wrote below it "accepted."

"Turgot will not enjoy being overridden," she chuckled.

"No."

"He will be most annoyed."

"Yes."

"He is still to remain at court?"

Louis turned away from her. "Yes."

She went thoughtfully from his presence. In accepting the order Louis was actually attempting to bribe her. This realization increased her anger against Turgot, but how useless it was to rage against him! She sought out the Comtesse de Polignac, now installed at Versailles, and confided in her fully.

"Gabrielle, what shall I do?"

Gabrielle laughed lightly. "I'm not interested in court intrigue, but I think I know an excellent way of dealing with Turgot. I would shake him off the same way I shake off an unwanted lover."

"That sounds amusing, but . . . *how?*"

"Listen . . ." said Gabrielle.

Marie Antoinette listened, laughed and clapped her hands. "Gabrielle, how clever you are!"

Later she went to Louis.

"Louis," she said quietly, "any man who works as hard as you do is sure to grow weary of it all. Forget state affairs for a while, forget your stuffy old council meetings. How long is it since you hunted boar? Go hunting again! How long is it since you worked at your bench? Can you remember? I vow I can't."

To encourage him she went riding with him and followed the hunt, even to the extent of spending days on end at the Choisy hunting lodge. At Versailles itself she persuaded him to spend long hours in his workshop and kept him busy designing and making for her a special little boudoir clock.

Thus, as much as possible, she kept him well removed from Turgot and at the same time took it upon herself to lead the court attack against the now quite harassed comptroller-general. Whenever Turgot appeared in public she and everybody else contemptuously turned their backs on him. No one ever spoke to him. Several times, in the King's name, she summoned him to the royal anteroom and, safe in the knowledge that Louis was busy at his bench, kept him waiting for hours. Spite? Yes indeed! She acknowledged it willingly and renewed her attacks. She had quite forgotten that she had once resolved never again to be involved in court intrigue . . .

In desperation Turgot was forced to write a letter of protest to Louis. He received it one evening after a morning's hunting and an afternoon laboring with the workmen who were knocking down a wall in order to enlarge his apartments. Worn out with the heavy exertions of the day, he gave the letter to Marie Antoinette.

"What shall I do now?" he asked helplessly.

She looked at him quickly. In recent weeks he had grown quite sluggish of mind and, he was eating more heavily than ever, a sure sign that he wanted to escape from the cares of state.

"First you must have a meal," she said. "I'm sure you need it badly."

He agreed with alacrity. "My belly does seem rather empty."

She sat at table with him, pretending to eat, and she read Turgot's letter. Among other things Turgot drew attention to the bad example of the late King's shameful reign and asked if Louis wanted a similar state of affairs to develop and ruin his own reign. Was his Majesty willing to sacrifice himself and his people to the vaunting ambition of scheming, grasping courtiers? He hoped and prayed that such was not the case. Marie Antoinette shrugged. That was neither here nor there; what infuriated her was Turgot's suggestion that she, the Queen, was the chief cause of it all. Finally, issuing what he obviously considered an ominous warning, Turgot drew Louis' attention to the weakness which in his opinion had brought Charles the First of England to the scaffold.

"The man is out of his mind," she cried.

Louis barely glanced up from his plate. "One would think so."

"You must take immediate action against him."

"Yes."

She realized in time how fatal it might be to come between Louis and his concentrated enjoyment of food.

"Your plate is empty," she said, and rang the bell.

Afterwards, when he could eat no more, she referred to the letter again.

"Turgot has done his best to insult you."

"It would seem so, Marie." He yawned disgustingly. "Yes, indeed."

"What are you going to do?"

"Send for him. Yes."

"And demand his resignation?"

"My hand is forced. Yes."

She felt a twinge of apprehension. Turgot, face to face with Louis, could be most persuasive.

99

"To send for him, to argue with him, that would be beneath the dignity of a king. Write to him, as he has written to you."

"Very well."

"Do it now, Louis."

He yawned again. "Turgot loves the people."

"But he seems to pity the King!"

"I sometimes pity myself. Ah well, this is the end of poor Turgot."

Count Mercy alone was bold enough to express disapproval of Turgot's dismissal. He came to her while the court was celebrating what everybody called the Queen's victory, and he shook his head sadly.

"The King of France," he said, and she knew he meant the Queen, "has in my opinion made the greatest blunder of his life. The late King, if I remember rightly, once said 'After me the deluge.' I, unfortunately, am forced to say 'After Turgot, the deluge.'"

"A deluge would be quite exciting."

Mercy sighed deeply. "May I ask your Majesty's future plans?"

"Future plans?"

She was barely listening. Turgot had gone and all she could think of at the moment was the informal party Gabrielle was to give in her apartments that night. She herself would give one in return tomorrow night at the Little Trianon.

"No one can doubt now that you are the real power at court," Mercy went on. "You may dismiss whom you please, appoint whom you please. You—"

"Oh come," she interrupted with a laugh, "I have no interest whatever in ruling France, and court intrigue, if continued too long, bores me. Now that Turgot has gone, all I want is to enjoy myself."

"So it was out of caprice, nothing else, that you brought about Turgot's ruin?"

"Possibly."

"A pity, that. A greater pity if, still out of caprice, you bring about your own ruin."

"Your seriousness is far too depressing, Mercy. I won't listen to another word."

"As your Majesty wishes, but before I go—"

"Well?"

100

"Your Imperial mother has decided to send his Imperial Majesty, your brother Joseph, on a state visit to France."

"It will be nice to see Joseph again after all this time, but why this sudden decision?"

Mercy smiled faintly. "Your Imperial mother feels that your brother, always a forceful person, might succeed where you have failed in giving your husband the courage to—ahem!—face the surgeon's knife."

Taken by surprise, Marie Antoinette blushed deeply.

"Splendid!" she cried, with forced gaiety. "It might be quite amusing."

FOUR

"NO, BY HEAVEN NO!" THE EMPEROR JOSEPH CRIED. "THIS PAINTED creature standing before me is not my little sister Toinette!"

Marie Antoinette laughed and flung her arms round her brother's neck.

"Dear Joseph, how like you to tease me immediately!"

But after they had embraced Joseph held her at arm's length and gazed at her sternly.

"I had heard that the ladies of Versailles wore heavy layers of rouge on every occasion, but I was not prepared for a sight like this. I should like to scrub your face till blood, not paint, reddened your cheeks. It's shameful, Toinette, shameful!"

She looked at him uncertainly. "You are only pretending to be angry with me, of course. Just as you always did."

Joseph smiled for the first time. "They were happy days, the days of your childhood."

"They were indeed, Joseph."

"You were natural and carefree. You laughed and sang and were gay. Now you have a strained look, and the air of brightness you assume is as artificial as the color on your cheeks. Ah well, I'll change all that, by heaven I will!"

She sent for refreshments and presently, while he ate, sparingly and fastidiously, she looked at him with increasing disappointment. Quite clearly he had not been teasing her, and how solemn he had grown, how very serious! His face had a thin, ascetic look; his eyes, once so merry, held little now but disapproval. She could only conclude that as Emperor, sharing the cares of state with their mother, he was taking life far too gravely. There might well have been fifty years' difference in their ages, not fourteen. And his clothes! She looked at them in horror. Not even the humblest French government clerk would have garbed himself so plainly.

"Darling Joseph," she said gently, "surely the Emperor should dress more lavishly."

102

"Why?" he demanded. "I pride myself, first and foremost, in being a philosopher."

"I fail to see the connection," she laughed, "but perhaps you have the look of one. Lean and hungry. Not, of course, that I have met any philosophers."

"One would scarcely expect to, at Versailles."

She quickly changed the subject. "Why did you arrive without warning? Louis and I intended to give you a state welcome. Everything was planned for a grand meeting on the road. Louis is away hunting. He has been sent for, of course, but still . . ."

"I travelled incognito," Joseph said happily. "I followed no fixed route, and once I crossed the French border I was able to see your country through the eyes of an unimportant traveller. What I saw and what I heard distressed me sorely. To be frank, Toinette—"

"Yes, yes," she said hurriedly. "We shall discuss all that later. Meanwhile—" Quite at a loss, but determined to prevent a long lecture on the state of France, she sought desperately for something to say. "Surely you travelled with a suite, Joseph!"

"A small one, yes."

"Then special arrangements shall be made, apartments prepared—"

"My suite," he interrupted, "have been installed at a modest hotel near the Austrian Embassy."

"But—*Joseph!*"

"I myself have a room at the Embassy, a quite comfortable room, large enough to hold my camp bed and the small amount of baggage I brought."

Marie Antoinette could scarcely believe her ears. "The Holy Roman Emperor proposes to sleep on a camp bed in a small room at the Embassy! Are you out of your mind?"

"Obviously my little sister thinks so, but *I* am quite satisfied with the arrangement."

"Heaven preserve us from philosophers!" she cried.

"And heaven preserve France," Joseph said mildly, "from frivolous, painted, overdressed women." He looked fixedly at the low neck of her green, gold-embroidered gown. "By overdressed I fear I mean underdressed." He rose from the table at which he had been eating and peered at her closely. "If you sneeze, you shameless creature, your nipples will become visible."

She clapped her hands. "Dear Joseph, you have given me an

idea for a new game. Pepper, large quantities of it, scattered liberally about the *salon*. The winner shall be the one who sneezes last. Gabrielle will love it."

Angrily he took her by the shoulders and began to shake her.

Marie Antoinette burst into sudden tears. "And I had looked forward so much to your visit!"

Joseph took her in his arms and patted her shoulder absently. "I had looked forward to it too. Ah well, I see my duty plainly. I shall strive, while here, to bring about a very necessary change in you. If I succeed my time will not have been entirely wasted."

She withdrew quickly from his arms. "Bring about a change in Louis. That is all I ask. That is all you came for."

Joseph nodded thoughtfully. "I shall do my best. It will be a source of satisfaction to me if I succeed when everybody else has failed." He looked at her with a surprisingly gentle smile. "Perhaps I have been harsh with you, Toinette. Louis, unable to give you one important thing, has given you everything else. Very dangerous, really, the pleasure-seeking of an unsatisfied wife, the more so when she is a Queen. I am referring now to the way you have been allowed to play at politics. Oh yes, the sooner your husband turns himself into a real man and asserts himself the better." His gentle smile turned to one of tight severity. "What is this talk I hear about your having taken a lover?"

To irritate him she smiled slyly. "I prefer to keep my private life—private."

"I want the truth, Toinette." For a moment the tone of his voice quite frightened her. "Come, the truth! Have you at any time taken a lover?"

"No! No, Joseph, I swear it."

He gave her a look of approval. "That was wise of you. Had you taken a lover you might have become pregnant. Had you become pregnant your husband would have been faced with a ticklish problem. He is, I understand, a kindly young man and a fool where you are concerned. He would, if I judge rightly, have hesitated to set you aside and have your child declared a bastard. If that had happened he would have done himself and his dynasty a grave injustice. But why have you restrained yourself from taking a lover?"

Marie Antoinette pursed her lips. Why? She had asked herself that same question many times. Gabrielle, in her easy-going way, had brought many presentable young gallants to her *salon*, had said serenely, 'There you are, Marie, take your pick.' She shuddered delicately. The very memory of it made her flesh creep. To select a man that way, in cold blood . . . horrible, quite horrible! Still, there had been one, an amusing fellow who had made her laugh and warmed her heart with his subtle flattery, yet when submission had seemed an attractive necessity her whole body had revolted and she had ordered him haughtily from her presence. Amazing, really, that at the critical moment she had thought of nothing else but Louis in his coronation robes, the lost, bewildered expression on his face.

"Come, come," Joseph said sharply, "*why*?"

She smiled on him sweetly. "Because at heart I am and always will be a virtuous woman."

"Splendid, my dear, splendid!"

Her mind flew back to what he had first said. "From whom did you hear that I had taken a lover?"

"We-ell, now . . ."

"I am entitled to know, Joseph!"

"The Prince de Rohan."

"Oh, but how horrible!" She remembered how the prince had said "How very unwise of you" when she had told him she never wanted to see him again. This, then, was what he had meant. "What did he say? Tell me, Joseph, tell me!"

"He made no definite charges, merely uttered broad hints which were taken up by others and eagerly repeated. Much damage has been done, but we must do our best to forget it."

"I shall never forget it, never!"

A little silence fell. She wondered what to do now with this brother who was such a disappointment to her and suggested half-heartedly that he might like to make a tour of the palace. He replied that palaces were no novelty to him; far rather would he pay a visit to the poor quarters of Paris.

"Goodness, Joseph, why?"

"You have never been there yourself?"

"Never!"

"A Queen should know how all the people live," Joseph said warmly. "Otherwise, how can she have complete sympathy with them, or they with her, for that matter?"

Fortunately at that moment word came that Louis had returned and was waiting to receive his brother-in-law. Taking Joseph by the arm, trying to think of him only as the big brother

105

who had been her childhood hero, Marie Antoinette led him to the royal apartments. In the inner anteroom, the Oeil de Boeuf, she paused for a moment.

"You will find Louis rather shy," she warned.

"Quite, quite. Shy and tongue-tied. Something of a nincompoop."

"Louis is anything but a nincompoop!" she snapped.

Joseph smiled thinly. "To spring to his defense does you credit."

The brothers-in-law met without formality.

Watching them, Marie Antoinette decided that in her eyes Louis, though shorter and fatter than Joseph, showed up to greater advantage. Against the lean and critical Joseph, Louis seemed more honest, more sincere, more kindly than ever. He really was a good man; stupid, yes, but good, while Joseph was just a carping, bloodless philosopher. Poor Louis, she saw, was a great deal more embarrassed than she had expected. His mind was obviously clouded by disturbing thoughts of the real reason for Joseph's visit.

"Well," he asked, when the polite words of greeting had been said, "what do you think of your sister now? You find her changed after seven years?"

Joseph's nostrils twitched. "I have already reprimanded her for the excessive use of paint."

Louis shrugged. "It happens to be the fashion. It detracts in no way from her natural beauty."

A silence fell and became intolerable. What now? Marie Antoinette asked herself. A cosy little chat, frankly intimate, about Louis' personal problem? She glanced at Louis. Still ill-at-ease, he was striving, she knew, to think of something else to say.

Joseph broke the silence with an inane little laugh. "We must have a few long private talks, you and I, Louis."

"Er—yes, indeed," Louis stammered.

"About the state of France," Joseph added, "the riots of a year or so ago. And—oh yes, about the part France is likely to play in the American war."

Louis' face cleared, and snatching as it were at a slight reprieve he spoke at length about the revolt in America of the English colonists.

"The Declaration of Independence of—let me see, ah yes, July 4th last year, revived the interest here. That was soon after Tur-

106

got's dismissal. I remember asking him if he thought there would be war in America. He was sure there would be."

"In a word, Turgot was sympathetic toward the colonists."

"Even as I was, and still am."

"We see eye to eye in that, Louis, but we must remember always, you and I, that we are monarchists by profession."

"Of course," Louis agreed. "But the Americans have right on their side, and right, Turgot was sure, would prevail."

"During my journey here," Joseph went on, "I spent days at a time in cities and towns. Everywhere, I heard people applaud the Americans, and more than once I heard it said that France would be drawn into the struggle."

Louis shook his head. "That would mean war with England, and that is the last thing I want. Irresponsible people say we must avenge our defeat in the Seven Years' War, but war, Joseph, quite apart from the fact that I hate it, would ruin my country."

"It may be forced upon you," Joseph said sagely. "Especially with such people as Lafayette regarding it as nothing but an opportunity for high adventure."

"So you have heard of Lafayette?"

"His name was spoken wherever I mixed with people during my journey."

"An irresponsible young man!" Louis said, with considerable heat. "My minister of war, Vergennes, whom you must meet, tells me that Lafayette has actually purchased a warship of some sort and is loading it with arms. The English ambassador has already protested, but what control have I over private individuals? None whatever!"

Joseph tried to make a joke. "You could throw him into your infamous Bastille."

"The Bastille," Louis declared warmly, "is not as infamous these days as people think. Some of the apartments are quite luxurious. Why, to spend a few months there myself would give me a happy release from the cares of state. Pon my oath it would!"

"I must see the place," Joseph said. "That, and all the other sights of Paris. I must also visit the infirmaries, the factories, the whole of the poor quarters of your capital."

"You shall see everything, everything."

"I also want, if it can be discreetly arranged, to meet the American delegation now in Paris."

107

Louis shook his head. "I can do nothing for you there. I have never received the American delegation at court. I have no wish to provoke England too far."

Bored with all this talk, Marie Antoinette said, "If you mean Monsieur Franklin and his friends, Monsieur Deane and Monsieur Lee, I—"

"Yes, those are the American gentlemen," Joseph said.

"I can arrange a meeting any time you wish," she concluded.

"*You* can?" Louis asked in surprise.

"I have met them already, Louis. Privately, of course, in Paris. So charming, so very amusing! Especially Monsieur Franklin. If all Americans are the same I gladly say 'Down with England!'"

"Even to meet them privately was most unwise," Louis protested.

"They have saved me more than once from boredom, Louis."

Joseph laughed shrewdly. "Charming and amusing, but cunning too. Clearly they intend to obtain French aid, if all other means fail, by flattering the Queen."

Louis cleared his throat. "I have come to two decisions. Lafayette shall be restrained, and you, my dear, must never meet the American delegates again." He rose and moved just a little hurriedly to the door. "Come, Joseph, I must show you my stables and then my workshop."

More amused than angry, Marie Antoinette reflected that Louis, emboldened by her brother's presence, was showing a surprising strength of will.

Joseph came to her apartments an hour later to bid her *au revoir* before returning to the Austrian embassy.

"My dear Toinette, I am quite impressed with Louis. He is not the fool I had been told. Weak, admittedly, but his grasp of things is amazingly sound."

She hesitated for a moment. "Have you spoken to him yet about—well, you know what I mean."

Joseph shook his head. "It might be fatal to press the matter too soon. I shall move slowly, gain his complete confidence. Only when I judge the moment opportune will I *strike*. But have no fear. Success will crown my efforts in the end."

During the next month Joseph succeeded in making himself surprisingly popular, if not at court, certainly in Paris. He visited the factories, where he talked at length—"man to man," he called it—with the working people; he spent hours at the poorhouses,

108

tasting and ladling out the soup; he listened to the debates of the Parlement of Paris, the lectures at the academies; he went to the markets and talked earnestly with the porters and the fishwives.

"What a sensation I am causing!" he told Marie Antoinette. "Never before has an emperor been known to hobnob with the people like this!"

"You go too far," she said indignantly. "The people will soon be expecting their own King to do the same."

"Louis would gain a better grasp of the state of his country if he did, my dear."

She changed the subject quickly. "I believe you went hunting with him this morning."

"Well—yes."

"Is it true you fell from your horse?"

"Mmmm—yes."

"And such a quiet horse, carefully selected!"

"I made the mistake," he said haughtily, "of speaking to it in German. Er—have you heard that Lafayette has defied the King?"

Marie Antoinette nodded. It really was a most exciting, even inspiring, story. Ignoring Louis, Lafayette had gathered about him a large band of young men and pressed on with his plans. Arrested for this, he had escaped, his warship had been dispatched to a Spanish port and there, joining it, he had sailed gallantly for America.

"You seem to admire the young hothead," Joseph remarked.

"I can only think of him as a valiant prince in a fairy story. And do you know—" she laughed gleefully—"my dear Léonard is busy designing a new headdress to commemorate the event. Something bold, with large sweeping lines. I must confess I suggested it myself."

"Incorrigible, incorrigible!"

She refused to be annoyed. "Tonight, Joseph, I shall take you to a masked ball at the Opera, and later, *much* later, you shall visit some of my friends. Finally, at four or five in the morning, we shall have a late supper with Gabrielle."

The evening was not a success. Joseph was as bad a dancer as Louis; the masked ball bored him. The visits to the three great houses she chose provoked him to a horrified indignation. "Gambling dens, all three!" he raged. "I shudder to think how much money you lose in a week of this sort of immoral entertainment."

She told him airily that she never kept an account of such expenditure. What, after all, was money? At worst, a pest, if you lacked it; at best, a means of exchange for the things you wanted.

The visit to Gabrielle de Polignac's apartments was disastrous. They entered her *salon* unannounced, almost unnoticed. The game which in fun Marie Antoinette had suggested was being played. The air was thick with pepper. In all parts of the room ladies were sneezing, some delicately, some with complete abandon. "Disgraceful!" Joseph cried, his eyes goggling at the contrived result. Marie Antoinette, overcome by the atmosphere, sneezed in his face.

"Have a care, Toinette, have a care!"

"You needn't alarm yourself," she said, and sneezed again. "There, you see! Nature has made me much too firm. My dignity and respectability are safe." She took him by the arm as he too was overcome by the pepper. "Supper will not be served for ages. We may as well go and see Louis."

Louis, of course, was in bed, and sound asleep. Only by shaking him vigorously was she able to wake him.

"Joseph," she said gaily, "is distressed by my gambling debts." Louis tried to rub the sleep from his eyes. "Well, so am I."

"As a matter of interest, how much do I owe?"

"Half a million livres. That was the last report. You signed an order for that amount a few days ago."

"Shameful, shameful!" Joseph cried.

She smiled sweetly. "Has my signature been honored, Louis?"

"Yes," Louis said shortly and turning on his side drew the sheet over his head.

"I can only hope and pray," Joseph said sadly, when they had withdrawn from the royal bedchamber, "that heaven will forgive and protect you, and by some means known only to heaven save France from ruin."

Airily she said: "When are you going to speak to Louis?"

"Soon, soon." He looked at her for a long moment. "Tonight has not been entirely wasted. It has given me an idea. I know now how best to approach him. The fault, I fear, is his, not really yours."

"I thought that was always understood."

"I am referring to the aimless, wasteful life you lead. Goodnight, Toinette, and, if God has not turned his face against you, God bless you."

110

Two days later she asked the question again. "When are you going to speak to Louis?"

And again Joseph replied, "Soon, soon."

They were at the Little Trianon, having walked through the park from Versailles in the warm May sunshine. Marie Antoinette had made good use of it since Louis had given it to her and had indeed found it a retreat from the formality of Versailles. Often she gave small supper parties, and sometimes, when the guests had departed, she spent the night here with only one waiting woman in attendance.

"I had heard that it was a grand elaborate palace," Joseph remarked, as he continued the inspection he had come to make, "but it is really only a villa."

"What else had you heard about it?" she asked sharply.

"Gossip has it that the tradition established by Louis' grandfather is being continued."

"In a word, the old King's mistresses have been replaced here by the new Queen's lovers."

"In a word, yes. You have of course spent vast sums of money on redecoration."

"Of course! And I shall spend a great deal more. For one thing, a small theater will soon be built in the grounds and a little model village."

"I quite understand. The child still plays in the nursery."

She stamped her foot. "You try my patience sorely, Joseph. In one sense you came to France to rescue me from the nursery. For heaven's sake do so and leave me in peace!"

Joseph embraced her quickly. "Forgive me, Toinette. My attitude has been, I admit, a little severe."

The next morning, while making her toilette, she learned that Joseph, coming out early from Paris, had walked for an hour in the park with Louis. The two had then taken breakfast together and were now closeted in Louis' workshop.

"Workshop?" she echoed.

"A most formidable sound of hammering can be heard," she was told.

The lengthy toilette continued while, impatient for news, she grew unbearably tired of the strict etiquette of her morning dressing. To make matters worse Madame Adelaide presented herself, and this, of necessity, complicated and lengthened the procedure still more.

111

"Your Majesty . . ." Madame Adelaide murmured, and curtsied briefly.

The lady of honor, caught thus in the act of handing Marie Antoinette her shift, froze and remained motionless, waiting. Madame Adelaide, remembering the order of precedence invoked by the presence of a princess of the blood royal, nodded curtly.

"Very well."

The lady of honor curtsied. "Your royal Highness . . ."

Madame Adelaide nodded again, even more curtly. The lady of honor gave her the Queen's shift. Madame Adelaide then handed it to Marie Antoinette. The ritual continued, with Madame Adelaide eager to ask questions but restrained by the presence of the lady of honor, the chief *femme de chambre* and all the others.

"The Emperor is with the King," she ventured cautiously.

"So I believe."

"In the workshop."

"Yes."

"A loud hammering can be heard. I heard it myself."

"Quite possibly it is Joseph knocking Louis' head against the vice. Or Louis doing the same with Joseph's."

"What nonsense! They are the best of friends."

"The mirror, if you please."

A waiting woman handed a gold-framed hand-mirror to the chief *femme de chambre;* the chief *femme de chambre* handed it to Madame Adelaide; Madame Adelaide held it before Marie Antoinette.

Madame Adelaide whispered, "I am praying like fury for your brother's success."

Marie Antoinette giggled. "That, no doubt, was just what God was waiting for."

The mistress of the robes entered, bearing the heavy pattern-book in which patterns of all Marie Antoinette's gowns were filed for easy reference. Marie Antoinette made a quick selection, a white gown delicately embroidered in gold.

"White for purity," she said solemnly.

Madame Adelaide cleared her throat. "If I may have a word with your Majesty in private . . . ?"

"Presently, presently."

Léonard was the next to appear, breezily, importantly, so very conscious of the prosperity which the queen's patronage had brought him. He was followed a few moments later by Mademoiselle Bertin. Soon the two of them, with Marie Antoinette putting in an amused word now and then, were arguing spiritedly about the headdress which was to follow the one inspired by Lafayette.

"The accent shall be on frugality," he declared slyly.

"Why that, Léonard?" Madame Adelaide demanded.

"In honor of her Majesty's brother, the Emperor."

Marie Antoinette laughed happily. "But how does one express frugality in a headdress?"

"Something flat, your Majesty. Very plain. A loop here and there that droops."

"Never!"

"For one day only, your Majesty? Just one little day?"

"Not even for one little hour, Léonard!"

Léonard threw up his hands. "This is sheer insurrection, your Majesty."

Madame Adelaide had had enough. "Pray dress her Majesty's hair and have done with this argument."

Léonard bowed. "The Lafayette style, your Majesty?"

"No," Marie Antoinette decided. "I have chosen a simple gown. I shall therefore wear my hair in a simple fashion, loose about my shoulders."

"Name of a name of a name!" the little hairdresser wailed.

At last it was all over, yet still the brothers-in-law were closeted in the royal workshop. It was the same at midday when a light meal was taken in to them, after which, not hammering, but a steady filing noise was heard.

It was not until the late afternoon that Joseph emerged and presented himself in Marie Antoinette's drawing-room. Wearily he sank into the easiest chair he could find.

"I am quite worn out, Toinette."

"So, I imagine, is poor Louis."

"All morning, while I tried to talk, he hammered and hammered at a piece of metal. He flattened it, he bent it, he straightened it out again. It was almost impossible for me to make myself heard."

"So you failed with him, Joseph!"

"On the contrary, I succeeded."

"You—?"

"He has given his word. A solemn promise. If nothing else, he is a man of his word."

113

"Tell me what you said, how you persuaded him!"

Joseph smiled thinly. "I told him that not only did you lead an aimless, useless, frivolous life, but were quite out of hand in all things. I said, in simple direct language, that you needed a real man to control you. I pointed out a fundamental truth. I said—and I repeated myself to give weight to my words—that no man who has failed, one way or another, to master his wife in bed can hope to master her elsewhere. I told him that he must master you, not just for his own sake, but for his country's sake. After that, I assured him, full of the confidence he now lacks, he will have no trouble in keeping your nose out of state affairs and sweeping aside the court intrigue which is ruining France." He paused, drew breath and concluded triumphantly, "All very simple, and Louis agreed with me."

Quite speechless for once, Marie Antoinette was staring at him with her mouth unbecomingly agape.

Mildly he said, "You owe me a great debt of gratitude, Toinette. You might at least say thank you."

She began to laugh then, hysterically.

"You must admit," Joseph told her sternly, "that Louis, once he is a real man, will keep you happy and contented. Really you must."

"And himself also," she all but sobbed.

"Yes indeed, I pointed that out to him."

Her hysterical laughter broke out again, but quickly, on a sudden thought, she controlled herself. What an idiot this would-be philosopher was! So carried away was he by his theory that he had failed utterly to see the obvious flaw in it. Louis was weakly indulgent because he was forced by circumstances to deny her the one thing that gave marriage real meaning. But in denying her this one thing he denied himself also. Once denial was no longer necessary, either to her or to him, her power would surely be increased. It would be infinite, infinite!

"Yes indeed, Joseph, I do owe you a debt of gratitude," she said docilely. "Thank you, thank you a thousand times. I will never, never forget it."

114

FIVE

WITH HIS EYES CONSTANTLY STRAYING TO THE LOUIS XIVTH CLOCK, Louis was talking excitedly about the American war, talking, Marie Antoinette knew, for the sake of talking, and making very little sense. Still talking, he went with shuffling steps to the clock.

"Fast. It needs adjusting." He put it back five minutes. "There!" He stared at it, then put it back another five minutes. "Better, better!"

Poor Louis, she thought, putting back the clock would cause no delay now. All preparations had been made; in a few moments the message would come from the surgeon, Lassone.

"Those American delegates, confound them," he said frenziedly, "are pressing me to sign a treaty of friendship and commerce."

"Ah, so you have received them at court."

"Certainly not. That would only bring another protest from the English ambassador. They are dealing with Maurepas and Vergennes. Most persuasive gentlemen, I'm told. *Most.* Really, my dear, I do believe that wretched clock is at least *twenty* minutes fast."

"I thought it was a trifle slow," Marie Antoinette teased.

"*Slow!*"

"Do you intend to sign a treaty with the Americans?"

"And provoke an unwanted, disastrous war with England?"

"I see nothing wrong with friendship," she mused. "They are such charming people, the Americans. So friendly, so engaging, so—" she sought for a word—"so vigorous. Not in the least like the English I have had the misfortune to meet."

"Dear me, are you still meeting them secretly, Marie?"

"Not secretly, Louis. Informally. Monsieur Franklin is very charming, but Monsieur Deane I particularly like. Last week he sent me a beautiful phaeton of American make and some handsome bay horses. And yesterday he sent two barrels of a fruit called cranberries. They make delicious pies, or so Monsieur Deane says. I had them delivered to your own personal chef. You shall sample a cranberry pie during your convalescence."

115

Louis uttered a little moan. "My convalescence!"

"There have been barrels of apples too," she hurried on, "and walnuts and butternuts. A very pleasant trade in American goods and produce could be established. I myself, Louis, would gladly support a treaty of friendship and commerce."

There was a scratching at the door. She looked at Louis; he scowled and averted his head.

"Enter!" she said.

A page came in. "Monsieur Lassone awaits your Majesty's pleasure."

"Pleasure!" Louis ejaculated.

The page withdrew.

"Courage, darling, courage."

He looked at her wildly. "The clock was slow, after all. Courage, you say! I am the greatest coward in the world! It should have been performed when I was a baby. What fools the physicians were not to have recognized the condition then. It will hurt a great deal more now! Pon my oath it will!"

She tried to keep her temper. "Joseph said—"

"Joseph! He knew quite well how much I shall suffer and hurried back to Vienna in case I reproached him."

"He had to go, Louis. State affairs made his presence in Austria necessary. He said—"

"I remember well the things he said. All of them." Louis smiled briefly. "Especially the things that forced me to give my word." He squared his shoulders. "I trust he was right. Otherwise I shall regret having given it."

"Shall I come with you as far as the operating room?"

"Operating room!" he gasped. "A torture chamber, no less. Knives! Knives everywhere! I dreamed about them last night. Provence said—"

"I can well imagine what your scheming brother said! How he would like to make you break your word! Surely you know his game, Louis!"

Louis nodded. "I do, of course. Next in the line of succession he would be the last to want me to have children."

"A disgraceful attitude to take."

"Disgraceful, yes."

Almost without his knowing it she was leading him now from her apartments. Smiling brightly, head high, she tripped along at his side as he lumbered forward. As if by magic the corridors and anterooms were crammed with people. So thick was the throng of sightseers in the Oeil de Boeuf that it might well have been a special public holiday. Marie Antoinette ignored them all. Let them stare, let them gossip, let them pass their lewd remarks! One's privacy could only be shattered if one *noticed*. Therefore one did not notice.

Alone with her at last in the cabinet, Louis clung to her like a child.

"Stay with me during the ordeal. Give me strength with your presence."

"Louis, what a thing to ask!"

"You fear you might faint? Very well! Stand by the window. Turn your back while the torture is going forward. All I ask is the reassurance of your presence. Please, Marie!"

"Very well," she agreed.

Monsieur Lassone was waiting respectfully in the inner room. Behind him stood his assistants.

"Hold out your hands, Lassone," Louis ordered. "Hold them high."

Lassone, his face grave, held out his hands, palms down.

"Perfectly steady, thank heaven!" Louis cried. "You must have nerves of iron."

Marie Antoinette stationed herself at the window with her back to the little group.

"Help me on the table," she heard Louis plead. "My legs are collapsing beneath me."

A silence fell, to be broken, as she waited, by little nervous utterances from Louis.

"Make haste, I beg of you—

"Your hands are still steady, Lassone?—

"Keep the knife hidden, the sight would kill me!—

"Hurry, hurry! The beating of my heart is choking me!"

A moment later, or so it seemed to Marie Antoinette, Lassone broke into a gentle little laugh.

"There, your Majesty! So quick, so simple!"

"You have quite finished?"

"Quite, quite."

"Ha-a-a!" Louis moaned.

"His Majesty," Lassone announced, "has fainted."

Marie Antoinette went that night to spend an hour or so at the patient's bedside. She found Maurepas in attendance, and for once it was Maurepas who was the listener. Louis, supported by an assortment of pillows—they were behind his back, his neck, under his knees—was talking excitedly.

"Ah, there you are, my dear! I was telling this wretched Maurepas how brave I was, but I doubt if he believes me. Not once did I cry out, but does he believe me? No, he sits and smiles and shakes his head."

Marie Antoinette looked sternly at Maurepas. "His Majesty was amazingly brave. I give you my word, Monsieur."

"Mind you, Maurepas, it hurt! A most *searing* pain. And now, if I move, I suffer agonies. It will be some weeks, they tell me, before I can sit a horse again. Please leave us, Maurepas."

Maurepas hesitated. "I came on most urgent business, Sire."

"Be brief, then!"

"Your Majesty, I spent a most disagreeable half-hour this afternoon with the English ambassador."

"What, pray, is troubling Lord Stormont now?"

Marie Antoinette was quick to recognize in Louis' voice a new strange ring of authority, even a hint of haughtiness. She looked quickly at his face. Though he was blinking short-sightedly his head was high, his chin thrust out. He almost looked belligerent if one could ever imagine the mild-mannered Louis looking belligerent.

"I am growing tired of these carping English protests," he said.

"Well, what was the trouble?"

Maurepas, no less surprised than Marie Antoinette, swallowed quickly.

"Lord Stormont's spies have discovered the private trading venture."

"*What* private trading venture?"

"The one set up by Beaumarchais, Sire. We discussed it some time ago. Vergennes himself—"

"Wait! As far as I recall the Beaumarchais venture was only suggested, not *approved*. The man was to set up a private company for the purpose of trading anywhere, but mainly in America. The goods in question would, of course, be arms and ammunition. It was suggested that the government should help Beaumarchais by lending him, secretly, the sum of a million livres. You speak as if that sum had already been granted."

Maurepas coughed. "It has, your Majesty."

"Without my actual consent? Scandalous!"

Smoothly Maurepas said, "Your Majesty was of the opinion, at the time, that if the matter was to remain secret the less you knew of it the better. The loan is a good investment. It will pay excellent dividends."

Louis shook his head in self-reproach. "The fault is mine. I should have shown more firmness. How much does Lord Stormont know?"

"He knows that Beaumarchais is selling arms in America. He merely suspects the source of Beaumarchais' capital."

"Then we have nothing to worry about."

"Nothing, except that the English might consider the venture, a warlike provocation."

Louis was silent for a moment. "I have been neglectful of my duties. May God forgive me if unwittingly I have brought my country close to war with England."

"The risk of open war is not very great, at present."

Louis laughed quietly. "I think Lord Stormont frightened you a little."

Maurepas looked nettled. "The whole point, Sire, is this: it is important to us that the Americans should win this war they are fighting with England."

"In what way is it important to us?"

"If England wins, our colonies in the West Indies, a very rich source of revenue to us, will be in grave danger. England must not win."

"*Must not* is all very well, Maurepas!"

Maurepas smiled. "She is, however, far too occupied at present in America to turn on France. Of that we can feel quite sure."

Louis said briskly, "Send for Vergennes. My mind is made up on one point. Preparedness. Our military and naval forces must and shall be strengthened."

"But Lord Stormont will—"

"To the devil with Lord Stormont!" Louis barked.

The change in Louis grew more pronounced during the period of his convalescence. He became more self-assertive, even a little aggressive. Clearly he was proud of having found the courage to submit at last to the surgeon's knife, and never grew tired of speaking jauntily of the ordeal through which he had passed.

Soon he announced solemnly that he was tired of his bed of sickness.

"Tomorrow I shall rise and go forth cautiously."

119

This he did, though he insisted, quite unnecessarily, on walking with the aid of a stick. Thus equipped he visited the stables and the kennels, and he pottered for a time in his workshop, after which he went gloomily to his cabinet, his intention being to receive Maurepas and Vergennes, but instead he sent for Marie Antoinette.

"Is anything the matter?" she asked. "Maurepas and Vergennes are in the anteroom. They say you have kept them waiting at least an hour."

"It will do them no harm."

"Goodness, what a long face!"

Louis looked at her musingly. "Neither the horses nor the dogs, nor anything in my workshop, held my attention for long. To tell the truth, my dear—" he cleared his throat—"I am looking forward with the utmost impatience to my complete recovery. I—I hope it is the same with you."

To her annoyance she found herself blushing. "I expect it is, Louis."

He, too, blushed. "It will seem strange after all this time."

"Yes."

"Very strange."

"I wish—" she began, and broke off.

"Yes, my dear? You wish . . . ?"

"I wish we were two ordinary people, not King and Queen."

"Even a king is a man, a queen a woman," he said eagerly.

"Yes, but an ordinary man knows nothing of what it is to be a king. Ordinary people at least have privacy. It's horrible to have the whole court watching, waiting for your recovery, gossiping about it, making up dirty stories."

"Versailles is a vile place!" he said violently.

"I wish we could go away when the time comes, but no! The whole court is watching and waiting." Her voice rose indignantly. "Do you know what that wretched Maurepas suggested? He suggested that we should go back to the very beginning, pretend that I had just arrived from Vienna, and—and—"

"I know, Marie. And be put to bed with pomp and ceremony. He suggested it to me too. The rest of them, I fear, will insist."

"Oh, *Louis!*"

"We shall be quite alone in the end."

"Yes, but they will stand outside in little groups, laughing, speculating. They will do that every night. Yes, Louis, *every night!*

120

Not till I am pregnant will they be satisfied. It makes me feel like an animal in a cage. I can't help it, Louis, I hate the thought of it."

"So do I."

"Is there no escape?"

"None," Louis said miserably. "It is our misfortune that destiny has made us what we are."

"Will the date of the event," she demanded bitterly, "be preceded by an official announcement?"

"Yes, undoubtedly."

Shyly she asked, "Have you been able to decide on a date?"

Louis nodded and blinked at her. "I had a consultation with Lassone and Maurepas this morning. Lassone said three days from today, for a certainty. Maurepas immediately suggested a week from today, which is my birthday. It does seem appropriate."

Her eyes narrowed. "Has it been announced yet?"

"No. Maurepas is waiting for my final decision."

"Let it be announced then!" she cried, in sudden excitement. "The 23rd, your birthday!"

Puzzled by this quick change he looked at her uncertainly. "My dear—"

"Louis, how *slow* you are!"

He gave a loud shout. "But not as slow as you think, you scheming little minx!"

"You can actually read my mind?"

"I can actually read your mind!"

"Tell me what you read!"

He lowered his voice to a conspiratorial whisper. "It will be possible for us to—well, for us to be together before then, secretly."

"Yes, secretly!"

He took her quickly in his arms but she squirmed free.

"No, Louis! You must court me first, like an ordinary man courts an ordinary woman. You agree? *Do* please say you agree!"

"Of course I agree!" he shouted.

"Oh thank you, thank you!"

He looked at her sadly. "But Marie, it is something I have never done before. Courting won't come easily to me. I—I'm such a clumsy fellow at the best of times." He shuffled his feet, fingered his chin. "Perhaps you can tell me how I ought to go about it."

She pouted. "Now you are spoiling it."

"Flattery," he said, smiling. "One begins with flattery."

121

"Yes! You tell me how beautiful I am, and I, believing it, deny it coyly."

"You are very beautiful," he said gravely.

"That, Monsieur, is a gross exaggeration."

"It is the solemn truth."

"You will gain nothing by flattery."

"But *is* it flattery?" Louis said earnestly. "Only when one speaks falsely can praise be flattery. I state a fact. No more, no less. The sun rises every day. That is a fact. You are very beautiful. *That* is a fact. When you smile on me I am the happiest person in the world. If the sun fails to rise tomorrow, that will be the end of the world. If you fail to smile on me tomorrow, that also will be the end of the world." He looked at her anxiously. "Am I saying the right things?"

"Dear Louis, you are suddenly inspired. You may kiss my hand if you wish."

He seized her hand in a grip that made her wince. The lingering touch of his hot lips brought a throb of response to her throat.

"Tell me it is not too late, Marie!"

She stood back from him. "You go too fast, Monsieur."

He made a despairing gesture. "Either I go too fast or not at all. I would never make a polished lover. Dalliance is foreign to my nature. I have waited so long, Marie. All these years! God forgive me, but my need of you is driving me crazy."

He took her swiftly in his arms. Frenziedly he kissed her cheeks, her brow, her throat. Unable to move in his powerful grip she remained stiffly in his arms, fighting down the urge to respond, more afraid of herself than of him, afraid most of all of the old bewildering frustration.

"Let me take you now, love you completely now!" he urged.

She began to struggle. Delay seemed imperative, delay and more delay. Yet her heart was beating heavily in her breast and a compelling warmth was surging through her body.

She laughed shakily. "Maurepas will lose patience in a moment and enter whether you send for him or not."

"One can always lock the door!"

"But Lassone said—"

"He was overcautious. I know that now!"

"Louis!"

A shamefaced look crossed his face. He released her and stood back, hanging his head.

Miserably he said, "Naturally you turn from me in disgust. I am not a very romantic figure, am I? Too fat, too clumsy. Almost always tongue-tied. Something of a fool in the eyes of my ministers . . ."

Impulsively she flung her arms round his neck. The shamefaced look, the misery of the self-disparagement, nothing had ever moved her so deeply before. She longed to hold his head against her breast and comfort him like the great baby he was.

"It isn't far to the Little Trianon," she whispered.

They made their escape separately from the palace and met in the park. They entered the Little Trianon separately and met again in the newly decorated boudoir, a gay, entirely feminine room with Watteau canvases on the walls.

"I am spending such a lot of money on my Little Trianon. Do you mind, Louis?"

"Dearest Marie, I love you."

He took her in his arms. His embrace this time was amazingly gentle.

"You must forgive me if at first I am like a child learning to walk."

She was tense to begin with, remembering that first night and the many others, even more disastrous, that had followed it. She quickly sensed in Louis a like tenseness, compassion swamped her and drawing his hot face against her breast she felt her whole body relax.

Afterwards, laughing merrily, she said, "For a child you walk very well."

"I must have hurt you a little," he said contritely.

She stretched happily. "It soon passed."

"You found it enjoyable?" he asked anxiously.

"Yes," she said simply. "And you?"

"A magnificent diversion. What an idiot I was, delaying so long. All those wasted years. Think of it, Marie, a full seven years!"

"We can make up for them, darling."

After a moment he leaped up. "I have a terrific appetite. I was never so hungry in my life. Those cranberry pies were delicious. What a pity there are no more."

"Monsieur Deane sent another barrel this morning."

"He did? Splendid! I quite agree, these American friends of yours must be very charming fellows. American cranberries, cooked by a French chef—what more could one ask!"

123

Part III

ONE

COUNT MERCY, STANDING AT MARIE ANTOINETTE'S SIDE, GLANCED across the crowded ballroom and laughed gently.

"It is a pleasure, your Majesty, to see such a remarkable change in the King."

She gave him a merry look. "He has changed? I had scarcely noticed."

"His Majesty has appeared at the last three balls. And he has remained each time till the end. He has danced a great deal and has appeared to enjoy himself."

"Well fancy that!"

"According to court gossip he has been taking dancing lessons."

"Really?"

"His dancing has certainly improved."

"You have my word on that, Mercy." She gave him an innocent smile. "His dancing has also improved."

Mercy's eyes twinkled. "The Queen, then, is doubly a happy woman."

She blushed quickly and glanced beyond Mercy's shoulder at the gay scene of the ballroom. With the musicians taking a brief respite the ladies and gentlemen of the court were gathered together in little groups, laughing, joking, flirting. This was Versailles at its best, Versailles as she had always wanted it to be. Her eyes fell on Louis, engaged for the moment in an earnest conversation with Maurepas and Vergennes. As Mercy had said, there was a remarkable change in him. His gesture, as he wagged a finger at Maurepas, proclaimed his new self confidence.

124

"Her Imperial Majesty, your mother," Mercy murmured, "is growing a trifle—well—anxious."

Rarely angry these days, Marie Antoinette gave way to a sudden little spurt of rage.

"Let her grow anxious!" she cried.

Nevertheless, she was growing a trifle anxious herself, and was well aware that the whole court, gossiping in its usual malicious way, was suggesting that in spite of everything either she was barren or Louis was still impotent. She remembered that she had written enthusiastically to her mother immediately after Louis' birthday, saying that daily she expected the happy event of a royal pregnancy. And that was six months ago. It was disappointing. It was the only thing that clouded her new-found happiness.

"One begins to suspect," said a smooth, sneering voice, "that nothing at all took place on that allegedly important birthday, any more than it did on the night of your marriage."

She turned quickly. Provence was standing a pace behind her.

"Eavesdropper!" she raged.

Provence bowed. "There are no secrets at Versailles."

"You," she said scathingly, "should be pleased if what you say is true."

He bowed again. "I gladly admit it. I wager nothing did happen."

He bowed for a third time and sauntered away.

"What a pig he is!" she exclaimed, but she smiled as she remembered that there was at least one secret not known to the court.

"A pig, I agree," Mercy said. "But cunning, dangerous. Watch him, my dear."

The Abbé Vermond was approaching, and with him, to her annoyance, was the Prince de Rohan, who had been recalled from Vienna and replaced.

The abbé bowed. "Your Majesty . . ."

"Good evening, Vermond."

The Prince de Rohan bowed. "Your Majesty . . ."

She looked at Mercy. She looked again at Vermond. She stared at a point beyond the prince's left shoulder.

"How odd, I thought I heard someone else speak." She gave her complete attention to Mercy. "As you were saying, my dear Mercy . . ."

Vermond and the prince moved hastily away.

125

"That was not very kind," Mercy said gently.

She shrugged. "Let him come a hundred times, my treatment of him will never vary."

"He is truly sorry for what he did. He wants to apologize."

"He has actually approached you, Mercy?"

"Yes."

"Let him approach everybody, nothing will change my attitude."

Louis joined them, followed by Maurepas and Vergennes. All three had a conspiratorial air. They looked amazingly pleased with themselves, like three boys playing some desperate game of make-believe. Yet a moment later, when the English ambassador approached, they seemed to draw together, as if guiltily seeking each other's protection. With fixed expressions they looked in silence at the Englishman while he stiffly begged his Majesty to excuse him.

Louis laughed with forced joviality. "What, leaving so early, Lord Stormont?"

The English Ambassador bowed. "Discretion is the better part of valor, your Majesty."

"Whatever did he mean?" Marie Antoinette asked, when Lord Stormont, withdrawing, was beyond earshot.

Louis laughed gaily. "He must have noticed the approach of our American friends."

"They are here tonight, the Americans?"

Louis beamed on her. "I took your advice. I decided it was time to receive them officially."

Marie Antoinette was puzzled. "Did I really advise you to do that, Louis?"

"You remarked once that my behavior was a little churlish. I agree that it was."

She glanced quickly at Vergennes. "So your minister of war has won you over to his own way of thinking."

"The decision was my own," Louis avowed stoutly. "I take a risk, I admit, of provoking England beyond the limits of her endurance, but there are times when one must endeavor to live dangerously." And jauntily he added, "Yes indeed!"

Vergennes smiled contentedly. "The American victory at Saratoga made a difference to all of us."

"Ah, here they come," Maurepas murmured.

Known already, but privately, to most members of the court,

the three American delegates were making an almost royal progress to the King's side. Beneath the formality imposed by etiquette Louis, in speaking to them, displayed an easy geniality. Marie Antoinette was quick to see that the American spokesman, Monsieur Franklin, white-haired, benevolent and plainly dressed, was making a good impression.

"Assure your Congress of my warmest friendship," Louis said.

With that the Americans bowed, withdrew from the royal presence and mingled with the crowd in the ballroom.

"How deeply does your warmest friendship commit you?" Marie Antoinette asked.

Louis smiled. "More deeply than you imagine." He gave Maurepas and Vergennes a look of defiance. "My dear, I think I may let you into a little secret."

Maurepas frowned; Vergennes looked indignant.

"I have at last signed a treaty with the Americans," Louis went on. "Friendship, alliance, commerce."

"Does Lord Stormont know?"

"I imagine so, otherwise I would not have trusted a woman with the secret." Louis laughed knowingly. He seemed to have grown in stature and looked much older than his twenty-three years. "I suspect that Stormont is now waiting for instructions from his government."

"Your fondness for cranberries," Marie Antoinette laughed, "has certainly given you great courage."

Louis roared with laughter. "Yes, it has indeed! From cranberry pie to the baking of a quite different pie." His laughter faded and he grew very serious. "It was not an easy decision to make. I feel, in part, that I am deserting a fellow king, siding illogically with republicanism in its opposition to monarchism. But my sympathies lie with America; the shortsighted English king can take care of himself. First and foremost I want my own people to know that I am a king of a different caliber. And I want America to know that I have faith in its future and admire its fight for freedom."

For Louis this was a long speech, but Louis, with the new confidence in himself, was in the habit now of making long speeches. Though as of old Marie Antoinette's interest in a serious Louis strayed easily, she was more tolerant now and at least pretended to listen. She looked at him with a gentle smile on her lips. Surely, she thought, I must really be in love with him.

A few days later she learned from Louis that the English ambassador had made a formal request for his passports.

"In short, England has broken off diplomatic relations with us."

"Will it mean war, Louis?"

"Vergennes says no. England is not in a position to fight a war on two fronts."

"And what does Maurepas say?"

"Maurepas says yes. And, cynic that he is, he thinks war might not be a bad thing just now."

"Whatever makes him think that?"

"He says that when domestic affairs are in bad shape, a war, stirring the people to a high state of patriotism, is an excellent diversion to have."

"Goodness, I didn't know domestic affairs were in bad shape. Not any more. I thought France was the happiest country in the world."

Louis smiled fondly. "Since we no longer have Turgot to preach economy and to do his best to limit your spending, naturally you believed that."

She laughed merrily. "I find his successor, Monsieur Necker, a much more reasonable man. And so do the people, I'm sure! A comptroller-general who believes in loans, not heavy taxes, is sure to be popular. I *like* Monsieur Necker."

"Loans have to be repaid in time, Marie. I tell you, my dear, if I were not so happy in my private life I would be worried to distraction by the state of France. The agitators are still busy, but working quietly now, waiting and planning. Beneath all this excitement about the American war lies a sinister unrest."

"Then perhaps, as Maurepas says—"

"Yes, yes, perhaps! But war with England would bring only a short respite from insurmountable difficulties. Wars cost money; wars have to be paid for. I hope I have not done an unforgivable thing in bringing my country close to war. I hope that today, March 15th, will not be remembered in history as a black day for France."

"Goodness," she cried, "is it as late in the month as that! Oh Louis, what a forgetful woman I am!" She felt a vast excitement rising in her breast. "And for six months now I have watched the dates so carefully."

Louis looked at her blankly. "Really?"

"Dear Louis, slow-witted as ever!"

128

"Great heavens!" he shouted. "Marie, my love, surely you don't mean—?"

She flung her arms round his neck. "I shall have to consult the physicians, but I'm not mistaken. I know I'm not!"

Louis held her at arms' length.

"Have you fainted yet?" he asked solemnly.

"No, Louis."

"Have you been sick in the mornings?"

"Not once."

"In that case you must be mistaken."

"I can count!" she said angrily. "Also, I am a very strong woman. Why should I faint, why should I be sick? Simply because it is expected of me?"

Louis tweaked her nose. "It is at all events fashionable. For that reason alone you should welcome a small fainting fit, a little bilious attack." Quickly he drew her against his chest and embraced her violently. "Oh, my dear, it would be cruel to raise my hopes and then—"

"Louis," she panted, "you're suffocating me."

He released her instantly.

"Forgive me," he begged. "I—dear heaven!—I might have hurt you, done you irreparable harm." He hung his head. "I suppose this means that from now on I shall be condemned to live the life of a monk."

"Darling Louis, how I love you!"

"Send for your personal physician, Marie. Let him settle the matter, once and for all."

"Whether or not you are to live the life of a monk?"

"It amounts to the same thing," he said solemnly.

The physician was summoned, but all the irritating man would do was shrug noncommittally.

"One must wait and see," he said, complacently.

"Confound you, you should know your business better than that!" Louis roared.

The physician bowed. "My humble apologies, Sire."

"Accepted," Louis said huffily. "Meanwhile it would be advisable, I presume, if I—hum—slept alone. Yes?"

The physician hid a smile. "Not unless it is the royal wish."

"No possible harm could arise?"

"None whatever."

"You relieve me, Monsieur!"

129

The physician began to back from the royal presence.

"Wait!" Marie Antoinette said.

"Your Majesty?"

"This is a private matter, Monsieur. If the court begins to gossip we shall know whom to blame."

But the court, in spite of the physician's silence, did begin to gossip. Other people could count, other people had watched the Queen, other people had kept their eyes on the calendar. Nothing was private, nothing was sacred, at Versailles.

"I hate the place!" Marie Antoinette raged.

"No, my dear," said Louis, smiling, "you love it. Nothing is dearer to your heart than the lavishness, the extravagance, the magnificent balls, the reckless card parties. Even the gossip, when it is not directed against the Queen, amuses you."

"Not now, Louis," she said softly, "not any more. Only one thing is dear to my heart now, the child that is growing in my womb." She smiled up at him quickly. "And only one thing amuses me, your fear that soon you will be forced to live like a monk."

Louis nodded solemnly. "Men are shameful creatures, but I have a remedy. I shall rise earlier than usual and ride for an hour or so, ride *furiously*. Then I shall work for hours at my desk, after which I shall ride again till I am ready to drop from exhaustion. Later in the day, if I have the strength left, I shall slave in my workshop, hammering at my bench. Utterly worn out I shall fall at last into bed with one thought only in my mind— sleep."

"Remember that I am a strong woman," Marie Antoinette reminded him, her heart full of love and desire. "Only towards the end will it be necessary for you to wear yourself out *that* way."

When at last her personal physician, after a lengthy consultation with his fellow physicians, declared that she was indeed pregnant, Louis was crazy with joy. He danced clumsily about the room, he sang in a harsh unmusical voice, he cried that if he were not so fat he would turn a dozen somersaults.

"A boy," he said, "it will of course be a boy."

"No one can be sure of that," Marie told him soberly.

He considered this for a moment. "Well, what does it matter? If a girl, a boy the next time, or the next. All I know is this, girl or boy my life will be complete. I shall be the happiest father in the world. Oh Marie, Marie, I love you so very much."

TWO

With pomp and ceremony his majesty the king was holding court. The Queen was close at his side, while nearby lounged the brothers, Provence and Artois.

"A heart-warming scene," Louis declared.

"Yes indeed," Marie Antoinette agreed, and glanced round the crowded audience chamber.

"This display of loyalty convinces me that I have done the right thing."

For weeks now, ever since Louis had declared war on England, members of the nobility had flocked to Versailles to pay their respects and express their unshakable loyalty, while whenever he appeared in Paris the cry of 'Long live the King!' rang out with greater fervor than ever before.

"A king must be strong when a show of strength is called for," he said contentedly.

Marie Antoinette smiled indulgently. Louis had certainly shown the world that on occasion he knew how to be strong. Or perhaps it was just a matter of Louis having lost his temper. Even though it was now acknowledged that he was a changed man, his sudden violent rage had surprised and startled everybody. "They want war, very well they shall have war!" he had cried. That was when news of *La Belle Poule* had reached Versailles. *La Belle Poule*, a French frigate, had been attacked by the *Arethusa*, an English frigate. An entirely unprovoked attack, that was clear to everybody, as clear as the fact that *La Belle Poule*, after a long and bloody engagement, had emerged victorious.

"I fell into a trap," Louis admitted afterwards; "England wanted war but preferred to tempt me to declare it."

Well, it scarcely mattered. The people were able at last to forget their troubles in an uprush of patriotism, and the clever Léonard, adding to his already large fortune, had designed his most popular headdress yet, *La Belle Poule*.

The stream of visiting lords and ladies continued. More people than usual were making their bows or being presented. It was

131

growing a little tiresome, but Marie Antoinette went on smiling brilliantly and laughing gaily. She knew she was now wearing what Gabrielle called her social smile, laughing her social laugh. A bright impersonal exterior covering a vast emptiness, the amusing Gabrielle said.

"You must come to court more often," she told a raddled old comtesse whose hair was set in the now outdated *La Belle Poule* style.

Behind this monstrosity stood a young man, waiting to make his bow to Louis before turning respectfully to her. Scarcely looking at him, Marie Antoinette brought the social smile to her face and prepared herself once again for the social laugh. A moment later, as he exchanged a few words with Louis, her heart missed a beat. Standing there slim and erect, he wore a strange, magnificent uniform, exotic enough to attract attention, even at Versailles, but she saw it through a haze. She knew her face had paled; she was sure her heart had stopped beating altogether. She had forgotten him long ago, yet now, in this shattering moment of recognition, she could remember only him and that brief meeting years ago at the Opera ball.

"My poor Marie," Louis whispered, as the young man stood there waiting, "is something the matter?"

"Nothing," she said faintly.

"You are overtired," he said tenderly. "This has been a long reception. I should have remembered your condition, not permitted it."

Still faintly, she said, "I failed to catch the young man's name."

"Count Axel von Fersen," Louis told her. "A member of a noble Swedish family."

Well, at last she knew his name! She repeated it to herself. Axel, she thought, dwelling on it, liking it, feeling, ridiculously enough, that it was of great importance to her.

"You have been to Versailles before, Monsieur le Comte?" she said, her voice quite controlled now.

The young man bowed. "Some years ago, your Majesty, before you were Queen." His eyes, betraying no recognition, held hers steadily. "But not having been presented to your Majesties since the accession I have blundered badly in coming here now, alone."

"Strict etiquette is not always to our liking," Louis told him affably. "In any case, your ambassador has already spoken of you, and warmly."

132

"Ah, then an old friend," Marie Antoinette said, her voice ringing foolishly in her own ears.

This, she told herself angrily, was dreadful. In a moment, having first grown pale, she would be blushing like a young and clumsy girl. She laughed quickly, a faint echo of her social laugh.

"A delightful uniform," she said, as she dismissed him with a nod. "We hope to see you here again, wearing it bravely."

The young count bowed, but before he could step back she leaned forward impulsively. A quick glance had told her that Louis, turning aside for a moment, was in conversation with Maurepas.

"My card party tonight," she whispered in German. "Come to it."

"Your Majesty is most gracious."

She watched him till he was lost in the crowd. Now why did I do that? she asked herself. Why? Well, for one thing, Louis was leaving in an hour or so for Choisy and a few days' hunting. That, of course, made her quick decision seem worse. Still, there would be dozens of people at the card party, there always were. Dozens of people, dozens of watching eyes! She would have to be careful, give nothing away. Give nothing away? What in the name of heaven *was* there to give away? And why all this fluttering agitation? One would think she was planning a love affair. The utter nonsense of it! A love affair, and she with a loving, doting husband, a husband she loved to distraction. And pregnant too, pregnant these last five months! How Gabrielle would laugh when she heard about it! Conscious suddenly that eyes were staring at her, she looked up quickly.

"Ah, Provence," she said brightly. "Are you as bored with all this as I am?"

Provence said, "You tried not to recognize him, but you failed miserably."

"Tried not to recognize whom?" she asked haughtily.

"The Swedish count. Who else?"

Her heart was hammering in her breast. "I had never heard his name before."

Provence smiled thinly. "I well remember a masked ball at the Opera several years ago."

"There are so many balls at the Opera it is difficult to remember any one in particular."

133

"He was a handsome youth then. No one blamed you for making him your lover."

"This is infamous, Provence, infamous!"

"In maturity he is even better looking. No one will blame you for continuing the affair."

She was beside herself with rage now. "There was no affair. He went away. I never saw him again!"

Provence chuckled softly. "So you remember that night at the masked ball, after all. I admit you were never *seen* seeing him again, but no doubt you continued to meet him secretly in the Rue des Bons Enfants. He, of course, with so much at stake, would keep himself well hidden in Paris."

She remembered Maurepas' warning. "What are you plotting, Provence?"

"Plotting?" Provence smothered a pretended yawn. "Nothing, little sister-in-law. Secret love affairs fascinate me. Shall we leave it at that?"

Shaken, she watched him stroll away. To be accused of something you had not done! Intolerable! Yet at the same time to feel guilty about it! That was even more intolerable.

Play at the card tables that night had been in full swing for more than an hour when Count von Fersen made his appearance. While playing and waiting, angry with him but admitting to herself that she had stated no time, she found concentration impossible. Gabrielle, privileged always to sit at her right hand, chided her about her losses.

"How, pray," she mocked, "are we to finance the invasion of England if your Majesty will insist on gambling in this disastrous manner?"

"Ah!" Marie Antoinette said softly, and half-rose in her chair.

Count von Fersen, accompanied by the Swedish ambassador, had entered. The two men began to stroll among the tables, pausing here and there, as did the non-playing onlookers, to watch the sport.

"You were saying . . . ?" She sank back in her chair.

"I was making a joke," Gabrielle replied. Her eyes also were on the handsome young count. "Yes," she mused, "quite delightful."

"I beg your pardon, Gabrielle?"

"The Swedish uniform, and for that matter the man who wears it."

134

Marie Antoinette threw down her cards and rose quickly.

"I have had enough. Play bores me tonight. Give me your arm, Gabrielle. Let us watch the others."

Arm in arm they strolled from table to table. When at last, as if by accident, they came face to face with the Swedish count, Provence, as if appearing by magic, was standing at his side. A few polite words were exchanged, a comment or two on the American war, the intended invasion of England. In such company no more was possible and Marie Antoinette was ready to burst into angry tears. Drawing her aside, leaving the count with Gabrielle, Provence chuckled softly.

"This is surely indiscreet."

"What do you mean, Provence?"

"Indiscreet and over-bold. You should keep him hidden, not bring him to court for all to see."

She turned her back on Provence, but the count had gone, and so had Gabrielle. Again she was ready to burst into angry tears. Gabrielle of all people! Gabrielle, her best friend! Back at her table she made it clear, by a brief arrogant gesture, that she had no wish to resume play. She sat down. Her feet, as if of their own accord, began to beat a furious tattoo beneath the table.

"Marie, my dear . . ."

She looked up in surprise. "Well, what is it, Gabrielle?"

"Since play bores you tonight, why not an hour or so of freedom in my apartments?"

"Very well."

At the door of Gabrielle's *salon*, having maintained a stony silence, she paused.

"Gabrielle, forgive me."

"For what, Marie?"

"For misjudging you. I thought that in your usual predatory fashion you had reached out to take yet another lover."

Gabrielle smiled. "The handsome Swede? You and I are good friends. Most of the time we forget that we are Queen and subject—" she made a slight, mocking curtsy—"but now and then I have the good sense to remember my place. How long have you known him?"

Marie Antoinette blushed. "I met him today for the first time. No, I'll be honest with you. I met him once, for a very short time some years ago."

"And now, meeting him again, you have eyes for no one else."

135

"Oh Gabrielle, that can't be true!"

"You are quite deeply disturbed, my dear. Obviously you are, or your German accent would not have become so suddenly pronounced."

"Eyes for no one else . . ." Marie Antoinette whispered.

"I was not the only one to notice."

"Provence?"

"The wily Provence. Because of that I judged it wise to practice the utmost discretion." Gabrielle made to open the door. "Well, is it this far and no farther?"

"The count is in there, in your *salon?*"

"Alone and waiting."

"Oh Gabrielle, what a dreadful thing to do! Whatever will he think of me!"

Gabrielle's eyes widened innocently. "I merely told the count that your Majesty wished to know something of the Swedish attitude to our war with England."

"Oh . . . Oh, I—I see."

Gabrielle touched Marie Antoinette's arm affectionately. "I hope I have acted wisely. To me a lover is a passing diversion. While loving one man to distraction I am searching always for his successor. With you it would be different. This Swede, if you permit it, will become the great passion of your life."

"I—"

"Perhaps he already is."

"Oh no, that can't be true! Tell him I have changed my mind. Tell him I have no wish to see him."

"Liar!"

"Tell him you made a mistake. It is the King, not the Queen, who wants to discuss the matter with him. Tell him Louis will receive him when he returns from Choisy."

"How unsure of yourself you sound."

"Oh Gabrielle, what shall I do?"

"Follow your heart, my child," Gabrielle said mockingly.

Marie Antoinette hung back still, but Gabrielle, opening the door, gave her a gentle little push into the *salon.*

Once the door was closed behind her she walked forward slowly and, she hoped, with dignity. She tried to tell herself that she was a woman now, and a Queen, not an impulsive little girl. The young count, with his back to her, was studying a portrait on the wall. He turned at the rustle of her gown. Quickly she

136

reminded herself that she had parted from him in anger that night at the Opera ball and disliked him intensely.

"Your Majesty . . ."

He clicked his heels together and bowed stiffly from the waist.

She looked at him arrogantly. "So you were good enough to come, Monsieur le Comte."

"It would be impolite to ignore a royal command."

He spoke quietly, calmly, with far too much composure.

"You came for that reason only?" she said coldly.

He smiled for the first time. "It was an honor, your Majesty, which I could not deny myself."

"What brings you to France this time?" she asked abruptly.

"In the first place, I wish to seek service with the French army."

"Really? The King will help you all he can."

"Thank you, Madame. In the second place, my father is anxious for me to marry. Paris, I understand, is a good place in which to continue my search for a rich wife."

"A rich wife?" she almost snapped. What he should have said was that he would never, while she lived, take a wife or a mistress. But no, not even his eyes transmitted this obligatory message. Her arrogance came naturally now. "So yours is a noble but impoverished family, Monsieur."

"On the contrary, your Majesty. A quite wealthy family."

His voice betrayed a slight pique. Pleased, she fell to studying him carefully, comparing him as he now was with the handsome youth she remembered. His shoulders had broadened but he was still slim, with the same easy, fluid movements, except when he bowed in stiff formality. His blond hair was still thick but more carefully dressed; his cheeks, with their fresh clear skin, were perhaps a little leaner. The thought that he was a man now, not a callow youth, set her heart beating violently.

"Tell me," she said, since clearly he would only speak when spoken to, "do you find me changed since last we met?"

He bowed. "If I may presume to say it, your Majesty, you are a woman now."

She made a face. "Just a woman? Not a pretty woman, not an ugly woman, just . . . a woman?"

"Your Majesty," he said, his voice quite impersonal, "is possibly the most beautiful woman in the world."

"Only . . . possibly, Monsieur?"

137

He looked momentarily contrite. "I apologize for my rudeness."

Then he glanced at the door, his first sign of uneasiness. "Your Majesty wished to know something of my country's attitude to the war between France and England."

"Oh nonsense! I am not interested in the war, except, of course, for the new fashions which will inevitably arise out of it."

The count's uneasiness increased. "In that case, your Majesty—"

"You will withdraw when I dismiss you," she said pettishly.

"As you wish."

What a stick he was! A toy soldier in his pretty uniform. No blood ran in his veins, only ice. He cared for her no longer, *that* was clear. No longer? Had he *ever* cared for her?

"Do you still find my eyes flawless?" she demanded.

"Your Majesty, this is most embarrassing—"

"Flawless, but still soulless, Monsieur?"

He averted his head, remained stubbornly silent.

"Are you afraid to reply because I am now Queen of France?"

"Not afraid, no."

"But it would be bad manners, a breach of etiquette! How stupid of me to have forgotten that! Yet that night at the Opera ball you refused, even when you knew who I was, to take back your words."

"They had been said. No good could have come of my retracting them."

"Ah, you are still frank underneath the polish you have acquired, but you have learned caution."

A delightful smile lit his face. "So it would seem, Madame."

Determined to break down the barrier which stood between them, she said earnestly: "This *salon*, which belongs to the Comtesse de Polignac, is the one place in the vast cage of Versailles where I may find freedom and be myself. Informality is the rule here. I call the comtesse Gabrielle; she calls me Marie. It is the same with all her friends when we meet here. Would you please remember that . . . Axel?"

"Your Majesty—"

"The name is Marie, just Marie."

"I—Madame— No, your Majesty, I find it impossible."

His discomfiture was pathetic. He was hidebound by etiquette, quite hidebound. Either that, or he felt no warmth toward her, no warmth whatever.

138

"You can at all events speak frankly, even if you must remember my rank." She was pleading with him now. "Please tell me, Axel, *please*, that the soullessness has gone."

He looked at her for a long moment. "Very well—"

"But only if you think it really has gone!" she commanded.

He said slowly: "When I saw you at court today I saw only happiness in your eyes."

She looked at him eagerly, with slightly parted lips. Happiness at the shock of seeing him again. Yes, yes, of course! She felt it again now, a tender sort of happiness, verging on tears.

"Happiness," he went on, "when you looked at your husband; happiness even when you looked at that painted old comtesse and pretended, oh so cleverly, to be glad to receive her."

"Oh . . ." said Marie Antoinette, quite deflated.

"There is nothing soulless about happiness, your Majesty. Most certainly not in the happiness of a woman in love with her husband, a woman—forgive me—who is soon to be a mother."

"It won't be for months," she snapped. "Why, it doesn't even show yet!"

"And now, for a moment," he said, quite sadly, "the old soullessness returns." He took a deep breath, grew quickly confused. "Forgive me, I spoke hastily."

What an impossible man he was!

"Do you know what I think?" she said scathingly. "I think that if you could become completely informal and speak your mind you would want to lecture me like my brother did."

Surprisingly he said: "I should like to be a brother to you."

"So that you could lecture me?"

"No, Madame. So that I could watch over you, advise you if you needed advice, help you in all your little difficulties. Yes indeed, I should like to be a brother to you."

He should have added, *Since I can be nothing else to you.* He should have, but did he even feel like that? He gave no sign. Stiff, pompous, impossible. A hateful, disgusting young man!

"I want to go back to the card room," she said angrily. "Give me your arm."

He made no move. "To enter on my arm, after a considerable absence . . . would that be wise, your Majesty?"

The hint of reproof in his voice—brotherly reproof, no doubt he thought it!—spurred her on.

"Are you afraid of gossip, Monsieur le Comte? Are you afraid of a distorted story reaching the King's ears?"

"Yes, Madame, but not on my own account."

She remembered what she had once decided about him. A man who never acted impulsively, who could be trusted implicitly, who gave his word and, whatever the cost, kept it. He was that, and more. He would die for her without the slightest hesitation. But he was still hateful, intolerable, and capriciously she thrust these serious thoughts from her mind.

"I have asked you to escort me to the card room. Please do so." She watched him as he set his jaw stubbornly and remained silent. "This," she added icily, "is a royal command!"

Fersen bowed. "I regret, it is one I cannot obey."

He bowed again and walked swiftly from the room, leaving Marie Antoinette quivering with anger yet feeling a strange reluctant admiration. Rude, defiant, but yes, most certainly a man she could trust implicitly.

"Well?"

It was Gabrielle de Polignac, grinning widely.

"Well—what, Gabrielle?"

"He passed me just now, grim of face—oh so stern!—and biting his lip."

"Oh Gabrielle, he wants to be a brother to me, that and nothing else."

"While you, of course, long to be a sister to him."

"That would be better than nothing else."

"Dear me, such purity."

"There are times, Gabrielle, when your conversation is not as witty as you think."

"I warned you this might become the real passion of your life."

"I shall never see him again! Not unless I send for him, and I swear I shall never do that. Never!"

It was actually Louis who, a few days later, sent for Axel von Fersen. For an hour or more the two young men strolled together in the park where Marie Antoinette, promenading with her ladies, caught a passing glimpse of them. With their heads close together they were talking earnestly, oblivious of all else but the subject of their conversation. Seeing them thus gave her the oddest feeling. It was almost as if her heart went out to them equally.

Later, Louis spoke enthusiastically about the Swedish count.

140

"I like him very much. A most engaging fellow. We see eye to eye in many things. His judgment is remarkably sound. If he were not so engrossed with his military ambitions I would consider making him my minister of war in place of Vergennes, even though he is not a Frenchman. I feel, my dear, that I have made a new and valuable friend. Pon my soul, I believe I love him already as a brother."

"Does he feel like that about you, too?" Marie Antoinette asked brightly.

"We-ell, he *hinted* as much."

Unable to control herself she began to laugh quite violently. A brother to her, a brother also to her husband! Amusing, fantastically amusing!

"My dear, what *is* the matter?" Louis asked mildly.

"Nothing, Louis, nothing!" she gasped. "A picture crossed my mind of the King of France parading in one of those fetching Swedish uniforms."

Louis considered this seriously.

"No," he said at last, "I haven't the figure for it."

"How long is Monsieur le Comte de Fersen staying in France?" she asked casually.

"For as long as we can keep him."

"*We?*"

"When you get to know him better you will be just as eager as I am to make a friend of him."

"That is quite possible," she admitted faintly. "Do you intend this foreigner to come often to Versailles?"

"How ungracious you sound! And how impolite. This *foreigner!*" Louis looked at her quizzically. "Ah, I see it all!" He was hugely delighted with himself. "I have never had a real friend before—by that I mean one who is not a place-seeker, fawning on me yet laughing at me behind my back—and now that I have found one, you are *jealous*. No, no, don't deny it, Marie. Jealous!"

"Unutterably," she said lightly.

"I knew it, I knew it!"

"I shall, of course, endeavor to be polite to him."

"Ah, as I on every occasion endeavor to be polite to Madame la Comtesse de Polignac."

"You dislike Gabrielle?"

"To be frank, I find her tiresome. And I am naturally jealous of her, just as you are jealous of Axel von Fersen." Louis' heavy shoulders heaved with suppressed laughter. "The debt, one might say, is evened off, eh?"

In the weeks that followed Fersen, who had taken lodgings in Paris, came often to Versailles, but Marie Antoinette was never at any time alone with him. He appeared at balls, receptions and state functions; he was present once or twice when the King dined in public; he took an occasional interest in his Majesty's *coucher;* but he always remained an unobtrusive spectator. That he was becoming a close friend of the King passed unnoticed by everyone, even the watchful Provence.

Marie Antoinette met him once in Louis' presence, and at Louis' insistence. Fersen was grave, courteous, politely attentive, yet he seemed quite unable to meet her eyes. She was sure she knew the reason for this. He had made up his mind from the very first to maintain a wall of strict etiquette between them, but at the same time had been unable to resist the urge to come to Versailles and feast his eyes on her. Poor Axel, how he must be suffering! Then an alarming thought all but shattered her. He avoided her eyes because, in the last week or so, she had grown noticeably larger. Embarrassment? Perhaps, but more than likely —her heart beat happily again—resentment. He was tormented by the wish that he, not Louis, was the father of her unborn child.

"I understand," she said, "that you are to be given command of a French regiment."

"That is Axel's wish," Louis said, answering for Fersen, "but there are certain difficulties. The dear fellow is loath to cause jealousy among French officers."

"They will be smoothed out in time," she commented.

"Yes, of course. And meanwhile we must do something about finding Axel a suitable wife."

"I suspect," she said lightly, "that Monsieur le Comte will be a hard man to please when it comes to choosing a wife."

Louis laughed smugly. "With my own good fortune a constant example before him, naturally he will."

Fersen bowed, but his eyes, dark and steady, betrayed nothing of his feelings. If he had any, of course, man of ice that he was!

Carefully she said, "My dear friend Gabrielle is growing annoyed with you, Monsieur."

"Indeed, your Majesty?"

"Gabrielle is a very persistent creature and will force you in the end to attend her informal parties. Loving her as I do, I can only urge you, Monsieur, to show her more graciousness. Why not join us tonight? A small supper party, very gay and carefree, I assure you."

Fersen hesitated.

"Pooh!" Louis cried. "Our dear Axel is far too sensible to fritter away his time in fruitless activities. And in any case, I intend him to take supper with me tonight. I want his opinion on our plans for the invasion of England."

"The biggest factor in any invasion plans," Fersen said quickly, "is the weather."

"And the English have the luck of the devil when it comes to the weather!" Louis cried wrathfully.

Marie Antoinette rose. "Since you intend to begin your discussion now, I may as well go in search of one or other of the fruitless activities you *both* despise so much."

Louis allowed her to go without a protest, and as she went his voice, eagerly addressing Fersen, followed her.

"I still have the gravest doubts about the step I have taken, but I firmly believe that all people should be free. When I say all people, I naturally mean my own as well. What I have done in helping the Americans must surely show my own people that I am fair and just. And I do hope and pray that my help will make it possible for the Americans to establish themselves as a free and independent nation."

He sounded like an eager schoolboy, unsure of himself, begging for reassurance. Marie Antoinette lingered outside the door, waiting for Fersen to speak.

"I have only one fear," he said at last, "the fear that in helping to establish a free nation in the new world, France may be sowing the seeds of ruin for herself in the old world."

She moved on down the corridor. She loved the sound of his voice, its steadiness, the conviction it carried. If only he were King of France in place of Louis! For Louis, in spite of the new confidence he had found in himself, was still weak and ineffectual, even if at heart he was kind and thoughtful and eager always to do the right thing for his people. She checked these thoughts. What a disastrous effect Axel von Fersen was having upon her! A little more of this nonsense and she herself would be just as out of place in Gabrielle's *salon* as he would be if Gabrielle succeeded in forcing him there. Wonderingly she thought: He could do anything with me; under his influence I could become as serious a stateswoman as poor Mama.

"Pooh!" she said aloud, "this is idiotic. I shall send for Bertin and command her to design a gown that will hide completely my swollen stomach."

The cunning little dressmaker excelled herself once again, and in a matter of days was inundated with orders for copies of the new creation.

"Those silly husbands," Marie Antoinette teased her, "how you must be making them pay through the nose."

"What else is a husband for, your Majesty?" Mademoiselle Bertin chuckled and, privileged person that she was, added slyly, "Especially if he is in addition a king?"

"Indeed what else!" Marie Antoinette laughed.

With the days and weeks slipping by most rapidly she continued while she could to lead the gay life of her own choosing. There were exciting weekends at the Little Trianon, where the theater she had promised herself was now completed, the usual balls and card parties, and delightful evenings in Gabrielle's *salon.*

Meanwhile, only vaguely interested in state affairs, she was aware that Necker was raising new loans, that war fever, as Mercy called it, was still gripping the nation, and that the news from America was heartening, so heartening that nobody minded postponement of the plans for the invasion of England. She cared little for this, except that in her mind she associated the war with Axel von Fersen. The round of gaiety, which did not entirely satisfy her during the last weeks of her pregnancy, was an escape, she told herself, from it and from him. Especially from him. How she hated his politeness, his irritating aloofness! He would change, she tried to tell herself, when her child was born. He was waiting for that, restraining himself gallantly. Afterwards, noble fellow that he was, he would declare the love that was tormenting him sorely.

Soon it was December and she grew more conscious than ever of the watching eyes of the court. How everybody stared at her, from the lowliest servant to the highest-born noble.

She protested indignantly to Louis.

"They are anxious," he told her. "We are all anxious."

"I see no anxiety in their eyes, only curious calculation. Never have I been so aware of the fact that I am public property. Yes, Louis, public property!"

"Look at me, Marie," he begged. "Look at me and tell me if you can see anything but anxiety in *my* eyes."

Her heart warmed towards him. "I can see nothing but anxiety, Louis."

"And *love*, Marie."

She threw herself into his arms. "If only you knew what a coward I am! I have heard such horrible stories about child-birth."

"Exaggerations, all of them!" he said eagerly.

"I expect pain, Louis. I—I think I am prepared for it. What frightens me most, and horrifies me too, is the public ordeal. I think I would be really brave if I were an ordinary woman and could have my baby in private."

Louis made an unhappy gesture. "It is impossible for the Queen of France to break with tradition."

"But *why*, Louis?"

"Witnesses must be present. The people must be sure that you really have given birth to a child."

"Surely the word of the accoucheur—!"

"He could be bribed. The physicians could be bribed. A changeling could be slipped into the bed."

She turned from him angrily. "So nothing can save me from humiliation as well as pain."

A few days later the physicians and the accoucheur, conferring together, declared with concern that the royal birth was overdue. Louis, half crazy with anxiety, called them incompetent idiots and stayed at Marie Antoinette's side from morning till night. Touched by his agitation, she nonetheless made a sharp retort to the physicians' complaint.

"My child is as reluctant as I am to face a public agony."

The first pain came in the evening of the 18th. She would have delayed, but Louis sent at once for the physicians. In a matter of minutes, even before the official announcement could be made and the bells rung, the news spread through the vastness of the palace. Her apartments filled rapidly and she retreated to her bedchamber. Gabrielle was there, and so was Louise de Lamballe. Strangely, she felt more pleased to see Louise than Gabrielle.

"Go out and tell them it is a false alarm," she begged of Louise.

"His Majesty will send them away in any case," Louise assured her. "There is plenty of time yet."

At three in the morning labor began, and the courtiers, sent away earlier, were quickly roused by the servants they had left to keep watch in the corridors. There was no escape now, she realized that bitterly, and soon, as the bedchamber became crammed with ladies and gentlemen fighting for vantage points, she no longer cared. She lay on the special delivery bed which had been rolled into the room and through a shimmering, stifling haze stared unseeingly as the aristocrats of the court and the common citizens who had come out from Paris pushed and jostled each other.

The agony that followed seemed endless, yet in the middle of it she thought, for one brief moment, of Axel von Fersen, and raising her head searched for his face in the crowd. Good taste, of course, had kept him away. Either that or jealousy. Then quickly she forgot him and only Louis, the cause of all this pain, remained in her mind. Numbly she heard his voice. He was shouting hysterically, demanding quite ineffectually that the room should be cleared. The next moment she caught a glimpse of him, climbing it seemed up the walls of the bedchamber. Vision cleared for a moment; Louis, with frantic strength, was forcing open the windows which had been sealed against the cold of winter draughts.

"Air!" he kept shouting. "We must have air!"

She fainted then, and when at last she recovered consciousness she saw that it was daylight, that the room had indeed been cleared and that only Louis was at her side, Louis who was weeping and laughing at the same time, Louis whose fat ugly face, stained with tears, seemed the dearest sight in the world to her.

"What if the court *is* disappointed?" he was sobbing. "A boy would have belonged to the nation, not to us. She is ours, Marie, *ours*. She belongs to us, to no one else, to us, Marie!"

"A girl, then, Louis."

"A healthy child, a perfect child, Marie!"

She turned her face from him. "I shall have to go through all this again."

"Not unless you wish it!"

Her head rolled back on the pillow. She smiled weakly.

"I expect I shall, when the pain is a forgotten memory." And inconsequently she added, "I love you very much, Louis. Yes of course the child will be ours, all ours."

146

THREE

"A MONTH OLD TODAY," LOUIS MURMURED. "I CAN SCARCELY BE-
lieve it."

He was walking up and down the nursery with the baby in his
arms. Watching him, Marie Antoinette was delighted at the
little crooning noises he was making, and the gentle expression
on his face brought quick tears to her eyes. How happy she
was! Not even the presence of Madame Adelaide and the ever-
watchful, brooding Provence disturbed her.

"Please let me hold her," Madame Adelaide pleaded.

Louis glanced at Marie Antoinette, as if seeking her approval,
then tenderly he placed the baby in his aunt's arms.

"There, my dear aunt, your great-niece, Maria Theresa Char-
lotte. In effect, Madame Royale, a most important person indeed.
But hold her carefully, I beg of you!"

With the baby in her arms Madame Adelaide made little
crooning noises too and looked positively dewy-eyed. Louis
glanced at Marie Antoinette. His thoughts were easily read. How
splendid if, because of the baby, his wife and his aunt could
become friends again.

"Well," he said, turning to Provence, "whom does she resemble,
Marie, or me?"

Provence, lounging near the cot, shrugged his shoulders noncommittally.

"Marie, perhaps, but I can see no resemblance to you."

"Thank heaven for that!" Louis laughed. "I am far too ugly."

He carried the baby to the cot and placed her in it. A moment
later, his face showing mild curiosity, he stood back with a sheet
of paper in his hand.

"Someone has been writing verses." He began to read, and
quickly his face grew stern. "I never saw anything more disgusting in my life!" He screwed up the sheet into a ball and flung it
violently across the room. "Horrible! Unforgivable!"

Marie Antoinette watched the ball of paper roll on the carpet.
She saw that Madame Adelaide, alert now and quizzical, was

147

watching it too. Provence strolled forward and picked it up. The tense little silence was broken harshly by Louis.

"Give it to me!"

Provence pretended not to have heard, unscrewed the paper and began, quite monotonously, to read.

"Hold your tongue!" Louis cried.

But his brother went on reading, and as she listened Marie Antoinette felt her throat constrict in horror. Happiness fell from her, and where normally she could have cried out in indignation she remained helpless and silent as, line by line, Provence pieced together the rhymed accusation that she, the Queen, was an unfaithful wife, the mother of a child that was not her husband's.

"So it has come at last," Provence remarked thoughtfully.

"Well, well," said Madame Adelaide, softly, eyes darting curiously from Louis to Marie Antoinette.

"A vile dirty lie!" Louis shouted.

Provence shook his head. "That is what I thought myself when I first heard it, but—"

"When you *first* heard it?" Louis challenged.

"There has been . . . gossip. *But*, as I was about to say, when I made inquiries, gathered together little scraps of evidence, I was forced, regretfully, to change my mind."

"And then you wrote those verses," Marie Antoinette cried.

He smiled blandly. "I was never a versifier."

"You caused them to be written!"

"Certainly not, but when they came my way—"

"You seized on them gladly! You placed them in the cot for one of us to find!"

Provence bowed. "Needless melodrama, no doubt, but I always did enjoy a touch of melodrama."

Numb with the shock, Marie Antoinette could find no more to say. Neither could Louis, who stood with his hands gripped tightly behind him, his face flushed, his eyes filled with pain.

Madame Adelaide said eagerly, "You spoke of evidence, Provence . . . Am I to understand that you intend to make a charge?"

"You are, my sweet aunt."

"You can substantiate it with *evidence?*"

"I can."

Madame Adelaide pursed her lips. "It is your duty, then, to make the charge."

148

"It is indeed. But—" he turned to Louis—"please believe me, my dear Berri, when I say how deeply it grieves me to have to do so."

Louis made a rough gesture. "Please leave us."

"But Berri—"

"Go before I lose my temper and throw you out!"

Provence shrugged, smiled ironically and went quietly from the room.

"You also," Louis told Madame Adelaide.

"As you wish," she said, and with something of a swagger followed Provence from the room.

"It is of course a plot," Louis said, in a whisper.

"Hatched by Provence, supported by Madame Adelaide!"

Marie Antoinette was looking despairingly at Louis. Instead of coming to her, taking her in his arms, comforting her, he remained there at a distance.

"If you really believe it to be a plot, Louis, nothing else matters, and I shall be able to bear it more calmly."

"Yes, a plot, a vile plot."

"What action are you going to take against Provence?"

Louis shifted his stance uneasily. "He spoke of evidence."

"*Evidence!*"

"Undoubtedly false evidence. He has been misled by others. Otherwise he would never have *dared* . . . !"

Something of her old spirit returned. "If others have misled him they should be dealt with. Surely you see that!"

He came to her at last and took her in his arms.

"Dear Marie, I believe in you utterly. What else matters but that?"

She felt that his voice did not carry full conviction.

"Are you afraid to push this further?" she asked quickly.

"In one respect, yes," he admitted. "I want to be wise, do the right thing. My foresight was never good, but I think I can see beyond the end of my nose in this case. There are many unkind people in the world who always like to think the worst of others. Prove that Provence has been misled and those same people would still prefer to think the worst of you. An inquiry might do you irreparable harm."

She flung herself from his arms. "I prefer the truth. I am not afraid of the truth."

"Let things remain as they are, I beg of you."

"Never, never!"

Later she sent for Count Mercy and confided in him fully. The old man agreed that an impossible situation had arisen, a situation which might easily end her domestic happiness.

"I refuse to believe that Provence has been misled by others," she said.

"And so do I. This attack on you is his, and his alone."

"But supported by Madame Adelaide!"

"She is, of course, snatching at a chance to discredit you. Clearly a doubt has been thrown in your husband's mind. He is a man like the rest. He loves you, but he is possessive and jealous. Naturally he is."

"I hate him for it!"

"Of course you do, but how would you feel if you were he?"

She smiled faintly. "I'd be jealous and possessive and full of doubt."

"There, you see! So Provence must be challenged, must be made to bring forward his so-called evidence."

Louis, meanwhile, had locked himself in his workshop. His Majesty, the servants said, had no wish to be disturbed. Impulsively she was ready to fling herself at the workshop door and hammer at it frantically with her bare fists. With difficulty she controlled herself. Dignity—she must cling to dignity at all costs. Quickly she wrote Louis a short note. *What a coward you are! I have sent for Provence. Are you determined to leave me to deal with him alone?*

Louis trudged into her drawing-room a moment after Provence had entered.

"Lock the door, Louis," she commanded.

With a sigh he did so.

"This is most unwise," he mumbled.

"Unwise or not, I am determined to expose your brother's plot." Dignity, she warned herself, hold on to it, keep your temper. She turned to Provence. "You made an accusation. You spoke of evidence. We are all attention, Monsieur, the King and I."

Provence shrugged. "Very well." He looked for a long moment at Louis. "You will, of course, remember your celebrated 23rd birthday. A sort of coming of age, as it were, a belated realization of manhood. We put you to bed, remember, just as on the night of your marriage you had been put to bed. It was a new

150

beginning, to all intents and purposes a first night. The next morning the sheets were examined. The only possible conclusion we could come to was that in spite of everything the marriage had still not been consummated. Either that or her Majesty was not—forgive me—a virgin."

Louis' shoulders began to heave; he roared with laughter.

"No more she was, no more she was!"

Provence stared at him. "I beg your pardon?"

Still laughing, Louis gasped, "I had seen to that myself a few days earlier. We cheated you, and by heaven how we enjoyed it!"

Quite taken aback, all Provence could say was, "Oh . . ."

"Months passed before Marie became pregnant," Louis went on angrily. "Her utter faithfulness during those months cannot be called into question."

Provence rallied and renewed his attack. "Her Majesty went often to Paris, *alone,* during that time. She met her lover secretly at one of the houses she visited, just as she met him secretly, here at Versailles, in the apartments of Madame de Polignac."

Marie Antoinette's heart missed a beat. She steadied herself, started to speak, but Louis, his face quivering, spoke first.

"Name the man and have done with it!"

"Count Axel von Fersen, a friend of yours, I believe."

Louis' face cleared. "Impossible! Axel is the most honorable man in the world, the most steadfast of friends. I would trust him with my life."

"And your wife also? How foolish!"

Marie Antoinette laughed scornfully. "You must give us proof, Monsieur."

Provence took from an inner pocket two sheets of paper which he carefully unfolded and handed to Louis.

"The sworn statements of two servants employed by one of Madame de Polignac's friends, Victoire de Massone. Exact dates are given. Certain amusing, not to say embarrassing, details are briefly recorded. There is no doubt that her Majesty met, and—forgive me—consorted with Fersen on those dates."

Louis gave Marie Antoinette a lost, bewildered look.

"I—I should prefer to question the two servants myself," he said hesitantly.

"Whenever you wish," Provence agreed.

"Oh, but this is fantastic!" Marie Antoinette cried. "Monsieur

151

de Fersen came back to France several months after I became pregnant. What a fool you are to believe these statements, sworn or otherwise."

Provence merely smiled. "I maintain that he arrived much earlier and remained hidden in Paris until you decided, unwisely, to bring him to court. I suggest that he has come often to France, secretly, since your first meeting with him at that Opera ball."

"When was that?" Louis asked.

Marie Antoinette told him.

"So you have known him all these years," he said quietly.

"I met him once, Louis, just once before he came to Versailles last year. I talked to him for a short time at that masked ball. I— I never even learned his name."

She knew she sounded as if she was excusing herself, and that was horrible.

"I see . . ." Louis said.

Provence smiled. "Your faith in Fersen is still unshaken?"

Louis swept this aside with a vague gesture. "If Axel is guilty I shall read it in his face. He shall be sent for at once."

"You are too short-sighted to read anything in anybody's face," Provence sneered.

"Not when I stand close to them," Louis avowed. "In any case his voice will tell me all I want to know." He looked at Marie Antoinette uncertainly. "You have no objection to my sending for Axel?"

"None whatever!"

Louis dismissed his brother. A messenger was summoned and instructed to go in haste to Paris. Monsieur le Comte de Fersen was to return with him immediately to Versailles.

"And now—what?" Marie Antoinette demanded.

"Axel will obey the summons. We must wait for him with patience."

She rose quickly. "When Axel comes and you have talked to him, you will find me in the nursery. If, of course, you wish to see me."

At the nursery she curtly dismissed the child's nurse. Little Madame Royale was sleeping soundly. The impulse to take her in her arms and hold her fiercely against her breast was strong, but she restrained herself. Restlessly she moved about the room, picking up ornaments, replacing them carefully, yet wanting to fling them violently against the wall.

152

Sooner than she had expected, Louis came tiptoeing into the room. He went first to the cot.

"Sleeping peacefully, poor little mite," he whispered.

"Have you talked to Axel?" she asked, in a whisper also.

Louis shook his head. "He was not to be found. He had packed hurriedly and gone." His face was blank; he continued to speak in a whisper. "Strange, you must admit. Yesterday I talked to him, promised him the immediate command of a regiment. He was overjoyed. Tomorrow the appointment was to be publicly announced."

"And so you think—!"

Louis glanced at the cot. "Quietly, I beg of you! What I think is of no account. I, if it comes to that, am of no account either."

And again on tiptoe, shoulders drooping, he went from the room, closing the door behind him with the greatest care.

Marie Antoinette buried her head in her hands. She could well imagine Provence's words when he was told, his exultant look. "Flight, my poor Berri, means one thing only." Surely this was a nightmare from which she would soon awake. Why, she asked herself, had Axel fled like that? The answer came promptly. Provence, clever and cunning, must be at the bottom of it all.

She thought of Mercy. She had confided in him before, she must do so again. He had been at the palace earlier, but now, when she sent for him, she learned that he had returned to the Austrian embassy. She ordered her coach. Quicker to drive to Paris than to send for Mercy and remain here, helpless, waiting.

In Paris Mercy listened in silence to all she had to tell him, and tried to comfort her when, sobbing convulsively, she flung herself into his arms.

"Poor little Toinette," he said gently.

"What shall I do, Mercy? What *can* I do?"

"You must be brave and strong. Also, you must wait here patiently while I go to the Swedish embassy."

When Mercy came back he was smiling grimly.

"Well?" she demanded.

"I was sure," he said, "that Fersen would never leave Paris without notifying the Swedish ambassador. He has set out for England. It may be possible to intercept him at Calais."

"You think he should be brought back?"

"I do indeed."

"Why did he leave? Did you learn that?"

153

"He said the Queen's good name was at stake. Only by flight could he protect her. He said that, no more."

"Mercy," she said quickly, "do you believe I am telling the truth?"

"Of course." He looked at her, his head on one side, and chuckled. "I believe you because I have proof."

"Proof?"

"I questioned the Swedish ambassador, discreetly, of course. Fersen left Paris soon after you first met him at the Opera. He returned four years later and presented himself at Versailles. You were, as you say, several months pregnant then. He was never secretly in Paris. That can be substantiated. His Majesty will listen no longer to Provence when the facts are placed before him. Those letters are either forgeries, or the servants who wrote them were paid to do so."

"But what do I care for facts?" she said despairingly. "Louis has doubted me. Facts mean nothing."

"You would have doubted *him,* remember!"

She smiled wanly. "Yes . . . Very well, place the facts before Louis, have Axel intercepted, if you can."

"My own special messenger has already left for Calais. As for placing the facts before the King, I shall return with you at once to Versailles."

Marie Antoinette was surprised that it was almost midnight when they reached Versailles. She had no memory of having travelled to Paris in the dark. Utterly weary, she went with dragging steps to her apartments while Mercy sought an interview with Louis, Louis who for once had stayed up late. Not by chance, she was sure, she met Madame Adelaide outside the guardroom. With her was Louis' young sister, Madame Elizabeth.

"I knew, of course, that it was true," Madame Adelaide said exultantly.

"Quite horrible," Madame Elizabeth remarked, in shocked tones.

Marie Antoinette glanced curiously at this young sister-in-law. Odd to think that though the girl was often present now at state functions one scarcely noticed her. She was seventeen, not so pretty as she had been as a child, colorless really, especially in the dowdy muslin gowns Madame Adelaide made her wear. Completely dominated, of course, by the old-maid aunt, but

154

quite devoted, in a mouselike way, to Louis. She had been friendly enough in the early days, when Madame Adelaide had been friendly, but an enemy now that Madame Adelaide was an enemy.

"I have tried to comfort poor Berri," Madame Adelaide went on. "He sees his duty clearly. You will be set aside. Your child will be declared illegitimate."

"He actually said that?"

"At all events I said it, and Berri will take full notice of me now."

Unable to listen to more, Marie Antoinette went slowly to her bedchamber. Dismissing her ladies—how curiously they stared at her!—she flung herself fully clothed on the bed. Almost immediately, or so it seemed, Louis was bending over her, peering down at her, trying to speak and failing, trying again and succeeding in a low troubled voice which she scarcely recognized.

"Marie, I have listened to Mercy. I naturally believe what he told me. You need not worry any more."

"Thank you," she said politely.

"I—I shall do my best to apologize to Axel when he returns, *if* he returns. Mercy's messenger might not reach Calais in time."

"Thank you."

"Provence will, of course, apologize to you."

"That will be nice," she said dully. "He makes all this trouble and then escapes with an apology."

Louis sighed. "You wrong him. I spoke to him briefly just now. He admits that he was misled, fell into a trap. He is very grieved about the whole thing. Madame de Massone's servants, it seems, approached him with their lies, hoping to gain a substantial reward."

"Are they to go unpunished?" she asked incuriously.

"They will be arrested, flung into prison."

She turned her face from him. "Goodnight, Louis."

"Goodnight, Marie," Louis said miserably.

The moment he had gone she felt inexpressibly sorry for him and wanted to comfort him. The fault was no more his than hers. They had been caught up in a vile intrigue and in it their happiness had been shattered.

The next day and the next, she was torn between hating and loving him. She hated him when he came to her apartments, trying pathetically to make conversation; she loved him and was

155

sorry for him the moment he had gone. She was careful, most careful, never to be alone with him in the nursery, for there, she knew, her heart would melt completely and all would be forgotten.

On the morning of the second day he told her that Madame de Massone's servants had been arrested but had escaped before it had been possible for him to question them.

She laughed dryly. "That was fortunate for Provence."

"You do him an injustice," Louis protested weakly.

"He has not yet made the promised apology."

"Poor fellow, he is too ashamed to face you."

"Too disappointed, you mean!"

On the evening of the same day Axel von Fersen returned from Calais and came out to Versailles with Count Mercy. The old man, presenting himself at her apartments, told her of this, and added that Fersen was now waiting in the King's anteroom. Axel . . . she repeated the name to herself. Since the birth of Madame Royale she had given Fersen little more than a passing thought—until Provence's vicious accusation. How, she wondered, would she feel now if she came face to face with the man? And how would Louis feel when, in a few moments, he received Axel in the inner cabinet? He had spoken of making an apology . . .

"Mercy," she said quickly, "escort me to the King's apartments."

Mercy gave her his arm. "What mischief are you planning?"

"None, my dear Mercy. I am simply consumed with curiosity."

They entered the Oeil de Boeuf just as Fersen was being ushered into the cabinet. Marie Antoinette relinquished Mercy's arm and, head high, followed Fersen into Louis' presence. He turned at the rustle of her gown; it pleased her to see a faint red tinge his cheeks.

"So nice to see you again, Axel," she murmured.

She looked casually at Louis, who had risen abruptly from his desk and was looking flustered.

"We are most anxious, the King and I," she went on, "to know why you decided to leave France so suddenly."

Fersen held himself erect. The tinge of color had faded from his cheeks, his eyes were veiled. He bowed, turned from her and addressed himself solely to Louis.

"Your Majesty, Count Mercy has already told you why I left Paris."

"Of course, my dear fellow, of course."

"But who induced you to leave?" Marie Antoinette demanded.

156

Fersen half-turned to her. "His Royal Highness, the Comte de Provence sent for me. He spoke of an impending scandal. He linked my name with your Majesty's. I was horrified. I did what I thought was right. I left for Calais immediately."

"At Provence's suggestion, of course!"

"Yes."

"Creditable, most creditable," Louis commented, "but you should have confided in me first. I thought we were good friends, Axel."

"Provence!" Marie Antoinette burst out. "He wanted Axel out of the way!"

"No," Louis said, irritatingly. "He, too, did what he thought was right."

Anger surged through her veins. What a fool he was, this King, this husband of hers! What a kindly, well-meaning fool!

She struggled to control her anger. "Axel, your friend the King wants to apologize to you for the inconvenience you have been caused."

"No!" Louis said, with surprising sharpness. "Later, yes, but first I want to ask him a question."

Fersen bowed and stood waiting.

For a long moment Louis faltered, then drew himself up to his full height.

"Axel, you have been accused of loving the Queen. Is that true or false? Look at me, answer me! I shall know the truth from your voice. Come, my friend, answer me!"

So doubt was still there, nagging at him, giving him no peace! She thought quickly of all the things Axel had seemed to mean to her—before the birth of her daughter. What a part she had given him in her imagination! She was ready now, because of Louis' attitude, to revive it all, believe in it, even embarrass both Axel and Louis, here and now, by throwing herself into Axel's arms.

"Answer me," Louis insisted quietly. "True . . . or false?"

Steadily and gravely Fersen said, "To me the Queen is a symbol. A bright and lovely symbol. She is not a woman, she is a goddess, far removed from the reach of man. That way, yes, I love the Queen."

Tears sprang to Marie Antoinette's eyes. Never in her life had she been so deeply moved. She looked at Louis; there were tears in his eyes too.

157

"Thank you, Axel," he said. "You make me deeply ashamed."

Fersen bowed. "Your Majesty, if I may withdraw?"

Something in his voice made Louis' head shoot up. "You still intend to leave France?"

"Yes. I want to go to America. With your Majesty's leave I would like to fight with the French forces there."

"Then you shall, by heaven you shall!"

"Thank you," Fersen said simply.

Through a mist of tears Marie Antoinette watched him walk steadily from the room. She feared that she would never see him again. She was sure that he took her heart with her. She saw now that the love which lay between them, tenuous yet binding, was a love of the spirit, beautiful, tragic. I have grown up at last, she thought; I feel so old and wise . . .

"Perhaps I ought to envy him," Louis said slowly. "The love I feel for you is desire. Desire of the flesh. A weakness, but to me, life itself."

Deeply moved again, torn between Fersen and Louis, she watched Louis stumble to the door. He turned before opening it.

"I shall come to your bed tonight, unless you send word that you are too tired. If you do that I shall understand."

He opened the door and went quickly from the room.

Axel on the one hand, Louis on the other. For Axel, love undying, spiritual, pure . . . How inspiring it was! For Louis, an ache of the flesh rather than the heart.

A moment later the door was flung open and Provence strolled in.

"Poor Berri," he said insolently, "has sent me to apologize."

She looked at him stonily. "Do so then."

Provence made a gesture of mock-humility, "I regret, your Majesty, that I allowed myself to be carried away by the spite of others."

"You expect me to believe that you, and you alone, were not the instigator?"

"Berri believes it."

"But I do not!"

"And you would fling me into the Bastille?"

"Without the slightest hesitation!"

He shrugged irritatingly. "Ah well, no very great harm has been done."

"Except perhaps to you."

158

Provence looked surprised. "To me?"

"You have shown yourself to be something of a fool."

It delighted her to see a flush spread slowly across his cheeks.

"You must have known that your so-called evidence," she said pityingly, "could easily be disproved."

"How was I to know that those sworn statements were false?"

"Poor innocent Provence, misled by others!"

He smiled. "I am quite mortified."

"What puzzles me," she said, "is why you should go to all that trouble. My child is a girl. You are still the King's heir."

"Precisely what I pointed out to Berri. Proof, surely, that I was misled by others."

"How silly of me! You thought it was worthwhile to try to turn Louis against me. He would have grown stubborn then, and shunned my bed. No more children for me then, girls or boys. It was a gamble and you took it."

"What an active imagination you have, dear little sister-in-law."

She made an arrogant gesture of dismissal, but he lingered a moment longer.

Provence laughed lightly. "I have no immediate plans. I am happy to hold my hand. As you say, I am still the King's heir."

She waited until he had closed the door behind him, then she said aloud, "The King's heir, but not for a day longer than I can help!"

Lightly she ran to Louis' desk, found a sheet of paper, snatched up a pen and wrote: *Dearest Louis, I shall go early to bed, but I am not in the least tired.*

Because of Provence she was ready now to forgive Louis for the way he had doubted her, ready to forget that he had not yet made a fitting apology. And because of Provence she had pushed from her mind the still-haunting fear of another pregnancy.

FOUR

AT LOUIS' COMMAND THE CARRIAGE STOPPED AT A LITTLE CLEARING in the forest. At his further command the coachman was dismissed and told to return in half an hour. A strange quality in the King's voice made Marie Antoinette look at him curiously. Without glancing at her he slowly and deliberately closed the carriage windows. This done he fell back heavily in his seat.

"No possibility of eavesdroppers now," he muttered.

"Louis, is something troubling you?"

For answer he took from his breeches pocket a crumpled sheet of paper, unfolded it and placed it in her hand.

She glanced down at it quickly. "More verses!"

"A series of couplets," Louis said somberly. "Directed, I fear, against you."

She read them hastily. The complaints fell into three parts: her vast gambling debts, which, it was suggested, were an embarrassment to the country in time of war; Gabrielle de Polignac, referred to as the evil genius whose influence would one day ruin France; and her alleged unfaithfulness to the King.

"Infamous!" she cried.

"I—yes, I agree."

"Who gave you this? Provence, no doubt?"

Louis shook his head. "Maurepas found it in Paris. Printed, as you see. Copies are being distributed all over the city. As many as possible are being seized, but much damage has already been done." His voice rose thinly. "Your popularity with the people will suffer now."

"Oh nonsense! Provence will never deceive the people."

Louis said heavily, "If Provence is really at the back of this he shall be dealt with unmercifully. It is a cruel thing to do, especially now when we are expecting our second child."

"One would expect Provence to strike at such a time. He fears the child might be a boy." She glanced at the couplets again. "The suggestion that you are impotent is stressed again and again."

160

Louis' face broke into a slow smile. "And what has my wife to say about that?"

She smiled too. "Your wife has no complaints."

"Fortunately no reference is made to Axel."

"How could there be? Axel is in America."

She allowed her mind to dwell on Fersen, as she had done many times in the months that had passed since his departure. She felt now that she could regard him through the eyes of a mature woman, not those of a silly romantic girl. He was a true and noble friend, she told herself sternly, that and nothing more. And as a true and noble friend she loved him dearly and would be happy to see him again.

"Marie, my dear . . ." Louis said diffidently.

"Yes, Louis?"

"I brought you here so that we could have a private conversation. Privacy is impossible at Versailles, impossible!"

She sighed in mock alarm. "I fear you have something unpleasant to say to me."

Louis cleared his throat. "I fear I have. You have spent almost a million livres on the Little Trianon."

"Have I?" she asked in surprise.

"It would be wiser to spend no more at present. And the gambling debts, mentioned in the complaints against you . . . would it not be sensible, at present, at a time like this, to shun the gaming tables?"

She flared up instantly. "It is a harmless amusement, Louis!"

"But it makes a bad impression. And—" he plunged on unhappily—"the question of Gabrielle de Polignac—"

"Ah yes, Gabrielle, my evil genius!"

"Strong language, that, but perhaps a grain of truth in it."

"I do exactly as I please. Gabrielle *never* influences me."

Louis quailed before her anger but pressed doggedly on. "Yes, my dear, you do exactly as you please, but do you ever read the orders Madame de Polignac presents for your signature?"

"Never! Why should I? As *surintendante* of my household Gabrielle holds a position of trust."

"Her husband and her relatives and friends do very well for themselves. The husband, for instance, you made your chief equerry—"

"A pension of 12,000 livres only!"

"Yes, but he has full control of your private stables, free use of horses and carriages. Eighty thousand livres spent in one year on the stables is staggering. And you have repeatedly paid Madame de Polignac's debts, increasing your private expenses beyond all —hum—reason . . ."

She looked at the indeterminate expression on his face and thought suddenly, If only he would attack me vigorously, even attempt to thrash me, I might feel respect for him and do as he wishes. Then she rose and threw open one of the carriage windows. The crash made her feel better. She turned to the other window. Anger swamped her again as she struggled with it.

"Have a care!" Louis warned. "I beg of you, my dear, in your condition—!"

His warning came too late. A searing pain shot through her body and she fell back gasping. Louis caught her in his arms and placed her gently on the cushioned seat. Everything was growing hazy and the pain was intolerable. Afterwards her only memory of the hurried return to Versailles was of Louis' fat face hovering anxiously above her.

"The fault was mine," he had kept saying, "the fault was mine."

"It was a miscarriage?" she asked dully.

"Yes. Everything possible was done but the wretched doctors were helpless."

"Provence will be pleased."

"No, no, he is not as big a scoundrel as you imagine."

"Well, I shall take greater care in future. Not even the most scurrilous of verses will touch me." She laughed hysterically and felt immensely cunning.

Louis looked at her sadly. "Lassone fears that a further pregnancy may not be possible, now."

"Then Provence must be overjoyed."

Louis made a helpless gesture and remained silent.

She gripped his hand tightly. "I insist, Louis, on the writer of those verses being traced."

"I have already ordered Maurepas to institute a secret investigation. The writer shall be found and punished, whoever he is."

Her mind flew off at a tangent. "My gambling debts, are they truly monstrous?"

"They are, poor little Marie, but they shall be settled in full. I give you my word."

She had been on the point of offering to shun the gaming

162

tables, but Louis' voice, expressing a pathetic eagerness to please her in all things, made her change her mind.

"And being unlucky at cards, am I permitted to gamble just as much as ever?"

"Just as much as ever," he agreed.

"And spend more money on the Little Trianon?"

"Of course. If you find it necessary. Heaven knows, your extravagance is negligible, compared to the vast sums we are spending on the war."

Softly she went on, "Quite possibly my household expenses are much too high, so if you wish, dear Louis, I—"

"No, no. After all a queen must live like a queen."

She laughed wildly. "Gabrielle is a good friend, a faithful servant. She and her husband have remained unhonored too long. I should like to be able to address her as Madame la Duchesse de Polignac."

"Whatever you wish, whatever you wish. All I ask is that you rest and grow strong again."

"Thank you, Louis."

Marie Antoinette emerged from the illness with a new feeling of restlessness and strain. If the court physicians were right, if it was impossible now for her to bear another child, her life suddenly lacked purpose. She confided this to Mercy, upon which the old man smiled gently.

"And so the struggle continues."

"What struggle, Mercy?"

"The struggle within you, my dear. The struggle between the pleasure-loving Queen and the woman who wants only to be a contented wife and mother."

"What fanciful nonsense!" she laughed.

"One would scarcely expect you to recognize the struggle," he smiled, "but it is clearly taking place."

Her gambling debts having been paid, more were quickly incurred, but the ritual of the evening card parties failed to excite her now, but the hours spent with her baby daughter gave her a passing feeling of contentment. Still there was nothing exciting in contentment, nothing whatever!

A month after the miscarriage Louis came to her with a solemn expression on his face.

"My dear, the writer of those couplets has been found."

"Ah! Provence, of course!"

"No, Marie." He was looking utterly miserable. "Aunt Adelaide."

She looked at him in amazement. "I never thought she was as clever as that. Has it been proved beyond doubt?"

"Yes. Maurepas' spies found the original in her desk—written in her own hand. She has admitted the truth."

"Did she also write those first horrible verses?"

"She denied it. She said those first verses gave her the idea. I—Marie, my dear, I hope you understand how deeply grieved I am."

"Yes, yes, of course, Louis." But happiness was surging through her veins. This, surely, was the end of the old-maid aunt. "What are you going to do?"

He seemed not to have heard. "Why does Aunt Adelaide hate you so much?"

"Because I stand between her and her ambition to control you, to be the power behind the throne. Louis, what are you going to do?"

"She has left Versailles already. I thought it better that you should not see her again. The other two aunts have gone with her."

"What of your sister, Elizabeth?"

"She remains. I cannot permit her to remain under Aunt Adelaide's control. She is still—well, suspicious of you. But I hope, in time, to win her over. She really is a sweet child, devoted to me. I want her to be devoted to you, too."

"Is it exile for Madame Adelaide and the other two?"

"In a way, yes. Exile from court. I have sent them to Choisy, temporarily. A suitable place of—er—retirement will be found for them later."

With the departure of the old-maid aunts, Marie Antoinette sought Gabrielle's company more than ever, but Gabrielle, now Duchesse de Polignac, failed to make her laugh with the old accustomed ease. Something vital seemed to be lacking now in Gabrielle and her friends. The absence of seriousness, always pronounced in the Polignac set, grew at times quite irritating. And what a joke that was! Marie decided that she must be missing Axel von Fersen more than she had imagined. He, at any rate, was the personification of seriousness. It was strange, she thought, how in moments of extreme restlessness her mind turned involuntarily to Axel, just as, impatiently, it turned away from Louis, her husband. The struggle within her was not quite as Mercy saw it.

She learned from time to time that Axel was acquitting himself with distinction in the American war. She further learned that he was somewhat dissatisfied with the rank he held in the French forces, that of aide-de-camp to Marshal de Rochambeau. This came to her personal notice when the young Duc de Lauzun, who had taken his own regiment to America, returned to Paris and came out to present himself at Versailles. Intent on hearing more news of Fersen, she eagerly granted Lauzun a private audience.

"What brings you back to France, Monsieur?" she began by asking.

"I came with dispatches, your Majesty, but I would like nothing better than to remain at court." He made a foppish gesture.

"But what of your regiment in America?"

"I propose to give it to Monsieur de Fersen."

"To *give* it? Surely it is worth a handsome sum!"

"Axel and I are warm friends. It is not my habit, your Majesty, to sell my possessions to my friends."

"Tell me about Monsieur de Fersen," she suggested, trying to repress her eagerness. "He is well and happy?"

Lauzun smiled indulgently. "But serious as ever."

She laughed negligently. "I always found Monsieur de Fersen's seriousness most appealing."

"Appealing, yes, and also amusing. He even indulges in the lighter side of love-making with seriousness."

"Love-making?" she questioned sharply.

"There is in Newport an American widow by the name of Hunter."

"So, a widow!"

"Ah yes, your Majesty, but Mrs. Hunter possesses two attractive daughters."

Marie Antoinette saw that Lauzun was looking at her quizzically. Quickly she affected a lazy indifference.

"It is, of course, necessary for a soldier in wartime to seek diversion. As for your wish to make Monsieur de Fersen a present of your regiment, it will be necessary to refer the matter to the minister of war."

"I have already done that, your Majesty, and failed to gain permission. For that reason, Madame, I humbly seek your royal intervention."

Marie Antoinette dismissed him with a command that he should appear at her next card party. She then sent for the minister of war, the newly appointed Comte de Ségur who had replaced Vergennes. She anticipated no trouble in getting her way with him, for, to please Gabrielle, she herself had persuaded Louis to give Ségur the ministry of war. But now to her annoyance Ségur, a rugged, abruptly spoken individual who had lost an arm in battle, quite firmly refused her request.

"In my opinion, your Majesty, the young Fersen is not sufficiently experienced to command a regiment."

She held back the angry retort that came to her lips. She did so because Ségur's eyes, holding hers, were clearly asking the unspoken question, What is this young foreigner to you?

"It would please the King," she said quietly. "His Majesty has a high regard for Monsieur de Fersen."

Ségur showed no sign of wavering. "Indeed, Madame."

Then, lying glibly, she said that Louis believed that Fersen's ability was being wasted while he remained an aide-de-camp.

Ségur gave her a cold look. "The most I can do for Fersen is to make him second-in-command of some other regiment."

"You have one in mind?"

"Yes, Madame. The Deux-Ponts."

"Very well."

Ségur bowed and withdrew.

Now why, she asked herself, did I keep my temper? I have indeed grown up, she chided herself, with a rueful little laugh.

Restlessness soon beset her again, and seeking a new outlet for her energies she gave most of her time to amateur theatricals. Calling in professional aid, she staged and acted in a number of frivolous comedies at her theater at the Little Trianon. This she found enjoyable for a time but lacking in real satisfaction. Then to make things worse new couplets, undoubtedly from the pen of Madame Adelaide, were written suggesting that her stage lovers were also real-life lovers.

"Apparently exile is not sufficient," she told Louis angrily.

He agreed unhappily. "But Aunt Adelaide is cleverer this time. Inquiries have been made. It has been impossible to find proof. The verses *could* be the work of someone else."

She tried to ignore the verses, but more and more were written and circulated, and it was evident from the silence which greeted her now whenever she appeared in public in Paris, that much harm was being done. She was constantly accused of acting under instructions from Vienna; she was referred to contemptuously as the Austrian woman, sometimes as the Austrian whore; she was blamed for the war and the waste of money thereby involved. Mercy, who sympathized with her, said that the country was growing tired of the war and so many people were willing to believe all that was written about her and find in her a scapegoat. As for Louis, he was sure that if only she could have a son the people would take her to their hearts again. He had grown noticeably lethargic, was spending more time hunting, more time in his workshop, less and less time in the study of state affairs.

"I have Maurepas to take care of things," he said.

"Maurepas is old and not in good health," she reminded him. "He can't live forever."

"There will be others."

Louis, too, was growing tired of the war. Nothing spectacular had happened to delight and divert the people, and the plans for an invasion of England were continually postponed. Even the war in America, which was going well for the new young nation, failed now to excite the people of France. Agitators tried again and again to stir up the poor of Paris by declaring that while they went hungry French money, because of the hated Austrian woman, was being poured senselessly into the struggle.

Soon, affecting her more than she would have expected, came news from distant Vienna of her mother's sudden death. Yet coinciding with this news and embittering her, came a delayed letter from the Empress herself, the last she had written to her daughter. Mama raged about the verses, saying, in short, that Marie herself was chiefly responsible. It was heart-breaking to know that Mama did not understand that whatever you did Madame Adelaide and Provence and their supporters would remain your sworn enemies. "I cannot live much longer," the letter concluded. "Let me at least die happy in the knowledge that I have a grandson in France."

A few months later, making fools of the doctors, Marie was able to announce to the court that she was pregnant once again. Poor Mama, she thought, she died too soon. Much to her surprise she found tranquillity in this new pregnancy. Pamphlets as well as verses were written throwing doubt on the paternity of the expected child, but these lies scarcely mattered when Marie was finding a renewed interest in her daughter, the little Madame Royale, and even in Louis himself who insisted, when alone with her in the nursery, on being not a king but a happy family man. Formerly the restrictions placed on her by the physicians, who feared a second miscarriage, would have irked her. Now she accepted them gladly. She must have rest, early nights, and most of all, no show of temper. Well, why not? Why not, if the result was isolation from the court and delicious hours of heavenly privacy?

Her time came all too quickly, and with it, at Louis' quiet but amazingly firm insistence, no repetition of that first horrible, entirely public labor. Not public, at least in the traditional sense of her bedchamber being thrown open to all who cared to come, but public enough so that members of the royal family must be present to witness the birth. That meant the presence of enemies as well as friends, enemies personified in the detestable brother-in-law, Provence.

Earlier Louis had told the physicians: "Her Majesty must not be told whether the child is a boy or a girl until all danger is passed."

But the moment the heavenly release coursed through her body she demanded the truth. The physicians shook their heads, yet smiled. Then as she looked beyond them, seeing the horrible scowl on Provence's face, she understood. And only a moment later, it seemed, Louis' voice filled the room with a hearty roar.

"Your Majesty," he said, "the Dauphin, our son, insists on meeting his mother."

There stood Louis with the new-born child in his arms. Tears were streaming down his cheeks. His face seemed no longer ugly but quite touchingly beautiful.

"A son," Provence cried, his eyes flashing hatred, "may heaven be praised, a son."

In the days that followed, as she rapidly regained her strength, she learned that festivities, both in Paris and the little town of Versailles, had reached a pitch of feverish excitement.

Louis was delighted. "I knew this would happen. You, my dearest love, are the most popular queen France has ever known."

Marie Antoinette was not impressed. "It is nothing but public hysteria. The people will get over it. They were wild with joy when war broke out; now they hate the war. They will soon hate me again. Provence and Madame Adelaide will see to that."

"But everybody is rejoicing," Louis protested tremulously. "Deputation after deputation keeps arriving at Versailles. All the guilds; the blacksmiths as well as the goldsmiths, the shoemakers, the masons, every possible trade, even the chimney-sweeps! Why,

168

the poorest people in Paris are stopping each other in the streets, weeping for joy and shaking hands."

"But why? What possible difference can it make to them?"

"I think it gives them hope. The birth of an heir always gives them hope."

"Hope of what?" she asked. "Increased taxation? A dauphin means more royal expenditure."

Louis looked at her oddly. "It gives them hope of salvation. Hope that the little prince will some day prove to be a better ruler than the one they know today."

"Poor fools," she said.

Louis grasped her hand convulsively. "This is amazing, my dear, amazing!"

"What is amazing, Louis?"

"Your new-born seriousness. The resolve to work with me for the good of the people."

"I have made no such resolve," she said quietly. "It was just a passing mood because I—" She stopped abruptly.

"Yes?" he demanded. "Because you—?"

Because she had thought, for a long moment, of Axel von Fersen, the serious, noble-minded friend.

She said lightly, "Because I am still weak and therefore foolish. In no time at all I shall be ready to enjoy life again. After all, that is what is expected of me, isn't it!"

FIVE

With the little dauphin, Louis Joseph, lying contentedly in her lap Marie Antoinette was conversing carefully in German with her young daughter who was standing patiently at her side. Madame Royale, long past her fourth birthday now, was an increasingly interesting companion and, as everybody agreed, exceedingly clever for her age.

"And now, Mama," said the child, "I shall speak French and you shall reply in German."

"It almost sounds," Marie Antoinette chuckled, "as if you are the teacher and I the pupil. Well, what shall we talk about, Thérèse?"

"Let's talk about the war in America," Madame Royale suggested.

"The war in America is over, darling."

"Have the English been defeated?"

"Soundly defeated."

"Papa says France will soon make peace with England."

"Papa is right. The Americans have already made peace. Everybody in France will be happy to have peace again."

The door opened suddenly and Marie Antoinette looked up in annoyance. Ever jealous of the hours she spent alone with her children, she had given strict orders that no one was to disturb her this afternoon.

"It's only Papa," Madame Royale lisped.

Still at the door, Louis was saying over his shoulder, "Come, my dear fellow, the children are here with their mother. You must see them at once. The happiest sight in the world!"

A hand seemed to clutch at her heart. She knew without the slightest doubt to whom Louis had addressed himself. Nevertheless, when Fersen followed Louis into the room she stared at him disbelievingly.

He approached and bowed stiffly. "Your Majesty . . ."

Divested of his military uniform, he wore a neat plum-colored coat and light gray breeches, fresh from his Paris tailor, she suspected. Quite stylish but not in the least foppish, she decided, and certainly he looked more handsome than ever, suntanned, his blond hair like a halo, his eyes a darker blue, his face perhaps a little leaner.

"How welcome you are," she said, trying to keep her voice steady. "When did you arrive from America?"

"A few days ago, Madame. I landed at Brest."

She felt an impulse to tease him. "It took you very little time to have new French clothes made."

A broad smile lit his face. "I have a tailor who works amazingly quickly. He sat up all night. Within twenty-four hours of reaching Paris I was able to come out to Versailles."

"Enough of this talk of clothes!" Louis protested. "Come, Axel, I must present you to my son, Louis Joseph."

Louis bowed solemnly to the child in Marie Antoinette's arms. Fersen did likewise.

"A handsome baby," he said.

"Twenty months old, to the very day," Louis told him happily. "If he could speak fluently he would tell you how delighted he is to receive you at Versailles. And now my daughter, whom you will remember as a baby." He put his arms round Madame Royale's shoulder. "This, my pet, is Monsieur le Comte de Fersen."

Fersen bowed, and smiled on the child. "Your Royal Highness . . ."

"Charmed, Monsieur le Comte," Madame Royale said haughtily, but added with complete frankness, "I like the look of him, Papa."

"We all like the look of him," Louis exclaimed.

Fersen, catching Marie Antoinette's eyes for a moment, looked unexpectedly confused, but he recovered himself quickly and spoke to Madame Royale.

"Your Highness, I think, will soon be five."

"I am exactly four years, six months and three days," Madame Royale announced.

"Dear me," Louis remarked, "how the time does fly! It must be over four years since we last saw you, Axel."

"Well—yes," Fersen acknowledged.

A small tense silence followed. All three of them, Marie Antoinette knew, were suddenly very conscious of the circumstances of their last meeting.

Louis stirred himself and smiled benignly. "Four years is a long separation for friends such as we are."

"Yes, indeed," Marie Antoinette echoed faintly.

171

The beating of her heart had quickened. She felt that if she were to rise from her chair her legs would scarcely support her. She was barely conscious of Louis, now taking the baby from her lap, holding him in his arms and standing at her side, as if posing for a portrait.

"Well, my dear Axel," he demanded, "did you ever see a happier family group?"

"No," Fersen said gravely, "never."

It *was* a happy family group, Marie Antoinette told herself insistently. And yet in the midst of this domestic happiness, all she could think as she looked up at Fersen, straight and slim and handsome, was, How desperately I love him! She tried to thrust the thought from her mind, but it remained there, filling her with anger, self-contempt and joy.

"When I grow up," her daughter announced in a piping voice, "I think I shall marry Monsieur de Fersen. He is just like the fairy prince I am always dreaming about. Truly he is."

"Unfortunately, darling," Marie Antoinette told her tartly, "Monsieur de Fersen will be too old for you when you grow up."

"Then I command him," Madame Royale said imperiously, "to remain just as he is, at the same age, till I am twenty."

Fersen bowed. "You honor me deeply, Madame Royale. I shall treasure your words for the rest of my life."

The child clapped her hands. "Do you know why I like him? I like him because he doesn't talk baby talk to me."

"An advanced little minx," Louis chuckled.

"I insist," Madame Royale added, "that I shall marry him when I grow up."

"For all we know," Marie Antoinette remarked, "Monsieur de Fersen may be married already."

"No," said Fersen, shaking his head.

"What, you have not brought back an American wife?"

"Certainly not, your Majesty!"

She smiled at the vehemence of his voice and was ready again to tease him.

"We heard, of course, of the American widow and her two charming daughters."

The faintest look of annoyance crossed his face. "They were indeed charming. I admit it. But all I had in common with either of them was the study of languages. I taught them French, they taught me English."

172

Louis roared with laughter. "Good lord, man, what a waste of time!"

Fersen remained at Versailles for the rest of the day, monopolized completely by Louis, who took him to the stables, the kennels and kept him for an hour or more in the royal workshop. Marie Antoinette met him again at supper, taken privately in Louis' apartments. Here, questioned by Louis, he spoke of his experiences in America and dwelt at length on the decisive battle at Yorktown, at which he had been present.

"It brought an end to a war that had gone on far too long," Louis said thankfully. "All I want now is a lasting peace with England."

The talk went on, exclusively between Louis and Fersen. Marie Antoinette, barely listening, took no part in it. Axel, she kept saying to herself, Axel! The surging exhilaration in her breast was almost more than she could bear. She tried to steady herself, tried to listen intelligently to the conversation.

Marie Antoinette, looking from Fersen to Louis, became acutely conscious of the difference in their voices. Fersen spoke vigorously, decisively; Louis, if not exactly weakly, with a depressing apathy.

Louis sighed again. "France has participated in a great triumph over the old enemy, England. France has helped to establish a new and independent nation in America. It is gratifying, but oh, my dear Axel, the American war has cost us a thousand million livres, possibly more, and that gives my government a greater deficit than ever before. And perhaps of greater alarm than the financial situation is the attitude of the countless young hotheads who are now returning from America. Aristocrats, mind you, all of them aristocrats! Their ideas are nothing if not revolutionary. It is even possible that in helping the former subjects of King George of England in their revolt I have sown the seeds of a similar revolt in my own country."

Louis broke off with a somber laugh and added, "That, I am sure, is the longest speech of my life. But enough of my affairs. You can scarcely have any real interest in the predicament of a poor and helpless king."

"On the contrary," Fersen affirmed, "my interest is deep and sincere. As deep and sincere as my desire to be of service to both you and her Majesty."

"Thank you, thank you," Louis said emotionally.

Trying to speak casually, Marie Antoinette asked Fersen about his immediate plans.

"Do you intend to remain in France or return to your own country?"

But it was Louis who answered her with a satisfied laugh.

"The Swedish King expects Axel to spend some time in Sweden, at court there, where he is held in high esteem, but Gustav is also willing for him to find service here in France."

"You seem to know more about Axel's plans than he does himself," Marie Antoinette laughed.

"Ah, but I received a letter from King Gustav—a happy coincidence—this morning. In it was a request for Axel to be given command of one of the foreign regiments now serving under the French flag."

"Serving in France?" she asked carefully.

"Where else? We need Axel close at hand." Louis rose. "Wait while I go and find Gustav's letter."

"Was this letter written at your request, Axel?" Marie Antoinette asked, when Louis had gone.

"Yes," Fersen said curtly.

Splendid, splendid! His one wish was to be near her!

She said: "King Gustav must indeed hold you in high esteem."

Fersen frowned attractively, "His Majesty expects me to follow in my father's footsteps and become a Swedish senator."

"But in the distant future, I hope," she said lightly. "A senator would not be able to spend much time away from his homeland."

Fersen avoided her eyes. "Forgive my saying this, your Majesty—"

"It was to be Axel and Louis, Axel and Marie, in private—remember?" she challenged.

Fersen cleared his throat. "As you wish—Marie."

"Proceed!" she said, in mock imperiousness.

"I am most concerned," he went on earnestly, "at the change in Louis. He—"

"The *change* in him? What do you mean by that?"

"Oh, as a husband and father, as a family man, he is very happy, and I applaud and envy that happiness. But as a king he—well—he has become uncertain of himself, distressingly apathetic. He is afraid of the future and seems unable to do anything to make it secure. It breaks my heart to see him like that."

"Then you must talk to him seriously, Axel. You must instil in him some of your own decisiveness."

"No," Fersen said quickly, "that is your own especial task."

"Mine? Oh come, Axel, everybody knows that all I care for is pleasure."

"You also care for your family. That was evident when I saw you this afternoon with the Dauphin in your arms and Madame Royale at your side."

"And my apathetic husband at my side also, making a perfect family group?"

"Yes," he insisted, "yes!"

"You seem anything but sure of it, Axel."

"I was never more sure of anything, never!" With an obvious effort he grew calmer and went on in a steady voice. "The time has come for a strong determined person to take control of state affairs in France."

"Do you think me strong and determined?"

Fersen ignored this. "It is necessary for someone—for you—to put heart into the King."

"By taking control of state affairs? No, no, Axel, I have neither the ability nor the inclination."

"Perhaps not the inclination, but the ability, yes."

There flashed through her mind a vivid memory of him at their first meeting, the rather prim young man who had come to Paris to acquire a final polish. The mature man of today strongly resembled that earnest youth.

"You are lecturing me," she laughed. "In a moment you will tell me again that I am discontented with the aimlessness of my life."

"On the domestic side there is nothing aimless about your life."

"The domestic side of my life is my own concern," she told him angrily.

He became instantly contrite. "Forgive me. I was forgetting who you are, speaking too freely."

Her anger went as quickly as it had come. "I am Marie, you are Axel. You may say anything you like, anything. Do please continue."

He shook his head. "I have said enough. Shall we discuss something less dangerous? The latest fashion, for instance, in headdresses?"

"Gladly!" she agreed. "My hair is quite simply dressed today. No fantastic headdress. Had you noticed?"

However at that point Louis returned with the King of Sweden's letter. He gave it to her and she skimmed through it quickly, laughing a little over the formal way in which King Gustav had addressed Louis: Monsieur, my brother and cousin.

"Why," she cried, "the Americans have given Axel their award for courage in battle, the Cross of Cincinnatus. You never told us, Axel."

"A modest young fellow," Louis remarked approvingly.

"And King Gustav has made him a chevalier of the Swedish Order of the Sword."

Fersen bowed and blushed.

"Scarcely worth mentioning, of course," she twitted him, and glanced again at the letter. "Gustav makes no mention of the foreign regiment he would like you to command in France. Have you any preference?"

"Why not the Royal Swedish?" Louis suggested. "Count von Stedingk is about to resign."

"I could wish for nothing better," Fersen said.

Marie Antoinette smiled. "Stedingk spends more time at court than with his regiment. Command of the Royal Swedish will give you plenty of leisure."

"That," said Louis happily, "will be excellent. Consider yourself commander-elect of the Royal Swedish."

Fersen looked hesitant.

"Is anything the matter?" Marie Antoinette demanded.

"My father has yet to be consulted."

"What do you fear in that direction? You have the approval of the King of Sweden and the King and Queen of France."

A rueful smile lingered on Fersen's face. "My father, a just and excellent man, is perhaps—well—just a little—cr—"

"Stingy?" she suggested.

"Yes."

"What has that to do with it?" Louis asked blankly.

Fersen shrugged. "Stedingk is asking a hundred thousand livres for his regiment."

"Your father is a wealthy man."

"He would be the last person to agree with you."

"Leave everything to me," Marie Antoinette said decisively.

And she thought happily, The negotiations will take some time, and that will keep Axel close at hand.

"Yes, leave everything to Marie," Louis agreed.

She thought: If Axel is not already my devoted slave, he will become so by the time the Royal Swedish belongs to him.

"Wait on me tomorrow afternoon at three," she commanded, "and we will discuss the best way of attacking a niggardly father."

Fersen glanced inquiringly at Louis.

"You have my full approval," Louis said.

"I was thinking," Fersen said hesitantly, "of—forgive me—of the gossip of several years ago."

Louis waved this aside. "Gossip shall never stand between me and friendship. And in any case one of her Majesty's secretaries will be present." He tried to make a joke of it. "Naturally a secretary will be present. Marie is the laziest person in the world when it comes to letter writing."

She looked at her husband suspiciously. Was he placing her on her honor? No. He was much too trusting, much too simple.

She awoke earlier than usual the next morning, and her first thought was, How happy I am! Much to the surprise of her ladies she rose at once, while to their further surprise she spent only half the normal time at her toilette. The rest of the morning was a painful drag, and at two in the afternoon she found herself waiting impatiently in her drawing-room for Fersen to present himself. She decided to spend the time composing the formal reply to King Gustav's letter. Smiling at the phrasing, she began: Monsieur my brother and cousin. Smiling still, a secret little smile, she spoke warmly of Fersen's services in the American war, dwelt with pleasure on his excellent good qualities, which she herself had been quick to recognize, assured his Swedish Majesty that no time would be lost in finding the young soldier a regiment, and concluded that now and at all times she would do everything in her power to further the friendship which existed between Sweden and France. She signed herself King Gustav's good sister and cousin.

When at last Fersen presented himself she gave him the letter to read. As he did so she saw in delight that he wore yet another new coat, beautifully cut and of the finest cloth.

"Ah," she laughed, "the tailor has been busy once again, doubtless all night, on your behalf."

Fersen looked up, quite sheepishly, from the letter.

"And how smart the coat is," she ran on. "Not exaggerated, but in the best of taste."

Fersen colored and went on reading the letter.

Quite the peacock, she decided, even if a restrained one. The peacock spreading his feathers to attract the peahen? She chuckled giddily at the thought of herself in the guise of a peahen.

"Well, is it a suitable letter?" she asked.

"Hardly."

Her head shot up. "Indeed?"

Fersen grinned boyishly. "You have spoken of me in this would-be formal letter as Axel. Just Axel."

"Oh . . ." she said.

Yes, but was it any wonder? Really now, was it? All the time while writing she had wanted to scribble 'Axel' over and over again on the writing paper.

"Now how in the world did I come to do that?" she asked softly.

"Because of your insistence on the use of Christian names," he told her abruptly. "You will have to write the letter again."

"Presently, presently. First we shall discuss the letter to your father."

"I have already written to him."

Nettled but undeterred, she said, "Then I shall write to him also."

"That would not be wise."

"I beg your pardon?" she said haughtily.

"It would not be wise," he repeated.

"Why not, pray?"

"Well—" He stopped, his face flooded with confusion.

"Why not, pray?" she repeated softly.

"My father is a stubborn man. He would feel that his hand was being unduly forced."

"No, I disagree," she said. "I am positive that Senator von Fersen would feel honored at the interest taken in his son."

"Whether or not you are right, there is still the question of the hundred thousand livres."

She laughed mischievously. "Is your father proud, as well as stubborn and stingy?"

"Fiercely proud."

"Then I shall offer to advance the money myself."

Fersen was instantly aghast. "My dear Marie, that would be disastrous!"

"Thank you for remembering to call me Marie, and for putting 'dear' in front of it."

Fersen's face stiffened. "I beseech you not to write to my father."

178

Her blue eyes flashed angrily. "Very well!"

"You give me your word?"

"Apparently I must!"

Fersen bowed. "If I may be excused . . . ?"

Speechless, she nodded briefly and Fersen made a dignified but hurried departure. The moment he had gone she flew to a big mirror on the wall and looked at her reflection searchingly. Had she aged too much while he had been in America? Was that why, despite the shameless way she had tried to encourage him, he had preferred to remain aloof? She was not yet twenty-eight, and twenty-eight was scarcely old. Perhaps he disliked the new head-dress which Léonard had insisted upon this morning. She had thought that it made her look younger, sweeping up as it did in soft lines from her temples. She scowled critically. It gave her face a narrow look and it certainly lengthened her nose. What an idiot that self-satisfied Léonard was!

Carefully she went over all she had said to Axel and all he had said to her, both yesterday and today. She recalled his every gesture and glance. She took an eager delight in his hesitations, his passing confusion. No, she decided, it was not her aging appearance that was troubling him, but the picture he had in his mind of the royal domestic happiness. He was trying, as never before, to be strongly guarded. Admirable, of course, but quite stupid. Yet what could she do, apart from throwing herself into his arms and crying, I love you, I love you? He had spoken boldly of the ideal love he felt for her; let him now speak boldly of his man's love. His man's love? She had no real evidence that he felt such a love, none at all!

"I was never so unhappy in my life!" she cried.

She rewrote her letter to King Gustav and felt an impulse to break her word and write also to Senator von Fersen. After a struggle with herself she repressed the impulse and resolved meanwhile to treat the irritating young man with a steady reserve.

"I must remember my dignity," she admonished herself.

While Fersen waited for his father's reply he was often at court where he took part, quietly and inconspicuously, in the balls and card parties. She treated him with the utmost formality; indeed, in his presence she went out of her way to gossip cordially with others in whom she had no interest.

"It deceives no one," Gabrielle de Polignac told her once.

"*What* deceives no one, Gabrielle?"

"The softness of your eyes when you glance at him," Gabrielle chuckled, "gives the lie direct."

"Oh rubbish!" Marie Antoinette snapped.

"Apart from that, I never saw a more admirable display of discretion. How do you contrive your meetings?"

"You are an old and privileged friend," Marie Antoinette said, raging at Gabrielle for the first time in her life, "but often you go too far!"

Well used to losing at cards, she tried deliberately, when Fersen was playing, to lose heavily. If, for instance, he could win from her a hundred thousand livres, all would be well. Annoyingly enough she won from him, but only small sums, for he refrained always from making big gambles and seemed in actual fact to dislike the gaming table. Or perhaps it was a case of like father like son. Stingy, that was it! Stingy with his money, stingy with his emotions. What a *stick* he was!

"Lucky at cards, unlucky at love," Gabrielle mocked.

"Oh hold your foolish tongue!"

It was Louis who told her of Senator von Fersen's reply to his son's letter. The elder Fersen had pointed out that while the regiment would cost one hundred thousand livres the return in salary would be no more than five thousand a year.

"It would take twenty years, according to the senator's calculations," Louis laughed, "to recover the capital expenditure."

"He seems to have forgotten the resale value."

"No, he referred to that, but he suggested—" Louis was frowning now—"that resale would be problematical since France's position is shaky."

"He sounds a very gloomy man, Louis. Nothing can be done, then?"

Louis laughed again. "Oh yes. The senator puts forward an alternative. He will buy the regiment for Axel, providing Axel shows himself willing to make a good marriage."

"Oh . . ." said Marie Antoinette.

"So now we must find Axel a wealthy wife. A simple solution, really."

"You sound as if you have one in mind," she said carefully.

"Yes. The daughter of my comptroller-general. Necker is very rich, so Germaine Necker is perhaps the most sought-after girl in France."

180

"Have you mentioned her name to Axel?"

"Yes indeed, my dear."

She could feel her heart falling, falling. "Is he agreeable?"

"I believe so, except that he feels he might be betraying a friend of his, Baron de Staël. According to Axel the baron and Germaine Necker are in love and have a secret understanding. I told him to take no notice of that. Necker will give the girl to Axel if I insist."

She felt as if she were choking. "Have you spoken to Necker?"

"Briefly, yes. The next step, if Necker hesitates, will be to issue a royal command."

"I don't believe Axel really wants the girl."

"Ah, but he really wants the Royal Swedish regiment."

This was terrible, terrible!

"Louis," she said quickly, "the arranging of a marriage as important as this needs *finesse*. In short, a woman's touch. Why not leave it all to me?"

"Of course, if you wish, my dear."

"Thank you."

"But bring it off, bring it off. Axel, remember, would do anything to gain the Royal Swedish."

Anything, she thought bitterly, but allow her to write to his father, anything but accept the regiment as a royal gift. The marriage must be prevented, she told herself fiercely, at all cost, at any cost.

Yes, but how?

Ideas began to form in her mind. The first thing was to please Senator von Fersen, or at all events to *appear* to please him.

"Louis," she said, "I want you to write to Senator von Fersen. It will look better coming from you than from me."

"Very well."

"Tell him that in Necker's daughter we have found Axel an excellent wife. Add that nothing now stands between Axel and the possession of the Royal Swedish."

Obediently, Louis wrote the letter.

"Have it sent by special courier," she said.

"You consider the matter urgent, eh?"

"*Most* urgent, Louis."

At one of her card parties, one of the many she gave while waiting impatiently for the senator's reply, she became suddenly and furiously aware that her young sister-in-law, Madame Elizabeth, was making sheep's eyes at Fersen. She tried to ignore this idiotic sight, but it rankled. Madame Elizabeth, since the hurried departure of Madame Adelaide, had remained unfriendly and suspicious. Her attitude distressed Louis, who was constantly trying to persuade his sister that their old-maid aunt based her libellous verses on nothing more than personal enmity. In reality Elizabeth was Madame Adelaide's spy, Marie Antoinette concluded, watching, always watching, and no doubt concocting gossip herself.

When at last the senator's reply came Louis gave it to his wife with a satisfied smile.

"All appears to be going well, Marie."

She read the letter eagerly. Senator von Fersen was honored that the King of France should take so great an interest in his son, and he was delighted to know that the troublesome young fellow was about to settle down at last. He concluded by expressing the hope that Axel would serve King Louis faithfully and well in his new command.

"Obviously the senator has written separately to Axel," Louis remarked.

Fersen presented himself at Marie Antoinette's apartments the next day and begged the privilege of an audience. The moment he was ushered in she saw that he was deeply troubled.

"Your face should be wreathed in smiles," she admonished him. "Unless we misread your father's letter he has agreed to buy you the Royal Swedish."

"He has."

"Then why this air of gloom?"

"I have just come from Louis."

"Indeed?"

"He referred me to you. *You*, he said, were arranging the whole matter."

"What 'whole matter'?" she asked innocently.

"My father spoke of a marriage between me and Germaine Necker, a marriage which Louis was eager to arrange for me. Worse—" Fersen's voice rose on a high note—"my father apparently wrote to Monsieur Necker, giving what he was pleased to term his 'blessing.' Worse still, Monsieur Necker sent for me. After that I went at once to Louis, and Louis, as I say . . ." His voice trailed away.

182

"What did *Necker* say?"

"He, too, bestowed his blessing!"

"Ah, then we are all quite happy."

"Happy? Is Germaine Necker happy? Is my friend Baron de Staël happy? Am I, for that matter, happy?"

"You have the Royal Swedish."

"But at what a price! I have no wish to marry Germaine Necker. Nor do I intend to marry her."

Happiness flooded her heart. "She is an excellent match."

"I am not in love with her."

"Does that matter in an arranged marriage?"

"It matters to me! By heaven it does!"

Marie Antoinette had never seen Fersen like this—heated, deeply indignant, on the point almost of shouting at her. It was very pleasing, for it made him seem much more human.

"Your sentiments are admirable," she said, tempting him to further anger, "but most men who make such marriages have no trouble in finding love elsewhere."

"You must have read that somewhere!" He was speaking now as if to a child. "You with your happy marriage, what can you know of such things? For myself I do not want, I refuse to have, an unloved wife and the passing diversion of a mistress." His voice grew scathing. "Here at Versailles I could take a new mistress every day."

"My friend Gabrielle finds it strange that you don't."

He looked at her hotly. "With me it is real love with one woman, or nothing. You understand, or nothing!"

"I envy the woman you will eventually marry."

"I shall never marry."

"Why?" she asked, keeping her voice casual.

His eyes, luminous and intense, held hers squarely.

"I can tell you the reason now, Madame. Now, because you are so eager to force me into a marriage I do not want."

Eager! If only he knew!

"Tell me, then."

Still holding her eyes he said, "I fell in love once. It is quite a joke. I am still in love. I shall never love anyone else. For that reason I shall never marry. How can I when the woman I love is beyond my reach! Worse than that, she is quite pitiless. While at heart she is completely indifferent to me she delights in flirting, in playing the coquette."

183

"And is eager also," she added shakily, "to force you into marriage with someone else?"

As if not having heard he went on passionately, "Once I told her that to me she was a symbol. A bright and lovely symbol. Beauty incarnate, I said. Not a woman, a goddess. That way, I said, I loved and adored her. What utter nonsense!"

"Nonsense?" she demanded indignantly, but the tears were stinging her eyes.

"*You*, a goddess?" he went on. "I said that to deceive Louis, who is my friend. I said it to avoid hurting him. I went to America because I could no longer bear to remain here. I came back because I could no longer bear to remain away. A goddess? Never! A weak and often foolish woman, but a desirable woman. You have been that to me since our first meeting."

The tears were rolling down her cheeks now. She felt unbearably happy. Laughing and crying she flung her arms round his neck, caressed his blond hair, lay her hot cheek against his breast.

"What perfectly horrible things you have said to me," she sobbed. "You ought to be horsewhipped."

"Marie—"

She clung to him. "I prefer to be loved as a woman, though it was very nice being a goddess."

Gently he freed himself.

"I have made a dreadful mistake," he said sadly. "I see that now."

"I love you as much as you love me. That is no mistake."

Fersen shook his head. "What I said appealed to your emotions. My words moved you, emotionally."

She stamped her foot angrily. "How else do you expect a woman to be moved?"

"Emotions are often false."

"Then the whole of life is false! Oh Axel, my darling, why argue? I love you, you love me. Why *argue*?"

Bitterly he said, "The next step, then, is a secret love affair. Is that what you want?"

"Yes, yes!"

"Common enough at Versailles. Quite fashionable. Horrible too, and cynical."

"Yet you know nothing can destroy our love—nothing!"

184

"Nothing in this life, nothing in the next! Knowing that we can try to be strong, both of us."

"Strong?"

"You know what I mean, Marie."

"Yes," she said angrily, "I know what you mean. Having shattered the goddess, the pretty statue, you want to pick up the pieces and put it together again. Or perhaps you want to leave them scattered about and go away, as you did before."

"What else can I do but go away? You have a duty to your husband, your children. More important still, you have a duty to France."

"Mine was an arranged marriage, remember. And what do I care for France? We love each other, we want each other. How simple, how easy to forget the world."

"And afterwards, to hate each other?"

She was defeated and she knew it.

"What are you going to do?" she asked tonelessly.

Fersen smiled brightly. "I can either make the marriage you tried to force me into, or I can return to Sweden."

"What an idiot you are! I had no intention of your marrying the Necker girl. All I wanted was to make your father buy the Royal Swedish."

"Under false pretenses, yes."

"Oh nonsense! All your father asked was that you should show yourself *willing* to make a good marriage. It will be easy enough for me to induce Germaine Necker and your friend to elope."

"You are splitting hairs, Marie."

"What of it? I was most diplomatic."

"Trickery," Fersen commented, "is, of course, another word for diplomacy. Diplomacy of a sort. You will never save France by trickery."

She began to feel desperate. "What are you going to do?"

"I shall return to Sweden and tell my father that after all he need not spend a hundred thousand livres."

"I shall never see you again. Is that your intention?"

"Yes."

"Oh Axel," she begged, "surely we can have friendship if nothing else."

"Friendship would not be enough now. You know that."

185

"Go away if you must, but come back. Oh please, Axel, come back."

Fersen smiled gently. "If I can conquer myself and return able to say to you 'Marie, all I want is to serve and help you,' yes, I shall indeed come back."

"But soon, Axel, soon!"

The door opened, startling them, and Louis came lumbering into the room. Fersen glanced anxiously at Marie Antoinette. He was afraid, she knew, that Louis would notice her tear-stained cheeks. She gave him a reassuring smile. The short-sighted Louis, unless very close to her, wouldn't even notice what she was wearing.

"Ah, still here, Axel, splendid!" Louis said. "I have just received a letter from King Gustav."

Marie Antoinette looked at him anxiously. Perhaps she had gone too far. Perhaps the King of Sweden, interesting himself in the proposed marriage, was now commanding Axel to marry the Necker girl.

"You will receive a separate communication through your embassy," Louis went on, still addressing Fersen, "but I may as well tell you the news. I do not pretend that I want you to leave France, but duty to your King comes first."

"Leave France?" Marie Antoinette questioned.

"Gustav is making a tour of Europe. Some years ago, due to his father's death, his grand tour was interrupted. He is now resuming it. You are commanded, Axel, to join your King in Germany. He does you great honor, Axel."

Axel bowed. "I realize that, Louis."

"You will still command the Royal Swedish, of course. In fact, Gustav is particularly anxious that you should."

"I— In that case—"

"Is anything the matter, Axel?" Louis asked, squinting at him.

"Axel," Marie Antoinette laughed quietly, "had decided to reject it, after all. A point of honor—as far as his father is concerned."

Louis looked puzzled. "A point of honor?"

Axel cleared his throat. "I have decided against the proposed marriage."

"Ah, I see, I see. How many men do I know who are as scrupulously honorable as you!" Louis was growing quite emotional. "None, none! Even so, Axel, since Gustav wishes it, how can

186

your father really refuse? It would have been a good marriage, too."

Axel cleared his throat again. "Baron de Staël has a prior claim."

"Again the point of honor!" Louis cried.

"I beg you, Louis," Axel went on, "to support my friend's suit. He is in any case most eligible."

"I shall do so gladly," Louis agreed.

Musingly Marie Antoinette said, "This tour of King Gustav's— will his travels bring him to Paris?"

"Undoubtedly," Louis told her.

"Ah then, whether or not Axel commands the Royal Swedish, he will return to France, and quite soon."

"Quite soon," Louis agreed.

She gave Axel a lingering, happy smile. Life, she told herself, was short, but not too short. She could wait.

SIX

"So once again, Marie, you have done your duty."

Marie Antoinette nodded briefly.

Her duty, she thought, that and nothing more. Another child, another boy, Louis Charles, Duc de Normandie, had been born to the King and Queen of France. One daughter, two sons . . . The country at large had greeted the arrival of this second son with scant enthusiasm. Perhaps France was more than satisfied, now.

Ironic, she reflected, that Louis Charles had been conceived during Axel von Fersen's brief visit last year in the company of King Gustav. Because of this she had expected Provence and Madame Adelaide to move against her, but Provence had held his hand. What had he said before? *I can wait* . . . No doubt he could, but . . . for what?

She glanced incuriously about the crowded Hall of Mirrors. The greatest of the great were here tonight, archbishops and bishops, marshals, ministers of state, haughty nobles and their simpering ladies. A magnificent, glittering spectacle, everybody gathered here at Louis' bidding to celebrate the royal birth. Her eyes fell on the Abbé Vermond. There he was, moving in and out of the crowd, a withdrawn, self-important expression on his face. She had kept him at court because her mother would have wished it. He was still her confessor, but he was not, as he liked to tell everybody, her chief adviser. She watched him as he paused for a moment to speak to the Prince de Rohan. Both men glanced in her direction, upon which she immediately (and childishly too, she admitted) averted her eyes.

"Gabrielle," she told her friend, "I'm bored. Think of it! I, who always took so much delight in the splendor of Versailles—bored!"

Gabrielle laughed tinklingly. "Probably Monsieur le Comte de Fersen, alone in Sweden, is also bored."

Marie Antoinette held back the angry retort that came to her lips. Deliberately she returned in memory to Axel's visit with King Gustav. It had been a state visit, in spite of Gustav's insistence on informality, a visit during which she had seen Axel on countless occasions—at the parties she gave at the Little Trianon, at the state balls, at the Paris theaters—but only once, briefly and hurriedly, alone. She could remember every word of the whispered conversation, every single word.

"Have you conquered yourself, Axel? Can you say now that you want only to serve and help me?"

"I can, Marie."

"You lie! Oh tell me you lie!"

"I can say it only because, in three days' time, I am to leave again with King Gustav."

"Taking my heart with you, Axel!"

"Leaving mine behind."

"Nonsense, romantic nonsense!"

"My dear—"

"But a woman needs reality."

"We have one reality, Marie. My willingness to serve you."

"To serve me! But—how? And . . . from a distance?"

"The time will come. When you need me I will come. I swear it."

And so he had gone, and now duty to his King, or perhaps a fear of himself, still kept him in Sweden. He had gone, and what had followed? The endless round of court gaiety and with it, duty to Louis, which was also duty to France. And the result? Another child, and this formal glittering celebration.

Yet behind the restlessness, which she hid always beneath a false gay smile, remained and grew the image of a noble, faithful Axel von Fersen. She could see this image now, the grave thoughtful smile, the luminous dark eyes. He was here in spirit, ready and eager to serve her, to advise her. To advise her! It was love she wanted, not advice, however wise and right it might be. Nevertheless, she often asked herself, What would Axel advise?

At that moment the Princesse de Lamballe approached, and with her was Madame Elizabeth. The girl smiled faintly, a shy almost friendly smile, exchanged a few brief words and moved on with Louise de Lamballe. The girl! Now why do I always think of her as a girl? Marie Antoinette asked herself. Elizabeth was twenty-five and should have been married years ago.

"Louise is doing her best," Gabrielle remarked.

"Her best, Gabrielle?"

"In two directions. But for Louise's influence, Madame Elizabeth would never have tried to smile like that. She will be embracing you in public next!"

Marie Antoinette smiled. "That would be embarrassing. What is the other direction?"

"Madame Elizabeth is really a beauty who has never made the most of herself. Louise has worked hard. Did you see the new gown? Quite smart, quite stylish. But the hair is still impossible. It needs the attention of your dear Léonard."

Marie Antoinette shrugged. Well, why not? She would talk to Elizabeth later, and, if she was still disposed to friendliness, discuss with her a hair style suitable to her face and figure.

"Marie, my dear . . ."

Gabrielle had moved away and Louis stood in her place. She thought he looked ridiculous and uncomfortable in his gold-embroidered coat, so ridiculous that her heart softened and she felt for him a great new compassion. Only by thinking of him as a child in need of love, a lost pathetic child, was she able to take him now as a husband. She wondered if he had noticed her passive submission to duty, her quick evasion whenever evasion was possible. But if he had become an animal who reached out instinctively for an animal's natural satisfaction, then the fault was hers.

"Yes, Louis," she said, smiling gently, "what is it?"

"Cardinal de Rohan is here," he said propitiatingly. "Do please for my sake spare the poor fellow a kindly glance."

She saw that the Prince de Rohan, now indeed a cardinal, had approached closer and was hovering uncertainly among the courtiers who had followed Louis to her side.

"If the cardinal is present tonight," she said briskly, "I must be blind."

Louis sighed. "It hurts me to know that you still hate him so much."

"It is not that I hate him, Louis. Simply that so far as I am concerned he does not exist."

Curiosity getting the better of her, she glanced quickly in the cardinal's direction but was careful while so doing to look right through him. Instantly he began to bow and scrape and smile in the most foolish manner, just as if by accident she had nodded graciously. And to her horror he moved closer, walked slowly past her and mumbled, "I had hoped that your Majesty would be wearing it tonight." Would be wearing it? Wearing *what*? The man was surely out of his mind.

Following on the cardinal's heels came Provence, a languid mocking expression on his face, an expression reflected on the face of Artois who was with him.

"Surely, at this late stage," he murmured, "your Majesty has no real wish to add the cardinal to your string of secret lovers?"

"Not unless she is more bored than usual," Artois added.

Unable to think of a sufficiently scathing retort, she turned on her heels and sought out Louis. She found him in earnest conversation with Mercy and Calonne, the new comptroller-general who had taken Necker's place. Since the death of Maurepas Louis was placing great faith in Calonne.

"Yes, yes," the comptroller-general was saying heatedly, "that is what they are calling her now, Madame Deficit."

Not having noticed her approach, Calonne colored and fell silent. Louis cleared his throat while Mercy, ever the polished courtier, remarked smoothly that her Majesty was looking more charming than ever tonight.

"Madame Deficit?" she echoed. "A new name for me, no doubt. Well, why not? My debts are as usual quite staggering."

Calonne, whose witty tongue she had always liked, recovered his composure and bowed elegantly.

"Madame Deficit, your humble servant."

"A sense of humor is all very well," Louis grumbled, "but the matter is far too serious for laughter."

"Laughter, your Majesty," Calonne ventured, "is all that is left to us."

"You said *they* are calling me Madame Deficit," Marie Antoinette said. "Whom do you mean?"

Mercy looked grave. "Your Majesty's enemies at court, or the anonymous authors of this new pamphlet written against you."

So, after a short respite, the verses and the pamphlets were starting again.

"We have seized as many as possible, your Majesty," Calonne said. "At most it will be only a whisper."

Marie tried to laugh lightly. "I expect my private affairs are in utter confusion. To call me Madame Deficit is not unjust."

"No reference is made to your *private* debts," Louis told her heavily. "It is the *government* deficit for which you are blamed."

191

"Am I to blame for it?"

"No, of course not. The American war is as much to blame as anything."

"And your fondness for cranberries is to blame for *that*," she laughed, and gave him her arm. "As you said, Calonne, laughter is all that is left to us."

She inclined her head to Mercy and Calonne and walked quietly away with Louis.

"This," she said, "is unprecedented for a woman who likes to stay up till dawn, but I want to withdraw." And half-mockingly she added, "Have I your Majesty's permission?"

The pressure of his hand on her arm increased. "I, too, shall retire early."

She thought, No, no!

"Supper together, just the two of us," Louis went on eagerly, "then early to bed. An excellent, delightful thought, my love."

"As you wish," she said lifelessly.

"The physicians have assured me—" He looked at her hesitantly.

"Of course, Louis, of course."

They had assured her also that she was now fully recovered from the confinement, that the birth had been an easy one, that many more, equally easy, could be expected to follow. Desperately she determined to make Louis eat a heavier supper than usual. Then he would grow drowsy and might even fall asleep at the table. It was a mean trick, but the flesh revolted. She needed more time before that particular round of duty began again.

However at first Louis showed little interest in eating.

"I have an appetite, yes, but not for food!"

She forced a smile. "I myself am ravenous. Toy with a chicken while I make a real meal."

The sight of the food she ordered was too much for him and soon, while she pretended to eat, he attacked with greed and a rapidly glazing eye the numerous substantial dishes which were placed before him. So intent did he become on this all-engrossing occupation that he answered her curtly when she tried to talk about state affairs.

"Yes, yes," he said, "the deficit. Alarming. Quite."

"But why do they blame me for it? Why not Calonne?"

192

"People are fickle. You must try some of this kidney pie. Delectable. Sheer heaven."

She knew why they blamed her. They blamed her because Calonne, who was unpopular, was regarded as the Queen's tool. Gabrielle had wanted the ministry of finance for Calonne and Marie Antoinette, acquiescing, had made the appointment possible. The Queen's tool indeed! Say rather Gabrielle's.

She asked herself how Axel would feel about the appointment. Would he say that the choice of the witty, handsome, always agreeable Calonne was a bad one? She smiled as she remembered the wry look on Calonne's face when on the day of his appointment he had said to Louis, "Sire, I am in debt, a bad thing, surely, for a new comptroller-general." Louis had been amused and had paid Calonne's debts without argument. No, Axel would not approve of that, nor would he approve of the fact that Calonne, whenever she asked him for money, immediately sent her twice the amount required.

"Louis," she said tentatively, "perhaps you should let Calonne go and bring back Necker."

Louis' mouth was full but he managed to say, "Perhaps."

"It may have been a mistake, letting Necker go."

"Huh?" Louis grunted.

Gradually he was eating himself into the required stupor. It was, she thought, an unpleasant sight to see Louis intoxicated, not because of wine, for he drank sparingly, but because of food.

But would Necker *come* back? After all, he had resigned and had refused again and again to reconsider his decision. A rat leaving a sinking ship, somebody had sneered. Rats never returned to sinking ships. And if he did come back, what could he do? More loans instead of taxes? In all probability Necker would begin by insisting on personal economy. She smiled. Well, why not? Axel would say it was a good example to set the court.

"Louis," she said, pleased with herself, "I shall turn over a new leaf; I shall economize."

But Louis, slumped in his chair, head forward on his chest, was now asleep. Worse, his thick lips were loose and his chin was stained with gravy. Marie Antoinette rose in disgust, in self-disgust too. She had brought about his condition. Better to have submitted, briefly, to the demands of duty. She rang for a servant.

"Call his Majesty's gentlemen. They will know what to do."

193

The next day, as if inspired, she was still determined on personal economy. She sent for her friend and *surintendante*, Gabrielle de Polignac, and much to that lady's amazement expressed a wish to go through the household accounts.

"What a boring occupation," Gabrielle laughed.

"I am turning over a new leaf. No joking, please."

Gabrielle's eyes twinkled. "The new leaf, I vow, is already written on, and the writing is just the same."

Marie Antoinette's lips twitched but she said sternly, "I refuse to be amused."

Seated in a businesslike attitude at her writing table she began to go through the accounts. What a lot there were! How much easier to leave it all to Gabrielle and merely sign the usual signature, 'Marie Antoinette.' An unworthy thought, she could hear Axel saying. Yes indeed, she echoed, an unworthy thought. She looked up suddenly.

"Gabrielle, why did you want the ministry of finance for Calonne?"

Gabrielle shrugged. "He is an amusing fellow."

"A lover of yours, perhaps?"

"Perhaps."

"Had you any other reason?"

"He was badly in need of the perquisites of some office or other."

"It never occurred to you that he might or might not be the right man—the man capable of saving France from bankruptcy?"

Gabrielle stared at her aghast. "Marie, you must be sickening for something. Either that or you are contemplating taking over the ministry yourself."

Marie Antoinette stifled a giggle. "I still refuse to be amused."

She went on with her grim task. Two accounts she set aside, marking them 'Delay payment.' They were from the dressmaker and the hairdresser. Both, she was sure, had overcharged. And since through her sponsorship Bertin and Léonard were making large fortunes, that was intolerable. Then she paused, frowning over what appeared to be, not an account, but a letter from the court jeweler, Monsieur Boehmer.

"Gabrielle, what is this?"

Gabrielle took the letter and read it.

"Quite confusing," she commented.

Marie Antoinette read it again. "Boehmer speaks of an arrangement made between him and me, but fails to say just what sort of arrangement. Has any arrangement been made with Boehmer on my behalf, Gabrielle?"

"None whatever."

"He also speaks of some diamonds, the most beautiful ever seen. I have bought no diamonds from him, have I?"

"Not of late."

"And I owe him no money. He has made a silly mistake."

"Either that, or this is his way of tempting you to some foolish extravagance."

Marie Antoinette smiled. "Ah, that must be it. Well, the poor man will be sadly disappointed." She crumpled up the letter and tossed it aside. "And now, heaven help me, the rest of these accounts . . ."

Weary already of the task she had set herself, she nonetheless pursued it doggedly. At the end of an hour's work she sighed woefully.

"It seems to me that in trying to find a way to economize I only succeed in bringing to light the things I have done without and really need most badly. If I go on like this I shall spend *more* in the future, not *less.*"

"I knew you would regret this waste of time," Gabrielle laughed.

"The trouble is, I have no understanding whatever of high finance."

"The first lesson to be learned," Gabrielle mocked, "is how to spend more than one can afford and yet keep out of debt."

"It has never been necessary for me to keep out of debt," Marie Antoinette said, her brows crinkled, her eyes puzzled. "Money is, and always has been, beyond my comprehension." What had Mercy once said? *Completely isolated from reality, you have been reared in a little world of ignorance.* "Perhaps I should have been taught something about it when I was a child." She rose from the writing table. "I have had enough for today. What shall I do to amuse myself, Gabrielle?"

"You could send for Léonard and ask him to do something about Madame Elizabeth's hair."

"So I could, but I think a romp with the children would be more to my liking."

She went to the nursery and there, with mixed feelings, she found her sister-in-law playing with the children. Madame Eliza-

195

beth was down on all fours. The Dauphin, now almost four years old, was riding perilously on her back while the seven-year-old Madame Royale was tugging at her hair. All three were laughing uproariously.

Marie Antoinette stifled a pang of resentment and jealousy and joined in the laughter.

"What an exciting game!" she cried.

Startled, Madame Elizabeth removed the Dauphin from her back and rose to her feet. The sight of her flushed face and her hair not unbecomingly disarrayed reminded Marie Antoinette of what Gabrielle had said, *a beauty who has never made the most of herself.*

"You should play oftener with the children," she said gently.

Madame Elizabeth avoided her eyes. "Thank you."

"But she plays with us nearly every day," Madame Royale pointed out. "When you're not here, I mean, Mama."

"I love Louis' children," Madame Elizabeth said, a note of defiance in her voice.

Marie Antoinette kept her own voice still gentle. "They are also my children, Elizabeth."

"Of course."

All this, which was more than the children should have heard, was hardly promising, but Marie Antoinette was determined to persevere.

"I very much admired the gown you wore at the reception," she said brightly, "but I think if we went through my pattern book we might find something even more suitable. Shall we do it now?"

Madame Elizabeth hesitated for a moment. "Very well."

They went together to Marie Antoinette's apartments, the heavy pattern book was brought and finally they were left alone to study it.

Still persevering but on dangerous ground, Marie Antoinette said, "Thank you, Elizabeth, for admitting just now that my children are also Louis' children."

The young woman flushed. "It is better to forget old scandals."

"Did Louise de Lamballe convince you of that?"

"Yes."

"At the reception I felt that you were ready to be at least a little friendly. Was Louise responsible for that?"

"Yes."

196

Marie Antoinette smiled. "A truce, then, if not actual peace?"

Madame Elizabeth gave her a serious look. "Louise made me realize that I had been lacking in Christian charity."

"Ah, then your changed attitude comes under the heading of good works!" Marie Antoinette laughed.

"Yes."

"Then let us agree that my interest in your personal appearance also comes under that heading."

"You are laughing at me!"

"I would rather laugh at you than be angry with you. But better still, I would rather that we laughed together."

Madame Elizabeth considered this. "Very well, for Louis' sake I will try."

"But you still hold certain reservations?"

"I am forced to by past events."

Marie Antoinette held her peace. The little progress that had been made would go for nothing if she lost her temper and raged about the iniquity of Madame Adelaide's lies.

"There is very little wrong now with your choice of clothes," she said gaily. "All that remains is the need to find a more becoming hair style. Léonard, of course, will soon do that. And goodness, his clever touch is most essential, otherwise we might never find you a husband."

"I shall never marry!" Madame Elizabeth cried vehemently.

"But why not?"

"I want to remain at court near Louis. I know he will need me some day."

"My dear, I might also need you, some day."

Madame Elizabeth smiled briefly. "I hope I shall know my duty when you do."

Heaven give me strength! Marie Antoinette prayed silently.

Aloud she said, "And now, let us discuss hair styles . . ."

She returned to the household accounts the next day, and the next. Apparently she could dispense with some of her personal servants; it really did seem that there were many more than she needed. And she decided that it might help if she wore a gown twice, for thus she would cut in half that particular part of her expenditure. But how people would stare when the Queen appeared more than once in the same gown!

Still full of zeal she made up her mind, painful as the effort

197

might be, to embark on a serious study of French history, unearth the mistakes of past rulers and thus armed act wisely in the future. It was, of course, quite boring, and confusion rather than enlightenment was the result. Writers of the past held different opinions; they contradicted each other flatly. When it came to facts, one said one thing, another said another, so that it seemed impossible to discover what, in a given set of circumstances, had actually happened. It would probably be the same, she decided, when people wrote about her long after her death. This was true, when she came to think of it, even now, during her lifetime.

She persevered, but with little heart in her task. She talked to everybody about the state of France, yet few people at court, even if interested, were able to express an unbiased opinion. She needed Axel, needed him badly. And so pressing did the need of him become that, setting aside all else, she sat down to write to him. She wrote rapidly, impulsively, and so immersed did she become that it was some time before she noticed one of her ladies standing close by, waiting for permission to speak.

"Yes, what is it, Madame Campan?" she asked impatiently.

"The jeweler, Monsieur Boehmer, requests the privilege of an audience, your Majesty."

"I have neither the time nor the inclination to receive him. Tell him, if you wish, that the Queen, for the time being, is buying no more trinkets."

Madame Campan, smiling faintly, withdrew.

Returning to the letter, Marie Antoinette reread what she had already written. She had intended saying briefly that he, her only true friend, was sadly missed, but what had she really written? A love letter, long, involved, almost hysterical, but undoubtedly a love letter. Carefully, deliberately, she tore the sheets into a dozen pieces, then attacked the pieces one by one, tearing them into smaller pieces. Far better, she decided, not to write at all. After all one must preserve one's dignity.

A few moments later Madame Campan returned.

"You sent the wretched man away?" Marie Antoinette demanded.

"Yes, your Majesty, but before he went he insisted on confiding in me."

The tone of Madame Campan's voice was surprising. Usually so quiet and composed, she looked and sounded most agitated.

"Your Majesty," she burst out, "Monsieur Boehmer declares

198

that you ordered from him a diamond necklace valued at one million and a half livres, that the necklace was delivered and that, though months have passed, no payment has yet been made."

Marie Antoinette rose indignantly. "The man is out of his mind!"

"So I told him, your Majesty."

"You know that I neither ordered nor took delivery of such a necklace."

"I do indeed, your Majesty, and I told Monsieur Boehmer so. He wrung his hands, he wept, he declared that some dastardly trick had been played on him by the cardinal."

"By the . . . cardinal?"

"Cardinal de Rohan, your Majesty."

"*That* creature!"

Marie Antoinette remembered the cardinal's words when he had had the impudence to speak to her in public; she remembered Boehmer's letter in reference to an 'understanding' and some diamonds, 'the most beautiful ever seen.' There seemed now to be a connection between the two, but neither incident made sense.

"Monsieur Boehmer," Madame Campan added, "declares that negotiations for the purchase were made on your Majesty's behalf by the cardinal."

"This is beyond belief," Marie Antoinette cried angrily. "Send after Boehmer, have him brought back. I want to question him."

Boehmer, who had evidently lingered nearby, made his appearance almost immediately. His face was white and drawn. His hands trembled. He bowed obsequiously, then spoke in a low, stricken voice.

"I regret with all my heart, your Majesty, that this dreadful thing has happened."

"I have no real understanding of it," she told him sharply. "Tell me briefly and quickly what the trouble is."

"I am ruined, ruined!" Boehmer moaned.

"If you yourself are innocent you will not be made to suffer. Come, tell me all you know."

The jeweler gulped, steadied himself and went on with less agitation.

"I had long hoped, your Majesty, that those truly magnificent diamonds would some day grace the royal person, so you may

199

well imagine my delight when Cardinal de Rohan sent for me, informed me that your Majesty wished to possess them and discussed with me an agreement for payment."

"Continue," she commanded, striving to control her indignation.

"The cardinal said that the purchase was to be kept a secret from the King, who would not, at such a time, approve of so large an expenditure. He further assured me that your Majesty would be in a position to pay for the diamonds privately, by instalments. Four payments were suggested, to be made over a period of two years."

"That was sheer invention on the cardinal's part!"

"I—" Boehmer gulped painfully. "It *was*, your Majesty?"

"You seem reluctant to believe me, Boehmer!"

Boehmer, trembling, bowed humbly before her. "Your Majesty, an agreement was drawn up. Payment over a period of two years, the cardinal standing gladly as guarantor. This agreement was submitted to your Majesty, marked 'approved' and signed 'Marie Antoinette of France.' See, your Majesty—" he drew a document from his pocket—"I have it here."

She took the document, read it quickly and stared for a long moment at the signature.

"A good imitation, this signature, but not mine. In any case I never sign myself 'Marie Antoinette of France.' I am not a French woman. I always sign myself 'Marie Antoinette.'"

Boehmer threw up his hands. "Ruined, ruined!"

"I begin to suspect that the cardinal is, or very soon will be," she snapped. "He told you, then, that I had signed this agreement and delivered it into his hands? He told you *that?*"

"No, your Majesty. It was delivered into his hands, or so he said, by your Majesty's dear good friend, Madame Lamotte."

"Madame Lamotte? I know of no such person. It seems to me that Cardinal de Rohan, rogue that he is, is also something of a fool. Serious enough to forge my signature, sheer stupidity to invent a person by the name of Lamotte."

"Begging your Majesty's pardon, but Madame Lamotte is no invention," Boehmer blundered on. "I met her myself when I gave the necklace into her hands."

"Into *her* hands?"

"In the presence of Cardinal de Rohan, your Majesty. She being, as I understood, your Majesty's friend, was then to convey it at once to your Majesty."

"Which, of course, she did not."

"N-no, your Majesty."

"You cannot for one moment doubt the word of the Queen, Monsieur!"

"No indeed," he said earnestly.

"This woman, this Madame Lamotte—would you say that she is the cardinal's mistress?"

Boehmer gave the matter serious thought. "Since one knows the cardinal's shocking reputation, since the woman herself is truly handsome—yes, your Majesty, I think it possible."

"Then the cardinal and his mistress conspired to rob you and at the same time involve me in an unpleasant scandal."

Boehmer looked apologetic. "The cardinal made himself responsible for the payments, your Majesty."

Marie Antoinette frowned. "The guarantor, yes . . . But how could he conspire to rob himself? He is, I agree, stated guarantor in this document, but has he signed any other document?"

"By heaven, no!" Boehmer shrieked.

"So he cannot be held responsible. All you have is this forgery. And it is a forgery. That can be proved. Otherwise *I* would be responsible. Perhaps that was the intention! Yes, it must have been!"

What a rogue the cardinal was! Tired of trying to gain royal favor, he had hatched this plot. Boehmer was to be robbed and she held responsible. Remembering the cardinal's mumbled words, which must have referred to the necklace, she frowned. A moment later her face cleared. He had been feeling just a little above himself that night. There was no other explanation.

"But where is the necklace, your Majesty?" Boehmer groaned. "If I could recover it I might avert ruin by selling it elsewhere."

"Leave everything to me," she said. "Every effort will be made to recover the diamonds. The cardinal and his accomplice will be arrested, charged and brought to trial."

Boehmer bowed. "Your Majesty is most gracious." He backed from her presence repeating, "Most gracious . . ."

"One moment, Boehmer!"

"Your Majesty . . ."

"Sit at my writing table. Write down all you know of this shameful plot. The facts can then be placed clearly before the King."

Boehmer obeyed with alacrity and the moment he had finished Marie Antoinette snatched the pages from him and went at once to Louis, taking with her also the forged agreement.

"Louis," she cried, "read this!"

Louis began to read slowly, all too slowly, at times tracing a line with his forefinger, at others mouthing the words. Finally, blinking and shaking his head, he looked up at her, and said,

"I admit to being vastly taken aback."

"Is *that* all you can say?"

"Involved, confusing, quite shameful," Louis added. "Still, I feel sure that Cardinal de Rohan himself is not responsible for this incredible fraud."

"How can you say that, Louis! Fool he may be, but obviously he hatched the whole disgraceful plot."

"I myself am inclined to suspect this Madame Lamotte."

"Cardinal de Rohan is the ringleader. As you love me, Louis, he must be arrested. He must, he must!"

Louis shrugged. "Immediately?"

"We-ell . . . No, wait!"

She smiled. The cardinal was now Grand Almoner of France, and as such he would officiate in two days' time at a most important celebration, the Assumption of the Holy Virgin. The whole court would be present, and many illustrious visitors. Oh yes, she had in mind for him a really fitting humiliation!

"Let him be arrested," she said, "just before we lead the procession to the chapel on the Feast of the Assumption."

"That is scarcely kind," Louis protested.

"Can you blame me?"

"I beg you to change your mind, my dear."

"Never!"

During the next two days Louis conferred several times with his ministers and repeatedly asked her to reconsider her decision. He feared, he said, that the scandal of the cardinal's arrest might have unpleasant repercussions.

"Better to send him quietly into exile," he pleaded.

"Leaving him free, as Madame Adelaide is free, to make more mischief at a distance? No, Louis, he must be shown up, either for the fool he is or the rogue he is, or both."

Louis pleaded once more with her when on the Feast of the Assumption she sat in his library, waiting. Outside, as she could tell by the sounds of movement and the quiet hum of voices, the court was gathering in the Hall of Mirrors. The cardinal himself, she knew, would now be waiting in the council room, ready to come forth and take his place in the procession the moment she and Louis appeared.

"Ah well," Louis remarked, "no man is strong when faced with a headstrong woman."

"I may be headstrong, Louis, but I have right on my side. Give the order for the cardinal's arrest. Have him escorted under guard through the entire length of the Hall of Mirrors."

She thought suddenly, What would Axel advise? Axel, she knew, would agree with Louis. A quiet exile for the cardinal, an avoidance, if possible, of public scandal. Quickly she shut her mind to these thoughts.

"Well, Louis?"

Louis rose, but his face showed an unexpected determination.

"I shall have him brought here first."

"A waste of time!"

"Would you have it said afterwards that you were afraid to face him? Let him be brought here. Let him at least defend himself."

"As you wish, then, but nothing will make me change my mind."

A few moments later when the cardinal entered the library, she was quick to see that his face held an uneasy, shifty look, a look emphasized rather than masked by the magnificence of his pontifical robes. Had he seen Boehmer? Had he been forewarned? Boehmer had been sworn to secrecy, but one never knew . . .

"Sire," she said, addressing Louis with the utmost formality, "I prefer not to speak to this man. Please do the questioning yourself."

Louis gave the cardinal a pitying look. "Monsieur, is it true that you negotiated with the jeweler, Boehmer, the purchase of a certain diamond necklace?"

The cardinal paled. "It is, your Majesty."

"Where is the necklace now?"

The cardinal moistened his lips. "I— Sire, I imagine it is in the possession of the Queen."

"Imagine?" Louis said quietly.

"Certain doubts have been placed in my mind, your Majesty, but—but the necklace was purchased for her Majesty and—and conveyed to her by her friend, Madame la Comtesse de la Motte-Valois."

"A comtesse now!" Marie Antoinette scoffed.

203

Louis said, "Call the lady what you will, Madame Lamotte or anything else, her Majesty has never met such a person."

"But the letters!" the cardinal gasped. "So many of them! Written by the Queen, all of them, to her dear friend the comtesse!" He was beginning to sweat; his eyes were dilated with fear. "All I wanted was to serve her Majesty, to restore myself to favor. I—I was sure I had succeeded when I met her Majesty in secret."

"When he met me in secret?" Marie Antoinette burst out. "What nonsense is this? Ask him, Louis, ask him!"

"Please explain yourself more fully," Louis commanded.

Babbling now, the cardinal said, "It was late at night, in the park, near the Bosquet de Venus. Her Majesty spoke graciously to me, filling my heart with gladness. Unfortunately we were interrupted. I could do little more than kiss her Majesty's hand. But Madame de la Motte promised to arrange a further meeting."

Marie Antoinette was left quite speechless.

"Are you suggesting," Louis roared, "that the Queen was on the point of conducting a shameful love affair with you?"

The cardinal bowed his head. "I had been led to believe that I could feel hopeful in that direction."

Marie Antoinette recovered her voice. "This is ridiculous! For years I have despised this man. I have refused to receive him, speak to him. I—!" She gasped for breath. "And now I am accused of meeting him secretly, late at night!"

Louis gave his attention sternly to the cardinal. "It was late at night. I assume it was very dark. The meeting had been arranged by this mysterious Madame Lamotte. Did you recognize the Queen's features?"

"I— Sire, I would have sworn—"

"Did you recognize her voice?"

"She—she spoke only briefly, Sire."

"But graciously. You said graciously."

The cardinal mopped his brow. "Her Majesty—the person I met spoke with an accent. I was influenced by that."

"Accents are easily assumed, Monsieur."

"I—I admit, Sire, that I might have been duped." He was silent for a moment. "And then there was the money. The money I so gladly lent her Majesty."

"So now he claims he lent me money!" Marie Antoinette cried.

"In the first place fifty thousand livres, later a hundred thousand," the Cardinal blurted out.

"Doubtless he obtained a forged signature in receipt!"

"Did you?" Louis asked.

"There was no receipt, Sire. I gave the money to Madame de la Motte; *she* gave it to her Majesty."

Marie Antoinette's patience was at an end. "Order his arrest and have done with it."

Louis said: "There is one thing I fail to understand, Monsieur. You accepted as the Queen's signature a signature which her Majesty has never used, 'Marie Antoinette of France.' You are the Grand Almoner; you are also a prince of the illustrious house of Rohan. You should certainly be familiar with the normal signature, 'Marie Antoinette.'"

The cardinal shook his head in misery. "I was besotted with the belief that the Queen was about to smile on me again."

"A likely story," Marie Antoinette said wearily. "I do not believe a single word of it. He was in league with this woman."

Louis hesitated. "I want to believe you, Monsieur. Can you tell me anything else that will prove you indeed acted foolishly, that will show you were duped?"

The cardinal shook his head. "I am too wretched to say another word, Sire—except that I will gladly pay for the necklace."

Louis tried again. "Go into the next room. Sit there calmly for a few minutes. You might even pray, but only if you can do so with sincerity. After that, write down your explanation and let me see it before I finally make up my mind."

"Most gracious, most gracious," the cardinal stammered, and withdrew stumblingly to the next room.

"It was presumptuous of me," Louis said, shaking his head, "to order a prince of the church to pray. Worse, to suggest, by telling him to do with sincerity, that he is unworthy of his cloth."

"Which he is, and you know it. The man should be unfrocked, Louis!"

"I am only the King of France," Louis said, with a comical solemnity, "not the Pope of Rome." He came close to her, looked at her searchingly and, after a slight hesitation, said hurriedly, "You did not meet him secretly in the park?"

She laughed shortly. "Oh Louis, if I wanted to take a lover would I choose a man I have always hated so much?"

"Well, no. You would have chosen any one of the others gossip credits you with."

She felt both hurt and angry. "Once again you are beginning to doubt me!"

"No," he said, "it is only that I am bewildered, and realize how unattractive I am to any woman. Forgive me, Marie, please."

"I shall do so the moment you order Cardinal de Rohan's arrest."

"You make it very difficult for me," Louis complained. "I have discussed this vexing problem with my ministers. They feel sure he has been duped. He has gladly offered to pay for the necklace. Be satisfied with that, and of course the arrest and imprisonment of the woman Lamotte."

"Imprisonment without trial, you mean?"

"Yes, of course. My aim is to keep the matter quiet."

"He must stand public trial, Louis. He must be shown up."

Louis gave her a miserable look. "Wait and see what he writes in explanation."

Silence fell between them and remained unbroken until, after a tiresome long wait, Cardinal de Rohan returned, carrying a sheet of paper. This, with shaking hands, he pressed upon Louis, and Marie Antoinette watched a puzzled frown spread over the King's face as he read what was written there.

"Monsieur de Rohan," Louis said at last, "I find here a mass of incompleted sentences and contradictions. The whole thing is so mixed and confused I can make no sense of it."

"Sire, it is the best I can do."

For one disconcerting moment Marie Antoinette felt a stab of pity, but then she quickly hardened her heart and averted her eyes.

"Order his arrest," she demanded.

The cardinal flung himself on his knees at Louis' feet. There, to Marie Antoinette, he seemed a most contemptible sight, his scarlet cassock a horrible mockery. Louis turned from him, opened the door and called his Minister of the Interior, Baron de Breteuil. While the baron stood waiting and courtiers, aware that something was wrong, pushed and crowded behind him, Louis turned once more to the grovelling cardinal.

"Monsieur," he said quietly, "it is my kingly right to judge you summarily, or you may if you wish stand trial before the Parlement of Paris. Which do you choose?"

Marie Antoinette, anxious now, looked carefully at the cardinal. She had quite forgotten this special right of a king. Louis, in spite of her wishes, was offering the cardinal a way of escape from public trial. He would take it, of course he would!

But as she watched the cardinal rose to his feet and seemed to pull himself together, and the look he gave her was one of the utmost malevolence.

"Sire," he said strongly, "I have no fear of the outcome. I choose open trial before the Parlement of Paris."

Marie Antoinette could scarcely believe her ears. He had refused to trust in the King's clemency; he had refused what would have been exile and nothing more.

Louis, likewise surprised, whispered briefly in the baron's ear. The baron bowed and summoned the guard.

"Arrest Monsieur le Cardinal de Rohan!" he ordered, in a ringing voice. "Take him at once to the Bastille!"

Part IV

ONE

"A GREAT DEAL HAS HAPPENED SINCE LAST WE SAW EACH OTHER," HE said, when the first words of greeting had been exchanged.

"Yes, Axel, a great deal."

Marie Antoinette had not yet recovered from the shock of Fersen's sudden, quite unexpected appearance at Versailles and her voice, she knew, still trembled a little.

"Do you find me changed?" she asked.

He laughed in what seemed to her to be a brotherly, teasing way. "By that you mean, do I find you older in appearance."

"Naturally I mean that," she said, trying, and much to her surprise failing, to sound coquettish. "I am thirty-three, Axel."

"I see very little change. You are, if possible, more beautiful." How steady his voice was! "If there is any change at all it is in your eyes. They have a wiser look."

"Wiser?" she took him up. "I am still a frivolous woman, though heaven knows, I grow weary of the frivolity of my life, the pointlessness of it all."

"Then a little progress has been made."

"So you have come back to lecture me!" she cried rebelliously. "You were always fond of lecturing me!"

"I want to help you, Marie, as well as lecture you."

She looked at him searchingly. He was calm and controlled; he spoke in clear ringing tones; he seemed completely at his ease. Had he come back now, after four years, as he had said he would, to tell her that he had conquered himself? Was he able to say now, Marie, all I want is to serve and help you?

208

"Have you seen Louis?" she asked.

"Yes, for a few moments only. He was happy to greet me but seemed very preoccupied. My impression is that he has grown more lethargic than ever."

"I have tried to put heart into him, really I have!"

"And you have failed."

"How accusing you sound, Axel! Very well, I'll be honest with you. Often my patience failed me and in the end all I did was force my own decisions upon him." She changed the subject abruptly. "You have not yet asked about the children."

Fersen looked at her for the first time with a tender expression in his eyes. "My dear, I hesitated because of the death of the little Sophie, but I do want you to know how grieved I was when I heard about it."

Tears came quickly to her eyes. "Thank you, Axel."

Sophie, her fourth child, born after the trial of Cardinal de Rohan, had been sickly from the first. Worse, she had been ill-formed and had shown no sign of normal progress.

"It was a blessing really, Axel, but her death hurt me deeply. Tiny as she was, her face had such a mature, kind look. She had a special smile for me. I wanted her just for myself. Madame Royale is so independent and the boys, much as I love them, belong to France. I had thought to make Sophie my friend rather than my daughter. Losing her left me with a feeling of utter loneliness, even friendlessness."

"You are not friendless, you know that, Marie."

"Yes, Axel, I know that."

She held out her hands to him. He took them quickly in his and the strength of his slim fingers comforted her. She raised her face to his and found in his eyes the same comfort. The love of a faithful friend rather than the passion of a lover . . . was that sufficient? It seemed now, in this moment of gentleness and sympathy, that it was.

She released her hands. "Thank you, Axel."

"For what, Marie?"

"Your friendship and your strength."

"Thank you for accepting them, Marie."

She dried her eyes and laughed a little. She was beginning to feel very much herself again.

"You want to help me as well as lecture me," she teased. "Shall we begin with the unpleasant part of that statement? You are, after

209

all, the one person in the world who can say horrible things to me without making me too angry."

Fersen's eyes twinkled but his voice was serious. "Tell me first about the situation in France."

She shrugged. "I imagine the government is more deeply in debt than ever."

"But you scarcely care?"

"Why should I? Life at Versailles goes on just the same. If I try to help I am accused of meddling."

"And so you lost heart and continued to enjoy an unreal existence in an elaborate gilded cage."

"Not to enjoy it, to suffer it!"

"And to gather enemies on every hand. Do you realize that you are the most hated woman in France?"

"No," she said in surprise. "Am I?"

"I suspected as much while I was still in Sweden. For that reason alone I would have returned of my own accord to offer help—"

"Of your own accord?" she interrupted. "I thought that since the Royal Swedish is now yours you felt a need to pay an occasional visit."

"King Gustav sent me," he said briefly.

"May I ask why?"

"He sent me on what is really a secret mission. He has heard many rumors about the state of France and he fears that you are threatened with revolution. He assumes that the calling together of the Notables was a last desperate attempt to find a remedy, but a failure, nonetheless."

"A failure, yes. *My* failure, since it was I who forced the issue."

Fersen smiled. "But without quite knowing what it was all about?"

"What a fool you think me, Axel!"

"No, Marie. I think your trouble is unawareness on the one hand, defiance on the other, and between the two, boredom."

"You see?" she cried dramatically. "You *can* say horrible things and not make me really angry. I wonder why that is, Axel?"

A look of confusion crossed his face. Say it, say it! she tried to will him. Admit that you know the reason is my love for you. Admit it, admit it!

"And so," he went on quickly, "King Gustav sent me to watch and make reports. He considered me an excellent choice. No, no,

210

I am not flattering myself. I own a regiment which is engaged in the services of the French government. I wear the uniform of a French colonel. I have a legitimate reason for being here. Not even my own ambassador will suspect the true reason. What King Gustav wants to know, in the first place, is why you are hated so much, and what can be done to remedy it."

Marie Antoinette sighed. "If I am as badly hated as you say, it all began with the trial of Cardinal de Rohan."

"But your innocence was completely established."

"So was the cardinal's," she said bitterly.

"In Sweden we heard many evil stories of your part in the cardinal's arrest and trial. What I want is the truth. Begin at the beginning. Tell me everything, even if it pains you."

Speaking lightly, Marie Antoinette gave him precise details of what had happened up to the cardinal's arrest.

"The trial," she went on, "was delayed again and again until all the conspirators had been arrested. The main ones were the woman Lamotte, an actress by the name of Nicole d'Oliva and a forger calling himself Retaux, who had gone abroad and could not be found for some time. Meanwhile the cardinal remained in the Bastille, lodged there in quite comfortable apartments. *I* would have put him in a dungeon and fed him on bread and water!"

"How you hate the man, Marie!"

She brushed this aside. "Before the trial Louis begged me again to change my mind, but—"

"As I would have done, had I been here."

She smiled. "As indeed you did, Axel."

Fersen looked puzzled. "My dear Marie—"

"I often felt your presence. A too-active imagination, of course, but often you seemed to be standing at my side—" she made a face—"*lecturing* me."

"But to no avail, it seems!"

"I was pigheaded, I admit it. I knew that many members of the Parlement of Paris were relatives and friends of the cardinal, which was why he had chosen to stand trial before the Parlement. I also knew that most of the others were enemies of the crown— wealthy aristocrats, mind you, not poor peasants."

"It is from such groups that we must expect the greatest danger," Fersen commented.

"Even if I was pigheaded," she went on, "it would have been impossible at that stage to keep the affair of the necklace quiet.

211

I felt that without a trial to bring out the truth people would have believed that I had indeed ordered the necklace. Worse than that, they would have learned that the cardinal had paid for it and would have been sure that I had had a love affair with the despicable creature." She broke off abruptly. "Oh Axel, I am so *sick* of the wretched story. *Must* I go on with it?"

"Please."

"Very well. Retaux confessed to having forged my signature and to having written letters supposedly from me to the Lamotte woman, letters which completely deceived the cardinal. Lamotte was of course the ringleader. She was an adventuress of the most daring kind. She played on the cardinal's weakness for women and his well-known desire to gain my favor. She became his mistress and convinced him that she and I were firm friends. She took money from him, money which he thought he was lending to me. Finally she persuaded him that, secretly, I wanted the necklace, and he was fool enough to believe that by helping me to get it he would endear himself to me. The actress, Nicole d'Oliva, confessed to having impersonated me and met the cardinal late at night in the park. The trial proved that he was the greatest of fools and had been shockingly duped. He was completely exonerated and freed. He left the court surrounded by a great silly mob of cheering supporters."

"And you, entirely innocent, became the real victim."

"Yes. There were demonstrations against me, organized, no doubt, by the cardinal's friends. Verses and pamphlets were issued by the dozen, and still continue. I had been called Madame Deficit before; now the name became widespread. Disgusting gossip started. The cardinal helped to spread the story that he had been my lover. He boasted of it! Louis sent him into exile and appointed a new Grand Almoner. All that did was arouse more sympathy for the cardinal." A lump rose in her throat, tears sprang to her eyes. "Oh Axel, you make me so miserable, forcing me to remember all this!"

"I had to know, Marie."

She flung herself into his arms and sobbed convulsively. He held her quietly for a moment, stroking her hair, then he tilted up her chin and swiftly brushed his cheek against her tear-stained face. Still sobbing, she clung to him all the more.

"This," he said gently, "is hardly the haughty, dignified Marie

Antoinette I know." Smiling, he added, "Have you told me the sober truth, or have you exaggerated?"

She stepped back from him angrily.

"Ah," he said, laughing.

"You wretch!"

"The sober truth, then?"

"If you doubt my words, consult the records."

"I shall need to in any case. King Gustav wants a full report of the trial."

"And when you make your full report, do you intend to state that my innocence has made me the most hated woman in France?"

Fersen hesitated. "Well—yes."

"I think I can read your mind! You will say that I made a grave mistake when I insisted on the cardinal's arrest?"

"*Did* you make a grave mistake, Marie?"

"I have admitted it to nobody, not even to myself. But yes, I made a grave mistake. But how was I to know? Tell me, Axel, how was I to know?"

"It is easy to be wise after the event," Fersen said. "The real mistake, though, was your hatred."

"Ha! Another lecture now!"

"Hatred," he said gently, "is such a terrible emotion. Your hatred harmed *you*, not the cardinal."

"I am what I am. You will never change me."

"All I propose to do is make you aware of your danger. You will make the change yourself, then."

"What do you really mean by danger? Not very much, surely! I am hated, I admit, but not as much as you think. I have, I hope, the dignity and pride of a true queen, the ability to ignore it all."

Fersen looked at her in silence.

Quickly and urgently she said, "Tell me you believe none of the stories that are being circulated. Please, Axel!"

"I know and believe only one thing, Marie. You are, always have been, always will be, a faithful wife."

How insistent he was on maintaining only friendship between them!

"A faithful wife!" she cried. "People must doubt it when they look at Louis. Fatter than ever, lethargic, a disgusting glutton."

Once again Fersen looked at her in silence.

"You blame me for what he has become?" she demanded.

213

"Do you blame yourself?"

"No, but you make me feel I ought to."

"It might be better if I went away again."

"No, not that, Axel, please!" She touched his arm lightly. "I will do anything you ask, anything! Follow your advice in all things, Axel, all things! If only you knew what a difference it makes, this return of yours! And to know that you are able to remain here—it makes my life so full, so splendid. With you here I shall never, I promise, be bored again."

"You make me very happy, Marie," Fersen said softly.

"Tell me there'll never be any need for you to go away again!"

His face clouded momentarily. "I hope and pray there never will be."

His unspoken meaning was clear to her. Very well, she too would ignore, as he was trying so hard to ignore, the deep demands of the personal love that lay between them. Anything, anything, she thought desperately, to keep him here.

"I hope and pray the same," she told him earnestly.

Axel von Fersen came often to Versailles, where he mingled with the crowd and took an inconspicuous part in court activities. Everyone seemed to accept him for what, on the surface, he was, a foreign soldier who had served in the American war, a colonel now, smart and punctilious in his French uniform, taking a belated interest in the regiment which his father had bought for him. Gabrielle de Polignac, of course, smiled and made stupid remarks about the pangs of unrequited love, while Provence, watchful as ever, contented himself with an occasional sneer. Such, however, was Fersen's discretion, that his name never once appeared in the salacious verses which continued to be circulated in Paris. Marie questioned Gabrielle about this, Gabrielle who knew every scrap of gossip, both of Paris and Versailles.

"Why?" she demanded. "Why? One would expect Provence to make the most of Axel's presence."

Gabrielle smiled lazily. "Provence spreads many stories he knows to be untrue, but for an obvious reason he will never spread a story about you and Monsieur de Fersen."

"I can think of no obvious reason, Gabrielle."

"He hopes for the downfall of the present King, but being wiser than you think, he fears that eventually every member of the royal family may have to seek exile. Sweden would make a safe retreat. Fersen is very close to the King of Sweden. A word from Fersen and Provence would never be admitted there. It is as simple as that, Marie, or so I believe."

"Eventual exile for every member of the royal family? What nonsense, Gabrielle!"

"I have eyes and ears."

"An alarmist—you of all people!"

"Not an alarmist yet. Merely curious and watchful. We shall soon know which way the cat is going to jump."

"But to become so serious—*you!*"

Gabrielle chuckled softly. "I have grown used to easy living. I wish to continue to enjoy it, here or . . . abroad."

Suddenly Marie Antoinette thought that she was beginning to dislike Gabrielle very much, Gabrielle and her friends, so many of whom, with their empty-headed emphasis on pleasure, were not only bores but parasites. Axel, of course, was responsible for this change of heart. Of course he was! He had never spoken against Gabrielle, but he had never liked her, had always seen her as she herself was now beginning to see her. I should never have brought her to court, Marie Antoinette told herself; that was another of my mistakes.

"The Dauphin was not very well last night," Gabrielle remarked. "I thought you ought to know."

"He was better this morning," Marie Antoinette said quickly, wanting with all her heart to believe it. "He is not as sickly as you seem to think."

Gabrielle, for some time now, had been governess of the royal children, an important appointment, but one which she failed fully to appreciate. Of course she did! It meant that she must keep careful watch over the Dauphin, even sleep in his bedchamber, a circumstance which placed a restraint on other nocturnal activities.

"The physicians are no happier about his health than I am," Gabrielle went on. "They are afraid of the disease that killed his grandparents."

This disease, Marie Antoinette knew, was tuberculosis, but, terror-stricken at the thought of it, she tried always to ignore it.

"We must hope for the best," Gabrielle said kindly. "The child has at least a healthy mother. He may grow out of it."

Two weeks after his return, Fersen, alone with Marie Antoinette for only the second time in that period, gave her his opinion of what he considered to be the state of France.

"France is sick," he said, "and the sickness is a sort of high fever which no doctor has yet been able to diagnose correctly and treat."

Soberly she asked, "Tell me in what way I have contributed to the sickness."

"By doing nothing, Marie."

"Except on occasion the wrong thing!"

"I think you did the right thing when you influenced Louis to summon the Notables, even though it failed." His eyes twinkled. "I suspect, though, you scarcely knew what you were doing. Who, for instance, *are* the Notables?"

"Since you know already, why ask?" she parried.

"The Queen of France," he chided her, "should know more about French affairs than a mere outsider."

She laughed dryly. "I confess I once began a study of French history, but I soon grew tired of it." She paused and frowned. "I persuaded Louis to call the Notables together simply because he was against it."

"You have still not told me who the Notables are."

She smiled and affected the voice of a little girl repeating a lesson. "The Assembly of Notables is made up of nobles, bishops and magistrates. It had not been called together for many many years." She abandoned the little-girl voice. "Louis, who is a student of history rather than a maker of history, told me all about it. He was not in favor of calling the Notables together—the idea was Calonne's—because he felt that for a king to bow to the will of a group of aristocrats would mean an end of divine right."

"But Louis is a most liberal-minded king."

"He is also a king with hundreds of years of tradition behind him. He fancies himself as father of his people, even if his people no longer want a father."

"May I ask how you gained your way?"

Marie Antoinette found herself blushing. After the birth of her last child she had revolted against further expression of that sort of duty. To resume it had not been easy, and Louis' gratitude after so long a denial had sickened rather than touched her.

"It is easy," she evaded, "to gain your way with a weak husband. I gained it out of perversity, yet I was afraid Louis might be right. What understanding have I, with my upbringing, of anything but absolute rule?" She frowned as she grappled with vague ideas beyond her comprehension. "Perhaps it is just as well the move was a failure and now the country as a whole is to be represented by the Estates General."

216

"How did it fail?" Fersen asked.

"It failed when Calonne took the stand that the Notables were the King's servants and must do as they were told. He told them flatly that the King was the King and would do as he pleased, whatever they decided. Louis dismissed him and appointed Brienne in his place."

"At your suggestion?"

"Yes. It was a bad appointment, I admit it. But Brienne tried his best. He was helpless because he could think of only one solution, more tax edicts, and he got no help from the other ministers. They hated him because he wanted to reduce their expenditure."

"And Louis remained mostly aloof?"

"Aloof and sulky, but he did dismiss the Notables. After that the Parlement of Paris refused to register new tax laws and declared that they must have the approval of the whole nation. In short, they wanted the convocation of the Estates-General. Louis sent the Parlement into exile at Troyes." She laughed quite merrily. "Oh yes, Axel, I know all about the Estates-General. There are three Estates, the clergy, the nobility, the commoners. It is a hundred and seventy years since a king of France convoked them. Well, Louis refused to listen and made Brienne his prime minister."

"At your suggestion?"

"Yes, but only because I wanted someone else to take the blame for whatever happened. All the other ministers resigned and Louis withdrew once more to sulk. Agitators began holding meetings all over Paris. The cry was for the convocation of the Estates-General. I tried to make Louis see that he was trapped. He had very little money and no means of raising any. He compromised by bringing back the Parlement and asked them to debate the question of a loan. There was a terrible scene. The debate went on for seven hours. Poor Louis was present, trying to look kingly and dignified. He realized that things were going against him and lost his head."

"Yes," said Fersen, "we heard about that. He told the Keeper of the Seals that the loan had a majority vote and ordered him to register it."

Marie Antoinette nodded. "Everybody started shouting at once and Louis left them to it. I felt very sorry for him. He raged for a time, then he wept." The sight of him then had reminded her of the boy who had failed so miserably on their wedding night and all the other countless nights that had followed. "His condition humiliated me," she went on, "and I reminded him that come

217

what may he was forgetting that he, and he alone, was the supreme head of state, the law-giver."

She paused, seeing in her mind's eye the scene which had taken place in her drawing-room, seeing Louis as he brushed his tears away and shot up his head, the wig on it crazily aslant. He had seemed to swell, had become frighteningly immense; had regained a ridiculous pathetic dignity.

"He thanked me for reminding him, Axel, and after that he was like a man in the grip of a terrible fever. It lasted for several weeks. He made an attempt to reform the whole law-giving system. He roared that Parlement was in revolt against the King. Very well, he would deal with this disgruntled set of aristocrats who feared they might lose position and money. With a stroke of the pen— what a flourish that was!—he took from the Parlement of Paris, and all the other Parlements, the right to register royal edicts. What a howl of rage went up! Demonstrations broke out everywhere. Aristocrats who should have known better organized the people against the King. And it was I who was blamed, I whose effigy was burned in the streets of Paris. In the end, when it seemed that we were on the verge of revolution, Louis collapsed. He could hardly eat. Poor Louis, that was a terrible hardship. He said sorrowfully, 'I have lost my taste for food, God damn the Parlements!' I sent Brienne to him with orders to resign unless Louis would convoke the Estates General. Louis agreed. Since then he has eaten quite well, much too well."

Smiling, Fersen said, "And when I asked you to tell me about the state of France you shrugged, sounded bored and said, 'I imagine the government is more deeply in debt than ever.' What a fraud you are. You have been trying your best all the time to find a solution."

She laughed shortly. "I was playing the part the world has always associated with me, the part of a frivolous, indifferent woman. In reality I would still have played that part, but for you."

She could see that he was trying to ignore this.

"We must do our best, from now on," he said gravely, "to change the people's hatred, to make you the most loved woman in France. And with God's help we will."

"Perhaps I made another mistake in forcing Louis to convoke the Estates General."

"No," Fersen told her, "the world we know is changing. Louis

218

helped in the change when he took part in the American war. The people must have a say in government."

"At the expense of divine right?"

"Even at the expense of that, Marie." He frowned for a moment. "I, like you, have always believed in divine right, so I can appreciate the struggle through which Louis is passing."

"Well, enough for now," she laughed. "My head is whirling. Take me for a drive in the park, Axel."

He shook his head. "That would not be wise."

"Exactly what I expected you to say!" She rose. "Since I must drive alone, drive alone I shall." She walked to the door, turned and on a sudden impulse said, "Axel, we will have to face it sometime."

"Face what, Marie?"

"The undeniable fact that we love and want each other." She gave him a bright smile. "*Au revoir,* my dear."

TWO

Louis came slowly into the queen's drawing-room followed by Fersen. Looking from one to the other, Marie Antoinette was struck by the contrast: Louis heavy-footed, dull-eyed, wheezing like an old man; Axel alert, bright-eyed, younger in appearance than his thirty-three years.

"Well, our troubles are possibly at an end," Louis remarked, but quite without enthusiasm. "Necker has agreed to return. He showed no surprise when I asked him to become my comptroller-general again. Indeed, he came to me well prepared, with many apt suggestions."

Marie Antoinette hid a smile. Of course Necker showed no surprise; of course he came well prepared. She had talked to him first, but pleased as she was with his decision she wondered if she had, this time, done the right thing. Necker was probably the best of a bad lot and his re-appointment would be popular with the people if not with the nobility.

Louis placed his bulk in a chair, a too-slender chair that creaked as he sat on it.

"Necker," he said, "made one condition before agreeing."

Well aware of the condition, Marie Antoinette looked with tactful inquiry at her husband.

"He insists," Louis went on, "he insists that the Third Estate shall be made up of as many members as the First and Second combined."

"Really?" she said, as if in surprise.

"It will cause a lot of protest from the clergy and the nobility," Louis added, with a watery smile, "but as Necker pointed out, both groups are aristocrats, so aristocrats and commoners will be equally represented." He sighed deeply. "I think I have less to fear from the commoners than the aristocrats."

Marie Antoinette agreed. She was inclined, as Louis was, to lean more to the people than to the aristocracy. *The people . . .* she pondered. Always a mystery, always an unknown quantity. Upbringing had taught her that they had existed always to serve monarchy. Well, perhaps they would serve it now, to greater advantage, when they learned that both King and Queen placed more faith in their loyalty than in that of the aristocracy.

Louis rose suddenly, swinging the slender chair from beneath him as he did so. For a moment, in a little fit of impotent rage, he raised it above his head and shook it.

"It would give me the greatest satisfaction," he cried tremulously, "to smash this chair across somebody's shoulders."

Marie Antoinette asked quietly, "Have you anyone particular in mind, Louis?"

Louis' face crumpled. "Myself, just myself." He dropped the chair and turned quickly to Fersen. "Forgive me, my dear fellow. You must think me a sorry spectacle, by no means a kingly figure." And with a quick, unhappy glance at Marie Antoinette he hurried from the room.

"I do not propose," she said, looking stonily at Fersen, "to apologize for Louis."

"But you do propose," he said gently, "to give him sympathy and understanding."

"I—!" She shrugged, said obediently, "Yes, Axel, of course."

They were alone together for the first time since her impulsive reference to the thing which she was still convinced they would have to face. Was it because of her impulsiveness that he had absented himself from Versailles? With his regiment stationed at Valenciennes it was, of course, necessary that he should sometimes go there, but still . . .

"I assume," Fersen said, talking quickly, "that you spoke to Necker before Louis asked him to return?"

"Yes, Axel. Were you with Louis when he received Necker?"

"Of course not. I was waiting in the anteroom. Louis had asked me to wait on him this afternoon. He seems to have forgotten that. He looked at me vaguely when he came out with Necker and—well—brought me along here."

"And here abandoned you."

"Necker," he went on hurriedly, "returns at a time when many other men, however ambitious for power, would shirk the task. The price of bread has gone up; the worst weather for years has destroyed half the harvest, and—"

"Even God is against the monarchy," Marie Antoinette interjected.

"For the rest, there has never been so much unemployment. Half the people are out of work in the big towns, in Paris at least a quarter. Shares have fallen disastrously on the bourse. The people are ripe for mischief. Necker will be a magician if he can change things for the better before the Estates General meet."

"Are you telling me I have done the wrong thing again?"

"There was nothing else you could do, Marie. We can only wait and see."

As they waited, Louis stirred himself to make one definite, surprising move. He decreed that all male taxpayers over the age of twenty-five should vote in the election of the deputies, and he suggested that the deputies, once elected, should draw up a list of the people's grievances. "I am," he said, "the benevolent father of my people." But Mercy, who discussed this with Marie Antoinette, thought it an action likely to open the floodgates of revolution.

"For the first time," he said, "the French people will have complete freedom of expression. By this well-meaning foolishness, his Majesty will set the common people talking. I think I know the French. How they will talk and argue and theorize! Good heavens, my dear, they will probably never stop for a hundred years or more!"

"What else would you have Louis do?" she asked.

Mercy shrugged. "I confess I feel as helpless as the next man, and am most happy to be no more than an outsider. All I can suggest is that in giving the people liberty he should move slowly. The wine of liberty is a heady drink and should not be taken in great intoxicating gulps."

When at last the elections were over and the deputies of the three Estates were preparing to gather at Versailles, Marie Antoinette remembered Mercy's words. The talk, the arguing, the theorizing had begun with a vengeance. In Paris, even in the normally quiet town of Versailles, excitement had reached fever pitch. Freedom of expression had meant a new flood of agitators, a new flood of pamphlets. Demand after demand was issued—no more *lettres-de-cachet,* strict secrecy of letters carried by the post office, abolition of all monopolies, permission for commoners to seek employment in government offices . . .

"It almost seems that I have unwittingly started a revolution," Louis said wonderingly. "Well, well, it is a bloodless revolution. Aunt Adelaide, by the way, is very cross."

"You have seen her, then?" Marie Antoinette asked sharply.

Louis' face fell. "How indiscreet of me to mention it! It was not by my own wish, my dear Marie. She came to Versailles yesterday. She raged and stormed, but I do assure you, I refused to listen and I sent her—hum—packing. Pon my word I did!"

"What made her cross?"

"She resents the sweeping away of aristocratic privilege."

Marie Antoinette had almost forgotten the old-maid aunts, in spite of the harm they had done her. There were only two of them now, Madame Adelaide and Madame Victoire, still living in retreat, as it was politely called.

"Louis," she said, "something should be done to silence Madame Adelaide altogether."

"Would you have me throw her in the Bastille?" he laughed.

Louis was in quite a good mood. It was a long time since she had heard him laugh like that. He had, of course, enjoyed a good morning's hunting. One of the best for years, he'd told her. How easy it was for him to forget the cares of state while hunting and, if the hunting was good, be childishly happy. She herself, no matter what she did, could no longer forget the cares of state. It was, she thought angrily, a strange metamorphosis.

"Aunt Adelaide is not such a dangerous enemy as you think," he added.

"Nor Provence?"

"Provence still sneers at you behind your back, and it troubles me, but he is with us now in all we do."

"His one concern being to save his skin!"

Louis ignored this. "And Elizabeth, you know, is quite a good friend now."

"Only because she is scrupulously pious, Louis. If only you knew how weary I am of her Christian charity! It gives her face such a long-suffering expression, too!"

Louis laughed a little, but grew quickly serious. "Your real enemy now, and mine also, is Orleans."

Axel had said the same. The others, compared with the Duc d'Orleans, were no more dangerous than a swarm of insects on the night air. This cousin of Louis', Axel said, was an ever-present threat to the safety of the royal family. He was shrewd and cunning, even brave. He would never run for cover whatever happened; he would remain and reach out, through his popularity with the people, for a position of power.

Marie Antoinette had found Louis Philippe, Duc d'Orleans,

amusing enough in the early days and had enjoyed many of his balls at the Palais Royal. Amusing enough, that was, until, like Provence, he had tried to make love to her. She could still remember his quick flush of anger, the hatred in his eyes, when she had repulsed him. His antagonism had grown really pronounced when she had influenced Louis against making him Grand Admiral of the Fleet. Well, perhaps she *had* been activated by spite, but everybody knew that he had no real ability for naval command. A real ability, though, for sinister intrigue, *that* was obvious. It was at the Palais Royal, as Axel said, headquarters of the Orleans clique, that the greatest danger lay.

"Oh Louis," she said, close to the breaking point, "I wish I could have remained asleep."

"Asleep, my dear?"

"I was thinking of the old story of the sleeping princess, but *she* awoke to happiness, *I* only to confusion and despair."

"You talk in riddles," Louis said, as if humoring her.

"Until recently I was asleep and dreaming, dreaming silly frivolous dreams. It was easier, bored as I was with it at times, than the reality of today."

Louis' face softened. "Poor little Marie, what an unfair weight I have placed on your shoulders. I have not given you much happiness, have I?"

"I have not given you much, Louis."

"You have given me more than I deserve. What do I really care if the monarchy is tottering? Why struggle to save it? Let it fall, let it! We might have a chance of real happiness together then, just ourselves and the children."

"A vain dream, Louis."

"We might yet realize it!" he ran on eagerly. "Let us promise each other that if things become too insupportable we will abdicate and bury ourselves somewhere in the depths of the country."

"Escaping, you think, from our responsibilities?"

"I—" Louis hung his head. "The King is father of his people. A father has responsibilities. How you shame me, Marie." He squared his shoulders with pathetic resolution. "I have high hopes of the Estates General."

"I wish I felt the same, Louis." It was as if a cold hand gripped her heart. "I'll try and feel the same." And she echoed Fersen's words. "We can only wait and see."

THREE

MARIE ANTOINETTE BENT ANXIOUSLY OVER THE DAUPHIN'S BED AND laid her hand lightly on his brow. The physician's urgent message had reached her just as she was about to join Louis and accompany him to the religious ceremony which was to precede tomorrow's opening of the Estates General. The pallid, lifeless look of her eight-year-old elder son shocked her deeply. She glanced up at the physician who stood in silence at the other side of the bed. His somber face filled her with alarm.

The Dauphin smiled up at her. "How pretty you look, Mama."

"Today we open the Estates General," she told him. "A woman must look her best for so important an occasion."

"Today is not the opening," the boy said, pretending to be stern. "That is tomorrow. Today you and Papa go to church with the three Estates to ask God's blessing."

"I stand corrected, Monsieur," she said solemnly.

"You were worried because of me, Mama, and you forgot."

"Oh, not as worried as all that, darling. A few days in bed is all you need. It was just that I was, as usual, scatter-brained." She kissed him quickly. "Thank you for thinking me pretty."

"Are you afraid, Mama?"

"Afraid, darling? Of all those deputies?" The child was gazing at her with the wise eyes of an adult. "Nervous, oh yes, nervous, but not afraid."

"Nor am I, Mama."

His words, the tone of his voice, the resigned acceptance, struck terror in her heart.

"I want to watch the procession," he said. "May I?"

"Your Majesty—" the physician began, in mild protest.

"His Royal Highness," she said haughtily, "shall watch the procession from a couch on the balcony. Madame Elizabeth will be in attendance."

She kissed the boy again and went lightly to the door, where she turned to wave. The physician followed her from the room.

"Well, Monsieur?" she demanded, a sob in her throat.

"A serious setback, your Majesty."

"*How* serious?"

"His Majesty the King should be told without delay."

"Are you warning me to prepare for the worst?"

The physician hesitated. "I shall call the other physicians together, your Majesty. An immediate consultation."

She dismissed him with a curt gesture. It would be wiser, she decided, not to tell Louis yet. The news might unnerve him completely, might even make him refuse to attend today's ceremony. She returned for a moment to her own apartments. A quick glance in the mirror told her that her face showed nothing of the grief she felt. All she could see was a bright mask, the heron's feather in her hair and the silver-spangled skirt below the close-fitting purple velvet tunic. She called her ladies and attended by them went to join Louis.

"You are several minutes late," he said fretfully.

"A Queen's privilege, Louis."

His face was twitching nervously. "I like the feather. It adds a touch of simplicity to the extravagance of the rest of your attire."

"You think it too extravagant?"

"I think it most queenly," he replied, uneasily.

"Would you rather we went in rags to impress the Third Estate?"

"Dear me no. We must make a brave showing. After all, look at *my* clothes, only look at them!"

For the first time Marie Antoinette really looked at him and had difficulty in repressing a shudder. He was a mass of cloth-of-gold bespattered with diamonds. The whole effect made him look larger and bulkier than ever.

"You think I look like a King?" he asked pathetically.

"Unmistakably," she said gently.

They were joined by Provence and Artois, Provence jaunty, Artois rather sullen. Brilliantly arrayed attendants flocked about them as they made their way to the waiting coaches. When the procession began she glanced up at the balcony and saw the pale intense face of the Dauphin. She hoped he was enjoying this elaborate display. She must remember to ask him later what he thought of the pages in their brilliant liveries, and the royal falconers, each with a bird on his wrist, and Papa's dazzling cloth-of-gold. Tears pricked her eyes. Perhaps God was being merciful. One must try to look at it like that.

At the church of Notre Dame de Versailles the members of the three Estates were waiting. She acknowledged that she was probably on the point of hysteria, but how ridiculous they all looked, standing there with lighted candles in their hands.

Next came the procession on foot through the streets to the Cathedral of St. Louis. The deputies of the Third Estate led the way, those of the other two Estates followed, while Marie Antoinette and Louis, walking side by side, came last, following immediately on the heels of the Archbishop of Paris.

"I do hope," Louis whispered, "that we shall have no further trouble."

"Has there been trouble already, Louis?"

"Just a simple matter of dress," he said heatedly. "How quick they are to suspect insult."

"Dress? Insult?"

"The deputies of the Third Estate, confound them! Naturally the Estates must be distinguished by different attire, or nobody would know which was which. All three are wearing black coats and breeches, as councillors of state should, but heaven help us all, the clergy and the nobility have gold trimming on their coats, and the deputies of the Third Estate seem to think it a special form of heresy. I am beginning to regret my generosity to the Third Estate, by heaven I am!"

Louis was talking too much and too quickly, a sure sign that he was nervous and alarmed.

Cheering rose in the distance, wild, excited, tumultuous.

"That," Louis complained, "is for our querulous gentlemen of the Third Estate."

Marie Antoinette listened for a moment. "No, Louis. The people are cheering Orleans. Listen!"

Louis looked at her darkly. "What a rat he is, marching there with the Third Estate."

"Orleans, with the Third Estate?"

"A sudden crafty decision. He should be with the nobility, but no, he made a public announcement. He claims that he has been elected to the Third Estate, that by choice he is a commoner. And there he is now, marching, marching, and grinning from ear to ear, I vow!"

At the cathedral the royal party was held up while deputies of the Third Estate protested loudly at what they called the indignity of being asked to sit at the back of the cathedral *behind* the aristocracy. At one moment it even seemed as if a riot might break out.

"Such pettiness," Louis grumbled. "They care nothing for France, only for their vanity. Dear heaven, what have I done!"

"Please ignore them," Marie Antoinette begged. All she could think of was the pale intense face of her dying son. "For my sake, Louis, please!"

Presently, when the master of ceremonies had argued with the affronted deputies, and less touchy members of the Third Estate had joined him, peace was restored sufficiently for Marie Antoinette and Louis to take their places. The peace, however, was short-lived, for one of the bishops, addressing the congregation in ringing tones, spoke unwisely of the 'homage' of the First Estate, the 'respect' of the Second and the 'most humble supplications' of the Third. A heavy rumble of indignation rose from the back of the cathedral.

"No doubt they will debate these grievances, these so-called slights, when they meet in solemn assembly tomorrow," Louis groaned.

Immediately on the return to Versailles Marie Antoinette hurried to the Dauphin's apartment. There she was met by Gabrielle de Polignac. Gabrielle, whose mood was usually so untrammelled, had tears in her eyes, and without a word she threw her arms round Marie Antoinette.

"The physicians have had their consultation," Marie Antoinette said tonelessly.

"Yes."

"They hold out no hope."

"My poor Marie, none."

Still tonelessly, she said, "God is good. Not for my elder son the trials and tribulations of the future."

"The physicians want you to tell the King."

"Have they spoken to anyone but you, Gabrielle?"

"No."

"Very well. I shall tell Louis, but not until after tomorrow. He needs what strength he has for whatever tomorrow holds."

She went into the bedchamber where the Dauphin, after the excitement of watching the procession, lay pale and languid in the canopied bed.

"Did the people cheer you, Mama?" he asked.

She had heard no cheering on her own behalf. "Indeed they did, darling."

228

"Wildly?"

"They were beside themselves with joy."

"Please ask Papa to water my vegetable garden."

"Of course, darling."

He closed his eyes and turned his head on the pillow. Unable to control herself a moment longer she went quickly from the room. In the corridor she came face to face with Louis.

"Is anything the matter?" he asked.

She was thankful that by keeping well away from him his short-sighted eyes could see nothing of her distress. Clenching her hands she tried to keep her voice level and unemotional.

"Well, is there?" he said pettishly. "You know how anxious I am about him. My page told me he was in bed."

"Only a slight chill, Louis. He watched the procession from the balcony. The wind was bitter. I thought it better he should go to bed at once. Please don't disturb him."

"Just one little peep, my dear."

"No!" she said, her voice rising.

"Something *is* the matter." Louis came closer, took her by the shoulders and stared at her. "There are tears in your eyes, Marie. For pity's sake—"

She flung her arms round him and clung to him.

"I gave France a dauphin," she sobbed. "God has decided that France is unworthy of such a gift. God has been kind. We must think of it like that, Louis. We must, we must!"

Holding her gently, he said somberly, "We have another son, another dauphin."

"Louis, he wants you to water his vegetable garden."

"Yes. Very well. When I was his age I had a garden myself. It was my own entirely. It was all I ever wanted. People laughed at me. Fancy wanting a small piece of waste land when the whole park was my playground. But it was mine. My own territory. All I ever wanted, that little plot of land. Never did I want the whole kingdom of France."

He released himself from her clinging arms and went on tiptoe to the inner room. He spent an hour with his son, and returned to him again in the evening. Only when the physicians assured him that the end would not be just yet did he agree to go to bed.

"It is France I am watching die," he told Marie Antoinette. "The France I thought I knew, still love and would save if I could."

229

"If you can, Louis. Put it that way. Say, 'If I *can*.' Say it, Louis!"

"If I can," he repeated obediently, but there was no heart in him.

The next morning, pale, grave, yet carrying about him an unaccustomed air of quiet dignity, Louis went, with Marie Antoinette at his side, to preside over the new Assembly which had gathered in the large Salle des Menus Plaisirs. The three Estates rose as he entered the hall and greeted him with a brief staccato cry of Long live the King! But no acknowledgement whatever was made of the Queen's presence. Dignity, Marie Antoinette thought, I must preserve my useless dignity. Louis doffed his high-feathered hat and seated himself on the throne. Conscious of the many curious eyes centered on her, she wondered if the diamonds in her hair and at her throat were a mistake for a bankrupt Queen. They would in any case remind many people of the Cardinal de Rohan scandal. She held her head high. What of it, she thought defiantly, what of it!

The deputies seated themselves. A deep and deadly silence followed. Not a single cough, not a single throat-clearing disturbed it. Marie Antoinette, seated in the armchair which had been placed for her near the throne, glanced anxiously at Louis. After a slight hesitation he rose to address the Assembly. She rose also and ignored the quick almost angry gesture with which he expressed the wish for her to remain seated.

Louis cleared his throat. "Gentlemen, this is the most important day in my life and in yours . . ."

As his voice gathered strength and confidence, Marie Antoinette's mind flew back to her son. She remembered the boy's request, only this morning, that Monsieur le Comte de Fersen should wait on him. Dear Axel, she thought, it seemed an age since she had last seen him; there were even moments when it seemed that he was just a figment of the imagination. He had come up, she knew, from Valenciennes, and was staying at his modest quarters in Paris. She had written him a hasty note stressing the boy's request. Her eyes strayed round the hall, lingered on the tall colonnades, the gilded walls, rose to the delicately painted oval of the ceiling, returned, after a glance at the sea of faces, to Louis, rather breathless now, but still surprisingly resolute.

He was speaking of the inequality of the burden of taxation, admitting that he had made many mistakes, vowing that with God's help and the help of the three Estates he would now make a braver showing.

"And this I solemnly promise you," he concluded, "I shall endeavor to be not only a father to my people but an understanding friend."

He stood there in silence for a moment, his head and shoulders bathed in a beam of sunlight from one of the windows. Unconsciously he remained in it, a kingly, heaven-inspired figure, while a spontaneous burst of cheering rose.

Marie Antoinette waited for him to sit down before doing so herself, but still the Assembly ignored her. She fought back her tears and held her head still higher. The haughty Austrian woman! Well, why not? Her enemies had done their work well, but not by a single flicker of an eyelid would she let them see the aching despair she felt.

The Keeper of the Seals rose, rather in the manner of a puppet jerked up on strings, and spoke in a faltering voice of the King's wish to see taxation borne fairly by all three Estates of the realm. No response whatever greeted his words, and still falteringly he enlarged on his Majesty's plans for criminal reform as well as complete freedom of individual expression. A shuffling of feet was the only response. Moistening his lips he ended by pleading for the setting aside of all petty hatreds, jealousies and resentments.

A little spate of applause trickled through the hall, applause which indicated the happiness of the deputies to hear the last of *him,* applause which came to an abrupt end when the comptroller-general of finance, Jacques Necker, rose to his feet. He looked round the crowded hall with all the assurance in the world and a smile for everyone, and then began an involved and tedious speech which was to last for almost three hours.

Marie Antoinette listened as attentively as she could, but in spirit she was at the Dauphin's side, weeping over him yet thankful that now, that never in the future, need her son concern himself with the state of France. Out of the welter of Necker's words and elaborate phrases she learned that the expenditure of the government exceeded the income by fifty-six million livres. Though money meant as little as ever to her, she recalled that Necker, in a recent private audience, had admitted to a deficit three times as great as that. The man was either a fool, or in spite of his air of assurance, quaking with fear. Or perhaps he was simply playing, hopelessly, for time.

"And so," he concluded breezily, "his Majesty requests the loan of eighty million livres."

A murmur of indignation ran through the hall; voices rose harshly in anger. One, shrill and piercing, reached her ears. She found herself repeating the phrases silently, automatically— "The secret has leaked out . . . we have been called here to find more money for the Queen to squander . . . down with the Austrian woman!"

Louis was on his feet, stepping down from the throne. He offered her his arm, and together, not hurrying but seeming to be flying in fear, they withdrew from the Salle des Menus Plaisirs. They walked in silence, followed by silent attendants. Soon, though neither had suggested it, they went, as if by a compelling instinct, to the Dauphin's apartment. They found Fersen sitting by the bed, seemingly relaxed and chatting quietly with the boy. He rose and bowed.

"Axel, my dear fellow . . ." Louis murmured, but he had eyes only for his son.

"Monsieur de Fersen," the Dauphin said, "has been telling me about the American war."

His face, with its hollow pale cheeks, had a more wasted look. His large eyes were far too bright.

Marie Antoinette kissed his brow. "I hope Monsieur de Fersen hasn't tired you too much, darling."

Presently, leaving Louis with the boy, she went to her own apartments. Fersen dutifully accompanied her and asked her to tell him how things had gone at the opening of the Estates General.

"I had hoped," she said quietly, "that the Estates General would be a new beginning. I see now it is a certain end. I feel it in my heart."

"Tell me what happened."

She told him briefly, saying finally, "Yesterday, grievances and hurt vanity, today—open resentment. I am so weary of it all, Axel, and disgusted with myself that in bringing back Necker I have made yet another mistake."

"He had no option when it came to asking for a loan. And it is understandable that he should minimize the deficit."

232

"We-ell, yes."

Fersen laughed lightly. "On the surface the unadmitted deficit seems fantastically large, yet what does it amount to per head of your population? Six livres, no more."

"How quick you are at arithmetic!" she laughed, and laughing still, added, "So if I and Louis, and everybody else in France subscribed six livres each our troubles would be at an end. So very simple, Axel!"

"It is good to hear you laugh, Marie, make a joke."

"A joke? Was it a joke? Demand six livres from everybody in France and the revolution people persist in predicting would be on us overnight. Demand it of the deputies of the touchy Third Estate and it would start in a moment. We should never have listened to Necker when he demanded so large a representation of the Third Estate. I see that now."

"France," Fersen said thoughtfully, "is still a rich country. A deficit of six livres per head is negligible. If Necker is the clever financier we believe him to be—"

"*If* he is?" she interrupted.

"No one doubts that he is. My 'if' was stupid."

"But you have certain misgivings about him?"

"I have heard rumors. Only rumors, mind you. Rumors that he is secretly a traitor to the King he serves. It is said that he holds republican leanings and is friendly with the Duc d'Orleans. He believes, or so people say, that the monarchy is tottering and nothing can save it."

Marie Antoinette sighed. "We must refuse to listen to rumors. And Axel—" her voice shook—"I am too weary to think of anything else but my son."

In the early hours of the next morning when Marie Antoinette and Louis, having been urgently called, had sat up through the night at the Dauphin's bed, Louis said much the same.

"Did I make a brave showing at the Estates General? They all claim that I did, but I neither know nor care. My heart wasn't there in that gilded chamber, nor was my spirit. My only concern is my son."

The Dauphin rallied the next afternoon and demanded of his father a full and faithful account of the condition of his vegetable garden.

Louis hung his head. "I regret, Monsieur, that I have neglected my duties as assistant gardener."

"Papa," Marie Antoinette told the boy, "has been very occupied with the Estates General."

Occupied indeed! she thought. Louis was just as helpless now as she was, as Necker, whether he be traitor or faithful servant, was. All day long the Assembly had been in a ridiculous uproar, with the deputies of the Third Estate declaring and insisting that they and they alone represented the people. An argument had begun about the question of voting and might well go on for weeks with the Third Estate gloating over the fact that they could always cause a stalemate.

"When Papa next addresses the Estates General," the Dauphin said, "he must tell the deputies that I have decided to grow enough corn in my garden to provide bread for the whole court. That will help us all, won't it, Mama?"

"Indeed it will," she agreed.

Day followed day, week followed week, and the argument continued among the deputies. Vital issues were ignored. Vanity only was the motivating power. Report after report reached Louis. He thrust them all aside.

"Let them argue and quarrel. My son is my sole concern."

When Necker insisted on an audience Louis and Marie Antoinette granted it reluctantly.

"I am at my wits' end," Necker said. "I can make only one suggestion. The way things are going the stalemate will soon end by the ranks of the Third Estate being swelled with deserters from the privileged classes."

"Do I hear a sneer in your voice?" Marie Antoinette asked. "Are you not a member of the privileged classes yourself?"

Necker remained silent.

"Tell us what your suggestion is," she demanded.

"The privileged classes, your Majesty, the First and Second Estates, are beginning to say they can place no faith in the King."

"Can the King place faith in them?"

"Possibly not."

"Your suggestion, please, and quickly!"

"Simply this, Madame, that the King shall make a bold bid and set himself at the head of the Third Estate."

Louis spoke for the first time. "All three classes have an equal right. How can I show any one of them especial favor?"

Necker shrugged. "When the desertions begin the Third Estate will outnumber the other two. I make my suggestion because of

234

that and because certain liberal-minded deputies of the Third Estate are already hoping for it."

Marie Antoinette tried desperately to give quiet thought to the question. She recalled the touchiness of the Third Estate, the easily hurt vanity, the readiness to call her the Austrian woman. She recalled also that members of the privileged classes had already called her that, with equal contempt and hatred.

"I can see nothing but disaster in such a move," she said, "but let my husband speak for himself."

Louis was looking most unhappy. "After the sorry example of the last few weeks, what faith can I place in the Third Estate? I can place little faith in the other two, I admit. Let it be known, Necker, that I am ready to arbitrate in this senseless quarrel between the Estates."

Necker bowed and withdrew.

They learned, a day later, after yet another sleepless night at the Dauphin's side, that a man called Mirabeau, apparent leader now of the Third Estate, was declaring himself certain that the King's offer was a trap, no more, no less.

"So we have another enemy, this Mirabeau," Marie Antoinette remarked to Necker.

"I think he could be won over, Madame. Because of him, in spite of what he is saying, the Third Estate sends the King every assurance of loyalty."

"But they still want me to take sides," Louis said sadly. "Did you anticipate this, Necker, when you insisted on so large a representation for the Third Estate?"

"No," said Necker, stoutly.

"Are your secret aims for France the setting up of a republic?" Marie Antoinette asked sharply.

Necker's face was impassive. "I have no secret aims, your Majesty. His Majesty's government needs money. I am trying to find the best way of persuading the Estates General to grant it."

Louis was smiling uncertainly. "They have a president in America," he said slowly, "not a king. Would my people respect me more if I renounced my throne, became a president and lived a humble life in a middleclass Paris suburb?" He laughed softly. "After all, I have a lot in common with the working classes. I am one of the cleverest clockmakers in France and I could, if necessary, build a house. Now I wonder, I *wonder* . . ."

Marie Antoinette was watching Louis' face. Something of a struggle was going on within him.

"Unthinkable, of course," he said, "but a very bold thought. Bold, like all dreams from which one inevitably awakes. They would remember who I really was beneath the play acting. And would calling myself President of France solve our financial troubles? No, Necker, my attitude is unchanged. I will help where and when I can, and give my protection equally, as a good father should, to all my children."

Protection! Marie Antoinette thought bitterly. It was Louis, not his 'children,' who were in need of protection.

When Necker had gone she said quietly, "Louis, the only children you have in France are those I bore you."

His face crumpled. "And that out of duty, only duty."

She went to him quickly and kissed him on the cheek. "No, out of love, Louis. Please believe me." Was it a lie? She scarcely knew or cared. Axel had begged her to be kind, sympathetic, understanding. She had tried many times; now there was no need to try when private grief had brought them closer together. "Do please believe me, Louis."

Louis embraced her clumsily. "God is good to me, Marie."

The stalemate between the Estates continued. The chief trouble was still the vexed question of voting. The privileged classes clung stubbornly to the old precedent of voting by body, one vote for each Estate. That way, any two could outnumber a third. Obviously neither the First Estate nor the Second would ever side with the Third, and for this reason the Third Estate demanded a voting procedure of one vote for each individual deputy. They demanded it more insistently now, since with the desertions from the other ranks they were sure of a majority vote.

"All this bickering," Louis protested, "when bread is scarcer than ever and we are threatened by famine. But do they care about famine? Not one of them, not one of them!"

The end for the little Dauphin was now close at hand. During the last hours Marie Antoinette and Louis never left his side, agony that it was to sit and watch his gallant, pitiful struggle.

"I told myself that God was being merciful," Marie Antoinette sobbed. "I was wrong, Louis. God is cruel to make a child suffer like this. He has done nothing to hurt anyone in his life, nothing, Louis!"

236

"Perhaps it is God's intention to make us suffer as we watch and wait," Louis mumbled.

"But why? *Why?*"

Louis made a helpless gesture. "One must submit, one must try always to have faith in God."

"Who is God? *What* is God? I no longer believe in God."

She said this again when the end came, tears streaming down her cheeks, her heart cold within her. Louis, so badly in need of comfort himself, tried clumsily to comfort her.

"To lose faith now, Marie, is to lose everything."

"Everything has been lost already. What is there left to have faith in?"

"In each other," he said. "And in the few good friends we have left."

"Friends? Have we any friends?"

"We still have some loyal subjects."

"Helpless, all of them, as we are."

"We have Axel von Fersen."

"Ah yes, Axel . . ."

"And we still have two dear children, Marie."

"Yes. One a boy, the new Dauphin, heaven pity him."

"No, heaven bless him. A healthy child, my dear. Sturdy, full of life and courage. We must remember that and take comfort from it."

They retreated to their apartments and gave instructions that not on any account were they to be disturbed in their grief. Marie Antoinette herself refused even to see Fersen who sent messages meant, she knew, to comfort her. Count Mercy, refused entry like the rest, sent a message that at first infuriated her. "This is the deepest grief that a mother can suffer," his message read, "but are you sure it is not being made a means of escape from a political situation you find intolerable?" She saw in time that possibly it was, on her part as well as Louis'. Yet who would not want to escape from the bickerings and petty jealousies of the three Estates? Nevertheless she roused herself a little and went to Louis. Put heart into him, she thought; that is what Axel would say. But put heart into him for what purpose? Either he remained aloof, helpless, or he placed himself at the head of the Third Estate.

Fractiously Louis said, "I have not touched food all day."

"Nor have I, Louis."

237

"Yes, but I have a large fat body. It will fall to pieces unless I eat. And the sight of food sickens me."

Patience, she thought; I have three children left, not two.

Louis said: "The Third Estate sent a deputation an hour ago and demanded an immediate audience."

"You sent the deputation away?"

"I begged it to take pity on a father's grief and leave me in peace. The demand was repeated. What a warning that is for the future! It was then that I sent the deputation away. There was, I'm told, an infuriated cry of Down with the King. I half-expected a demonstration in the anteroom."

Anger swelled in Marie Antoinette's breast. "I came to you, Louis, to suggest that it might be wise for you to heed Necker and place yourself at the head of the Third Estate. What a stupid thought! I can see only one course. You must make yourself King in fact as well as name, not remain a helpless puppet."

He shook his head. "I am the wrong man for that. Even if I were the right man it would be too late."

She disagreed, but she felt no urge to argue. "And the fault is mine. I persuaded you to convoke the Estates General."

He showed no sign of having heard. "Marie, I hate Versailles. We insist on privacy but have no real privacy. I want to go away for a time. I have been thinking of Marly. We could go there and recover, perhaps, from our sorrow. Besides—" he added broodingly—"I always did have a good appetite at Marly."

She found herself smiling indulgently. "Anything you wish, Louis, anything . . ."

FOUR

NOT EVEN AT MARLY, THE COUNTRY RETREAT SO MUCH FAVORED BY the fourteenth Louis, was real privacy possible. Necker continually sent them news of further bickerings in the Assembly and the brothers, Provence and Artois, paid them many visits. Artois, a little shame-faced but quite obviously disliking Marie Antoinette as much as ever, was the spokesman now. He suggested a personal truce, a forgetting of old grudges. The royal family, he told her, must present a solid front to the world; the whole structure of the monarchy depended on that.

"The people are beginning to convince themselves," he said, "that they can manage without a king, but the aristocracy needs a king, otherwise there will be no aristocracy left in France."

"A feverish speech," she told him dryly. "The speech of a drowning man clutching at a straw."

"A not inconsiderable straw," Artois laughed, but his eyes were resentful. "In short, the army."

Louis, present at this 'personal truce,' showed a flicker of interest.

"I will never resort to armed force!" he cried.

Artois looked at him pityingly. "The army, with things as they are, should be kept in readiness for any emergency."

"The army is always ready for that," Louis said vaguely.

Artois returned to Marly a few days later with the news that in the King's absence the Third Estate had announced that they and they alone now represented the French nation.

"They have issued a declaration," he said heatedly. "They have decided to call themselves the National Assembly."

"A good name," Louis murmured.

Artois' eyes flashed. "But Berri, you great idiot, the declaration has been issued without royal sanction. The impertinence of it!"

Marie Antoinette quickly spoke up in support of the detested Artois. "In other words, they are saying 'To the devil with the King'!"

"They knew you would never sanction the declaration," Artois added. "It is sheer defiance."

Louis stirred uneasily, "True, true."

"One deputy asked if the Americans consulted the King of England before making their declaration of independence. Everybody cheered him. It is a revolt, a deliberate, insolent revolt."

"Well, what can I do, my dear brother? Call out the army, as you keep insisting? Oh no, not that. No, never! Take up arms against a section of my people? Never, never! I know my history only too well. That was the fatal mistake made by Charles First of England. And he went to the scaffold."

"I would rather go to the scaffold fighting!" Artois cried.

"And really," Louis went on quietly, "I see no harm in a National Assembly. Anything, anything, so long as they stop arguing and get down to real business. Let it be known that I shall feel respect for them if they find a way to feed the people."

Artois was back again two days later with further news.

"They have set up a committee to discuss the grain shortage. The result? More talk, more argument. Nothing whatever done to sweep away the private monopolies which are the prime cause of the shortage. Necker could do it, but he is too afraid of Orleans, who is at the back of more than one monopoly. Either afraid of him or in league with him. They are being seen together in public, Necker and Orleans. Necker smiling, smiling, caring only for the applause of the mob."

"Have you proof of all this?" Louis asked.

"No, but Necker's actions condemn him. Dismiss him, Berri. Better still, hang him, and Orleans too."

"With whom would you replace Necker?" Marie Antoinette asked.

Artois scowled. "God knows."

"Yourself, perhaps?"

Artois smiled slyly. "I am not as eager as all that to put my head in a noose."

Louis shook his head sadly. "Talk and argument—we are no better than the Third Estate."

"You place no faith in rumors," Artois went on, "but the latest, which I believe to be true, is that Orleans plans to seize the army and overthrow the crown. In a word, to set himself up as President of France. Do you propose to remain in hiding and allow that to happen? Do you, Berri?"

240

Louis humped up his cumbrous shoulders. "No. I shall return to Versailles. I shall call the three Estates together and address them." He pondered on this for a moment, said it would take some time to prepare his speech, quoted a date and added, "Meanwhile the Salle des Menus Plaisirs shall be closed and kept closed. There shall be no more senseless argument until I make my speech."

Marie Antoinette looked at him wonderingly. This, surely, could be little more than another sudden, soon-to-die spurt of awareness.

He said, "Let the three Estates be acquainted with my decision."

Immediately they returned to Versailles Louis began to spend long hours at his desk preparing his speech. Marie Antoinette offered to help. He sternly shook his head. "This is *my* especial task." The spurt of awareness and energy was running more strongly than she would have believed. It almost seemed as if a real king might rise from the ruin and confusion that surrounded her. Meanwhile she gave most of her time to her two remaining children, shunned Gabrielle de Polignac's *salon* and found a little comfort in the quiet companionship of the Princesse de Lamballe. She thought often of Fersen, now busy with his regiment at Valenciennes, and longed to feel the reassurance of his presence. Promising herself that all she wanted was the companionship of a friend, she wrote to him, asking him to come to Versailles.

Fersen arrived two days later, during the early evening, and entered her apartments unannounced and unnoticed, which, at Versailles, was something of a miracle. She greeted him eagerly but he seemed not to hear and stared at her for a long moment in silence, his face pale, his stillness disconcerting.

"My poor Axel," she said gently, "have I changed so much since the death of my son that you scarcely recognize me? Have I?" His continued silence alarmed her. "Is something the matter, Axel?"

"You know nothing, then, of this Tennis Court Oath?"

"This—*what*, Axel?"

"You have heard nothing? No one has told you?"

"I have been in my apartments most of the day, the children with me. For once, people have left me alone."

His voice more controlled, Fersen went on, "The deputies of

241

the Third Estate found themselves locked out of the Salle des Menus Plaisirs and set up a great roar of indignation."

"But they knew they would not be admitted until Louis was ready to address them."

"Someone must have blundered. They certainly expected to be admitted as usual."

She smiled wryly. "I can well imagine their indignation."

"A wild scene followed. It was very nearly a riot. They went in a body to the Jeu de Paume, the nearby tennis court, shouting and gesticulating as only the French can. Someone—it was Bailly, president of the new National Assembly—flung himself onto a table and declaimed the proposed oath. He asked them all to swear with him that they would never disband until the King had granted them a constitution."

"And they swore?"

"All but one man, and to save his life his friends smuggled him away."

Looking at Fersen curiously, she said, "Axel, I have never seen you so disturbed before. I can see nothing very terrible in this oath."

"Perhaps I exaggerate, Marie, but to me it is a threat, not only to the King's position, but to his very life."

A little shudder passed through her. "By that you mean also *my* position, *my* life."

"Yes." He looked at her with burning eyes. "I, too, have sworn a solemn oath. I have dedicated my life to the Queen of France. I have sworn to stand between her and all danger."

"Because you are a royalist?" she whispered. "And she a Queen?"

"Because she is a woman."

"The world is full of women."

"There is only one woman in the world," he said. "The woman I love and adore. The woman I am ready to die for at any moment."

Her eyes filled with tears. There he stood, loyal, steadfast, but uneasy now because she had forced him against his will to speak of his love. The knowledge of this filled her with shame, yet his words had brought her fully to life again. The pain and grief and fear of the last few weeks melted away. Her very soul reached out to his; an intolerable longing filled her whole being. Further denial, she told herself hotly, would be a monstrous sin. Ab-

242

jectly she was ready to plead with him, to say, For pity's sake, have done with this torment.

"To die for me would be splendid," she said brokenly, "but far rather would I have you live for me." She had moved close to him instinctively; now she lifted up her face to his. "For me and for yourself, Axel."

Gently, with all uneasiness gone, he put his arms about her. For a moment his lips touched her brow, and still he held her in a light, passionless embrace. Never before had she felt so much at peace, nor so strangely satisfied. An immeasurably deep emotion had taken hold of her. It was heaven itself.

He released her, saying in a whisper, "Thank you, Marie."

She spoke in a whisper too. "Oh, my dear, never, never, whatever the future might hold, will I forget this moment."

He said, "I want you to go to Louis. He must act, and act quickly. And wisely too, I pray God."

She went obediently, going by way of the little corridor that connected Louis' apartments with her own. She found the anterooms filled with ministers and courtiers. All fell silent at her approach, made way for her, stared curiously. The magic still on her, she barely noticed them, acknowledged not one of the bows, many of which were openly mocking. She found Louis crouching over his desk, his eyes intent, his lips pursed. He looked up vaguely from his papers.

"Louis, you know about this oath, this Tennis Court Oath?"

"Of course."

"What are you going to do?"

"Complete my speech. Deliver it at the appointed time."

"Three days from now! Oh Louis, how ridiculous!" The magic was fading rapidly. "You must act at once. Nothing quite so bad as this has happened yet."

"Yes, yes," he growled. "Artois wants me to call out the troops, scatter the deputies, arrest Orleans. You know my views on the use of armed force." He squinted up at her. "I regard it as nothing more serious than an hysterical outburst. Please leave me, Marie. This speech needs all the concentration I possess."

She refused to accompany him when he went at last to the Salle des Menus Plaisirs. She felt that to invite again the humiliations of the opening of the Estates General would be the height of stupidity.

After it was all over Fersen, present in the hall as a public spectator, gave her an account of the proceedings. Louis had told the deputies quite amiably that after a period of two months they had not been able to agree even on the question of voting. Firmness began to creep into his voice when he asserted that he, the King of France, was the defender of the laws of France. He then commanded one of his secretaries of state to read the speech and make known the royal wishes.

"The first," Fersen said, "was that the declaration made by the self-styled National Assembly, being illegal and unconstitutional, should be declared null and void. That put the Third Estate into a bad mood. I doubt if they really listened after that to the reforms Louis suggested, reforms which could bring an end to all your troubles."

"Tell me the rest," Marie Antoinette said.

"When the secretary of state had finished Louis addressed the deputies again. He seemed unaware of the sullen silence. He said he wanted them to work with him for the public good, and he added that if they saw fit to desert him he would carry on alone. After that he ordered the Assembly to break up and left the hall. The members of the First Estate followed him, but a portion of the Second remained seated with the deputies of the Third. I expected a riot. Mirabeau sprang to his feet and cried, 'Only bayonets will drive us out!' A stupid, melodramatic thing to say. They can return tomorrow, and the next day and the next, to continue their useless arguments."

"They left the hall in the end?"

"Yes."

"Did Necker make a speech?"

"Necker was absent. A silent protest, that."

"What shall we do, Axel?"

"Dismiss Necker, call out the troops, arrest Orleans and his supporters. Make the reforms Louis wants the Assembly to make."

"Louis might dismiss Necker, but he will never call out the troops. Nor will he carry out his threat to carry on alone."

"He seems to have gained a new strength, Marie."

"It will desert him at the critical moment."

As she had expected, Louis was willing to make only one move, the dismissal of Necker, but she argued against it. She felt it would be dangerous to dismiss a man whom the hoodwinked and emotionally disturbed people regarded as a hero. Louis, showing signs of weakness again, agreed with her.

"So for the time being, Necker remains," she said.

"For the time being, yes."

"What is the next move, Louis?"

She could see by his face that he was rapidly becoming his old bewildered self again. He remained silent and unhappy.

"Perhaps Artois is right, after all," she suggested.

"Perhaps, but must I keep repeating myself? I will never resort to armed force. Call it weakness if you will. *I* prefer to call it love of my people."

"You have no 'next move' to make," she said.

"Yes, Marie, I have. Perhaps you know that more than half the deputies of the Second Estate have joined the National Assembly, so—"

"There is no National Assembly. You declared it illegal."

"Yes, yes, an unauthorized body, I know," Louis said quickly, "but circumstances force me to acknowledge it. I—I shall now command the First Estate, and what is left of the Second Estate, to join it, thus creating one single body."

"With voting by head."

"What other method is there for one united assembly?"

"The revolutionaries will outnumber the rest." She realized that for the first time she had used the term. "You understand that, Louis?"

"Yes, but I am hopeful, quite hopeful."

"Of what?"

"I think wisdom may prevail."

She turned to leave him. "You are signing the death warrant of monarchy." At the door she paused. "Promise me one thing, Louis. Send troops to Paris."

"Troops!" he cried. "My dear, you know my—"

"Oh, not to take up arms against the people," she said impatiently. "Merely to keep the peace. Paris is seething with discontent. There are demonstrations all the time. The ordinary law-abiding people, the people in whom, perhaps, we can place a little faith, need protection from the hotheads."

Louis' shoulder drooped. "I see the sense of that. Troops shall be sent to Paris, then, but under orders never at any time to resort to violence."

245

"Whatever the provocation?"

"Whatever the provocation!"

News that the King had sanctioned and ordered the gathering of one united assembly seemed to please everybody except the aristocracy. Large excited crowds flocked out from Paris, stationed themselves outside the palace and chanted insistently for the King. A little timidly Louis appeared on the balcony and faced the restless milling mass. At the sight of him there rose a thunderous cry of Long live the King! A few people even cheered Marie Antoinette when she had steeled herself to stand at his side.

"One can almost believe that our troubles are at an end," Louis whispered tremulously.

It was a forced optimism and Marie Antoinette felt none of it. She sensed defiance in the cheering, not approbation. The King, for once, was an obedient little boy, bowing to the people's wishes. That was splendid, but let him be warned, the obedience must continue.

She remembered this impression when the troops, forty thousand mercenaries, began to arrive in Paris. Demonstrations were immediately organized, demonstrations which quickly became undeclared warfare between ragged groups of shrieking Parisians and the foreign soldiers who, knowing little or no French and under orders never to draw their swords, fell into an intimidated bewilderment.

With jails broken open and prisoners freed, with shops pillaged and lawlessness spreading everywhere, the National Assembly, expressing a hurt indignation, demanded that the King should withdraw the troops.

"What shall I do?" Louis asked.

"Tell the National Assembly that the troops, helpless as they are, are there for the Assembly's protection as much as anybody's."

Obediently Louis did so.

The rioting continued.

Again Louis asked, "What shall I do?"

"Tell the National Assembly this time that you will withdraw the troops if the Assembly itself will withdraw from Versailles and sit at, say, Soissons."

"Why that, my dear?"

"The unrest in the Assembly might not then spread so quickly

246

to Paris. It was a mistake to convoke the Estates General at Versailles so close to what *might* be called the stronghold of monarchy."

Again obediently Louis followed her suggestion.

The National Assembly refused to move. An impasse had been reached. Paris, by day and by night, Fersen reported, was like a boiling cauldron, with the names of Orleans and Necker, the people's heroes, on every lip. And at this stage Necker, fully confident of his power, challenged Louis by offering to resign.

"Accept," Marie Antoinette said, without the slightest hesitation.

"My dear," Louis protested feebly, "you said—"

"This," she stressed, "is a heaven-sent opportunity. You are not dismissing Necker, merely allowing him to go at his own request."

"How clever you are, Marie!"

"Clever?" She laughed derisively. "No, Louis, only desperate."

The following morning Fersen came out hastily from his lodgings in Paris. Others had arrived at Versailles before him, a stream of agitated courtiers babbling confused reports, but it was to Fersen that Marie Antoinette and Louis turned for an unbiased story of conditions in the capital.

Fersen said: "The news of Necker's dismissal was spread immediately by Orleans' agents."

"*Resignation,*" Marie Antoinette corrected, "but why split hairs? I fell into a trap of my own making."

Fersen went on: "I think everybody in Paris stayed up all night, forming little groups, shouting for Necker and Orleans; and then, this morning, the groups converged and marched into the Place Louis Fifteenth. A clash occurred when the troops tried to stop the mob from marching into the Champs Elysées."

"Was there any bloodshed?" Louis asked anxiously.

Fersen hesitated.

"There has been none up to now," Louis said, "for which I have continually thanked God." He looked pathetically at Fersen. "Axel, my dear fellow, tell me the worst."

"A man was—"

"Killed? Pray heaven not that!"

"Not killed, injured by a sword thrust."

"So my orders were disobeyed!"

"What else could the troops do but draw their swords?" Fersen asked quietly. "They were being attacked. Rocks and stones were hurled at them. I tell you, Louis—"

But Louis was paying no attention. "The first spilling of blood . . ."

"A little blood was spilled but the man wasn't seriously injured."

"The first spilling of blood . . ." Louis seemed in a daze from which, only slowly, did he recover, and recovering cried heatedly, "I shall withdraw the troops at once, at once!"

"Delay a little longer," Marie Antoinette begged. "This may be the turning point."

The dazed expression returned. "One day more, then . . ."

Fersen was back the next day with further news. He came straight to Marie Antoinette's apartments. The children were with her when he was announced, but she sent them quickly away.

"Well, Axel?"

"There was more rioting and pillaging during the night. The troops might as well have been withdrawn for all the use they are. The street women are busy in any case seducing them."

"Louis has forgotten all about withdrawing the troops," she said. "He was out hunting this morning, a sure sign that he wanted desperately to forget his problems. I tried to tell him that Paris is on the verge of revolution. He shrugged and said, 'Why should I care?' He does care, of course. He said, 'What can *I* do? The National Assembly have usurped my power. They are now the King. Let them deal with the situation.' He is right. He can do nothing."

"The newly created guard might restore order," Fersen said.

"I know nothing of a newly created guard. Created by the National Assembly, you mean?"

"No, by the municipal council of Paris. It has only just been set up and is composed of what I imagine to be responsible citizens, more anxious to save their own property than anything else, but still . . ."

"Axel," Marie Antoinette said suddenly, "I want to go to Paris."

Fersen stared at her in amazement. "The sight of your coach, surrounded by your personal guard, would incense the mob afresh."

"I want to go as an ordinary woman, not as Queen. Please take me, Axel."

248

"This is sheer madness, Marie!"

"I want to see things for myself. I have lived in isolation too long. After all, what do I know of Paris? The theaters, the Opera balls, the fine people in their grand houses, that is all I know of Paris. Please take me, Axel."

"Never!" he said vehemently.

Without a further word he turned on his heels and left her. Angry with him at first, her anger soon passed. Yet the desire to go to Paris remained with her. Unless he takes me, she promised herself, I shall go alone.

Fersen came to Versailles again the following morning. Feeling that he would avoid her if possible after what she had asked of him, she had a watch kept and when told that Monsieur de Fersen had gone straight to the King's apartments she smiled fondly to herself. She found Louis' anterooms strangely deserted and entered the inner cabinet unannounced. Fersen sprang punctiliously to his feet at the sight of her; Louis, sprawled in a chair, barely moved, but he smiled on her benignly.

"Axel tells me that the situation in Paris is quieter," he said.

"Quieter, yet hardly quiet," Fersen hastened to add, "but perhaps the situation will soon be under control. Honest people of all classes, even a sprinkling of aristocrats, are at the town hall, offering their services in the new guard. I understand that most of the riff-raff have been unarmed."

"And the troops?" Marie Antoinette asked.

"Ah," said Louis, "the commander, a wise man, has withdrawn them to the other side of the river. He felt, and I applaud him, that bloodshed would be avoided that way." With an effort he lifted himself from his chair. "And now, to encourage my children further, I shall order a complete withdrawal of all troops." He glanced slyly at Marie Antoinette. "You approve, my dear?"

"You do as you think best, Louis."

Smiling quite happily he trudged from the room.

Marie Antoinette turned to Fersen. "Axel—"

"*No!*" he said promptly.

She laughed in forced merriment. "How well you read my mind. But if, as you say, things are quieter, it will be quite safe for me to go to Paris."

"You know nothing of the violence of the mob, the ugliness of the dregs of the city hunting in a pack."

"You still refuse to take me?"

"By heaven I do!"

"Then I shall go alone."

"Paris today is no place for a woman alone."

"Ah, but I have made arrangements. A shabby old carriage and a broken-down horse are ready at the stables of the Little Trianon. I have given all the servants a holiday. Clothes are ready too, for me to change into. The clothes of a common working woman. Dressed like that, with no paint on my face and smears of dirt on my cheeks, no one will recognize me. I shall leave word here with one of my ladies. If anyone misses me it will be understood that I am spending a few quiet hours alone in my boudoir at the Little Trianon."

"I repeat," Fersen said desperately, "Paris is no place for a woman, even a working-class woman."

"You fear some horrible villain might rape me?"

Fersen's concern deepened. "Marie, you are on the verge of hysteria."

"Stand by and watch me go if you must," she said, controlling herself, "but go I shall."

Fersen glanced down at his uniform. "My clothes are hardly suitable."

"I have workman's clothes ready for you in the stables."

"Marie, I beg of you—"

She shrugged and walked to the door. "Au revoir, Axel."

"Wait!" he cried.

"You will take me?"

"I have no option, you irritating, stupid woman!"

She pointed a finger at him. "Dear Axel, how I love you!"

"All workmen, of course, possess carriages."

"Pooh! If anyone questions us we'll say we stole the carriage from an impoverished aristocrat. But what an adventure, Axel! Just think, a workman and his wife, or his girl, off to see the sights! What fun it's going to be, what fun!"

FIVE

Seated at fersen's side in the open carriage, admiring the deft way he handled the old horse, Marie Antoinette felt almost happy. A workman and his girl . . . ! It was a delicious thought. Her mind flew back to the deserted stables where they had changed their clothes after walking separately through the park to the Little Trianon. Axel had got there first and changed so quickly that he was ready and waiting before she herself had arrived. And afterwards he had been careful to stand outside, looking most embarrassed even then.

When they reached the city and became involved in a stream of other carriages, Axel, who had been silent most of the time, remarked that it would be wiser for her not to speak too much if they got caught up in the crowd.

"Why, Axel?"

"Your accent might give you away."

"My French is perfect now."

"The accent is most pronounced when you grow excited."

"You have an accent too."

"There are plenty of foreign workmen in Paris."

She laughed merrily. "You want me to remain dumb, wear a vacant expression on my face? Very well then! Something like this, Axel?"

Fersen glanced at her quickly. "Half-witted—splendid!"

Presently, after much difficulty, so thick was the traffic, they reached the Place de Greve. Here, close to the Town Hall, their carriage was forced to a halt, quickly surrounded and swarmed over by frantic people anxious to gain a better view of the agitators who, standing on chairs and boxes, were addressing all who cared to listen. Some of the people had a frightened look, but most of them wore a demented air, the sight of which made Marie Antoinette move close against Fersen's side.

"You said Paris was quieter," she whispered.

"Some new alarm has shaken the people," he whispered back. The din was deafening; everybody was talking and shouting

251

and gesticulating at once. The nearest agitator, shaking his clenched fists in the air, managed to make himself heard. The troops had not really withdrawn across the river, he yelled; they had merely gathered there to consolidate their numbers and would soon be marching into the city.

"To devastate it, burn it to the ground!" he shrieked.

Anger rose in Marie Antoinette's breast. She was ready to shout that he lied, but the pressure of Fersen's hand on her arm restrained her.

Immediately beneath her, in the press of people that surrounded the carriage, a tall young man, neatly dressed, with a pale intelligent face, shouldered his way towards the agitator.

"Idiots!" he shouted at the people he pushed aside, "This man is an Orleanist agent, paid to mislead you! Let the troops come! Let them, I say! Their orders are to protect you. And by heaven, how you need protection!"

A momentary silence fell.

The agitator, his face contorted with malice, pointed a finger at the tall young man.

"A royalist! Listen if you must and watch Paris burn!"

A howl of rage broke out. Fists were shaken in the young man's face. He was seized by a dozen screaming men and women, but towering above them he shook himself free and leaped into the open carriage at Marie Antoinette's side. A burly red-faced man in a butcher's apron leaped up after him. For a moment, with the crowd milling round it, it seemed as if the carriage would be overturned. Fersen jumped down and caught Marie Antoinette in his arms as she fell.

"I warned you," he said in a fierce whisper.

She clung to him. "Forgive me. I had no conception."

Someone had whipped up the horse. The crowd scrambled away in all directions and the carriage, rocking crazily, disappeared with the tall young man and the butcher wrestling desperately. A strange nostalgia touched Marie Antoinette's heart. It seemed that with the tall young man went all hope, all sanity.

"Down with the traitor!" a woman shrieked.

Poor misguided creature, Marie Antoinette thought; what she means is down with liberty.

"To arms!" another cried.

The agitator took it up gleefully. "To arms, citizens! To arms!"

"To arms, to arms!" the crowd roared.

252

Somebody began to beat a drum. The crowd stiffened, a shuddering sigh rose. The drum-beat went on relentlessly, imposing a semblance of order, transmitting to all a compelling feeling of purpose.

"To the Bastille!" a piercing voice commanded. "All the arms we need are there. Storm the Bastille! Seize the arms! Save yourselves, citizens, save yourselves!"

"To the Bastille, to the Bastille!" the crowd roared.

Unable to escape now, Marie Antoinette and Fersen were carried forward on wave after wave of screaming people. Sobbing uncontrollably, gripped by an emotion that was part anger, part pity, Marie Antoinette clung to Fersen's arm as the mad rush bore them forward. Women collapsed around them, to be thrust brutally aside or trodden underfoot. Pikes and sticks were brandished above their heads, jagged stones were waved in their faces. And all the time, ringing out like an insane litany, the obsessive cry rent the air, *To the Bastille, to the Bastille!*

"Where are we, Axel?"

"In the Rue Saint-Antoine."

Suddenly a halt was called. Above them loomed the graystone towers of the Bastille.

"The cannon have been withdrawn," someone cried wonderingly.

Of course they have, Marie Antoinette wanted to shout. Later, according to Louis' orders, they were to be taken out of the embrasures and dismantled. Let the people see that their King was a peace-loving gentleman, never tempted for one moment to take up arms against his beloved subjects.

"Withdrawn?" a voice thundered. "And *why?* Let me tell you, citizens! Withdrawn to be fully loaded. Why stand here like sheep, waiting for the slaughter? March on, citizens, march on!"

"March on, march on!" the crowd roared.

Carried forward again, Fersen tried, while shielding Marie Antoinette with his body, to edge his way outside the frantic mob. Fists were shaken in his face, claw-like hands tore at his clothing. At last, fighting for breath, he found shelter in the doorway of a perfume shop on the ground floor of a building set against the encircling wall of the fortress.

"Madness to have come," he gasped. "I'll never forgive myself."

He held her close and the warmth of his embrace was a comfort beyond description. It drove out fear and the nightmare

253

horror of the screaming mob, a mob shaken by yet another howl of rage.

"What is it now?" she whispered.

"They are held back by the first drawbridge."

"Ah, but look, look!"

Two men had scrambled up to the roof of the building above them and were trying to reach the Bastille wall. They succeeded, amid hoarse cheers from the watching crowd, and were soon easing themselves gingerly towards the chains which supported the drawbridge. And meanwhile the soldiers within the fortress stood helpless and bewildered. Oh, those pitiful orders from Louis! Would he stand in the midst of the crowd himself and submit without protest to a murderous attack? He would, kindly idiot that he was, she knew he would!

The two men were hacking now at the chains while the crowd chanted "Down with tyranny, down with oppression!" The drawbridge fell with a shattering crash. Several people who had pressed too close were injured and one man was killed instantly. The injured were swept aside by the vanguard of the mob which poured over the drawbridge and streamed into the inner courtyard. Only then, and firing in the air, did the soldiers attempt any sort of defense. The crowd swayed in sudden indecision, turned and retreated in a cursing body to the outer courtyard.

Fersen took Marie Antoinette by the arm in a firm grip.

"I must get you away from this!"

But they were caught in the retreating vanguard, borne back on its crest towards the Rue Saint-Antoine. Here the ever-increasing rearguard, aware only that shots had been fired, unhesitatingly believed the cry that the Governor of the Bastille, ordering the drawbridge to be lowered, had planned to trap and slaughter the innocent in the inner courtyard.

"Spread the news!" the agitators cried. "Let all Paris be warned!"

Pandemonium broke loose. People flung themselves about in all directions, cursing the governor, crying wildly for his blood. Carried this way and that, half-suffocated by the press and stench of human bodies, Marie Antoinette and Fersen found themselves thrust into a doorway, and there, seeking what little shelter they could, they clung desperately.

Presently Fersen said, "Ah, a deputation. And from the Town Hall, by the look of it."

Marie Antoinette was conscious of a lessening of the aimless confusion about her.

"Responsible citizens, all of them," Fersen added.

Responsible citizens! Unbelievable that at this stage there should be even one responsible citizen left in Paris! She could see the members of the deputation now. One man was carrying a flag, another was solemnly beating a drum. Reluctantly the crowd made way for them. The purpose of the deputation, if one could believe the story passed from mouth to mouth, was to ask the governor permission for a detachment of the new municipal guard to enter the Bastille.

"And guard the fortress against the excesses of the mob," Fersen added.

"To the devil with that!" the agitators screamed, when some of the crowd seemed ready to hang back and wait.

The governor of the Bastille was now standing on the battlements, and with him the leader of the civic deputation was trying vainly to engage in a shouted, hoarse-voiced parley. His words, and those shouted back by the governor, were distorted and lost amid the wild screams of the mob.

"Ask somebody what is happening," Marie Antoinette whispered.

Fersen spoke to a young woman standing in front of them. She turned and grinned up at him. She had the common, pretty face of a streetwalker; her cheeks were heavily painted, her breasts were bare.

"Some other time, sweetheart," she said, her voice rising to a strident laugh. "No business on a day like this, not even for the King himself."

He spoke to her again, repeating his question louder.

"Oh, *that!* Well, now, the governor seems willing to admit the deputation, but not the people. Keep out the real guardians of freedom? Not bloody likely."

A moment later she edged herself against Fersen. "You're a real handsome fellow, aren't you? Maybe if you ask me again—"

"What is the governor saying now?" he interrupted.

"He says he'll come down. Brave talk, that! You can have me for nothing if he does. *That's* what I think of the word of a stinking aristocrat."

Muskets were being distributed among the crowd now. They had been taken, rumor had it, from one of the arsenals, that of

255

the Invalides. Eager, grasping hands reached out for ammunition, and soon a spasmodic attack, unorganized, piecemeal, was being made on the soldiers in the inner courtyard. The fire was returned half-heartedly.

"Get me away if you can, Axel," Marie Antoinette begged.

Dragging her by the arm, sometimes half-carrying her, Fersen struggled against the flow of the mob. Carts filled with lighted straw were being pushed into the inner courtyard in an insane, hopeless attempt to burn down the Bastille. Fresh groups of people were arriving all the time, pressing wildly forward, crying shrilly that they were here to save their gallant brothers from massacre. Some dragged cannon with them, set them up and began an indiscriminate, inexpert bombardment.

"Fools!" Fersen raged. "They are killing each other!"

A great cry rose. The chains of the second drawbridge had been severed. The mob surged forward in another great wave. Battling against it, near exhaustion, Fersen was carrying Marie Antoinette in his arms. That much she realized before, with the world turning sickeningly over, she lost consciousness.

She recovered to find herself lying in the shelter of a wall. Fersen was bending anxiously over her.

"Are you strong enough to stand?"

"Give me a few moments more," she begged. The reverberating howl of the mob sounded distant and unreal in her ears. "What is happening now, Axel?"

"The Bastille has been taken. The governor is at the mercy of the mob. They are carrying him to the Town Hall."

She made a tremendous effort. "I think I can stand now."

With Fersen supporting her she began to walk blindly, going she knew not where, nor hardly cared. She knew presently that she was in an open carriage and that Fersen was whipping up the single horse.

"How did I get here?" she asked stupidly.

"I lifted you in. It was unattended. I took it."

She recovered her strength during the drive back to Versailles but her mind was still dazed and her heart felt dead within her. Only one compelling thought moved her. The children, she must get back to the children. She changed into her own clothes while Axel waited outside the stables.

"Meet me in Louis' apartments," she said, when she was ready. She thought he was looking at her oddly. "Is anything the matter,

256

Axel?" She laughed quickly before he could speak. "My face, of course, is in need of paint and powder."

"I can see a change in you," he said gravely, "that paint and powder will never hide."

A little shuddering sigh escaped her lips. "I am not the same woman who went so gaily to Paris. Fun, that was what I called it. Dear heaven, what a blind fool I was!" She turned to leave him. "Remember, Axel, what we did today is our own horrible secret."

Within the palace all seemed calm and safe. The familiar surroundings, the guards who stiffened to attention as she passed, almost convinced her that Paris was an untroubled city. Surely, while resting during a walk in the park, she had fallen asleep in the sun and suffered a nightmare.

She went first to the children, spoke to them for a few moments with forced gaiety, then hurried to her own apartments. The attendants on duty there stared at her curiously. She dismissed them with a quick, curt gesture, and unaided changed her gown and carefully painted the rouge on her cheeks. After that she thought of Axel again. Meet me in Louis' apartments, she had said.

The royal anterooms, especially the Oeil de Boeuf, were crammed with people, and the atmosphere, she sensed, was that of consternation masked by the jauntiness of bravado. She walked forward steadily, inclining her head to right and to left as courtiers, eyeing her critically, bowed before her. Her eyes fell on Axel. She gave him but a passing glance and went, still steadily, into Louis' inner cabinet. The room was empty. She moved about it aimlessly until, a few moments later, Louis entered hurriedly, followed by Axel.

"Ah, Marie my dear," Louis said vaguely. He swung round and faced Axel. "Well, my dear fellow, what news from Paris now?"

Marie Antoinette stared at him in amazement. It was inconceivable that, as his tone suggested, he should know nothing of what had happened.

"Not by any means as quiet as you thought this morning, eh?" Louis went on, as Axel hesitated. "Various reports keep reaching me. Confused, all of them, contradictory. Some wild talk about a mob marching on the Bastille."

Marie Antoinette and Axel exchanged a quick glance.

Louis laughed uneasily. "An exaggeration, of course. What use is the Bastille to the mob?" He tried to make one of his rare jokes. "Would to heaven the agitators took it over and remained in residence there. In the most comfortable apartments, of course! Why, they would never want to leave the place!" He was talking quickly now, seemed unable to stop. "A grim, shameful prison, eh? It was once, but not now, good gracious no! Why, only a handful of prisoners there these days, and plans are being made to pull it down, have a nice big square there instead. When we can afford it, of course. The Place Louis Sixteenth, the architect wants to call it—" He pulled himself up abruptly and blinked at Axel. "Well?"

Axel said quietly, "The attack on the Bastille was made to obtain arms, not to free the prisoners."

"Ah, you have the facts! And—and there really has been an attack on the Bastille? Come, my dear Axel, tell me all you know. The reports were, as I say, confused, contradictory . . ."

Before more could be said a messenger was announced, a messenger who presented a wild-eyed appearance, his eyes dilated with fear. In a low shaken voice he related much of what Marie Antoinette had seen. When he had finished Louis dismissed him and remained silent for a moment. His hands, she noticed, were trembling.

"And I had ordered the complete withdrawal of all troops from Paris," he said at last, in a whisper.

"The order was given too late, Louis."

Her fault again? Just another of her many mistakes? She tried to tell herself that the mob would have risen in any case, would have been incited to rebellion whatever she had done or not done.

Still in a whisper, Louis said: "Please leave me, both of you. This is a shattering blow."

They left him.

The crowd in the Oeil de Boeuf were clustered around the messenger, who was telling his story again. No notice whatever was taken of Marie Antoinette and Axel, but Axel, punctilious as ever in the presence of others, bowed her out of the anteroom and followed respectfully on her heels.

"What are you going to do now, Axel?" she asked.

"I had thought of going back to Paris—"

"In your so very attractive uniform? Are you crazy?"

"—but," he continued, "I should be at Valenciennes with my regiment. It is only that I hesitate to leave you."

"You may be of greater use at a distance. I shall send for you the moment I need you."

258

"If you give me your word—"

"I give you my word, Axel."

He began to speak eagerly now. "I have a plan. The moment you give the word I'll take you and the children across the border to the safety of Belgium."

She considered this gravely. "Why should I run away? Hopeless to remain, but I should despise myself if I ran away."

Back in her own apartments she found Artois waiting for her. He was pacing up and down, up and down. She was sure that in his eyes she could detect a quite lively fear. Speaking jerkily he urged her to force Louis to take drastic action, now, at once, before it was too late.

"Isn't it too late now?" she asked listlessly.

Artois stared at her wildly. "Yes. Yes, I expect it is. Of course it is! No one would listen to me before. Why should I talk now just for the sake of talking? Only one thing is left, now."

"And that?" she asked incuriously.

He made no answer, merely stared at her insolently.

Only one thing . . . His meaning was clear enough. Was Artois to be the first to go, the first to desert? The first terrified little rat deserting the sorry ship of monarchy?

He turned on his heels and went quickly to the door.

"Wait!" she cried.

He swung round. "Well?"

"Since your desires for violent action against the people are now well known to the people, you are one of the most hated men in France. It would be better for the King if you left the country at the earliest possible moment."

She could see by his crestfallen look that he had not expected this of her.

"Only Berri can dismiss me," he said insolently.

"You wish to remain and brave it out?"

"I— Oh damn you, Marie, I want to save my skin."

"Very well then, let us not talk of dismissal. Let us say that only the King can grant your request for permission to leave France. And by heaven, Artois, grant it he shall!"

Artois gave her a half-admiring look. "Your Majesty is the only man at court, but you have reached your manhood too late."

She shrugged aside the half-compliment. She had gained her point; preserved her dignity. Nothing else mattered.

When Artois had gone she dismissed the ladies who came chattering about her, but alone she found the room full of horrible shadows, full of echoes of the screaming, demented mob. Quickly she went to Gabrielle's apartments, but only the maids were there, all busy with obvious preparations for flight. She realized then that it was night time and quite late. Gabrielle, still royal governess, would be in the Dauphin's apartments. Unless, of course, she had fled already. She went there slowly, hating now to face the friend of so many years, hoping against hope that Gabrielle had indeed deserted her post.

But Gabrielle was sitting placidly in the outer room, reading a book. She rose languidly at the sight of Marie Antoinette.

"You seem surprised to see me, Marie."

"When are you leaving, Gabrielle?"

Gabrielle shrugged. "After the violence of today things will quieten for a while before more violence breaks out. Tomorrow, the next day . . ." She shrugged again. "The sooner the better, of course."

Again it was a matter of preserving one's dignity. "You understand, surely, that you cannot leave Versailles without my permission?"

Gabrielle laughed lightly. "I never gave *that* a thought. How can you keep me here, Marie?"

"I have full authority to throw you into prison."

Gabrielle smiled maliciously. "The Bastille, for instance?"

Marie Antoinette bit her lip. "You are hated almost as much as I am. Perhaps more, by some people. For my sake, for the King's sake, it would be better if you went, and quickly." She felt tears sting her eyes. "Send for Madame Campan. She shall take charge of the children immediately and remain in charge until I can find someone else. You are dismissed, Madame. For your own sake, leave France quickly and quietly."

She went quietly into her son's bedchamber. Little Louis Charles was sleeping peacefully, his cheeks rosy, his arms lying on the coverlet. A lump rose in her throat. She touched his cheek lightly with her lips. He stirred a little and chuckled in his sleep. She tried to console herself with the thought that there must be many mothers in Paris this night as anxious as she was, but fear drove it from her mind. Perhaps Axel was right, perhaps she ought to escape and take the children with her . . .

She returned again to her own apartments and there she found

260

Louis sitting apathetically in a chair. He spoke without looking at her, spoke as if repeating a long-rehearsed sentence.

"Not a revolt this time, a revolution."

He remained immovable in the chair. His voice came again, dead, monotonous.

"They murdered the governor of the Bastille. They all but tore him to pieces. Then they murdered him. His head was carried through the streets on a pike."

He moved slightly. "I blame myself. Yet I still feel it was right not to resort to violence against my people."

He rose unsteadily. A hint of life came to his voice. "It was the work of agitators and the dregs of the city, not of honest god-fearing citizens."

He smiled uncertainly. "When the full truth is known the people as a whole will shrink in horror from this day's work. I want to think, I *insist* on thinking, that this will be the end of unrest and terror, the beginning of sanity."

He looked at her eagerly. "It will be, tell me that it will be, Marie!"

SIX

AWAKE BEFORE LOUIS, MARIE ANTOINETTE SAT UP AND LOOKED DOWN at him. In sleep his face had the peaceful, innocent look of a child. She wondered if her own face was as untroubled as his when sleeping.

During the ten weeks since the storming of the Bastille Louis had come to her bed every night, not to make demands of her, but to seek of her the warmth and comfort and protection a child sought of its mother.

He stirred, woke instantly, heaved himself to a sitting position and yawned noisily. She had grown used to his first words after waking. "What of the weather?" he always asked. "Will it be a good day for hunting?" She fell back on the pillow, waiting for the familiar question.

Louis said, "I forgot to tell you that I had sent for Axel. He should arrive today. He will come straight to you."

"Why that?" she asked in surprise.

"My dear, you, I and the King of Sweden are the only people who know anything of Axel's unofficial reason for being in France. Well, I need an intermediary, somebody who can get secret messages out of France to Sweden. In any case, Axel is the only man I feel I can trust completely in anything."

"We have known that for some time, Louis."

"Granted, granted. However, I must take every precaution. I know I am closely watched and must regard many at court as spies for the National Assembly. It would be unwise for me to be seen anywhere, at any time, alone with Axel. Because of that I have a request to make of you."

"Anything you like, Louis."

"I shall give you the communications I want smuggled out and you shall give them to Axel. The sort of game one plays as a child, eh?"

"Except that it is grim reality now."

Louis sighed. "Dear Marie, it is only by pretending to play a desperate childish game that I can keep up my spirits."

"Then let us by all means pretend."

"Thank you." He yawned and stretched. "What of the weather? Will it be a good day for hunting?"

She answered as always. "I hope so, Louis."

Lying back on the pillow she glanced at the drawn bedcurtains. This dim enclosed little world, this silken tent . . . a womb from which with reluctance one emerged each morning. She heard footsteps in the room. The routine of the day was beginning. She listened to the footsteps, those of her chief *femme de chambre*, as they crossed to the door in the panelling which led to Louis' apartments. She heard the door open and the whispered words exchanged by the *femme de chambre* and Louis' *valet de chambre*. New footsteps advanced into the room, a hand drew back the curtains on Louis' side. The valet stood there holding a silver-embroidered dressing-gown and a pair of red slippers.

"Ah well, we begin another day," Louis said.

He dangled his feet out of bed, the slippers were placed on them. He slid to the floor with a dull thud. The valet helped him into his dressing-gown.

"*Au 'voir*, my dear."

He padded away, followed by the valet. The *femme de chambre* closed the connecting door, re-crossed the room and went out to the anteroom. Marie Antoinette sighed in relief. It was known that she was not to be disturbed for another hour. An hour entirely to herself! How delicious the thought!

In this undisturbed atmosphere, with familiar routine moving steadily forward, one could almost believe that nothing of any great moment had happened. The Bastille had been taken by the mob ten weeks ago and was being pulled down. Well, fancy that! How surprising! She repeated the words aloud. "How surprising!" But it was useless. The horror through which she had passed became even more real as she lay in the enclosed silence of the curtained bed.

She began, step by step, to recall the events which had followed the fall of the Bastille.

She remembered how, the next day, Louis had gone to address the National Assembly. She could see him now, unattended, unguarded, dressed in plain somber clothes, eager to give the impression that he was just a man of the people, a good citizen deeply concerned at the turn of events, not a king nobody wanted.

What had he said to the Assembly? He had said that the order of withdrawal issued to the troops in Paris was an order that would be obeyed. Cheers then from the deputies, many of them still shaken by the violence of the day before. He had said, "Help me, I need help; help me, I trust you. Help me, you representatives of the people, to save the people." Words, words, words! But again they had cheered him and risen in one emotional body to accompany him back to his apartments.

And then what? Another day, and the desertion of friends and enemies alike had begun. After Artois and his family, Gabrielle and hers, others had followed, going with a sort of hurried unhurriedness. Now a steady stream was 'emigrating.' A new fashionable word, that! Not deserters, dear me no! *Émigrés*. Familiar faces disappearing all the time. Even the old Abbé Vermond had gone, his destination Austria, his declared reason being his wish to raise help, if possible, at the court of her brother Joseph.

And yet, there had been no repetition of the violence which had attended the storming of the Bastille. Bailly, elected President of the National Assembly, had become Mayor of Paris, while Lafayette, the same Lafayette who had led his band of aristocrats to the American war, had been appointed commander of the municipal guard, now known as the National Guard. The National Guard! A few aristocrats, a mixed body of middleclass gentlemen, an earnest collection of commoners—amateur soldiers, most of them, soldiers who, in wet weather, carried umbrellas as well as swords. An inspiring sight! The charge, one might say, of the Umbrella Brigade.

And after that? An order—an order, not a request—that the King should pay a visit to his people of Paris. Just the King, mind you, not the Queen. The Queen's presence might rouse the mob. She had feared a trap for Louis, had watched him start off for the capital believing she would never see him again, because he had been escorted to Paris by a horde of men carrying scythes and pick-axes. Yet he had come back safely, an exhausted, almost vacuous expression on his face. And pinned to his hat was a three-colored cockade.

"What," she had asked, pointing at it, "is that?"

"The badge of revolution. I can almost believe that I am one of the leaders."

And then, with bewildered eyes, he had told her in short jerky sentences what had happened in Paris.

"At first a few people cheered me. That gave me hope. They were silenced by agitators. A shot was fired. It missed me, killed a

264

poor innocent woman. Bailly offered me the key of the city. On a velvet cushion. The irony of it. He gave me this cockade. I put it in my hat. The whole mob cheered then. The cheers sounded like imprecations. At the Town Hall somebody addressed the people. He said many fine words about me. I could be depended on always. I would shed the last drop of my blood for them. I think I waved my hat. They seemed to go wild with joy, or a sort of unholy glee. Then I was allowed to— Then I came back to Versailles. The cheering when I left sounded like real cheering. They called me the father of the people. Their father the King . . ."

Louis had brightened then, adding with that terrible hopefulness of his, "All will now be well. Yes indeed, Marie."

After that, as week followed week, a strange brooding had hung over Versailles, while the National Assembly, still sitting in the Salle des Menus Plaisirs, had begun, vote by vote, to take from Louis the last shreds of royal authority.

And what did Louis do now? He still muttered that all would be well, he hunted madly, seeming to care for little else, yet obviously he was concerned at the course of events, otherwise why should he send like this for Axel?

And she herself? Life now meant the etiquette and routine of the dwindling court, the gaming table occasionally, the children, the writing of useless letters to Joseph, and above it all a resolve not to look back at the past, not to search too deeply the problematic future, to live for the day and that day only, to act when action was necessary, not after much thought, but as the instinct of the moment took her. Yes, and even to say, as Louis said, All will now be well.

Nonsense, all of it. She saw that now. But what else could she do?

She heard the door open, heard again the footsteps of the *femme de chambre*. The quiet hour alone had passed. She felt more pleased than sorry. It was rarely good to be alone now with one's thoughts. The *femme de chambre* opened the curtains, held out the negligee, the feathered slippers.

"A beautiful day, your Majesty, but a nip in the air."

"One expects it to be cool at the end of September."

The slippers were on her feet, the negligee about her shoulders. She went to the window while another *femme de chambre* came in and wheeled away the night stool. Axel, she thought, I shall see Axel today. A feeling of exultation rose in her breast. To live for today and today only. She heard more footsteps behind her. The wardrobe woman now, to take away the pillows. Other serving women followed, bringing in the slipper-bath, the soap, the towels, the perfume. A significant little silence fell. They were awaiting her Majesty's pleasure . . .

She went to Mass at the usual time, followed from her apartments by the first equerry, the gentleman usher, several ladies of honor and one member of the royal family, Provence's wife. Surprising, when you came to think of it, that Provence and his family were still here. Perhaps by this hanging on, this show of courage, Provence still hoped to replace Louis. Amazing if that were true. What prince in his right mind would want to replace a battered figurehead, a plaything of the National Assembly?

Courtiers and their ladies were waiting to join the procession to the chapel. She glanced at them briefly, one by one. Who would be the next to go, to *emigrate*? Will it be you, Monsieur? You, Madame? Her heart leaped suddenly. She was staring at the face of Axel von Fersen. There he stood, erect, grave, immaculate in his colonel's uniform. Steadying herself she paused to greet him.

"Ah, Monsieur le Comte. So nice to see you again. You are very welcome."

Axel bowed. "Your Majesty is most gracious."

She extended her hand languidly; he kissed it and stood back. The procession continued. What did she care about Mass? About etiquette, routine? Nothing, nothing whatever! Merely a passing glimpse of Axel was enough to drive out fear, horror, uncertainty. I am no longer alone, she told herself.

It was not until the late afternoon that she was able to receive him in the privacy of her drawing-room.

"Ah, our old friend Monsieur le Comte de Fersen," she said casually, when the lady-in-waiting had announced him. "I understood that you had returned to Sweden."

But the moment they were alone she sprang from her chair and ran to him. Gently he placed his arms about her and held her for a few moments. It was still the same. Nothing had changed. The magic was renewed with intensity.

He released her and she told him why Louis had sent for him, explained that he must not feel hurt if Louis affected not to notice him.

"You do understand, Axel?"

266

"Of course, Marie. I am ready at any time to serve you both. You know that. Is Louis planning an escape?"

"An escape from what?" she asked bitterly. "He is free to come and go as he pleases. An escape . . ." She dwelt on this. "Perhaps he is planning an escape, but he would never admit it. All he appears to want is to maintain through you a secret correspondence with your own King."

Axel was frowning now. "I went to Paris before coming to Versailles. I spent the night there. Paris is still a volcano, ready to erupt again. What troubles me is this. Louis, as you say, is free to come and go as he pleases, but here at Versailles he has no protection from the mob. A handful of loyal guards, a detachment of that ridiculous National Guard. Versailles could be taken more easily than the Bastille." He paused; his voice shook with emotion. "What really matters to me, *you* have no protection here."

"Axel, are things suddenly worse in Paris? What have you heard there, what have you seen?"

"I have heard that bread is still scarce; I have heard the agitators outside the Palais Royal, paid by Orleans to preach to the mob, to keep the resentment simmering. I have seen the hooligans roaming the streets; I have seen the countless pamphlets; I have also seen, heaven pity them, the National guards with their umbrellas."

She seized on one word. "Pamphlets . . . Do they blame me again for the scarcity of bread, or are they content to write about my sexual excesses?"

Axel's silence was sufficient answer.

"Is it strength or weakness that prevents me from saying 'Axel, help me to escape'?"

"Strength, Marie."

"Strength that has come too late."

"For your own protection you must bring troops to Versailles."

"I shall speak to Louis when he comes back from yet another day's hunting."

"It will have to be a foreign regiment, Marie. French soldiers might refuse to obey orders."

"Mercenaries then."

"I pray God this is not bad advice."

"Bad or good, Axel, it must be followed. Either I must escape with the children or see that they have full protection here. Are you staying at your old lodgings in Paris?"

267

"No, Paris is too far away. I have found new lodgings in the town here."

She spoke to Louis that night. He hesitated and grumbled. His temper was not very good; the day's hunting had been the worst he could remember. But when she spoke of the danger to which the children might well be exposed he agreed at once.

"The Flanders Regiment," he decided. "Is Axel in good health?"

"Yes, Louis."

"Tell him I love him and place the utmost faith in him. I hope you have found a comfortable apartment for him in the palace."

"You want him to stay *here?*"

"Of course."

"You must be crazy!"

Louis came closer to her until her face was in complete focus. He stared broodingly for a long moment.

"Dear Marie," he said at last, "you have loved him for many years."

"Yes, Louis."

"And always you have denied that love."

"Always."

"I would give you to him gladly."

"Thank you."

"All I want is your happiness."

"You have always been most kind."

The crazy formality of this fantastic conversation!

"My kindness, as you call it, has been repaid a hundred times. Follow your heart now. I shall never blame you, never reproach you."

"I have never been unfaithful, Louis. I never want to be."

"Ah, this physical faithfulness," he said enigmatically, and abruptly left her.

Axel took very little part in the life of Versailles. Occasionally he was present among the spectators when Marie Antoinette and Louis dined uneasily in public, but most of his time was spent in Paris. He went there in plain clothes and mingled with the crowds, watching, listening—preparing himself, he said, for any emergency that might arise. Sometimes Marie Antoinette met him, as if by accident, when promenading with her ladies, but the real meetings took place in the park near the Little Trianon when she walked there unattended and he, out for a quiet ride, dismounted to walk at her side.

268

One such meeting took place the day after the arrival of the Flanders Regiment. It was a calm, clear autumn day with bars of yellow sunlight streaming through the half-denuded branches and setting fire to the piled-up fallen leaves. She watched him dismount, then went forward to greet him as he led the horse by the reins. Conscious of the unbearable golden beauty of the day, she knew, with an ache in her heart, that this was a place more suited to a lovers' tryst than a discussion of the progress of the revolution.

They spoke quietly, almost in whispers.

"Well, Axel?"

"A rising murmur of protest."

"Expected, of course."

"A cry of indignation. The King has brought troops to Versailles. The King places no faith in his people. His people are hurt."

"If that is all, Axel—"

"Orleanist agents are whispering that a foul plot is being hatched."

"As if sensible people would believe that! How many men are there in the Flanders Regiment? Not enough to protect us if severely attacked."

He touched her arm lightly. "My dear, you must go back to the palace. To come here unattended is dangerous."

She clung to his arm. "My dearest Axel, we shall continue to meet here at this hour, day by day, whilever we can. Here in this little world of our own."

They embraced for a lingering moment before parting.

She turned from him and walked slowly away. A light breeze had risen. The autumn leaves danced merrily before her. She glanced back once. Axel was following at a distance, keeping her in sight, watching over her.

At the palace she found Louis returned early from the hunt at Meudon. She saw at once that he was in the best of humors.

"The hunting was good," she commented.

"Excellent, excellent!"

She thought he looked his best in riding clothes, far better than in robes of state, infinitely more at ease. After the exertions of the day a healthy glow tinged his cheeks and his eyes were clear. A much happier sight than slumped over the table after a too-heavy meal, florid and loose-mouthed.

She went with him to his inner cabinet. He went to his desk and examined the papers which had been placed there for his attention.

"Ah," he cried, "the palace guards request permission to give a banquet for the Flanders Regiment. A long time since I had such a request. The old courtesies are reasserting themselves. We shall put in an appearance at the banquet, of course."

He peered at another paper, then frowned.

"What is it, Louis?"

"A message from the Assembly. Their debates continue. We now have reforms aplenty. The new Constitution on the one hand, the Declaration of the Rights of Man on the other. I am invited to grant royal sanction to the first principles of the one, the full declaration of the other."

"Invited? Not . . . *commanded?*"

Louis laughed mirthlessly. "The Assembly sometimes displays good manners."

"The royal sanction!" she cried. "The sanction of a figurehead! Refuse these measures and they will be passed in any case."

He pondered over this. "That is true enough, yet why ask for the royal sanction at all? We have a revolution, but the Assembly seems in no way inclined to set up a republic. Is it any wonder I never know what to do for the best?"

The day after the banquet, which had been held in the Salle d'Opera, Marie Antoinette met Axel at the usual time and place. It was another beautiful day, and in the pale blue muslin gown she had chosen, and with her hair dressed in a simple fashion, she felt free and young and happy.

"The news of the banquet nearly caused a rising in Paris," Axel said.

Her happiness began to fade. "But *why*, Axel?"

"The cost, the extravagance. Another example of the spendthrift Queen's amazing recklessness."

"Regimental funds paid for the banquet."

"No regiment is supposed to have funds in this would-be democracy."

She said sadly, "The spendthrift Queen . . ."

"Always the scapegoat. The agitators see to that."

A foreboding of evil swamped her. "Do you really expect a rising?"

"I think we should at least be prepared for one, Marie. A bread famine would set off the powder, and a bread famine can be organized."

"By Orleans?"

"Yes, but Orleans is clever. His agents are well paid and cunning. No one can prove anything against him, yet grain is being held back—by him, I am sure. A sudden withholding of all supplies, if only for a single day, and Paris will wake up with no bread in the shops. A few cries of Famine! and everybody will be frantic."

Desperately she said, "Oh Axel, all I want, in the short time we have together each day, is to forget all this, to be just an ordinary woman walking in the autumn sunshine with a friend. Take my arm, Axel. Walk with me. Talk of anything—anything you like but not the revolution!"

They walked in silence for a few moments. The dry brown leaves broke crisply beneath their feet, the bars of yellow light through the trees spread a mottled carpet of sunshine on the path before them.

"This is heaven itself," she said, but the words meant nothing.

"It isn't easy to pretend, Marie."

He stopped. She turned at his side, her arm still linked through his, and looked up at him.

"What is it, Axel?"

"I was remembering the Opera Ball."

"So was I. That first meeting, and . . . all the other meetings."

"All the other meetings . . ."

She reached up and kissed his cheek lightly. He took her hands in his.

"How cold you are, Marie."

"The sun has gone behind a cloud."

"The sun is still shining."

"I can only see the clouds. And Axel, dearest Axel, the magic has gone."

"No!" he said.

"Nothing in its place but the pain of wanting, the torture of denial. How I hate the life I have been forced to lead!"

Axel took her in his arms and held her close for a moment.

"You see," she said brokenly, "nothing! Nothing at all! So ridiculous, the wanting, when my heart is as cold as ice."

They began to retrace their steps.

"We must never meet again here like this," Axel said.

"You lack the strength?"

"I lack the courage you yourself possess. Little bands of marauders are roving the countryside. There might be some in the park at this moment. You must never come out again unattended, unguarded."

"As if I cared, Axel."

"I heard ghastly threats in Paris this morning. I was at the markets. The women are your worst enemies. They— Marie, you must promise not to come here again."

"Very well," she said wearily, "I promise."

"I shall see you at the palace every day."

"Of course, Axel."

But the next afternoon, restless and defiant, filled with an inexpressible longing, she went to the meeting place again, not alone this time, but attended by a footman who followed at a respectful distance. It had been raining all morning and now, though fine, heavy gray clouds hung low in the sky. She rested on a fallen tree, the footman out of sight but within earshot.

How changed everything was! She could find no beauty in the gray monotony, the dripping branches, the sodden leaves. *Here I was happy and here my happiness died.* A little spark of anger flared in her breast. Self-pity . . . *Dear God, protect me from that!* She fancied that her mother was standing near-by. *Well, Mama, are you satisfied now?* But that was another form of self-pity. She thought of her brother Joseph. He had urged her, begged her, to join him in the safety of Vienna. Well, why not? What else was left but flight?

The footman approached, deferential but anxious. Behind him followed a page. They stood before her, waiting for permission to speak.

"Well?"

"Your Majesty, a new rising. A great crowd of people marching out of Paris, advancing on Versailles."

Her first thought was, *The children!*

She leaped to her feet. *The children!* She was running now, unaware that it was raining again, that she slipped, sometimes fell, on the sodden leaves. Once, with the page helping her to her feet, she shouted in his face, "The children!"

272

SEVEN

At the palace all was quiet; nothing seemed changed. Marie Antoinette looked back indignantly at the page as he hurried behind her up the Marble Stairway.

"Is this a hoax?"

"No, your Majesty. Monsieur de Fersen rode out ahead of the mob. It may be hours before the women arrive."

"The . . . *women?*"

"Thousands of them, your Majesty. All demanding bread."

In her drawing-room she found Axel pacing up and down.

"My dear!" he cried, aghast at the sight of her mud-spattered clothing.

"Tell me the worst!" she demanded.

For once he seemed at a loss. "Marie, no one knew where you were."

"*You* should have known, Axel."

"My *dear* . . ."

"*Tell me the worst!*"

"It was what I feared. No bread in the Paris shops this morning. Carts of flour which should have arrived last night failed to arrive. The cry of 'Famine!' was soon ringing through the city. I went to the markets. I mingled with the women there. I saw the agitators at work. This is a man-made famine, but who is to know that? I went with the crowd to the Town Hall. I never saw such a horde, and all women. The mayor seemed helpless. So did your precious commander of the National Guard, Lafayette. What can men do against a horde of frantic screaming women? Somebody shouted 'To Versailles! Make the King feed us!' With that the march began. I wasted no time in coming to warn you."

"Louis is at Meudon. Has anyone been sent to tell him?"

"Yes. But Marie, their rage is directed against—"

"Of course! Against me!"

"The flour carts were rolling into the city when I left, but it was too late then. I questioned one of the drivers. Orders, from whom he seemed not to know, had delayed them."

Marie Antoinette felt a wave of uncertain relief. "If it is only women—"

"Ah, there you have the cunning of the agitators. Will Louis send troops out against women? And you saw the women during the storming of the Bastille."

She shuddered. "I saw them."

It seemed an age before Louis arrived from Meudon. He came straight to Marie Antoinette's apartments. He was wet to the skin, his clothes were torn, his face was a mass of scratches. She learned afterwards that his first thought had been for his family. Outstripping his companions, scorning all roads and bridle-paths, he had driven his horse in as straight a line as possible, over hedges, through undergrowth, to the palace.

"But . . . *women?*" he said, when Axel had repeated his story. "I visualized an attack similar to that made on the Bastille. Now you say . . . just women."

"But a demented mob, Louis. The dregs of Paris. I beseech you, send your family to a place of safety. Rambouillet, for instance. Remain yourself if you must, but send your family."

"Just women . . ." Louis repeated. "Bread? They shall have all that can be found at Versailles."

Axel turned to Marie Antoinette.

"No," she said, "my place is here."

Louis went to his own apartments to confer with his ministers. It was known now that the vanguard of the marching women was close to the palace, lined up and waiting in the Avenue de Paris. Impatiently Marie Antoinette hurried after Louis. She found him silent, impassive of face, while his ministers argued, advised, contradicted each other. She called for silence and addressed Louis as quietly as she could.

"What are your orders for the troops? Surely that is the first thing to be decided."

He looked mildly shocked. "Would you have me make war on women?"

"You propose to stand by and let them invade the palace?"

"No, no. The troops and the palace guards shall prevent that, but on pain of death must harm not a single woman. It is only a wave of hysteria." He laughed lightly. "All women are given to hysteria at times. It will pass."

A messenger had been ushered in, and urged forward now by one of the ministers he approached and bowed. Marie Antoinette

274

stared at him in speechless horror. Blood streamed down his cheeks; his clothes hung on him in shreds. His agitation was pitiful.

"They tried to stop me from reaching the palace," he said, "but I managed to break through. They surrounded me for a time, those female furies, tore at my clothes, scratched my face, made indecent assaults on my person. One of them, a burly hideous specimen, demanded that I should feel her breasts. She screamed hoarsely, 'Go on, timid little gentleman, feel them, feel them!' She dragged her gown from her shoulders. Dear heaven, what breasts! Two pistols, your Majesty. She, like many of the others out there in female attire, was a man."

Louis' impassivity fell from him. He turned quickly to Marie Antoinette.

"Fersen is right. You must take the children to Rambouillet."

The messenger interrupted hurriedly. "It is no longer safe for anyone to appear outside the palace, still less her Majesty and the royal children. Guards trying to reach the palace from outside are being attacked as I was."

Marie Antoinette looked at Louis. "Your Majesty, what orders for the troops?"

"The same as before. To guard the palace, prevent the mob from forcing an entry. But no violence. I hold on to my resolve till the end. No armed force against my people, no blood to be shed at my command."

Another messenger, his condition no better than that of the first, was ushered in.

"Sire, they cry for bread, but their real purpose is to take you by force to Paris. An end to the extravagance of Versailles, they keep shouting, the King shall live modestly at the Tuileries."

One of the ministers, speaking up urgently, suggested that a detachment of horse should be sent to Paris to destroy the bridges.

"Paris will then be cut off, and with Paris cut off, Sire, it will be a simple matter for you to ride at the head of the Flanders Regiment and scatter the mob. Strong action, your Majesty, is essential."

Louis shook his head stubbornly. "Must I repeat, and repeat again, never will I take up arms against my people."

"It is either that, Sire, or flight with the troops to Rambouillet."

Louis' head shot up. "Flight? Never!"

Marie Antoinette heard somebody mutter that the King was afraid, but she knew that to be untrue. Now, if nothing else, Louis

275

was a brave man. She heard somebody else mutter that he was stupid. No, she thought, not really that, not unless kindliness and stupidity went hand in hand. She thought she could see him now as a king shorn of everything but a new-found kingly courage.

The next messenger to arrive came from the commander of the National Guard. Lafayette was on his way, the scribbled note read, with the National Guard to restore order.

"Good!" said Louis. "All will now be well."

Doubting it, Marie Antoinette withdrew to the Oeil de Boeuf. There she found Axel waiting, and attended by him she made a quick tour of the palace. The corridors were lined with courtiers, each ready, as many of them fervently declared, to lay down his life for the royal family. So not all friends had deserted, she thought emotionally.

Leaving Axel, she went to see the children. It was later than she had realized; they had already been put to bed. She spoke for a few moments with the new royal governess, the Marquise de Tourzel, a calm pleasant woman of her own age. She was a widow whose husband, a hunting friend of Louis', had been killed a few years ago in a hunting mishap. The children adored her, Louis Charles especially. After Madame de Tourzel had promised to remain dressed all night and ready if need be for flight, Marie Antoinette returned to Louis. A confusion of stories, rumors and contradictory reports were reaching him all the time. How helpless she felt, shut up in the palace like this, listening, waiting, hoping, despairing.

More and more women had arrived and were standing out there in the rain. She could hear their distant, shrill cries and the spasmodic musket shots. The wine stores of Versailles town, Louis told her, had been plundered and many of the women were drunk and crying crazily for the blood of the Queen. The head of the Austrian whore, or nothing! Louis' people, his beloved people! And the streetwalkers were busy, seducing the troops who stood guard outside, cold to the bone, waiting for definite orders which never came.

Lafayette reached Versailles at midnight. Here to restore order? Here at the head of his umbrella-equipped men? He smiled weakly when Louis questioned him. Not wanting to alarm the King unduly he had refrained from putting the truth in his message. He was here simply because his men would have come without him, so incensed were they by a report that innocent women were being raped and murdered by devil-ridden foreign troops. Marie Antoinette looked at him sorrowfully. Where now was the dashing, romantic aristocrat who had gone so gallantly to the American war?

"Of course, we know now that the report was false," he said with forced cheerfulness. "I shall have no trouble controlling my men."

"Order them to put up their umbrellas," Marie Antoinette said scathingly.

"They have already done so," he replied quite seriously.

Dear God, was this a grim revolution, or a farce staged at a Paris theater?

Louis, in spite of his bewilderment, gave an optimistic little laugh.

"Never fear," he told everybody, "Lafayette will restore order, and later I shall talk to the people, promise to remove my court to Paris." And he added to Marie Antoinette, "Go to bed, my dear. Get a little rest."

Rest!

She went to her own apartments, talked reassuring with her ladies, saw Axel again. Once more he spoke of an escape to Rambouillet.

"All I ask is permission to command a small detachment."

"You would cut a path for me through the mob? Louis would allow it, you think?"

Axel looked at her miserably. "I have already asked him."

"What sanctuary would I find at Rambouillet? The mob would follow."

She went to see Louis again at two o'clock. He was alone now in the inner cabinet, slumped in an armchair. He leaped up at the sight of her.

"Marie, I thought you had gone to bed."

"Sleep would be impossible. In any case, it is well known that the Queen always sits up gambling till dawn."

"But a little rest, even if you were unable to sleep . . . I do urge you to go to bed. I, of course, will stay here all night. Things are not as bad as they might seem. There has been no attempt to break in. Our friends are on guard in the corridors. Outside we have the National Guard."

"And the Flanders Regiment?"

"They are standing by."

"And our personal guards, the Swiss?"

277

"Loyal and steadfast, every single one of them."

"And if attacked, what then? They are to stand at attention, allow themselves to be murdered?"

"Marie, you break my heart."

"Listen!" she said.

Together they went to the window. Flickering lanterns, dotted here and there in the courtyard beneath, gave the only light they could see. They were conscious of, rather than saw, the close-packed mob below. A dull muttered roar rose from it, and now and then a shriek, an insane crude laugh.

"Quieter, much quieter, Marie."

"Yes, Louis." He was asking for reassurance. "Much quieter."

"The light of day will bring sanity. This is just a bad dream. Tomorrow we will forget it. Promise me now you will go to bed."

"I promise."

But first she went again to the children, stealing on tiptoe into their bedchambers. They were sleeping undisturbed. She thanked Madame de Tourzel for watching over them, remembered her promise to Louis and went to her own apartments. Axel was there, and several of her ladies. She dismissed all but two.

"And you, Monsieur," she said formally to Axel, "I—"

"There is a guard outside," he interrupted, "and beyond him, in the outer anteroom, several more." He placed his hand on his sword. "Nevertheless, your Majesty, I beg permission to remain here, inside, as an additional guard."

For a moment she was unable to reply. It was as if something pent up was bursting in her breast.

"Granted," she said, as steadily as she could.

She went into her bedchamber. Her two ladies undressed her and withdrew to the anteroom. The stillness of the bedchamber, emphasized by the dull roar of the mob outside, was well nigh unbearable.

She lay back on the pillows and stared up in the darkness until her eyes ached. She tried desperately to think of nothing whatever, and for a time succeeded. Not conscious of sleeping, she knew that from time to time a light momentary sleep overcame her. She knew because of the constant struggle against the black palpitating nightmare.

A few hours later—she learned afterwards that the time had been six o'clock—she sprang up fully awake and flung open the bed curtains. The noise outside had changed in tempo, had be-

278

come louder, more menacing. Surely it was inside the palace as well as out there in the courtyard! Snatching up a negligee she went barefooted to the door and slowly opened it. Axel was standing at the far door of the anteroom, facing it, his sword drawn. The two ladies were sitting bolt upright in chairs, frozen, wax-like figures. She went forward slowly, unnoticed. As she did so the door was flung open in Axel's face and a guard half-entered. The din rose then, deafeningly. She heard the exultant screams of rage, the tearing ugly sound of doors and panelling crashing asunder.

"For God's sake save the Queen!" the guard shouted.

Axel pushed him from the room, slammed the door and barred it. The din continued, muffled but unabated. He turned his head for a moment and saw her. The two ladies remained unmoving in their chairs.

"Marie!—"

His voice was drowned by a scream of agony outside. Inconsequently she thought, They have killed the poor guard.

Shouting, Axel made himself heard. "Louis' apartments! Take the children there. Hurry, Marie, hurry!"

She ran to him. For a brief moment he held her close. How wrong to have thought that the magic had gone; it was still here between them, its strength intensified. Gently he freed himself.

"As you love me, hurry, hurry!"

Automatically she went back to her bedchamber. The two ladies, coming at last to life, followed her. One slammed and barred the door; another found her Majesty's slippers. Still moving automatically Marie Antoinette entered the passage which led to Louis' apartments. Two thoughts battled for supremacy in her mind: the children, Axel—Axel with only a door between him and certain slaughter. She reached the Oeil de Boeuf. All was unnaturally quiet, a deathly silence. Frantic now, she ran to the inner cabinet. Not a sign of Louis. Back she flew to the Oeil de Boeuf.

"Marie!"

Louis was entering from the outer anteroom. He carried the Dauphin in his arms, a sleepy child rubbing his eyes. Their daughter followed, clinging to Louis' coat, whimpering a little. Behind them came Madame de Tourzel.

"Oh Louis, I searched everywhere for you."

"I searched for you too."

He gave his son to Madame de Tourzel. "Take him to my cabinet. You will be quite safe there." He rumpled his daughter's hair. "Go along too, my pet. And up with your chin! Remember who you are!"

When they had gone Marie Antoinette said, "So they managed to break in."

"Yes . . ."

She could see the struggle going on within Louis, the struggle against bewilderment, personal hurt, disbelief.

"As soon as I heard the uproar," he said dully, "I went out to the vestibule. I was in the guardroom, you see. My only thought was for you. I should have gone back through the Oeuil de Boeuf, reached your apartments that way. But I scarcely knew what I was doing. The mob had swarmed up to the vestibule, men and women in one screaming pack. They had carried fifty or more of the bodyguard with them."

"And the bodyguard still under orders not to fire a single shot," she remarked tonelessly.

"I—yes, I fear so."

"Many of them had been murdered?"

"Yes," he said in a whisper.

"Oh Louis, Louis!"

"The fault was mine. I admit the responsibility."

"Of course, of course."

Louis avoided her eyes. "I was frantic when I realized that some of the mob had forced their way into your outer anteroom. I shouted at them, I pushed myself in amongst them. Derisively they jeered 'Long live the King!' But they made no attempt to harm me."

"They murdered the guard outside my door. Did they— Louis, did they also murder Axel?"

"Thank heaven, no. Axel joined me. He is in the guardroom now. He came out wearing a cloak to hide his uniform and he shouted fiercely—forgive him, my dear, but his words saved your life—he shouted fiercely that the Austrian whore had escaped. There was a stampede then, back through the vestibule, back down the stairway. Six of them were carrying the body of that noble guard above their heads. They—they flung it down the stairway." He covered his face with his hands. "And those were my people, my children."

Marie Antoinette looked at him incuriously. She felt drained of all feeling.

"What did you do next, Louis?"

280

"I found Madame de Tourzel with the children. I brought them here."

"Where is Lafayette?"

"I have seen nothing of him since he went to bed."

"To bed? The commander of the National Guard?" She shrugged. "A traitor, of course."

"No, Marie. You wrong him. He was, and still is, at the mercy of his men. He was genuinely convinced, as I was, that the presence of the National Guard would restore order."

"Waving their umbrellas. Saying to the streetwomen, come share them with us."

"Marie," he asked pitifully, "what am I to do now?"

"Listen!" She had heard a disturbance in the direction of the King's anteroom, or beyond it, in the guardroom. "Are your loyal bodyguards, obeying orders, being murdered one by one?"

He straightened up. "One thing is left to me."

"Louis!" He had moved quickly to the anteroom door.

"I can try a personal appeal."

Feeling had come back overwhelmingly. "Indeed you can! You can say to your people, your children, 'Behave yourselves; go home and take a little rest.' "

He flung open the door. The anteroom was empty, but the sound of raised voices, coming obviously from the guardroom, was louder. He trudged across the anteroom and flung open the guardroom door. Following close behind him she saw, not the mob, but a group of bodyguards. Some were carrying their wounded companions; others lay dying on the floor.

"Lafayette!" Louis shouted.

She saw Lafayette. He was picking his way through the guardroom. Quite fastidious, he looked, in his spotless uniform. He approached Louis and bowed before him.

"I came the moment the news reached me, your Majesty."

"Taking time first to dress yourself with care!" Louis cried, with unaccustomed asperity. "Well, about your business, man! Your duty is to restore order, even at this late stage. Restore it!"

Lafayette gave him a sickly, hurt smile, remembered to bow and withdrew in considerable haste. He returned an hour later, facing Louis and Marie Antoinette again in the inner cabinet.

"Your Majesty, the mob has been removed from the palace."

"Splendid!" Louis said ironically. "They are still outside. Come with me to the window."

Lafayette obeyed.

"What do they want?" Louis asked.

Lafayette turned. "Sire, they want you to show yourself on the balcony. They still demand that you should go to Paris."

Louis touched his brow, stroked it lingeringly. Watching him intently, Marie Antoinette knew she had never seen him more confused, more at a loss. Compassion swamped her. The hurt had gone deep. A bewildered father, scorned and attacked by his blood-crazed children.

He moved slowly, like a sleepwalker, towards the balcony.

"I am here to do their bidding."

Lafayette opened the windows. Louis stepped out, Lafayette immediately behind him. Marie Antoinette followed but hung back out of sight. A roar rose from the mob.

"To Paris! The King to Paris!"

Fumbling for words, Louis said, "They still think of me as their King. Lafayette, my dear fellow, speak to them. My mind is a blank. Speak to them in my name."

Lafayette stepped forward and held up his hand. Silence fell. He cleared his throat. "Your King," he said, in a voice that carried over the unearthly stillness, "will do as you wish. He is anxious to please you in all things. He will go with you to Paris and take up residence at the Tuileries."

The stupidity of it, Marie Antoinette thought. Louis should have spoken, Louis should have berated them for their unforgivable behavior. Louis should have asserted himself now, when all seemed hopeless. Yes, but how could a kindly King, weak in his kindness, do that? It needed the violence of a tyrant.

"The Queen!" a woman shrieked. "Bring out the Austrian whore!"

The whole mob took up the cry. "The Queen, the Queen!"

Louis bowed his head and retreated from the balcony.

"My dear, is it too great a thing to ask of you?"

She drew away from him, horror twisting her heart.

Lafayette had retreated from the balcony also.

"Your Majesty," he begged, "just a brief appearance. Nothing else will satisfy them."

"I am not the plaything of the mob," she said chokingly.

"Your Majesty is . . . afraid?" Lafayette whispered.

His challenge had roused her anger. What now of pride and dignity? She glanced down at her crumpled negligee. Her hair,

282

she knew, was in disarray about her shoulders, her face pale and stiff. A regal sight indeed!

"Your Majesty—" Lafayette began.

She brushed him aside and stepped onto the balcony. Silence fell immediately. She swept the crowd below with a slow glance, from left to right, from right to left. A haze, heavy and chill as the grayness of the sky, dimmed her vision. Her actions, she knew, were automatic. Faintness all but got the better of her. She steadied herself, held her head high, remembered idiotically the words spoken by Louis to their whimpering daughter. *Up with your chin, remember who you are!* A gasp rose from the crowd. Behind her Lafayette whispered, "Never in my life have I seen a more queenly sight."

An isolated voice screamed: "There she is! Fire and be done with the miserable whore!"

"Shame!" came a chorus of protest.

"Long live the Queen!" another voice cried.

The cry was taken up till the whole courtyard echoed and re-echoed with it. Lafayette touched her arm. She stepped back from the balcony.

"There!" he cried, trembling with excitement. "Your Majesty, without a single word, evoked an amazing flood of loyalty."

Bitterly she said, "I know the French. I know their hysteria, their rapidly shifting loyalties. Well, Monsieur, what now?"

"To Paris, Madame. Yourself, the King, the royal children."

"At once, you mean?"

"It must be at once, otherwise the mob will storm the palace again."

"So much for the loyalty I evoked!"

Louis said, "Let us make our preparations, then."

"We go, of course, to a prison."

"No, no, my dear. The Tuileries is a royal palace."

"How long have we to prepare ourselves?" she asked Lafayette.

"An hour at the most, Madame, otherwise—"

Marie Antoinette sent a message to Madame de Tourzel, asking her to prepare the children for the journey to Paris, then she went back to her bedchamber. Some of the mob had been there after Axel had first sent them away. The panelling had been shattered, the bed curtains slashed, the pillows opened up by sword thrusts. As she looked round numbly at the desolation the room began to dance before her eyes. Weakness, held unconsciously at bay until now, was getting the better of her. She found herself falling, and after that lay on the floor, her body shaken by uncontrollable sobbing. Presently she felt a hand on her shoulder. Through eyes that still refused to focus properly she saw the figure of one of her ladies.

"Your Majesty, my heart bleeds for you."

Marie Antoinette raised herself to a sitting position. The lady, weeping herself, reached out to help her to her feet. She dashed the helping hands aside.

"You should have contempt for me, not pity."

She was on her knees now, a moment later shakily on her feet.

"Help me dress, Madame."

Presently, with Lafayette in the anteroom, raising his voice, urging her to make haste, she remembered that at some stage she had gathered together her jewelry. How very silly! Of what use was jewelry now!

Dumbly, frighteningly calm, she joined Lafayette and went with him to Louis' apartments. Louis was standing in the middle of the inner cabinet, clutching at a portfolio of papers. His eyes were glazed, his fat cheeks pallid and sagging.

"They are eager to begin the procession."

"Procession, Louis?"

Lafayette said, "The people wish it. They are intent on leading the royal family to Paris. The coach is waiting. Coaches also for members of the court. Deputies of the Assembly to follow at the rear."

"Ah yes, the deputies. What hand have they had in this slaughter, Monsieur?"

"None, your Majesty. Many were struck dumb with terror last night. The mob invaded the Salle des Menus Plaisirs, taunted the deputies, took charge of the debate that was in progress. Some of the women sat at the president's side; others lay down in the hall and slept."

Louis giggled suddenly. "For once the people were really represented in the Assembly. Delightful, delightful!"

His giggling ceased as suddenly as it had come.

He offered his arm to Marie Antoinette. "The coach is waiting, Madame."

She saw that Madame de Tourzel was in the room with the children. Louis' sister Elizabeth also. And goodness! even Provence and his family.

284

She was aware next that they were all passing slowly down the Marble Stairway. She noticed, with an incurious sort of horror, that the splashes of blood on the marble had begun to dry. Somewhere close at hand a little group of courtiers raised a feeble cry.

"Long live their Majesties!"

Thank you, ladies and gentlemen.

Had she actually spoken the words?

They moved out to the courtyard. Yes, the coach was indeed waiting. Behind it, other coaches; in front of it, the mob in disorganized order. She saw men and women waving pikes. There were heads on some of the pikes, yes, several heads.

They were all in the coach now. Strange there should be room for so many people: herself, Louis, Madame de Tourzel and the children, Madame Elizabeth, Provence and his family. Louis was leaning out of the window, was stupidly asking someone to save, if possible, what was left of Versailles. Over his shoulder she caught a passing glimpse of a familiar face, tense, pale, with burning eyes. Why, to be sure, that was Axel von Fersen.

Afterwards only a few conscious memories of that nightmare drive to Paris remained in her mind. She remembered going through Passy and seeing there, on the terrace of the house of one of his friends, the Duc d'Orleans, a most interested spectator. How the rabble had cheered him! She remembered the endless stream of female faces at the coach windows, the curses, the spray of spittle. And then, shrieked over and over again, the word *boulanger*. French had deserted her; all her thoughts had been in German. Boulanger, boulanger? Of course, how silly! Boulanger—baker. The mob was chanting something about bakers and bread. Who need go short of bread now? Here was the chief baker, his wife and his oven boy.

And then they were at the gates of the city. The mayor of Paris was waiting to greet them. He offered Louis the keys of the city on the inevitable velvet cushion. Cushion? It was a bowl of blood, the keys floating on the thick red surface.

Next, she knew that they had entered the Tuileries Palace, that Louis, complaining of cramp, was stamping his feet, flinging out his arms.

"Marie, do you know what the time is?"

She looked at him vaguely. "The time, Louis?" Her mind cleared for a moment; she pointed a finger at him. "Of course, so important to a clockmaker. Not the baker and his wife, the clock-maker and his wife. In what part of the city do you propose to set up business? After all, we must earn our keep. We can't live for-ever on my diamonds."

"Poor Marie," he said gently, "how weary you must be. The drive to Paris took nearly seven hours."

"Nearly? Be exact, Louis. A clockmaker must be exact."

"Six hours thirty-four minutes, my dear."

"Good, good!"

"Dear sweet Marie," he begged. "Be of good cheer. See, I am full of confidence again. The bewilderment is passed. I can even begin to believe that our arrival in Paris will bring peace and a new understanding."

She laughed with a shrillness that appalled her.

"Peace and a new understanding! Well, why not, Louis, why not!"

Part V

ONE

"BERRI," MADAME ADELAIDE SAID FRETFULLY, "HAS REFUSED TO receive me."

Marie Antoinette gave her a deliberately blank look. "I beg your pardon?"

"Berri—" Madame Adelaide began again, then flushing, understood. She curtsied ironically. "His Majesty the King has refused to receive me."

"I sent him a message," Madame Adelaide went on. "He referred me to you."

Marie Antoinette studied the old-maid aunt as she stood stiffly before her. Ancient, she looked now, thin faced. A withered twig of a woman but still as strong as a horse. Almost Marie Antoinette had grown to like her again, if only for one reason: unlike so many others, Madame Adelaide had shown no eagerness to emigrate.

"To be precise," Madame Adelaide added, "it was my request that he referred to you."

"So you have a request, Madame."

Madame Adelaide gave Marie Antoinette a beady-eyed darting glance. "As your Majesty knows I am a most religious woman."

Marie Antoinette smiled. "We need not argue about that."

"Thank you! Well then, from a religious point of view, if from no other, the position of the royal family is now intolerable."

Marie Antoinette understood. "Ah yes, the civil oath."

It had long been the aim of the National Assembly to separate the throne and the clergy. Soon after the arrival at the Tuileries the possessions of the clergy had been confiscated and given over

287

to the use of that nebulous body, the People. This had been followed a year later by a decree demanding that the clergy should swear allegiance, no longer to the King, but to the people, the people as represented by the National Assembly. Louis had been horrified and had resisted with an amazing stubbornness, but intimidated in the end by threats of new risings he had been forced to grant the royal sanction.

"Yes indeed, the civil oath!" Madame Adelaide's cracked old voice rose indignantly. "Only priests who have taken the civil oath are permitted to attend us. I ask you, can one truly make a confession to a renegade?"

Marie Antoinette laughed lightly. "You actually find confession necessary?"

Madame Adelaide, her eyes twinkling suddenly, tried to ignore this jibe.

"Your Majesty, I want to worship God in godly surroundings. I seek permission to go to Rome and take Victoire with me."

Marie Antoinette studied her in silence.

Haughtily Madame Adelaide said, "No doubt you think it a plausible excuse!"

"No, Madame. You were never a coward."

"Royal permission is granted, then?"

"Knowing how much it costs you to ask it of *me*—"

"Wait!" Madame Adelaide interrupted. "It *is* a plausible excuse. There now, you know the worst. I *am* a coward. My nerve has failed me. I want to run away."

"Knowing how much it costs you to ask it of *me*," Marie Antoinette repeated, "royal permission is granted."

"You will be glad to be rid of me, of course!" Madame Adelaide challenged.

Marie Antoinette considered this. "No."

"Not after the way I have wronged you?"

"When are you leaving?" Marie Antoinette asked.

"As soon as possible, providing the new rulers of France will permit it."

"Having received royal permission, do you propose now to apply to the National Assembly?"

"Certainly not! I refuse to accept the authority of the Assembly. I shall start off, hope for the best and defend myself with my tongue."

Marie Antoinette smiled. "A powerful weapon, in all conscience."

Madame Adelaide's face crumpled again, and this time tears filled her eyes, spilled down her raddled cheeks.

"Dear little Marie," she said brokenly. "I have always loved you, underneath, always. Can you forgive me for the dreadful things I have done to you?"

"With all my heart," Marie Antoinette cried impulsively.

"It was my pride and vanity. I wanted to rule poor Berri. Mind you—" she was in control of her tears now—"he might have been a stronger King if I had."

Marie Antoinette embraced her quickly. "Dear Aunt Adelaide, you must come back as soon as you can."

"Back?" Madame Adelaide snorted. "Back to what? Will there ever be anything to come back to? Can you tell me of anything that has happened since you came to the Tuileries to give you real hope of restoring the old order? Can you, child?"

"Child! How strange to be called that at my age!"

"I am seeing you as you were when you first came to France, remembering so much."

"The way you wagered your favorite horse, and lost it, for instance?"

"Yes." Madame Adelaide was on the point of weeping again. "Please answer my question, Marie."

Obediently Marie Antoinette looked back over the past year. She thought of those first few days, here at the Tuileries, a long-neglected palace, dirty, unfurnished, full of the echoing loneliness and despair she felt herself. The settling down, as Louis called it, had not been easy, though in Paris there had been a growing atmosphere of relieved tension, an apparent desire on many people's part to forget, to return to the old familiar gaiety. Was the worst over? That had been the question on everybody's lips. A few, Count Mercy among them, had shaken their heads. A short respite only, a critical pause in the progress of revolution.

Louis, always so quickly optimistic, had echoed this opinion. He was more miserable than he had ever been and fell into a sulky drifting with the tide. The real reason for this, she had soon discovered, was the fact that he was no longer able to hurt, except in the Bois de Boulogne, and then under the 'protection' of a detachment of National guards. "My liver is out of order, food no longer agrees with me, I need violent exercise." He went but little to the Bois, took exercise of a sort by stumping up and down the echoing corridors of their prison.

And the Tuileries was, as she had expected, a prison. Oh yes, they were permitted to go where they chose in the city, even to spend short periods at St. Cloud, but by the ruling of the National Assembly they had freedom only within an area of twenty miles from the Town Hall. Held by an invisible chain, they could go no further than the chain permitted, while within the Tuileries a mockery of etiquette and routine continued. There was still the public dressing and undressing, still the dining in public, but now it was a National guard, not a royal bodyguard, who stood behind the King's chair.

The National Assembly now held their sessions in Paris, using the former Tuileries riding school. They had moved to the capital to be close to their King, not out of love of him, but to keep a possessive eye on him, hold him down beneath the weight of their heavy thumb. They had passed and were still passing decrees by the score, decrees which, by their ruling, still needed the farcical royal sanction.

"Well?" Madame Adelaide asked.

Hesitantly Marie Antoinette said, "Mirabeau . . ."

"Mirabeau?" Madame Adelaide questioned sharply.

Marie Antoinette realized she had made a slip. Her dealings with Mirabeau were secret.

"His speeches in the Assembly reveal a certain sanity. That was all I meant."

She saw in Mirabeau a faint hope of safety and was using him only as a means to an end. Mirabeau wanted a constitutional monarchy. Well, why not, if it would give her a breathing space, and a stepping-stone to the restoration of absolute power. Mirabeau believed that nothing could be achieved while Louis remained at the Tuileries, a prisoner on parole. He advocated a flight to Normandy, where the people, in spite of the insanity elsewhere, were still fiercely loyal to the throne. This she had learned after a secret meeting with Mirabeau at St. Cloud. Louis, when she had discussed it with him, had shaken his head. He had given the National Assembly his royal word not to leave Paris, and in any case, if he went to Normandy he would risk civil war.

She thought of Axel, whom she also met secretly when at St.

Cloud. He had lodgings in Paris again, and when it was known that the royal family were going to St. Cloud he stayed nearby at the chateau of a friend. Axel's plan, too, was flight, but flight to the border, the rallying of foreign aid, the march back to Paris of a forceful, triumphant King. It sounded grand and inspiring, but Louis remained stubbornly against it. Nevertheless, working through Axel, she had put out feelers abroad, but no real interest had been raised. She had felt that she could rely on her own Austria, but the sudden death of her brother Joseph had been a bitter blow. Another brother, Leopold, was Emperor now, and Leopold, with whom she had never been friendly, was showing little enthusiasm.

"Well?" Madame Adelaide said again.

"I can see hope in one direction only, and that not yet."

"Escape to the border? Foreign aid?"

"Yes. Or failing that, exile."

"Not exile, Marie! Never that!"

"You are going into exile yourself."

"A coward, I admit it." Madame Adelaide clutched at Marie Antoinette's hand. "I beseech you, never permanent exile for you and Berri. Never resignation!"

"Never resignation, Aunt Adelaide. I promise you that. You have put new heart in me today."

"Then, child, I go not too unhappily."

Later in the day Marie Antoinette went to Louis' bedchamber. His apartments were above hers, on the first floor of the palace, and connected by a small, newly built stairway. Louis was still in bed. At the sight of her he put down the book he had been pretending to read and stared at her blankly.

She sat down by the bed. "I think you look a little better today, Louis."

"Yes. Yes, the physicians assure me that I am improving rapidly. The fever, or whatever it was, has passed. It was aggravated by all the worry about the civil oath. I shall be up and about in a day or so. Though what there is to get up for, God only knows."

"Madame Adelaide," she remarked, noting that he was inclined to talk lengthily, still feverishly, "wants to go to Rome."

"Yes. I referred the request to you. Well, let her go. Perhaps they are right, these *émigrés*. Perhaps flight is the only solution. Perhaps Mirabeau is right, or Axel. After all, why *not* leave the National Assembly to blunder on alone until things get completely out of hand, until the people demand the return of their King."

"Why, Louis—!"

"No, no," he said wearily, "I have given my word. Mirabeau is our only hope, but he must compromise. He must find a solution which will not force me to break my word. And no risk of civil war. Remember that, Marie."

After a long silence—it did seem that they had nothing else to say to each other—she rose and left him. Back in her own apartments she was surprised to find Madame Elizabeth waiting for her.

"Aunt Adelaide is going to Rome," Elizabeth said.

"Yes. How embarrassed you look, Elizabeth. Do you want to go with her?"

Elizabeth shook her head violently. "No! No, no, no!"

"Then, my dear—"

"I want to stay. I want to help if I can. I— Aunt Adelaide spoke to me just now. She—she made a confession. None of the terrible things she said about you was true. Not one! I—Marie, I feel so *ashamed*." She flung her arms round Marie Antoinette and wept bitterly. "Can you ever forgive me?"

"Of course. It is very easy to be misled. But Elizabeth, I think you ought to go for your own sake. I think I ought to command you to go."

"No, please! Not unless you want to punish me."

"Punish you?"

"I can't leave Louis. I can't leave you. I want to stay and help and make amends."

"Make amends," Marie Antoinette laughed, "by ceasing to suffer me with Christian charity."

Elizabeth smiled wanly. "How insufferable I must have been. I see that now."

Louise de Lamballe entered the room unseen by Madame Elizabeth. She hesitated for a moment, smiled understandingly at Marie Antoinette and went softly away. Louise had come to the Tuileries the day after the forced arrival and had been here ever since. For what it was worth she held again the position of *surintendante* and was always a source of comfort when it was possible to accept comfort. But I do wish, Marie Antoinette thought now, she would go while she can and find safety, if nothing else, abroad.

292

A few days later a deputation from the National Assembly approached Louis. It was suggested—in other words it was commanded—that he should pay another series of visits to the factories and workshops of the city. He had engaged in this occupation soon after the arrival at the Tuileries and the people, or so everybody said, had been quite pleased.

"Am I expected to accompany you?" Marie Antoinette asked.

"It is the hope of the Assembly that you will."

"Very well." She smiled, ready for the moment to tease him. "I know you will be happy if a few clockmaking establishments are also visited."

"Yes indeed," Louis laughed.

The series of visits began and were stoically continued, stoically as far as Marie Antoinette was concerned. As for Louis himself, he grew boyishly enthusiastic, talked at length with the men at the benches and often suggested that this or that method would be easier and quicker. Watching and listening, Marie Antoinette conceived an odd feeling about the spirit of their reception by the workpeople, a feeling which for a time she was unable to describe.

"I have enjoyed myself immensely," Louis said, after a week of such activity. "I know they were all very glad to see us."

"There was certainly something unusual about the way they received us."

"Ah, you noticed that? So did I. A real genuine enthusiasm."

"Enthusiasm?" She thought she saw at last what it was. "Enthusiasm if you like, Louis, but a quite appalling enthusiasm."

"My *dear*—"

"We have become a sort of possession. We do indeed belong to the people. Some of them were ready to pat you on the back. A king with no authority. Not really a king at all. A tame domestic animal! Yes, Louis, just that!"

"Marie—"

"Soon," she ran on indignantly, "we will with practice be able to perform all the tricks required of us. Go to the factories, the Assembly will command. Obediently we will do so. Visit the workers' homes. Well, why not? Take a glass of wine with the streetsweepers. Gladly! Democracy, my dear Louis. Constitutional monarchy. Such a grand phrase!" She paused for breath. "Dear heaven, Louis, is that going to be the fate of the kings and queens of the future, the life of useless, quite tame domestic animals? But behave yourselves, little royal figureheads, or out comes the whip. Given a salary, of course, a sort of stipend. Paid to grow bored. Paid to forget the purpose for which you were born!"

"Dear Marie," Louis mumbled, "how much more you believe in divine right, absolute monarchy, than I do."

"What else can I believe in? What else have I ever known?" Hatred tore at her heart, hatred of the mob, hatred that covered fear. "Louis," she added, "we must do as Mirabeau suggests."

He ignored this. "In spite of all the changes that are being forced upon us we must endeavor always to love this country, this France."

"Why should *I* love it?" she burst out. "What has France done for me except to label me the Austrian whore?"

"It was our own kind who began that sorry libel, Marie."

"Whoever began it, we now have a revolution and the people believe the libel. Oh Louis, have you forgotten what happened at Versailles? Have you forgotten that I would have died there but for Axel? What would you be doing now, Louis, if they had murdered me? Would you be visiting factories, wagging your head sagely, saying 'All is now well'? Would you, Louis?"

"Marie," Louis said slowly, "that carnage at Versailles still troubles my sleep with ghastly nightmares. Had you died then I would have sought out your murderers and torn them apart."

The simple conviction of his words touched her heart, dissipated her anger. She embraced him swiftly. But poor Louis, she thought, there is no room in this violent world for a gentle, loving heart. To survive one must grow hard, hard!

"Let us go to St. Cloud for a short respite," he said.

They went to St. Cloud for a few days, travelling as usual under the "protective" custody of the National Guard. There she met Mirabeau again, as she had met him before, late at night in a secluded part of the grounds. It was a calm clear night, the air crisp rather than chilly. The stars, she thought, had a brighter, larger look. A setting, surely, for romance! Would Mirabeau be numbered some day with the rest of the lovers ascribed to her?

She found him pacing restlessly up and down, his black cloak flying out behind him, swishing like a whip when he turned. He was a man of tremendous, almost frightening energy, a man seeking impatiently an outlet for his personal aims and ambitions. She

294

reflected with distaste that this former leader of the Third Estate was by birth an aristocrat, an aristocrat who by his earlier actions was a traitor to his class. Sufficient justification, surely, in striving to use him and then, when he had served his purpose, cast him aside.

"Monsieur le Comte," she said softly.

He came to her side at once and bowed briefly. "Your Majesty."

She shuddered, as she had shuddered before, at the ugliness of his gross, pock-marked face. His harsh voice, which at times rose to a ragged thunder-clap, was just as repugnant. What had Louis agreed to pay him on the completion of his service? A million livres, no less. The sooner the service was completed and, always providing the money could be found, the debt paid, the better would she be pleased.

"Madame," he said, "the King must make up his mind, and quickly. I was accused today of selling myself to the enemy—the enemy of course being the royal family. I was threatened with personal violence—in short, hanging from the nearest tree. Not that I care, or go in fear of my life, but in me lies the fate of the crown."

"I think you over-estimate your own importance, Monsieur."

Mirabeau's ugly face broke into a grin. "That haughtiness of yours, Madame, will be the death of you yet."

"An exchange of insults will achieve nothing," she said impatiently. "I am charged, Monsieur, to ask you to find a peaceful solution to the King's problems."

"You believe a peaceful solution possible?"

"No."

"Madame, I urge you to force the King to accept my plan. He must act without a moment's delay. Otherwise, the constitutional monarchy I envisage will remain a dream."

"We have a constitutional monarchy already, Monsieur."

"No. We have nothing at all, except a King in chains." He flung back his cloak and seemed for a moment to be overcome by a spasm of uncontrollable fury. "The King misses the whole point of my argument. Only through civil war can he assert himself. Triumphant in civil war, he will then be able to set up a constitutional monarchy of his own design."

"And in this new regime, what position do you propose to hold?"

Mirabeau laughed heartily. "Does a name matter? Shall I not be the power behind the throne?"

She had expected this, but had not expected him to declare himself so boldly. Her resolve to use him and cast him aside strengthened.

"Make your secret arrangements," she said quietly. "Be ready to move the moment I give the word. The King will go to Normandy. I promise you that."

Mirabeau bowed low, a little mockingly perhaps, but his voice was charged with admiration.

"Madame, you are the only man at court."

She and Louis and the children returned the next morning to the Tuileries. During the drive Louis asked her about the meeting with Mirabeau. Evading the real issue she told him briefly that Mirabeau was working frantically to find a solution. She knew that nothing would persuade Louis to make the flight to Normandy, but something of Mirabeau's violent energy had gripped her. Louis must be removed to Normandy by force, just as he had been removed from Versailles to the Tuileries by force. Once that was achieved he would accept the situation.

On arrival at the Tuileries they learned that Madame Adelaide and Madame Victoire had been detained for a time at the border, but only for a time. True to her word, Madame Adelaide had indeed defended herself with her tongue. "Keep me here," she had raged scornfully, "and the world will know without doubt that the royal family is held in France by force." She had also cursed the frontier officials in a manner expected only of a Paris fishwife.

"A happy augury," Louis declared.

"Why that?"

"The National Assembly, when it comes to the point, is afraid of arousing too much indignation in the rest of Europe."

"I place no faith in the indignation of the rest of Europe. We must look to ourselves. Nobody really cares what happens to us."

Louis bubbled over with sudden, alarming laughter.

"The tame domestic animals! Imagine my little Marie in *that* role!"

More determined than ever to take Louis by force to Normandy, Marie Antoinette waited impatiently for the opportunity of another meeting with Mirabeau. He wrote to her frequently, letters which she burned as soon as she had read them, but she felt that the risk involved in writing to him was too great to be taken. Several times she brought up the subject of another visit to St. Cloud, but each time Louis shook his head.

"The feeling is growing that we go there too often, have too much freedom there. However, we shall go to St. Cloud for Easter. I have quite made up my mind on that."

"Why Easter in particular, Louis?"

"My dear, Easter is the most important religious celebration of the whole year. I—" he lowered his voice as if afraid spies were hiding behind the curtains—"I refuse to celebrate Easter at the Tuileries with none but renegade priests in attendance."

"But even at St. Cloud—"

He smiled darkly. "I am making secret arrangements. Real priests will be there."

Impatient of the delay, she began to form her plans for Easter, and then word came that Mirabeau had suddenly died.

"What did he die of?" she asked Louis, who broke the news to her. "He was in perfect health last time I met him!"

"No one seems to know. Perhaps it was a surfeit of women." Louis looked at her solemnly. "He slept with two the night he died." He cleared his throat. "Forgive me. I am not making a joke. A rather poor one, if I were. An inquiry will be held, of course."

The result of the inquiry was death by natural causes, yet the causes were not stated. Rumor, which spread rapidly, suggested that Mirabeau had been poisoned by his political enemies. Not that it mattered, she told herself wearily. There was no hope now of taking Louis by force to Normandy. She was trapped now, completely trapped.

On the morning they were to start off for St. Cloud Louis rose earlier than usual. He was in high spirits. He came a dozen times to her apartments, urging her to hurry, not to keep the coaches waiting. He stumped impatiently about the corridors, organizing the servants, chiding the members of the court for their slothfulness. He was like a boy planning a fishing excursion on the river.

When at last everybody was ready he ran out ahead of the little party to the Cour des Princes. He returned almost immediately, his face showing annoyance.

"Only one coach. I distinctly remember ordering six."

297

He ran back to the Cour des Princes. And then it came, distant but unmistakable, the howling roar of the mob. He returned once more, accompanied this time by Lafayette.

"A slight disturbance, my dear," he said, the old bewildered look on his face. "Apparently my reason for wishing to spend Easter at St. Cloud has got about. They—they don't want me to go." He looked pathetically at Lafayette. "Surely St. Cloud is within the limits of travel imposed upon us?"

Lafayette bowed. "Of course, your Majesty."

Marie Antoinette stirred herself.

"Organize your men, Monsieur," she commanded Lafayette. "Your duty, and theirs, is to protect us."

Lafayette, looking distressed and helpless, took his leave.

Louis said, "The coaches were stopped outside by the mob. Only one managed to get through into the courtyard. Someone, thank goodness, had the sense to close the gates and keep the mob out."

Marie Antoinette took her daughter by one hand, her son by the other. She moved forward resolutely.

"Come, Louis."

"I— Very well."

They went out to the coach followed by Madame Elizabeth and Madame de Tourzel.

"At least the mob is held back by the gates," Marie Antoinette said, when they were all seated.

"But dare we open the gates?" Louis demanded. "*Dare* we proceed?"

"Give the order, Louis!"

Louis did so, and this proved to be a disastrous move. The men of the National Guard regiment had been standing stiffly at attention in the courtyard, but now they fell suddenly into confusion. Lafayette, Marie Antoinette saw, was arguing and pleading with them, not issuing stern orders. Shouldering him aside they moved in an untidy body to the coach, surrounded it and shook their fists menacingly. The National Guard now, as well as the Paris mob! A mob in themselves, really, some of them shouting derisively.

"Great fat pig!"

"Austrian whore!"

"Back to the kennel where you belong!"

298

Louis thrust his head out of the window. "Less noise, I beg of you! Listen for a moment while I speak to you!"

Marie Antoinette laughed hoarsely. The ineptitude of it all! Louis might just as well have shouted "Shoo!" to a charging lioness. Madame Royale pressed herself against her mother's side, the little Dauphin began to cry.

"You are frightening the children!" Louis shouted. "Quiet, you idiots, quiet!"

But his voice was drowned by derisive cheering.

He withdrew his head. "I fear we have no recourse but to bow to the will of the people."

He opened the coach door and stepped awkwardly down, then he lifted the children down and held up his hand to Marie Antoinette. In silence, with fists shaken in their faces, muskets brandished over their heads, but unmolested, they re-entered the Tuileries.

When the great doors had been closed and barred Louis turned and stared at them blankly. He spoke at last, in little more than a whisper, but a whisper which carried strongly.

"The constitution to which I gave my foolish assent permits me to go freely where I please, unmolested, within twenty miles of Paris. I gave my word that I would never infringe that ruling. I gave my word to Paris. Paris gave its word to me. Paris has broken its word. I am free now to break mine."

Marie Antoinette looked at him in amazement. Now, when all hope had seemed vain, her heart grew full of it.

"Louis, you—you mean—?"

He looked at her somberly. "I am ready to plan an escape. I am ready to go to the border. Send secretly for Axel."

TWO

IN THE DREAM THE REVOLUTION WAS REPRESENTED BY A SINGLE monstrous female, broadshouldered, sneering, bare-breasted. Marie Antoinette could feel the wrenching downward pull of this creature's claw-like hands on her own slim shoulders. A dream, only a dream, she told herself as she struggled to wake. A dream, yet she could feel the pain of the strong fingers biting into her flesh.

"Wake up, my dear! Come, wake up!"

It was Louis' voice, shattering the darkness, rescuing her before the horror grew too great to bear. Did people die in their sleep because of a dream too horrible to support?

She opened her eyes. Her heart was still beating painfully. Louis, his hands on her shoulders, was shaking her gently.

"I've been awake for hours," Louis said. "I came down to rouse you. A momentous day, Marie. One can't afford to lie in bed on such a day."

She remembered then. Tonight at midnight, the flight from Paris.

"Mind you," Louis went on, sounding like a boy playing an earnest game of hide-and-seek, "neither of us must show any sign of untoward excitement. Normal routine, that is the order of the day."

"Yes, Louis."

"What time do we expect Axel?"

"Five this afternoon."

She relaxed on the pillows and thought of all that Axel had done for them. Their only trustworthy contact with the outside world, he had negotiated for weeks with General Bouillé, commander of the army of the eastern section of France. Bouillé, his loyalty to the King presumably beyond question, was on the surface a faithful servant of the National Assembly. His plan, which they were to follow in detail, was flight to the border fortress of Montmédy. His chief concern had been how to cover the flight without arousing suspicion, but happily the indiscreet

300

actions of a large concentration of *émigrés* beyond the border had given him a plausible excuse for making troop movements. They, the *émigrés*, were declaring an open intention of invading France to rescue their King; General Bouillé must therefore stand in readiness to repel such an invasion.

The next step had been the matter of passports. Passports were essential if they were to pass in safety through the gates of Paris. Axel had a friend, a Russian woman, a widow by the name of Korff. Marie Antoinette frowned now, as she had frowned many times, at the thought of this widow. Very little was known to her of Axel's life in Paris. Just what had induced Madame Korff to apply to the Russian embassy for passports granting safe passage to herself, her children and servants? Yes, and then hand over the passports to the King and Queen of France? Axel had another friend, a wealthy Scot by the name of Crufurd, who had placed at their disposal his house in Paris. It was there that the large travelling coach had been hidden, there that clothes and other essentials had been stored.

Yes, Axel had been marvellous, not only when it came to meticulous, detailed planning, but in the way he had managed by a cheerful word to prevent Louis, so often irresolute, from changing his mind. Without Axel tirelessly helping them in every direction all hope of escape would have long since vanished.

Louis said, "Part of my disguise is a large brown wig." He laughed gently. "It is impossible, of course, to disguise my shape. Let us hope the guards at the gates will be too sleepy to take notice of a fat gentleman waddling across the courtyard."

She looked at him curiously. "Louis, are you afraid?"

He looked surprised. "Not in the least. Are you?"

"When I think of tonight, yes. So much depends on tonight. The risk of discovery terrifies me."

"Like all women," he said placidly, "you have too much imagination."

"Before we leave for Montmédy," he said, "I want one thing made quite clear."

"Yes, Louis?"

"My purpose, Marie, is to establish myself at Montmédy and gather about me all the loyal *émigrés* who care to join me. My position two hundred miles from Paris should be a strong one. There I shall issue a manifesto to the people deploring the high-handed methods of the National Assembly, pointing out their mistakes. I shall point out that the poor are starving, their privations worse than ever before. Whose fault is that? Mine, shorn of power as I am, or the National Assembly's? The good sense of Frenchmen will assert itself. They will gladly turn to me again."

"Of course, Louis," she said patiently.

"A joint co-operation between King and people. That is what I want. In a word, moderation. But one thing I will have. Freedom for the clergy. An end to the iniquitous civil oath."

"What if the Assembly sends an army against us?"

"To avoid civil war I would go gladly into permanent exile."

Louis went back then to his own apartments, and for Marie Antoinette the routine of what, at the Tuileries, was a normal day began with the entry of the waiting women.

During the afternoon, attended as ever by a detachment of National guards, she took the children for a drive as far as the Jardin Boutin. Neither had been told of the plan of escape; neither seemed suspicious. Unnaturally quiet they were, these days. Even the thirteen-year-old Madame Royale had little to say for herself; not actually cowed, but quiet and watchful and ready to cling to her mother. It was the same with the Dauphin, who was now six. He was still a healthy child, but far too nervous for a boy of his age. The horror of that drive from the palace of Versailles to the Tuileries, half-forgotten, had been revived by the violent demonstration at Easter. She could see it in both children's eyes. For that reason if for no other the escape tonight must be completely successful.

Groups of idlers stared at the coach as the drive continued. It was, she felt, a brooding silence. The Queen and her children taking an airing in the June sunshine, but held tight like dogs on leashes. "Watch them well," an old crone screeched at the guards, "they'll make a dash for it one of these days." Many people, she knew, were expecting an attempt at escape, and had been ever since that man Marat had warned the people in his newspaper that an escape was planned.

Back at the Tuileries she spoke to the officer in charge of her escort.

"Thank you. A pleasant drive. Will the weather be as good tomorrow?"

"There is every sign of it, Madame."

"Then the same drive tomorrow, at the same time."

No untoward excitement? Certainly not! But if only she could feel pleasure in this glib little deception, pleasure instead of that crawling, griping pain in the pit of her stomach. Too much imagination? So much simpler, life without imagination.

She took the children to Madame de Tourzel and had a few words with that lady in private.

"All goes well, Madame?"

"All goes well, your Majesty."

"We must remember soon to call you Madame Korff."

Madame de Tourzel, holding the passports, would impersonate the Russian, Madame Korff. The royal children would be her children; the King and Queen and the King's sister would be her servants. Unless suspicions were aroused, only 'Madame Korff' would need to speak while the others cowered back in the darkness of the coach, breathless, waiting . . . Imagination! Fight against it, fight against it!

Marie Antoinette went next to Louis' apartments. It was almost five o'clock. She found him busy at his desk. He was working, he said, on the manifesto. A few moments later Axel slipped quietly into the room. He wore plain clothes instead of the former conspicuous uniform. She noticed for the first time that he was looking older; there were lines she had never seen before on his handsome face, and his fine dark eyes betrayed a little of the strain he felt. Well, she was looking older too. There were streaks of gray in her once-beautiful hair. At thirty-six, she thought, an old, old woman . . .

"You were not recognized or challenged?" Louis asked.

"No."

"Splendid!"

They listened while Axel outlined the plan of action from then till midnight. Normal routine would continue. Dinner would be taken in public. Madame Elizabeth would join them at table, so would Provence and his wife. Marie Antoinette told herself there was much to be said in Provence's favor. He had shown no fear, had given no sign of wanting to escape himself until the plan was confided in him. Now he too was going, first to Belgium, then to Montmédy.

"I suggest ten o'clock for the King's *coucher*," Axel went on.

"Agreed," said Louis.

The public undressing, if only to show that no change had been made in established routine, was more necessary than ever tonight. Lafayette would be present and probably a few deputies.

303

They would drive up in their carriages, and drive away again afterwards, satisfied that his Majesty was going obediently to bed.

"The carriages will be waiting, as usual, in the Cour des Princes," Axel said. "I shall arrive shortly after ten in a plain carriage and leave it with the others. It will cause no comment. Meanwhile—" he turned to Marie Antoinette—"you will prepare the children. We have already spoken of the unused apartment on the ground floor, the one with a door opening onto the courtyard. You will take the children there with Madame de Tourzel and see them into the carriage. As for your part, Louis—"

"Quite simple," Louis said. "I have been undressed, I have gone to bed. It is known that I sleep soundly. I am sleeping soundly. All I have to do is get up, dress and steal down the stairs."

"But your valet," Fersen pointed out. "If you disturb him—"

"Goodness gracious," Louis wailed, "the piece of string!"

Marie Antoinette had forgotten that when sleeping in his own apartments Louis did so with a length of string attached to his valet's thumb. It was an old tradition. If his Majesty needed any attention during the night, all he had to do was tug at the string and the servant, sleeping on a camp bed in the same room, was instantly awakened.

"Clumsy as I am," Louis said, "I shall contrive not to disturb him. But this carriage of yours in the Cour des Princes, Axel, is there a change of plan? Are we all to drive away in it?"

Axel shook his head. "Madame de Tourzel and the children only, the children on the floor. I shall then drive it to the Place du Petit Carrousel. Carriages are often left there by people visiting friends in the neighborhood. I shall be just another coachman waiting for the rest of my passengers. You, Louis, Marie and Madame Elizabeth will join me there."

"But to be separated from the children," Marie Antoinette protested, "even for so short a time—"

"Wiser that way," Axel said. "An escape is half-expected. A carriage full of people might be held up at the gates. As it is, no one would expect the King and Queen to *walk* away from the Tuileries, boldly, even in the dark."

"You have thought of everything," Louis said.

Marie Antoinette smiled in spite of herself. "But one thing worries Louis. His shape is familiar to all the guards."

Axel smiled too. "For the past week or so a trusted friend of mine has attended the *coucher* every night. He wears a brown wig and a cloak similar to the one Louis will wear. He is a very bulky gentleman. The guards have often jeered at his resemblance to the King. He is a familiar figure now. Tonight, after attending the *coucher*, he will delay his departure until Louis is safely away."

Louis roared with laughter. "What a delightful joke!"

"Where do we join the travelling coach?" Marie Antoinette asked.

"Just within the Saint-Martin gate. Then we drive up to the barrier, show the passports and proceed on the journey."

"It sounds so simple, Axel!"

"It *is* simple, Marie."

"You propose to leave us—where?" Louis asked.

"At Bondy."

"You will join us as soon as possible at Montmédy?" Marie Antoinette asked.

"As soon as possible," he assured her.

Louis rose and came lumbering forward from his desk. He flung an arm round Axel's shoulder.

"Some day when all this fuss is over, you shall have a place of honor at my side. If the worst happens I shall always remember you as the truest friend a man could ever have."

Marie Antoinette followed Axel out to the anteroom. Carefully she closed the door behind her.

"Axel, before you go—"

He turned to look at her. "Yes, Marie?"

"Much money has been needed for all these arrangements. Where has it come from?"

"Friends have provided it," Axel said brusquely.

"Tell me their names. I want to remember them."

"Their names are of no importance."

His continued brusqueness told her all she wanted to know.

"There is just one friend, Axel. How did you manage to raise so much money?"

"That is my own business."

Marie Antoinette stamped her foot. "I want to know! Tell me!"

"I have expectations. It was possible to raise mortgages in Sweden."

"Axel!"

"It was the only way," he said simply.

"Axel," she said quickly, "promise me one thing."

"I would promise you anything. You know that."

"If the worst happens your part in all this will become common knowledge. Promise me you will get out of France and stay out."

Axel looked at her in stubborn silence.

"The mob would tear you to pieces, Axel. It would break my heart."

"I cannot make such a promise."

"You said you would promise me anything."

"That was rash of me."

"How angry you make me! I command you to make that promise. I, the Queen, command it!"

Axel smiled. "Your Majesty has not the right to command anything of a foreigner."

Tears sprang to her eyes. "Why do you want to remain in France? To be near the widow, Madame Korff! Yes, that must be it!"

He looked aghast. "My dear Marie—"

"Have you known her long? Is she in love with you?"

"She has never been shameless enough to tell me so."

"Why else should she oblige with passports?"

"Sympathy for the royal cause."

"Oh nonsense! You knew she would refuse you nothing. That was why you approached her."

Axel smiled faintly. "I see I had better admit it. Otherwise—" he glanced at the door—"you will make a terrible scene and bring Louis out to inquire."

Marie Antoinette lowered her voice. "And her payment for this service rendered?"

"Marie, she obtained duplicate passports. She pretended that the originals had been destroyed by accident. She needs the originals. How dare she remain in Paris after the duplicates have been shown at the Saint-Martin barrier? She leaves tonight, at the same time, by another route."

"Her payment, her payment!"

"She will continue to love me and hope that I will join her in Belgium."

Her anger collapsed suddenly. "Forgive me, Axel. I am deeply ashamed of myself, and very very grateful to Madame Korff."

He embraced her quickly, in the old way.

"It is still here between us, Marie, the magic of our love."

"No," she said wilfully, "no!" She clung to him demandingly. "Something more human has driven it out, promising a greater magic. We are not and never have been the lofty spiritual creatures you like to imagine."

He kissed her full on the lips; she clung to him passionately.

"So," she said, holding him away from her, "you really are a man of flesh and blood." She laughed bitterly. "Is it because it is all so hopeless now, because we can have no more than a moment or two alone like this? Does it give us a sort of cowardly courage?"

Footsteps which she had ignored before were passing along the corridor again. Those of the guard, of course, and this time they stopped outside the door. Axel looked at the door, and waited. The footsteps resumed and grew faint. He went quickly to the door, opened it quietly and looked out. He glanced back at Marie Antoinette, whispered "Till tonight," and stepped out into the corridor. She ran to the door and watched him until he disappeared from sight before the guard turned to retrace his steps.

It was six o'clock. Four hours to Louis' *coucher*, two more to midnight, six in all before they could expect to leave Paris. The terrible drag of waiting, waiting. It was like being suspended in mid-air, expecting to fall, holding yourself against the sickening plunge . . .

During dinner, with the National guards behind their chairs, she wondered if the little party looked to others as grotesque as they looked to her. Elizabeth was much too silent and Provence was talking a great deal more than usual, while his silly wife, for no reason at all, kept giggling. Louis, ridiculously calm, talked about the old days at Meudon. He said how grievously he missed his shooting and declared that tomorrow he would ask the Assembly to relent like the good fellows they were and permit him a few days of freedom in the woods at Meudon. She thought of the children, in bed now, unaware of the rude awaking which lay before them. Adding her own voice to the conversation she spoke of the drive she intended to take with the children tomorrow. She knew she spoke too loudly, looked too challengingly at the handful of deputies who, with the members of the public, had drifted in to watch the animals at their food.

She retired to her apartments to change into the gray silk gown she had chosen for the journey. She wished she could put forward the hands of the clock. Its steady relentless ticking infuriated her.

307

One of her ladies remarked that the King's *coucher* might take longer tonight; the Mayor of Paris had put in an appearance and seemed intent on lecturing his Majesty about the rights of man.

Presently Provence was announced. She dismissed her ladies.

"Well, Provence?"

"Berri has gone to bed at last."

She looked at him impatiently. "You have come to bid me farewell?"

"Yes. I have already taken leave of Berri privately."

"We will meet again at Montmédy."

"For all we know we may never meet again."

"You expect failure?"

"I regard it as a distinct possibility."

"Let us say *au revoir* and have done with it."

Provence bowed. "Very well, but first—" he moistened his thick lips—"I have done much I now regret. I hated you and wronged you. Those first verses, I admit I caused them to be written. I—"

"For pity's sake, Provence!—" Dear heaven, was this to be a repetition of the farewell scene with Madame Adelaide? Not if she could help it! "The past is the past. Let us look to the future. If we meet at Montmédy, well and good. If not, I wish you well, wherever you may be. Now go, Provence, before I remember how I used to despise you."

At the door he turned. "If ever they carry your head through the streets of Paris on a pike, the expression on the dead face, I vow, will be haughty still."

"By heaven it will, Provence!"

With Provence gone, she went to her daughter's bedchamber on the first floor. Madame Elizabeth, ready for the journey, met her at the door. Inside, Madame de Tourzel was sitting waiting, a tense expression on her face. She held in her hands the hat and veil which Marie Antoinette was to wear. She rose quickly and made an attempt to control her obvious fear.

"You feel capable of coping with any questioning that might arise at the barrier?" Marie Antoinette asked her gently.

"With the help of God, yes. I can even speak with an accent that might pass for Russian."

They woke Madame Royale by gently shaking her. The girl sat up at once, her eyes wide in alarm.

"Mama!"

"There is nothing to fear, darling," Marie Antoinette said, and marvelled at the composure which had descended upon her. "Monsieur le Comte de Fersen is going to look after us all. You liked him once, remember, and fell in love with him, but being fickle you transferred your affections to the Russian ambassador."

"Are we going away, Mama?"

"Immediately. Come, Madame de Tourzel will dress you."

The girl jumped out of bed. "It was the Spanish ambassador, Mama."

Leaving Madame de Tourzel to her task, Marie Antoinette went next to her son's bedchamber. In sleep, the fear that haunted his waking hours was gone. The long dark lashes brought a lump to her throat. She stroked his brow, then touched him lightly on the shoulder. He turned and blinked up at her.

"A little expedition," she told him. "In the dead of night. Can you think of anything more exciting? And at the end of the journey, thousands and thousands of soldiers to care for us and do our bidding."

"And I the general, Mama," he lisped.

"Naturally."

She lifted him from the bed. He almost fell asleep leaning against her as she dressed him in the girl's clothes which his aunt Elizabeth had hidden earlier under the bed. She smiled at the thought of his indignation when, waking in the coach in the morning, he became aware of his petticoats.

Carrying him in her arms she returned cautiously to her daughter's room, ready at the sound of a footstep to slip back out of sight. Elizabeth had already started out. If no one sounded the alarm, if the palace remained undisturbed, Elizabeth was a lucky mascot. While waiting she put on the hat and adjusted the veil.

Madame de Tourzel spoke in a whisper. "Your Majesty is ready?"

"Yes. I think we may assume that Madame Elizabeth is now safely on her way to the Place du Petit Carrousel. Go ahead of me. The apartment downstairs. I will follow with the children."

At the door they waited, listening, listening. They could hear no sound, no echoing footsteps. Guards were often lax at this hour of the night, or busy with the girls they had smuggled into the palace. They waited a moment longer.

"Proceed," Marie Antoinette whispered, in an agony of suspense.

Madame de Tourzel opened the door and without hesitation moved silently along the corridor. Marie Antoinette followed, holding her son close against her breast; only half-awake, he was

309

scarcely conscious of what was happening. Her daughter stayed close at her side, silent except for her spasmodic, quickened breathing.

At the top of the stairway Madame de Tourzel turned, nodded and began to descend. Halfway down she stopped and drew back. A guard, passing below in a leisurely manner, paused, yawned and moved on out of sight. They continued the descent, a little huddled group now, drawn together by mutual fear and hope. Thus they reached the door of the unoccupied apartment and Madame de Tourzel, holding the handle firmly to prevent all noise, slowly pushed it open. A moment later they were within the room, the door closed and barred.

Madame de Tourzel half-turned. "Your Majesty is ready to continue?"

Marie Antoinette nodded briefly. The beating of her heart all but choked her; even a whispered word was impossible. Still in a huddled group they moved across the room to the outer door. The weight of the Dauphin was beginning to tell now. Her arms ached intolerably, but when Madame de Tourzel made a move to take the boy Marie Antoinette stood back defiantly.

"Open the door," she commanded. Her voice was a horrible croak; no one would ever have recognized it. "Quickly, quickly!"

Madame de Tourzel opened the door an inch, another inch—they could hear the sound of coaches rolling out of the courtyard—then wide enough for them to pass through to the dimly lit, heavily shadowed Cour des Princes. The balmy air of the June night played about their faces, cool and pleasant, but to Marie Antoinette at that moment, hot and stifling. A shadow moved. She drew back with a little gasp. The shadow became a man, obviously by his dress a coachman. A yellow light from one of the courtyard lamps fell across his face. Axel!

He turned without a word and strolled towards the shadow of a carriage. Madame de Tourzel, at a nod from Marie Antoinette, followed him. Footsteps echoed unnervingly in the distance. Marie Antoinette hung back; her daughter clutched at her gown. The footsteps died away.

"That was Papa, I know it was!" Madame Royale whispered.

"Let us hope so. Come, child, quickly!"

Half-running, stumbling at times under the weight of her son, Marie Antoinette reached the carriage. Madame de Tourzel was already seated. Axel, in complete silence, bundled Madame Royale in at her side. Steeling herself for this temporary parting, Marie Antoinette passed her son up to Madame de Tourzel's waiting arms.

"The children on the floor," Axel whispered, then leaped up on the box.

Marie Antoinette tried not to speak, but one word, *Godspeed*, escaped her lips.

She lingered for a long moment as the carriage rolled across the courtyard. *Godspeed, Godspeed!* She turned to retrace her steps, then stopped and listened anxiously. The clop-clop of the horse's hooves continued steadily, grew distant, faded altogether. Relief flooded her heart. No hold-up at the gates, no inspection of the carriage, no questioning . . .

She waited for a few moments in the empty apartment. The only sound she could hear, a sound which seemed to echo loudly through the whole room, was the beating of her heart. She tried to steady herself and stepped out once more into the courtyard. How odd, she thought, as she walked towards the gates, I am going out alone, in possession of nothing but the clothes I wear. Old memories jostled each other in her mind. That first day in France—how clearly she remembered it! The pavilion on the island, the undressing ceremony, the stripping off of everything that was Austrian. They would strip me now of my French clothes, leave me naked in the darkness.

The carriage came upon her from behind before she had noticed its approach. She stepped quickly aside, and it rolled past so close she could see the pale face of the occupant in the inner dimness. Lafayette! The commander of the National Guard going home after satisfying himself that all was in order at the Tuileries. Instinctively she thrust out her tongue. So much for you, Monsieur! She ran behind the carriage to the gates where the guards, having saluted Lafayette, turned lazily away. With head erect, and walking steadily, she followed the carriage out into the darkness. The ease and simplicity of it all made her want to cry.

And now, she told herself, the Place du Petit Carrousel.

She knew the way, it was after all such a short distance, but the darkness confused her. She knew in a moment she had taken a wrong turning. Uncertain footsteps approached. A man, drunk and reeling, clutched at her. She shook herself free and ran from him as he fell, his curses echoing lewdly behind her. She ran on blindly in the ghastly vacuum of darkness. Once again she heard footsteps. She stopped; the footsteps drew rapidly closer. On she ran until a wall blocked her way. She pressed the flat of her hands against it and sobbed impotently. A Queen! Come, your Majesty, remember your royal dignity! She turned and faced the man. He bowed swiftly, beckoned her to follow him. She laughed insanely. Axel's valet; she knew him well by sight. Would it always be thus, Axel reaching out to guard and protect her?

There were other carriages in the Place du Petit Carrousel, just as Axel had said. In the darkness she would never have known which was hers, but the valet led her unerringly to the coachman who stood patting his horse. Without a word Axel helped her into the carriage. She saw, as she sank into her place, that all the others were there: her son, now fast asleep in Madame de Tourzel's arms; her daughter, sitting bolt upright with big staring eyes; Madame Elizabeth crouched forward; Louis—how unmistakable his bulk, more than filling a corner seat.

"Late," he said. "We were growing anxious."

"I lost my way." She reached out and took the sleeping boy from Madame de Tourzel. "You escaped without difficulty?"

A slow chuckle came from Louis' throat. "My valet noticed nothing. The real trouble was dressing myself. My fingers were all thumbs, and with my breeches on back to front I thought I had suffered a stroke."

"The guards at the gates showed no suspicion?"

"None. One of my shoes was unbuckled and I bent before their very eyes to do it up."

"Papa," Madame Royale remarked shrilly, "had his shoes on the wrong feet."

"Little minx," Louis chided her, "you must remember not to call me Papa again till we reach Montmédy. My name is Durand. I am Madame Korff's body servant. Madame de Tourzel is Madame Korff. Mama is Madame Rochet, your governess. You are, of course, Madame Korff's daughter. Aunt Elizabeth is Madame Korff's travelling companion."

With Axel on the box, the carriage was moving at a brisk pace, and soon Louis, leaning out of his window, was announcing the closeness of the Saint-Martin gate.

The carriage stopped. Marie Antoinette could see in the nearby shadows the big travelling coach, the four horses, the coachman and the two bodyguards. They made the change silently and swiftly, the carriage, a hired one, was driven away and abandoned.

"Ready?" Axel asked.

"Ready!" Louis replied cheerfully.

Axel climbed up beside the coachman. They were on the move again.

"And now for the barrier," Louis whispered excitedly. "Quiet, everyone, quiet!" He seemed in the highest, most boyish spirits. "Only Madame Korff is allowed to speak when they demand the passports. How is your Russian accent, Madame Korff, eh?"

But no speech was necessary. Axel jumped down from the box, obsequiously asked for the passports and casually presented them to a sleepy official, grumbling meanwhile about a crazy foreign mistress who would insist on travelling late. A moment later he was back on the box.

"I can scarcely believe it," Marie Antoinette whispered, as the coach passed through the barrier.

Louis settled down in his corner. "Not far to Bondy, but time enough for a little doze. Wake me when we get there."

Bondy was reached half-an-hour later with Louis sleeping peacefully. Angry with him at first for his apparent lack of feeling, Marie Antoinette began to gather confidence and hope from the sight of this great sleeping bulk. While Axel superintended the changing of the horses—the coach was to be drawn by eight, not four, from now on—she leaned forward to touch Louis on the knee. She saw that his eyes were half-open; she had a strong feeling that he had sat thus, simulating sleep, the whole time.

"You are not as calm as you pretend, Louis."

He opened his eyes fully. "Goodness, yes."

"I think you merely wanted to inspire us all with confidence."

He smiled slowly. "Well, well, perhaps I did."

"Thank you, Louis."

"But note, please—" he thrust his head out of the window for a moment—"no suspicion is felt here. The ostlers are going about their business quite normally. What else is needed to inspire confidence?"

"When we are missed in the morning at the Tuileries—"

"We shall be a hundred miles away."

Axel came to the window. "The horses are changed. All is ready."

313

A cold hand clutched at Marie Antoinette's heart. "This is goodbye, Axel."

He said in a quick low voice, "We are not at Bondy on time. It is necessary to be at Chalons by midday tomorrow. Let the coachman keep that well in mind. I expect no delay at the posting stations. The courier I sent ahead has served us well here. It will be the same at each of the other stations."

Louis touched him on the shoulder. "Have no anxiety on our behalf."

Axel took some papers from his pocket and handed them to Louis. "This is the itinerary. You will find all details clearly stated." He seemed inclined now to linger. "You will be hungry in the morning. You will find all you need in a hamper under one of the seats."

"Ah, you know what an appetite I have!" Louis laughed. He fumbled in his pocket, brought out a sealed packet and gave it to Axel. "These are important documents. I want them delivered to Count Mercy." Mercy, recalled to Vienna by the new Emperor, had now been sent to Brussels. "I charge you, Axel, to see that they reach him. They must be delivered in person. Afterwards, you shall join us at Montmédy." Louis smiled. "So there is no real need to say goodbye."

Axel stood back from the carriage, removed his hat and waited there, erect, unmoving, as the coach rolled forward. Marie Antoinette watched till his dim figure faded into the general darkness.

"Those documents," Louis said quietly, "are of no consequence whatever. I want Axel safe in Belgium, in case we fail." And he added simply, "I love him dearly."

Marie Antoinette tried to speak and failed. Never before had she so much appreciated Louis kindliness, his gentle loving heart. There he sat in the darkness of the coach, a great ungainly hulk of a man, but no longer, as so often he had been, a figure of fun. Her heart swelled painfully in her breast. She felt a great enduring respect for him. What if he *had* failed as a king? He had never failed in those deep and simple things that really mattered.

"And now I really do intend to go to sleep," Louis laughed. "Otherwise I shall be tempted to open that hamper and make a hole in the contents immediately."

314

THREE

Shortly after dawn Louis came awake with a great thunder-clap of a yawn. Marie Antoinette, who had done little more than doze for a few moments at a time, moved her cramped legs and glanced at the children. They stirred with Louis' second yawn, opened their eyes and stretched.

"A clear sky, a beautiful summer's day," Louis announced, blinking out of the window. "A good omen, surely. And better still, I never felt so hungry in my life."

The little Dauphin was fingering his girl's clothes in wonderment, then alarm, then a vast disgust. His sister, bright-eyed now, her face free of any fear, was quick to tease him.

"My sweet little sister," she laughed.

"We are going to a party, darling," Marie Antoinette told him. "Fancy dress is essential. Look at Papa in his great brown wig. And Aunt Elizabeth, how prim she looks, dressed as a lady's companion. A real English Miss, but quite refined, of course."

The boy giggled uncertainly, then squirmed in his seat.

"Mama, when can we stop? I am in great discomfort."

Madame de Tourzel spoke up then, her nose in the air. "Provision has been made. An appropriate utensil is under the King's seat."

"*My* seat indeed!" Louis roared. "I have been known to spend a full day in the saddle and still hold my water." He took his son in his arms, then reached under the seat. "The dear Axel, he thought of everything." He steadied the boy between his knees. "There, young man, skirts are more convenient on occasion."

By this time Madame Royale had found the hamper.

"Breakfast, Papa!" she cried, and threw open the lid.

"Wait!" Louis commanded. "Monsieur Durand will serve breakfast." He snatched at the hamper and peered into it. "Heaven bless the thoughtful Axel!"

He lifted out the silver plates and handed them round; he seized a bottle of champagne with one hand, a whole chicken with the other.

315

"Champagne for breakfast! Now *that's* a treat! Occasionally I've taken a sip of Burgundy, but never champagne. Champagne for breakfast! One rarely makes merry at breakfast, but by heaven, this shall be the merriest meal we have ever eaten!"

He glanced sharply at Marie Antoinette. She responded with a quick laugh. Strangely enough, so infectious was Louis' mood, real or simulated, she had never felt so gay in her life.

"A celebration! What could be better, Louis!"

"Ah!" he cried, diving deep into the hamper, "Burgundy also, but first the champagne." His face fell. "Two bottles of—yes, *water*." His face cleared; he looked impishly at the children. "For you, of course, my pets."

Madame Royale pouted. "I want champagne too, Papa."

"The King's young daughter a drunkard? Never!"

But he gave her a sip, and his son a sip, and with a hearty ringing laugh he proposed a toast.

"To Montmédy, and curse the National Assembly!"

At the next posting station Louis got out.

"A brisk short walk while the horses are changed, that's what I need."

He returned after a few minutes. His eyes were beaming, his cheeks glowed healthily. Quite forgetting himself he had removed the brown wig and was swinging it in his hand.

To her horror Marie Antoinette saw one of the ostlers staring at him, staring, staring. And then, as she watched, the man approached. Perhaps he had been to Paris on holiday. He might even have been in the crowd when they had been dragged from Versailles to the Tuileries. The nightmare horror of that terrible journey came back to her. Any moment now the ostler would give the alarm.

"Goodday to you, my man," Louis said genially. "And a very good day it is!"

The ostler fell on his knees at Louis' feet, reached up to kiss his hand.

"Well, well," Louis laughed, "like many others you are taken-in by my distressing resemblance to the King."

The man got to his feet. There was a puzzled expression on his face as he watched Louis climb into the coach.

"You saw that, Marie?" Louis said emotionally. "How humble it makes me feel. And how grateful to be in the country. Only in

Paris has the cankerous evil eaten into the nation. And what hope it gives me, what hope!"

With the fresh horses ready, the coach moved on again. The ostler ran alongside it for a few yards.

"Long live the King, whoever you are!"

Half-an-hour later the coach came to a jarring halt. The children were thrown forward; the Dauphin rolled on the floor, but unhurt, remained there for a moment, chuckling. Louis leaped down to the road.

"A slight mishap," he reported. "A broken trace. No cause for alarm."

"Even the slightest delay . . ." Marie Antoinette said, anxious now for the first time since Axel had left them.

Louis looked at his watch. "We are well behind our schedule, I admit, but we are so far from Paris that even if the alarm has now been given they will never overtake us." He studied his watch again. "For so heavy a coach we are making good time. Seven miles an hour. Almost eight." He slapped his heavy thighs and laughed merrily. "Yes, the alarm will have been given at the Tuileries. What a state Paris will be in! And poor Lafayette—to have slipped through his fingers so easily! Will the mob rise and tear him to pieces, I wonder?"

With the damage more serious than first believed, the repairs took an hour. Louis contented himself with marching up and down the road, shaking up his liver, he said, and making his great stomach rumble with hunger.

"Thank heaven there's still plenty to eat in that hamper!"

En route once more, he settled down in his seat, opened a map he had brought and gave the children what he called a timely lesson in geography. He also took from his pocket the itinerary drawn up by Axel.

"Ah," he said, "once we pass through Chalons and reach Pont de Sommevelle we shall meet Bouillé's first detachment. After that, not even the most timid amongst us need fear arrest."

They reached Chalons at four in the afternoon. Axel had said that they must be there by midday. Four hours late! Marie Antoinette felt her heart sink, though she tried to tell herself that anxiety and the lack of sleep were getting the better of her. Four hours late, but well on their journey, with not a single demand anywhere for the showing of passports. She thought of the ostler who had cried 'Long live the King!' Was he a loyal man or just a cunning one? Pah! the stupidity of tormenting oneself like this.

At Chalons, further increasing this new anxiety, the ostlers were slow and seemed deliberately to delay. Worse, the arrival of this unusually large coach had caused excitement in the town, and now little groups of idlers were gathering about it. She caught odd snatches of conversation. Obviously the travellers were rich, obviously, they came from Paris where all the rich people lived. More obviously, nay undoubtedly, they were yet another party of aristocrats making good their escape. Suddenly the idlers fell back a few paces, and one of them cried, "Monsieur le Maire!" She saw a solemn self-important group arriving. The Mayor of Chalons, leading a delegation!

"Have no fear," Louis said. "I insist that this is a loyal town."

He climbed stiffly down from the coach and removed his wig. Well, why not? What disguise was a wig in broad daylight? She watched a man step forward and bow stiffly from the waist.

"God bless your Majesty," he said.

A cheer rose from the group of townspeople behind him.

Louis shook himself like a great dog. "Long live France, the France we all love!"

He climbed back into the coach. There were tears in his eyes. "By heaven, in the new regime I shall make Chalons my capital!"

On the outskirts of the town, just as the coach was gathering speed again, a single horseman, riding furiously, drew alongside. His face appeared at the window for a moment. His eyes had a wild, mocking look.

"Fools!" he shrieked. "The wrath of the people will stop you yet!"

He veered away, dug in the spurs and disappeared in a cloud of dust.

"Take no notice," Louis said placidly. "In every community at least one fanatic."

"He has ridden ahead of us to give warning," Marie Antoinette said in a whisper.

"Then he will ride full tilt into Bouillé's detachment." Louis looked at Axel's itinerary again. "Yes, I thought so. Young Choiseul is in charge of the detachment. Forty or fifty hussars. From then on, detachment after detachment, all the way to Montmédy. My dear, I am absolutely famished. Is there any more chicken in the hamper?"

318

The contents of the hamper had been sadly depleted but there was still a small ration for each of the travellers and a last bottle of Burgundy. The coach, rattling along at a good pace now, passed through village after village without incident. A steady eight miles an hour, Louis commented, when, an hour and a half later, they entered Pont de Sommevelle. Except for the ostlers at the posting station no one was in sight.

"We are late, of course," Louis said. "Choiseul would hesitate to keep his men in the town. Obviously he would. He withdrew them after waiting for a time, but posted a man to keep watch." He half fell from the coach, stretched his arms, began stamping his feet. "In a moment or two— Ah, here he comes!"

A horseman, but not in uniform, rode up to the posting station. He was covered in dust; his horse was near exhaustion. Marie Antoinette looked at him anxiously and waited, fear in her heart, while he dismounted and approached Louis. Quickly he introduced himself. He was the courier, sent ahead by Axel to warn the posting stations of the change of horses required. Questions and answers followed. He had seen no troops anywhere, had been afraid to arouse suspicion by asking questions.

"We shall press on to Sainte-Ménehould," Louis decided. "Obviously we can do nothing else."

They reached Sainte-Ménehould at eight o'clock, and by now Marie Antoinette was feeling utterly weary. Her eyes were paining her, the lids tight from lack of sleep. She was sure that the number of people in the streets was suspiciously large, and while the horses were being changed idlers drifted up to stare in silence, then drifted away again. She caught sight of a few soldiers in the near distance. They remained there, their manner sheepish.

She touched Louis' arm. "The soldiers—not one is carrying arms!"

Presently an officer approached. He introduced himself as the commander of the detachment. He had received word, he said, from Choiseul who, holding the opinion that the date had been changed, had finally left Pont de Sommevelle an hour before the party's arrival there.

"Fool!" Marie Antoinette cried.

"We were late by four hours," Louis said. "No one can blame him."

It had been apparent to Choiseul, the officer added, that to remain longer would arouse suspicion. That was the position here in Sainte-Ménehould. Suspicion, and rumors that the King was to pass through the town in flight from Paris. He had disarmed his men because of the hostility of the townspeople.

"I tried to allay suspicion," he said, "by speaking of a convoy I have been ordered to guard—a large amount of money being taken to headquarters to pay the troops. The postmaster, a fierce revolutionary, laughed in my face."

Louis was silent for a moment.

"It will be better to brazen things out," he said at last. "We will proceed without escort. We have come thus far without it, in any case, and safely enough. Stand by and watch; come to our aid only if an attempt is made to stop us."

No attempt was made and the coach rumbled out of the town without incident.

"So far so good," Louis said calmly. "Clermont is our next stop. According to Axel a Colonel Damas will be there with a hundred or more dragoons."

Marie Antoinette sat back and closed her eyes. Colonel Damas, yes, providing he had more sense than Choiseul. She was stiff and sore; the swaying of the carriage, more pronounced now on rougher roads, made her feel desperately sick. It was the same, she knew, with Madame de Tourzel and Elizabeth. As for the children, they were much too silent now; the tension she herself was feeling had been conveyed disastrously to them.

"God, am I hungry!" Louis grumbled.

Food, she thought, was the last thing she wanted.

It was half-past nine when they reached Clermont. With heavy gray clouds in the sky, it was growing rapidly dark.

"We have gained a few minutes," Louis announced. "Splendid!"

Marie Antoinette spoke briefly to Madame de Tourzel. "Tell the ostlers to hurry."

To her infinite relief she saw an officer approaching.

"Colonel Damas?" Louis asked, in a whisper.

"At your Majesty's service."

"Your men are in the town?"

"Yes, but small demonstrations keep breaking out against them. Everyone seemed to know that the King was expected."

"Surround the coach with your men," Marie Antoinette interposed, "and escort us out of the town."

Louis agreed. "But no violence, mind you. Not a single shot to be fired."

320

"Not only will you escort us out of the town," Marie Antoinette added, "you will accompany us to the next posting station."

"That is understood, your Majesty."

Presently, at a steady pace, the coach moved through streets lined with angry, shouting townspeople. What had Louis said? *Only in Paris has the cankerous evil eaten into the nation.* Despair got the better of her and deepened when coach and dragoons alike were held up by a solid mob of people, a mob as hysterical as any she had seen in Paris. Colonel Damas issued a sharp order. His men exchanged glances with each other and then, as if at a given signal, refused to obey.

"So this is the end," she said.

"Wait!" Louis cried.

A pathway had been made for the coach.

"You see! All the people object to is an armed escort."

"A cat playing with a mouse, Louis. They know, they must know, that a greater mob will be waiting at the next stop."

The next stop was the town of Varennes, which they reached at eleven o'clock. All was dark and silent; the posting station was closed and quite deserted. It was one of those still summer nights, heavy with an oppressive blackness exaggerated rather than relieved by the fitful yellow glow of the coach lamps.

"We must go on!" she cried.

"My dear, the horses are ready to drop."

"*We must go on!*" she insisted.

Louis gave the word reluctantly. The coach moved slowly through the town. Why, she tried to reason, should this stillness be so frightening? After all, at this time of night one would expect most people to be in bed.

"I remember Varennes," Louis remarked. "Any moment now we should pass under an archway in the wall, and then over a bridge."

Hard on his words came a sudden reverberating shout.

"Halt!"

Voices in the darkness echoed it until the single word, repeated again and again, became an angry roar. Torches flared up. The coach was surrounded by screaming men and women. The smoking yellow light from a dozen flames revealed the outline of the archway.

A head appeared at the coach window; a harsh voice demanded the names of the travellers. Madame de Tourzel was quick witted enough to reply, quick witted enough even to assume a foreign accent.

"My name is Korff. I am a Russian subject. I am travelling with my children and servants. I am in possession of valid passports."

"Show them, then!"

A hand was thrust into the coach. Madame de Tourzel placed the passports into it. A group of men, each one carrying a flaming torch, gathered at the coach window.

"The passports are in order," said one.

"Except, idiot," said another, "that the signature of the President of the National Assembly is missing."

"A Russian subject is not answerable to your Assembly," Madame de Tourzel snapped.

There was a pause. No one had yet suggested that the body-servant, Durand, pressing himself back against the cushions, was Louis, King of France. The pause was drawn out agonizingly while the group at the window was jostled by other citizens, some carrying muskets, others pikes. A cry rang out in the darkness, "Block the bridge!" A musket was thrust into the coach, a high thin voice shouted, "Move, and take the consequences!"

A handful of dragoons appeared, stared helplessly at the coach and drifted away. A man, calmer than the rest, pushed his way purposefully to the coach window. He announced, with some importance, that he was a grocer and, in addition, procurator of the local commune.

"Your name, Monsieur?" Madame de Tourzel demanded.

"My name is Sauce, Madame."

Sauce! To Marie Antoinette, at this moment, an insanely funny name! Only by clenching her fists and biting her lips was she able to prevent herself from bursting into shrieks of laughter.

"If I can be of any small service . . ." Monsieur Sauce suggested.

"We wish to proceed. Naturally we wish to proceed."

"We-ell . . ." Monsieur Sauce glanced about him.

"The passports are in perfect order!" Madame de Tourzel cried.

"Forgeries!" someone in the crowd shrieked. "We all know the King is in the coach. Let the big fat pig come out and show himself."

Monsieur Sauce shrugged. "You see, Madame? Undoubtedly a misapprehension, but for the present I can do nothing, save place my humble premises at your disposal."

322

Louis made a rumbling noise. "I am devilishly hungry. Can you provide us with food?"

"Gladly," Monsieur Sauce said.

"Then, my good fellow, we place ourselves willingly in your hands."

Louis got down from the coach. One by one he helped the others to alight, took his still-sleeping son in his arms and commanded his daughter to take a firm grip on his coat. Thus he led the little group through the crowd and looked neither to right nor to left. A woman tipped his wig over his eyes and a man remarked loudly that if this red-headed woman was indeed the Queen she was not the raving beauty he had always been led to believe. The crowd rocked with laughter. Its mood, though threatening, was quite playful.

Monsieur Sauce led them into his shop, which smelled of strong cheese and spices, and up a narrow flight of stairs to two small rooms. One contained a bed, in which the children were immediately placed. The other contained a few rough chairs and a small table with a candle flickering on it. Louis sat at the table and reminded Monsieur Sauce that he was hungry. The grocer-procurator brought cheese, bread and wine. Marie Antoinette sat in an uncomfortable armchair and refused to eat. Madame de Tourzel and Madame Elizabeth withdrew to the other room, where the children were sleeping.

On the wall facing Marie Antoinette was a rough plaster portrait of Louis. Monsieur Sauce, seeing that this held her attention, laughed uncertainly.

"A strong resemblance, Madame, to the gentleman here, just as there is a strong resemblance between Monsieur's head and the King's head on the coins of the realm. No one in Varennes has ever seen the King in person, so naturally the misapprehension continues. A search is now being made round the countryside for someone who knows the King by sight or personally."

"It is clear that you are a good subject of the King."

Monsieur Sauce looked uncomfortable. "These are difficult times, Madame. I try always to do my duty."

With his mouth full of bread and cheese Louis said, "It is inconvenient for Madame Korff to be detained like this. Worse, it is an insult to her own country. It would be unfortunate if, because of a few hotheads, serious trouble were to arise between Russia and France." He took a swig of wine. "Why not go down and tell the people that?"

Monsieur Sauce bowed and withdrew.

"He knows who I am," Louis remarked. "His loyalty is beyond question but his position is intolerable. However, delay is now our only hope. After all, Bouillé is just twenty-two miles away with a whole army." He rose and came to her side. "Do please eat something, Marie."

She turned her head away. "No."

"Just a little nibble of cheese to keep you going."

"Louis, *no!*"

Monsieur Sauce returned. During his absence the excited shouting outside had grown louder. The man's face as he approached Louis was lined with unhappiness.

"Monsieur, they refused to listen to me. More and more people are gathering in the streets and the bridge has been firmly blocked."

An uncertain silence fell. Absently Monsieur Sauce refilled Louis' glass; absently Louis drained it. There was a disturbance on the stairs. A middle-aged man, followed by three excited youths, flung himself into the room.

"You are indeed the King," he said, pointing a finger at Louis. He spoke half angrily, half jokingly. "Come, be a man, admit it."

"I am Durand, body-servant of the Russian lady," Louis told him mildly. "Who, for that matter, are you?"

The middle-aged man cocked his head on one side. "My name is Drouet. I am the postmaster of Sainte-Ménehould. I received a warning from the postmaster at Chalons. I reached Varennes before you did. Come, admit your identity!"

Monsieur Sauce gave him a stern look. "I am in charge here. Our one concern is to keep our heads and see that injustice is prevented."

Drouet and his companions withdrew reluctantly, but Drouet himself was back a few moments later, dragging by the arm an elderly man who came, it was obvious, with the greatest unwillingness.

"This," Drouet announced triumphantly, "is Magistrate Destez. He has been often to Paris. He has seen the King and Queen many times. Come, Monsieur Destez, remember your civil oath! Speak the truth."

"Damnation!" Louis cried, with a great bellow of anger. "Why pretend? Why should I cringe in dark corners like a rat?" He tossed the useless brown wig in Drouet's face. "Yes indeed I am your King. You understand, man, *your* King!"

Drouet ran from the room and clattered down the stairs shouting, "The King! He admits it, he admits it!"

The magistrate turned and followed slowly.

"I never liked that wretched wig," Louis grumbled, and placed another slice of cheese in his mouth.

The tumult outside rose deafeningly, and then more footsteps were heard on the stairs. Monsieur Sauce flung himself against the door as if, futilely, to barricade it with his body. The handle turned, pressure was applied.

A voice said, "I beg you, permit me to enter. My name is Choiseul."

Marie Antoinette sprang up. "Choiseul!"

Monsieur Sauce stood back. Choiseul entered swiftly and closed the door behind him. He went straight to Louis and fell on his knees at his feet.

"Sire, I have men outside, standing guard. I await your Majesty's orders."

"Your men are loyal?"

"Well . . ."

"Loyal, but somewhat intimidated by the crowd, eh?"

"They stand firm for the moment. Therefore all haste is necessary. My plan, Sire, is this: sufficient of my men shall dismount and place their horses at your party's disposal. Guarded by the rest of my men it should be possible for you to make an escape."

"How many men have you, Choiseul?"

"Forty."

Louis turned to Monsieur Sauce. "How many people would you say there are in the streets?"

In a whisper Sauce said, "Upwards of ten thousand, for a certainty."

"Armed, many of them, with muskets and pikes. Escape? I doubt it! In any case, nothing will induce me to risk the lives of my wife and children."

Marie Antoinette made a weary gesture. "I would rather die here than be murdered in Paris."

Louis shook his head. "Bouillé is only twenty-two miles away. His arrival here with a large superior force will intimidate the mob. Rescue without bloodshed is more than probable." He turned

325

to Choiseul. "Can you send a trusted messenger to General Bouillé?"

"I have already sent two men, your Majesty."

"Splendid! Bouillé will be here by four in the morning. Five at the latest. We are safe enough till then."

No longer caring, Marie Antoinette said, "By that time troops will be here from Paris."

"Touch and go," Louis admitted, "but let us hope for the best."

Marie Antoinette woke at four o'clock. She found it hard to believe that she had slept at all in the hard uncomfortable chair. General Bouillé? Not a sign of him, only the steady murmur of the mob in the street below. At five o'clock there was a report that peasants, armed with scythes and sickles, were streaming in from the surrounding countryside. She fell into a fitful doze, from which she woke to hear Louis in conversation with a stranger. She opened her eyes. The stranger was a young officer. She gathered that he commanded sixty hussars, but his men were at the other side of the blocked bridge. He asked Louis for orders.

"A king in chains can give no orders," Louis replied.

He meant, of course, *I'll have no bloodshed.*

He added calmly, "Bouillé will be here by six, at the latest."

Wide awake now, Marie Antoinette went to look at the children. Both were still asleep. She spoke briefly to Madame Elizabeth and Madame de Tourzel, who were sitting in chairs near the bed. Not believing it, she said, "General Bouillé will be here at six o'clock." She returned to Louis and wandered aimlessly about the small room. She paused at the window and stared at the pale pink morning sky. A day of beautiful sunshine lay ahead. She looked down at the mob in the street below. Many people were sleeping against the walls, others were sitting in little groups, drinking and talking in low voices. She saw soldiers among them, each with a young woman. From time to time these girls laughed immoderately. She turned from the window, only to be drawn back by a rising stir of excitement. People were springing to their feet, shouting wildly.

"Bouillé?" Louis asked, and joined her at the window.

"No," she said tonelessly. "A detachment of the Paris National Guard. I know one of the leaders. Lafayette's aide-de-camp."

"Ah, Romeuf! A pleasant fellow. Always sympathetic, always helpful. It could be worse."

"It could be worse . . ."

"You are angry with me, Marie."

"No, not angry. Not even disappointed. But I have made a new resolve. Strange, when all is lost, to make any sort of resolution."

"Tell me what it is."

"They will drag us back to Paris. In Paris I shall use every means in my power, however unscrupulous, to save our lives. I can feel nothing in my heart, Louis, but a cold hatred. That, per-haps, will help me in my flight."

Louis sighed. "I shall never blame you, whatever you do."

A few moments later Lafayette's aide-de-camp, Romeuf, came clumping up the stairs. He was followed by Bayon, one of the high-ranking officers of the National Guard. Marie Antoinette looked with loathing at their tri-color cockades. Romeuf sympathetic? He might be, but Bayon, with that arrogant smile on his face, never! Both men bowed briefly. Romeuf glanced cautiously at Bayon.

Bayon smiled thinly. "Romeuf, you have a duty to perform."

Romeuf took a document from his pocket.

"These are my orders," he said, and handed it to Louis.

Having read the document Louis said quietly, "It was expected that we should be obliged to return to Paris."

Marie Antoinette sprang forward and snatched the document from his hands. Her intention clear to him, Louis restrained her before she could rip it to shreds. In the senseless little struggle it fluttered to the floor at Romeuf's feet.

Gently Louis said, "It claims that we have been abducted by the enemies of the revolution. It enjoins all good citizens to help in carrying us safely back to our capital. It is signed by Lafayette."

Bayon said insolently, "You are ready to proceed at once?"

"Naturally, naturally," Romeuf interposed. "Go down and make immediate preparations, Bayon."

With a reluctant look Bayon obeyed.

Hurriedly Romeuf kissed Louis' hand. "Sire, is General Bouillé expected?"

"At any moment."

"I prayed for that. I delayed wherever possible on the journey, but Bayon was—difficult. I shall cause as much delay as possible now. The children cannot be disturbed yet, and your Majesties must have breakfast before starting off. I—" he hurried to the door —"everything possible shall be done, everything."

He was able to cause an hour's delay, but no more, by which

time several deputies had arrived from Paris, the coach was at the door and the mob was shrieking for a sight of the King.

"Bring out the fat pig! Bring out the Austrian whore!"

"Bouillé, was there ever such a man?" Louis asked sadly.

Marie Antoinette straightened her aching back.

"Remember my resolve, Louis, my hatred. I shall fight them now to the death."

FOUR

SHE WONDERED HOW LONG IT WOULD BE BEFORE THE GUARD NOTICED that her night light was burning on the table by the bed. She stared at the open door. Last night when she had lit the night light he had half entered the room and ordered her to put it out. Possibly, just possibly, he had fallen asleep in the armchair in the corridor and she would be left in peace to read, or at all events to try to read.

She glanced at the other door which led into her dressing-room. The grand apartments of the Queen! Just two small rooms on the ground floor of the Tuileries, that was all she had been permitted since the ignominious return to Paris, and always the bedroom door unlocked during the day, wide open at night, with a guard constantly on duty. A similar watch was kept over Louis, the children, Madame Elizabeth.

She gave a little start at the grating sound of a chair being pushed back in the corridor outside. A moment later the guard, a burly young man with pale cheeks and small suspicious eyes, advanced into the room. He stood before her, stretching and yawning, then he drew up a chair and seated himself by the bed.

"Since you can't sleep and won't let me sleep, we may as well spend an hour or so talking."

Marie Antoinette drew the sheet more closely about her. "Monsieur, I beg of you—"

His coarse laughed interrupted her. "Now that's what I like in women, modesty."

She made an attempt to speak imperiously. "Your orders are to keep watch outside, not to enter the room."

He leaned forward. "They've faded, the good looks, but I'll vow she's just as experienced as ever, this Austrian whore. That's another thing I like in women, experience." He twitched at the sheet. "Maybe you'd like me to close the door?"

She could bear no more. She felt the sting on the inside of her hands before she realized what she had done, then she saw the marks of her fingers on his cheek.

"Bitch!" he said, but he was on his feet, backing to the door.

He had of course gone too far and knew it. Shaking with indignation, ready to burst into tears, she sat up tensely, listening. She heard the creak of the chair as he seated himself again. The wisest thing, she knew, would be to put out the light, but sleep was more impossible than ever and the thought of complete darkness terrifying.

On a sudden impulse she got carefully out of bed, picked up the night light and carried it to the dressing-room where she placed it on a table which served as a writing desk. She closed the door with the utmost care and sat down at the table.

"Axel . . ." she whispered.

During the last three months she had written him many letters. Louise de Lamballe had smuggled them out—they were written in code—and had given them to Axel's friend, the Comte d'Esterhazy, who in his turn had sent them on to Sweden. Axel's replies, also written in code, had reached her in the same way.

"As I have told you before," she began, "my resolution hardened and hardened during the indescribable horror of the journey back to Paris and has never faltered since."

Deliberately, if only to harden her heart still more, she thought of that journey back to captivity. Most of all, and with a horror that would never leave her, she remembered the murder of a royalist on the outskirts of Sainte-Ménehould. A white-haired old man, he had ridden close to the coach and uttered a few words of sympathy. For that he had been torn from his horse and his bleeding head, hacked off before her eyes, had been thrust in her face. She dreamed of it often and woke from the dream sobbing.

She remembered the halt at Chalons, where they had learned from an overtaking courier that General Bouillé and a large force had entered Varennes almost immediately after they had left it.

She remembered . . .

No, she thought, I shall dwell no more on all that; I shall think only of Barnave.

Barnave was one of the three deputies sent by the Assembly to join them at Chalons and ride back in the coach with them, overcrowding it, making the heat even more insufferable. Antoine Barnave—she had heard mention of him as a supporter of the Duc d'Orleans, a revolutionary loud in his expressions of hatred, a man known among his companions as The Tiger. Yet on meeting him for the first time, watching him as he sat in the coach, she had found him mild-mannered and had noted his horror when told of the murder of the old royalist. She had made up her mind then that he might be exceedingly useful and had set herself to please and flatter him. And the result? Before the end of the journey he had shown her every courtesy, had even whispered that he sadly regretted the way he had misjudged a woman he had never met.

She went on with her letter. "You feel it is dangerous to negotiate with Barnave. I have survived too many dangers to care about that. When Barnave has served his purpose he will be cast aside."

Be hard, unscrupulous, remember that, remember it always!

It was now a fight against time, and in that Barnave was useful. Things had moved so fast that, once a violent revolutionary, he seemed now the most moderate of men. Pretend, then, to agree with him in his moderate aims, delay, delay, while Axel worked feverishly in his constant attempts to organize outside aid. Armed intervention from the royal houses of Europe, it was that or nothing now. Louis would not agree, but why confide in Louis? Better to keep one's own counsel, useless to point out to him that the new small party in the Assembly, the Jacobins, was a republican party, outnumbered so far, but likely to grow, and growing turn this mockery of a constitutional monarchy into a kingless republic.

She grasped the pen more firmly. "Today Louis has accepted, sanctioned—choose whatever word you wish—a new constitution, and accepting it has sworn never, under any circumstances, to leave Paris again. It gives him an alleged right of veto, but what a ghastly joke *that* is!"

The new constitution . . . She thought of one of its high-sounding phrases. *All Frenchmen are free and equal.* All except the King himself, of course.

"I have written many times since I last heard from you," she continued. "In your last letter you spoke of a secret mission on King Gustav's behalf, a visit to Vienna in an attempt to rally forces there. Write the moment you return. If there is any hope at all, tell me at once."

How thankful she was now that Louis had sent Axel to Belgium. It might well have been his head that had been thrust in her face.

"Dearest Axel," she concluded, "you speak often of coming to

331

Paris, but please, I beg of you, as you love me, as you know I love you, never under any circumstances attempt it. Your part in the attempted escape is known to everyone. An edict has been issued. Death for Axel von Fersen the moment he shows himself in Paris. Have patience. Wait with a strong heart. We will meet again. Believe that, Axel. *I* believe it. Adieu, my beloved. I embrace you with all my heart."

Carefully she read through the letter, lined out unnecessary words and phrases and then began the laborious task of rewriting it in the code agreed upon.

The next morning, after breakfast, Louis came briskly into her bedroom. He appeared to be in high spirits, and to Marie Antoinette's amazement he slammed the door and turned the key in the lock.

"What is this, Louis, a revolt on the part of the King?"

He smiled faintly. "No, my dear. The restriction concerning locked doors has been lifted."

"Lifted? Rather would I expect it to be intensified, with the doors locked on the outside."

"Believe me," he said eagerly, "completely lifted. Just one result of my acceptance of the new constitution."

"We have a share in the new freedom? What mockery is this?"

"And tonight," he went on, ignoring her scathing tone, "we are to make a state visit to the theater. Paris is returning gladly to normal."

"How can you believe such nonsense, Louis!"

"I— Because I want to believe it."

She shuddered at an old, old memory. "When I was a small child I was taken to a country fair, and there I saw a duck dancing on a little platform. Such a merry sight! I discovered afterwards that the platform was a sheet of iron, heated from underneath by a coke fire. We are the same as that poor frantic duck, Louis."

They went to the theater that night. Most of the people in the streets were silent, but a few raised a cheer and were not molested. It was the same at the theater. She laughed several times during the performance, quite hysterical laughter, for she saw, not the actors on the stage, but a dancing duck and the bleeding head of an old aristocrat.

A few days passed. It seemed that the people, unsure of the

332

position at first, were prepared to relax and enjoy themselves. There was public rejoicing, dancing in the streets, and with the grounds of the Tuileries thrown open a fete was held beneath the palace windows.

A week passed and the public rejoicing gave place to a steady calm.

"The revolution is over," Louis announced.

But Barnave, at one of his secret visits to the Tuileries, took a different view.

"It is a dangerous calm, Madame. If the Jacobins have their way a shattering storm will follow it. They are working quietly now, the Jacobins. Their quietness is in itself alarming. They are gaining new supporters every day. I know they are preparing plans for a republic."

"What can you do to counter these plans, Monsieur?"

"Strive, I and my friends, to keep the temper of the Assembly on a sane basis."

"You can do no more than that?"

The young man's face broke into a grim smile—he really was much younger than she had thought, and had about him not only the fanaticism but the earnestness of youth.

"The formation of a Queen's party is a distant possibility."

Marie Antoinette smiled too. "A *very* distant one, I'm sure. To put me forward as your leader at this stage would cause another revolution overnight. But why a *Queen's* party?"

"I admire the King for his gentleness and greatheartedness, but the Queen I respect for her strength of character, her bravery in adversity."

She found herself blushing, which was ridiculous.

"Do you by any chance see yourself the prime minister of a government set up in my name?" she asked.

"I have not yet looked so far ahead, Madame."

"But you are ambitious."

"Ambitious to see France happy again, with a settled government. That and no more. I want nothing for myself."

"A noble character," she taunted. "Yet I must admit that you have never at any time tried to bargain with me. You have not even looked at me as a woman, desired me and demanded that as your price."

Barnave grew quickly embarrassed. "Your Majesty!"

333

"You sound indignant. Is it possible that there is still a man in France who stands in awe of my royal blood and would never *dare?*"

Barnave hesitated.

"Speak up, Monsieur."

He said quickly, "Madame, have you looked at yourself lately in the mirror and really seen yourself?"

She felt utterly crushed. "What a brutal thing to say! You are as cruel as the rest of them. It is not my fault if I am old before my time and haggard."

"Forgive me," he said earnestly, "if I seemed to speak brutally. It was not my intention. You are old before your time but not haggard. Your face is careworn but still beautiful. The lines etched by suffering touch me so much that I feel nothing but compassion. I want to help and protect you as a son would help and protect a mother who had struggled so gallantly against insurmountable odds."

Shaking with anger she said, "You add insult to insult."

"Believe me, I speak from the heart."

She fought back her anger. "Let us discuss your aims and ambitions, not the face of a woman who died long ago."

"Gladly, Madame. My aims and ambitions are unchanged. I, and the deputies who are gathered about me, are the true constitutionalists. Our task is to oppose and destroy republicanism, save France and save the royal family."

That, for the time being, was sufficient, was all he or anybody else could do. If thus he could gain the time she needed he would have served her well. He had annoyed her, angered her, hurt her personal vanity, but he was good and sincere, he did indeed speak from the heart. She would reward him in the end, not cast him aside. She would raise him to a position of honor. A new order, perhaps; a special decoration. The Order of Truthful Men —men who spoke the truth and cared nothing for a Queen's feelings.

He was looking at her thoughtfully. "I have never tried to bargain with you, Madame, but I feel that I must now, in one respect."

"And that?"

"The Jacobins have a new rumor. They are saying that a secret emissary is in Vienna, placing before the Emperor plans for an invasion of France. The story has it that this emissary is none other than Count Axel von Fersen. You, Madame, are accused of being at the back of it all."

"Nonsense!"

"You give me your word?"

"Without the slightest hesitation."

Barnave seemed partly satisfied. "Fersen planned the escape, and escaped himself. No one can be blamed for believing he is continuing the work he started."

"The Swedish count is answerable only to the Swedish King."

"That is true, but—"

"You were about to bargain with me, Monsieur."

"I and my friends will continue our secret support, providing you give us your royal word never to bring in foreign military aid."

"I give you my royal word."

"Thank you," Barnave said quietly. "I accept it and trust you implicitly." He took a quick step towards her. "Permit me, your Majesty."

He kissed her hand swiftly, bowed and was gone.

Marie Antoinette sank back into her chair and remained there, unmoving, for several moments. The feel of his lips remained on her hand. Furiously she rubbed the skin where his lips had touched it. Yes, yes, she had a conscience and it troubled her. But was she, because of it, to grow soft, set duplicity aside? And in any case, if one wanted to argue the point, how could *she* bring in a foreign army? She could pray for it, and through Axel work for it, but the decision rested with the foreign powers.

Then she remembered Barnave's horror at the suggestion that he might desire her as a woman, and springing from her chair half ran to the dressing-room. But at the door, knowing what she would see in the mirror, her steps slowed and she moved reluctantly.

"So you," she said to the reflection in the mirror, "are Marie Antoinette of France. One would never know it. Your hair lusterless, almost entirely gray now; your eyes too prominent, your lips not lips at all but a narrow slit, and the Habsburg lip uglier than ever. I refuse to accept you!"

Another week passed, with the calm in Paris continuing, except for a mild excitement at the announcement that the King was to go in state to the Assembly, now known as the Legislative Assembly. Barnave, however, brought disquieting news on the eve of Louis' appearance there.

"The Jacobins have increased their power and forced into being a new decree. The royal forms of address, Majesty and Sire, are dispensed with. The President of the Assembly, not the King, is to take precedence."

"A further calculated insult," Marie Antoinette remarked.

"I strongly advise the King not to attend."

"Why?"

"If I judge the temper of the people rightly, the King enjoys a quiet sort of popularity. Once I have spread the truth among the people, emphasizing the fact that the Jacobins are bent on humiliating him, I expect an outburst of enthusiasm."

She made up her mind at once. "The King will refuse to attend under the conditions imposed upon him. I promise you that."

Louis agreed without argument—"Whatever you wish, my dear—" and sent a message to the President of the Assembly. After that she waited anxiously, afraid that Barnave, no better able than anyone else to judge the temper of the people, had miscalculated. Almost immediately there was an outcry in Paris. The King had been insulted by the Jacobins. The King had taken a stand against them. Long live the King! Deputies who showed themselves in the streets were followed, jeered at, called guttersnipes. These crazy, unpredictable French! Had the tide turned? Was the Assembly to be the scapegoat now, not the King and Queen?

She wrote a triumphant little letter to Axel.

"The hateful decree was hastily set aside. Louis went in state to the Assembly. He was cheered in the streets and received with a grudging respect. In spite of the growing power and arrogance of the Jacobins we have enjoyed a small victory. It may even be possible to look forward to a counter-revolution."

But next came news that Provence, backed by Artois, had issued a manifesto. The royal brothers were now installed in comfortable quarters at Coblenz, where they had surrounded themselves with *émigrés*. In his manifesto Provence asserted that his aim was to preserve the French monarchy, which was an institution not much concerned with any particular king. He was ready to raise an army and fight his way to Paris. To rescue Louis? By no means! He declared himself regent of a vacant throne. Marie

336

Antoinette remembered how Provence had once remarked that he could wait. This, then, though he could not have suspected it at the time, was what he had waited for. His manifesto, she was sure, would stir the people to anger, and hourly she expected a storming of the Tuileries, but no, all remained amazingly calm.

"The people are angry," Barnave reported, "but their anger is directed against the Comte de Provence, not against the King."

"How odd, Monsieur!"

Barnave smiled wryly. "The King belongs to the people. They would never allow him to be replaced by Provence."

But if things remained calm in the capital the reverse happened in the provinces. The Jacobins, Barnave said, unable to make the progress they wanted in Paris, were striking at such places as Toulon, Melun and Avignon, organizing what he called a reign of terror. At Avignon, any man or woman who rose in the name of sane government was seized and imprisoned, and these initial actions were followed by a terrible massacre. Reports kept reaching Paris of bodies buried in ditches, some dead, some living. Official inquiries were made, solemn deputations sent to Avignon, but in the end the Assembly, timid now as Louis had so often been, granted an amnesty to the fanatical murderers.

"It is only a question of time," Marie Antoinette wrote to Axel, "before these waves of terror reach Paris. I pray God that time is not against us. Renew your efforts, I beg of you. Louis is now partly in agreement with our plan. He wants foreign intervention, but intervention by peaceful means. I held my tongue while he spoke of this. I enclose a letter from him to the King of Prussia."

After a moment's hesitation she added a few lines more.

"How I long to see you again, Axel. With no letters reaching me for what seems a desolate age, the longing grows and grows, has become more than I can support. If you are ready to take the risk of coming secretly to Paris, for pity's sake, Axel, take it."

But later, when re-writing her letter in code, she left out this cry from the heart and shuddered to think that she had ever written the words. Her duty was to gather strength about her, not grow weak and imperil the life of one she loved.

FIVE

SHE SAW ONLY THE BACK OF THE MAN WHO HAD SLIPPED HURRIEDLY into the room and was standing now with his hand on the door knob, his ear pressed against the woodwork. Barnave, evading the guards once more, but anxious. She saw his large enveloping cloak, for the February weather was bitter, and the big fur-lined boots. He turned and faced her.

"Axel!"

"Marie . . ."

"But I didn't send it! I know I didn't! I wrote it but I didn't send it!"

Axel came towards her slowly. His face was blue with the cold, but his eyes were bright and full of an undeniable happiness. He took her hands in his, they were icy.

"What didn't you send, Marie?"

"I wanted you to come. I begged you to come, but I thought of the risk. I couldn't bear it if— Oh Axel, has anyone recognized you? For heaven's sake tell me!"

"No one recognized me," he reassured her. "I slipped into the palace quite easily. A dreadful night, of course, dark and bitterly cold. Very few people abroad."

"Tell me why you came."

"I am under orders from King Gustav. I am travelling secretly, under an assumed name. I have a passport for passage through France to Portugal. Naturally I am not going to Portugal. I would have come in any case. Something beyond my control . . . Marie, I had to come."

She clung to his hands. They were warm now, pulsing with life. The slim hard fingers filled her with a new strength.

"I must see Louis," he said.

"Of course."

"There are many things to discuss."

"Yes."

"You are lovelier than ever."

"I am old and haggard."

338

"I can see only your eyes and what is in them."

"Dim eyes, and sad, but resolute still, Axel."

"All I can see is the life in them. I have been dead since we parted at Bondy."

"As I have been."

"It would not be safe to go to Louis' apartments. You must bring him here, Marie."

"Soon, soon."

"The routine of life at the Tuileries is unchanged?"

"Well, we may lock our doors at night. The guards are as watchful as ever, of course. I have hardly any servants. A maid or two, and two regular ladies-in-waiting. One I can trust—my old friend Louise de Lamballe. The other might be a spy. Louise is on duty tonight."

There was a scratching at the door.

Marie Antoinette looked quickly at Axel.

In a whisper she said, "That door there. My dressing-room. Hurry!"

She waited till he was out of sight, then said, "Enter!"

Louise de Lamballe came in.

"Ah, Louise, I was going to send for you. Please inform Louis that I am going to bed early and will see him tomorrow. And Louise, no formality tonight. I shall undress myself. All I want is to be left in peace."

"Of course, Marie."

"A little supper, though. You know my tastes. Champagne, chicken. Have it sent as soon as you can."

Louise looked at her hesitantly. "Is anything the matter, Marie? Bad news, perhaps?"

"Bad news? No, Louise, not that. Well, goodnight!"

"Goodnight, Marie."

Axel came out of the dressing-room the moment Louise had withdrawn. Marie Antoinette looked at him gravely. She knew exactly what she was going to do, what, without question or argument, was going to happen.

"I expect," Axel said thoughtfully, "it will be better to see Louis tomorrow."

"Better, yes. And Axel, until the maid brings the supper tray it will be safer for you to remain in the dressing-room."

"Of course."

She waited with a racing heart for the maid to come. Strange,

339

she thought, the same heavy palpitation when the mob screamed for your blood, but less fear now, no real fear at all.

The maid came at last and placed the tray on a small table.

Marie Antoinette said, "I shall need no further attention tonight. You are free to do as you please."

The maid curtsied. "At what hour will your Majesty rise?"

"Nine o'clock."

The maid curtsied again and withdrew.

Marie Antoinette called softly to Axel. He came and stood by her side at the table. She lifted the silver lid of the serving dish. The savory smell of roast chicken filled the room.

"You must be famished, Axel."

"Yes."

"As I am. As we both are, and have been for many senseless years."

She replaced the lid.

Axel went to the door and turned the key.

"Since the new constitution permits it," he said, and smiled broadly.

"Darling!" she cried in a choking voice. "Darling, darling . . ."

Afterwards, as she lay at peace in the curtained bed, she thought how it had happened with complete naturalness, a sense of supreme rightness. No arguments, no speech at all, not even a few murmured words of love. It was possible to believe that this was just a link in a chain, that between them it had always been like this, always would be. A continuation, that was it. A deep acknowledgment of the oneness which, beneath everything, had always been there. A renewal of a long-made pledge.

"Axel . . ." She knew he was awake.

"Marie?"

"Are you happy too?"

"Yes, very."

"How good it is! I can think of nothing else."

"An amazing happiness. Calm, full of peace."

"It is the same with me."

"Strange, Marie, it should have taken a revolution to bring it about."

"Strange, yes . . ."

She slipped out of bed. The lamps had burned very low.

"Nearly six o'clock, Axel. And goodness, how hungry you must be! Cold chicken and champagne for breakfast." She carried

340

the tray to the bed. "This reminds me of the hamper you packed."

They ate in silence, though they chuckled a little at the successful attempt he made to open the champagne bottle without noise.

"What am I to do," Axel asked presently, "when the routine of the day begins?"

"Ah yes, we must think of that, but we have three hours yet."

"I can hardly remain here in the Queen's bed until they come to make it."

"I should love you to. It would make me laugh to see their faces."

"We must be serious, Marie."

"Yes, Axel, we must be serious!"

"It is not a laughing matter."

"I can see laughter in your eyes."

"I can see it in yours too." He pointed a chicken bone at her. "Marie, *be serious!*"

"Immediately!" She considered the problem for a moment. "No," she said, laughing softly, "it would be *too* undignified."

"Under the bed, you mean? I could lie there with complete dignity."

"I would never be suspected of hiding anyone here. The cupboard in the dressing-room will be the best place. My bath will be wheeled in from outside, as usual. Afterwards, my dressing-table will be wheeled in from the dressing-room, as usual. Yes, you must hide in the cupboard, and remember to keep very still and quiet when the maids fetch the dressing-table."

They were asleep when, at nine o'clock, the maid scratched at the door. Axel seized his clothes and hurried to the dressing-room. A comical sight, Marie Antoinette thought, but there was a little lump in her throat. Perhaps all men looked funny under such circumstances. Louis must have looked funny, on the night of the escape, stealing away from his valet to dress himself. Louis, she thought . . . yes of course, there was such a person.

The maid scratched again and turned the door handle.

Marie Antoinette slipped from the bed, found her negligee and unlocked the door. A second maid appeared. The bath was trundled in. The water was not quite hot enough. The winter air of the room, she realized now, was bitterly cold. She bathed in haste and dressed in haste.

When breakfast was brought she shared it with Axel. Later she went to see the children and at one o'clock took a brief meal with Louis, then returned hurriedly and anxiously to her apartments. Incredible, of course, but Axel had succeeded the whole time, during the making of the bed and the cleaning of the rooms, in evading detection.

"Louis?" he asked.

"Later, Axel. Tonight. Please, darling, not till tonight."

He smiled at her. "I suspect you of planning to keep me here like this for days."

"That is what I want to do."

They looked at each other in silence and complete understanding.

"Axel . . ."

"Marie?"

"We have the afternoon. I gave orders that I was not to be disturbed. I said I had much to do, much to think about. A careful study of the latest debates of the Assembly."

Axel went to the door and locked it.

It was not until six in the evening that Marie Antoinette, reluctantly facing the necessity, went to fetch Louis. Two guards were on duty in the corridor. They barely glanced at her as she passed. She chuckled at the thought of what they had been so carefully guarding. A third guard on the stairs looked at her curiously, or so she imagined. Silly to wonder if he suspected. She had a high color, of course, and not from rouge. She touched her cheek tenderly. Axel was badly in need of a shave.

She found Louis busy at his desk.

"I am signing decrees with which I am totally in disagreement," he said sarcastically.

"Let them wait, Louis. A friend has called, a friend most anxious to see you."

"If you mean Barnave, I prefer to leave him to you."

"I speak of the only real friend we have."

"My God—not *Axel?*"

"Come with me, Louis. I have him well hidden in my apartments." She marvelled at the ease with which she was able to face Louis, the freedom from conscience. "Come quickly, but show no excitement."

"I know how to control my emotions," Louis said. "But . . . Axel!"

"It is not the first time he has risked his life for our sake."

342

Louis greeted Axel in silence. Having controlled his emotions in the corridors—indeed, having stopped to bid the guards a cheery good evening—he was now unable to control them. His face worked painfully, there were tears in his eyes. He embraced Axel with a frightening intensity and seemed unable to let him go.

Finally he managed to speak. "Axel, my dear fellow, Axel . . ." He stood back from him. "Weary and travel stained, I can see that." He peered closer. "Unshaven, too. Quite a villainous look it gives you. A disguise in itself, no doubt." He tried to laugh. "Not the immaculate Fersen, just a frightful revolutionary. Oh Axel, how very glad I am to see you. But dear heaven, the risk you took!"

Impatiently Marie Antoinette said, "Axel is here at the command of King Gustav." She turned to Axel, anxious now to hear all he had to say. "Tell us first about your visit to my brother Leopold."

"I found the Emperor deeply concerned, entirely sympathetic."

She looked at him sharply. "That doesn't sound very encouraging."

"But more encouraging than you might think. As soon as he heard of your arrest at Varennes he wrote to England, Spain, Russia, and Prussia. He suggested a coalition, a joint protest—"

"Protest! Just that, Axel, a *protest!*"

"Backed if need be by armed intervention."

"No," said Louis, seizing on this. "I cannot have armed intervention."

"Oh Louis," Marie Antoinette pleaded, "remember the atrocities at Avignon, the sanction given to them by the Assembly."

"My poor France is desperately ill but I cannot have invasion."

"What reply did Leopold get to his letters?" she asked.

"England was sorry, but preferred to remain neutral. Russia is too occupied with her war in Turkey to offer anything but sympathy. Spain was sure that a threat of armed intervention would endanger your lives."

"As it would," Louis said.

"And all three pointed out that the new constitution had brought peace again to Paris. The Emperor was impressed by that also. He thinks it better to wait and watch and—forgive me —hope for the best."

"And your own King?" Marie Antoinette asked.

343

"His Majesty King Gustav sees the danger clearly. He realizes that the revolution in France is a direct threat to absolute monarchy everywhere."

"A stalemate has been reached!" she cried.

Axel smiled. "King Gustav has a plan. That was why he sent me here. He is trying to stir England and Prussia to action, but meanwhile he feels that another attempt at escape should be made."

Louis sighed. "I have given my word."

She said, "Axel, have you and your King worked out a plan between you?"

"Not in full detail, but I have profited by the mistakes I made last time."

"Mistakes? You made none! You did everything possible. We were slow getting away. We were held up on the road. We lost four vital hours."

"Yes, but the escape was planned more like a royal progress than a desperate bid for freedom."

"I have given my word," Louis repeated. "Forgive me, Axel, if your secret mission has been a waste of time."

Axel was looking at Marie Antoinette. "It has not been a waste of time." He turned to Louis. "Is there no action I can persuade you to take, no action whatever?"

Louis, deep in thought, obviously upset by a struggle going on within him, stumped slowly about the room.

"I recognize a certain hopelessness in my position," he said finally. "I thought at first, after the new constitution . . . then there was that upset at Avignon . . . this rapid growth of republicanism . . . I do, I know, sit on the edge of a volcano . . ." Suddenly he gave way to a little spurt of anger. "What do they want of me? I am now what they demanded, a poor fish of a constitutional monarch. What are my powers? I have the privilege of saying, 'I disagree with you, but if you insist on going contrary to my wishes I am obliged to permit it.' I have, as a last resort, the right of veto, but dare I use it? I repeat, what do they want of me?"

Marie Antoinette said quietly, "They want your head, Louis, and mine also."

"The unhappiness of my poor France," Louis said. His anger had passed now, and he went on slowly, "Axel, this is my decision. This is what you must tell Gustav and the other kings. I suggest a gathering of the kings of Europe, a united front of royal heads. I suggest they should open up negotiations with the Assembly, reach an agreement for the guarantee of our personal safety. Further, an agreement which will allow me to leave Paris with my family and live at peace somewhere in the country."

"What if the Assembly refuses to treat with the kings of Europe?" Marie Antoinette pressed.

"If that happens, heaven forgive me, a threat of armed intervention. But mind you, Axel, only a *threat*."

Axel bowed. "Very well, Louis."

"And now—" Louis was glancing anxiously at the door—"it is most unsafe to keep you here. There is always the likelihood of a reversal of the present leniency, a sudden inspection by the guards of every hole and corner of the palace."

Marie Antoinette wanted to shout, *He's been here all day, all last night!* but she steadied herself and asked Axel where he would go, once he got safely away from the Tuileries.

"To the Hotel des Princes, in the Rue Richelieu. A friend has taken a room for me."

"And then?"

Axel smiled ruefully. "I had expected to stay there and organize your escape."

Louis grew suddenly agitated. "How unimpressed you are by the danger of your position! Stay at the Hotel des Princes tonight, if you must, but tomorrow, without fail, you must get out of Paris. You give me your word?"

"I give you my word, Louis."

"Thank you!"

Axel turned to Marie Antoinette, but before he could speak she cried, "No! We'll have no farewells, Axel!"

"No farewells," Louis agreed.

"Go quietly and confidently, as if you expect to see us again tomorrow," she begged. "Take with you our gratitude and thanks and love." Her voice was shaking now, almost beyond her control. "And remember this, Axel, your visit has given me a new, unthought-of strength."

Louis was at the door, unlocking it. He stepped out into the corridor, paused there for a moment, then thrust his head back into the room.

"The two guards are talking together at the other end of the corridor," he whispered. "Wait till I reach them. My fatness is of *some* use. They will step aside for me. I will step aside for them. A little collision, and there is your opportunity."

With Louis trudging purposefully towards the two guards, Marie Antoinette ran to Axel's arms. They embraced swiftly.

"Tomorrow you must shave," she said, sobbing.

"I promise."

"Now go. For pity's sake go!"

She followed him to the door. One glance in Louis' direction revealed him in what appeared to be a desperate struggle with the guards, except for the shout of laughter issuing from his throat.

"Hurry, Axel, hurry!"

Axel ran lightly in the opposite direction, turned, paused for a moment, waved and was gone. Marie Antoinette threw herself on the bed.

SIX

LOUIS POUNDED HIS DESK WITH A CLENCHED FIST. "SO THIS IS WHAT the kings of Europe want! Friends of mine? Brother kings, full of sympathy, ready only to help me? I tell you, Marie, they are no better, in their own cruel and grasping way, than a mob of revolutionary terrorists!"

Marie Antoinette could but agree.

The result of the appeal for help was disillusioning. Negotiations with the Assembly? Nothing of the kind! Austria would gladly hold out a helping hand, at the price of two or three French provinces. Prussia was reaching out greedily for Alsace-Lorraine. England wanted Dunkirk and as many French colonies as possible. Russia alone seemed content to forego territorial gains but was eager to turn what was left of France into an ineffectual third-rate power.

"Dismemberment," Louis said, whispering now. "A pack of wild animals waiting to spring on France and tear her apart."

Marie Antoinette thought of Barnave. He was useless to her now. Events had outpaced her own small scheming. Or was it that her own small scheming had brought about these events? She had not, of course, expected the rapacity of the foreign powers.

"These aims of my brothers of Europe," Louis went on, "are anything but secret aims. They are talking loudly, swaggering already. Their threats will unite my country as it has never been united before."

She was quick to notice pride of country strong in his voice.

"Will we be blamed, Louis?" she asked.

"Why not? We have been blamed for everything bad that has happened during my reign."

After that she waited daily for the storming of the Tuileries, but for a time all seemed quiet in Paris. And then one morning she heard from her window the first cry of 'Long live the Republic!' Yet there was no organized demonstration. Little groups of people gathered, cried 'Long live the Republic!' and drifted away. But they continued to gather, and soon it seemed that this cry, not the hands of the clock, marked the regular passage of time.

Meanwhile Austria and Prussia had formed an alliance and had appointed the Duke of Brunswick commander-in-chief of their joint forces. Next came news that her brother Leopold had died suddenly, and close on this the news that Gustav of Sweden had been assassinated. Axel wrote that though nothing could be proved, her brother had been poisoned, murdered as King Gustav had been. Spies of the revolution were busy everywhere, he said. And finally, while Austria and Prussia hesitated on the brink of war, the Assembly acted. It was Barnave who brought her the news.

"A declaration of war, Madame. France declares war on Austria and Prussia."

At first she refused to believe it. "But a country torn by revolution is in no position to make war." She laughed scornfully. "A series of charges made by National guards flourishing umbrellas —is that what is planned?"

"France recognizes the common danger. France will unite."

He sounded just like Louis, the same pride of country in his voice.

Hopefully she said, "Austria and Prussia might never have embarked on invasion. Now their hand has been forced. Yes, this rash declaration may be for the best, after all."

Barnave's eyes flashed angrily. "So it's true, as I was beginning to suspect. You were using me, Madame, and at the same time working for a foreign invasion."

"The Assembly has forced the issue, not I," she said coldly.

"What a fool I was! How easily your pitiful plight deceived me!" He took a quick step forward; she thought for a moment he was going to strike her, but to her surprise he seized her hand and kissed it. "I think you have signed my death warrant, Madame, but what I did I would do again."

"Why?" she asked.

But he seemed not to hear. "I never wanted the terror, the slaughter of innocent people. I was even too blind to foresee it. What I looked forward to, through revolution, was a steady improvement of conditions for the unfortunate. Liberty of choice and thought, equality of opportunity. Now I look to the future

348

with fear and doubt and dismay in my heart." He turned from her abruptly. "I wish you well, Madame."

Almost immediately the cry of 'Long live the Republic!' became a thunderous roar. Day and night it echoed round the Tuileries. From the windows of the palace Marie Antoinette watched the ordinary citizens marching out of Paris, a ragged determined army. Nursing her hatred, she refused to believe that they could hold up for one moment the trained experienced forces under Brunswick's command. Powerful enough when it came to attacking a defenseless family, but going now, poor fools, to certain slaughter. Brunswick's advance would be swift, rescue and freedom were close. She knew that attack by the mob might come first, but sternly she turned her mind from such a thought.

A month passed. Brunswick's advance was not as swift as she had expected. He was moving through the north, leaving a trail of desolation behind him, but his pace was all too slow. Incredible and surely futile, this stubborn opposition of a citizen army!

The second month drew to a close. Brunswick's advance continued, methodical, brutal, but with a slowness that was now an agony. Contingent after contingent marched through Paris; thousands fell before his murderous attack, but thousands more replaced them.

"I am proud of my people," Louis said sadly. "Tens of thousands of civilians, untrained for war, marching, marching, and dying."

"Were you proud of them when they marched on Versailles?"

"I never wanted freedom this way. My crown will weigh heavy on my head if I gain it like this."

"Have no fear. Unless Brunswick succeeds nothing will save us. It amazes me that we have not been attacked before now."

"*If* Brunswick succeeds," Louis corrected, "nothing will save us. Perhaps I should have exercised my right of veto, never consented to the declaration of war."

"Oh Louis, Louis! As if any notice would have been taken of you!"

He said eagerly, "It is a matter of feeling my way gradually. A small veto before a large one." He smiled at her hopefully. "It will surprise you to know that today I have vetoed two decrees. One concerns the clergy. The fanatics have renewed their attacks

349

on the church. They want a godless France now. Exile for all priests, whether or not they have taken the civil oath."

"And the second decree?"

"The Jacobins are trying to form what amounts to a private army, every man specially selected. The excuse is necessary preparations for the celebration of the storming of the Bastille. The undeclared aim is an attack on the Tuileries."

Gently she said, "You might cause the thing you want to prevent."

Louis laughed slyly. "I am quite prepared for an attack on the Tuileries, and this time I have a plan."

She sighed. "Well, what is your plan?"

Louis smiled irritatingly. "Wait and see."

He came to her the next day, quivering with excitement.

"My challenge has been accepted, but my strength recognized. The mob will march on the Tuileries, but not to attack us. A march of protest, that is what is being organized. Cap in hand, you might say, the leaders are going to *beg* me to accept the two decrees."

"And your plan *is* to accept them?"

"Certainly not!"

She was unable to get more out of him.

Two days later, at four in the afternoon, she heard the tramp of marching feet and the distant rising murmur of excited voices. Summoned by Louis, she hurried to the Council Chamber. She found him surrounded by members of the court. Madame Elizabeth had been summoned also, and had the children with her. They all moved in a group to the window and looked out across the courtyards to the Carrousel. The marching mob, some of them armed, was passing in an almost orderly formation.

Louis seemed quite pleased with himself. "They are marching round the palace, merely that."

"But any moment now—"

Even as she spoke all semblance of order fell from the mob and a mass of surging figures began to sweep into the courtyards.

"Louis, the palace will be surrounded in a moment!"

"Yes."

An officer of the National Guard approached.

"All doors are locked and well guarded, your Majesty."

"Well, that is my cue," Louis said. "I must go down now." He stood before Marie Antoinette for a moment, smiling on her. "I took the sacrament this morning, Marie. I have lifted my eyes to heaven. I am ready to die, if need be."

He was calm and immovable. His eyes were shining. He had the bearing of a man deeply inspired, but a man, she thought, out of touch with all reality.

"Louis, you spoke of a plan!"

"Yes."

"To make a human sacrifice of yourself?"

"I hope not, my dear." He embraced her. "Stay here with the children. You will be well guarded."

"Louis!"

"Put your trust in God. Hold on to your courage."

He kissed the children. "Wait here with Mama. Be fearless, as she is, as I hope I am."

She watched him trudge from the room, head and shoulders pushed resolutely forward. Long after he had gone she stared at the open door. Outside the yelling of the mob rose in waves, and with it a new sound, the splintering of woodwork as axes rose and fell. She realized that except for a dozen National guards she and the children were alone in the Council Chamber. She drew the children close and looked carefully at the guards. Friends, or enemies?

The officer in charge was issuing orders. She watched, stupefied, while his men pushed the heavy council table towards a corner of the room. The officer saluted and pointed to the corner.

"Your Majesty and the children will be safer there, behind the table."

"Thank you."

Was it her own voice? It had a strange dry sound. "Thank you," she said again, and led the children to the corner. "A certain amount of protection, yes. A heavy table. Put to better use now than when councillors of state used to doze over it."

The officer laughed; his men joined in.

"Long live the Queen," one murmured.

She looked at him gratefully. "If it is permitted, please go down and bring us news of the King."

The officer said sharply, "You heard, man. Obey the Queen's order."

The crash of axes had stopped but the ugly screaming of the mob was closer.

The guard who had gone for news of Louis returned hurriedly. "His Majesty insisted on all the doors being thrown open. The palace is now at the mercy of the mob."

"And the King—?" Marie Antoinette asked fearfully.

"He walked calmly to his apartments. The mob followed, a great press of them. And then he turned and faced them. He is standing with his back to a window, his arms folded. The mob is threatening him with bayonets but his face is quite serene."

"They will tear him to pieces!"

"No, Madame. His calmness has taken their breath away."

At that moment, with shrill cries and a pounding of feet, a score of women burst into the room, carrying the guards before them. Others pushed in behind. Thinking of Louis' calmness, Marie Antoinette steeled herself for the ordeal. She placed her arms round the children and begged them to remember what their father had said. Both, though white and terrified, held their heads high. Pandemonium broke loose. The women shrieked and cursed, and chanted the now-familiar chorus, "The Austrian whore, the Austrian whore!" Each wore a red cap, the symbol of the Jacobins; their clothes were filthy and torn; their faces reflected a blind contorted hatred. With flailing arms and clawing fingers they flung themselves on the guards.

"Wait!" Marie Antoinette commanded.

The women held back, momentarily.

"Stand aside," she ordered the guards.

The guards disentangled themselves and stood back.

She placed her hands on the table. "The Austrian whore," she said, slowly and distinctly, "is in good, if degraded company."

A young girl laughed shrilly. "That's right. Whores every one of us."

An elderly woman slapped the girl across the face and flung a red cap on the table.

"Stick it on the Dauphin's head. He's one of the people now."

Marie Antoinette picked up the cap. The sweaty filthiness of it made her flesh crawl. May heaven forgive me, she thought, and placed it on her son's head. He looked up at her, smiled uncertainly.

"Madame," she said, addressing the owner of the red cap, "we have not had the pleasure of meeting before."

"I was at Versailles!" the woman screamed.

"And now you are at the Tuileries, standing before the council table. Have you come to tell us all how best to solve our problems? Why not climb on the table and address this gathering? Let us pretend that this is the Assembly and you are the president.

A murmur of spontaneous laughter rose.

More sure of herself, Marie Antoinette recognized the need to keep on talking.

"We hear a lot these days about the rights of man. What about the rights of woman? What about the rights of a Queen, who is also a woman? Would you, Madame, prefer to change places with me?"

The woman hung back, scowling but silent.

"Go on, Thérèse," someone cried tauntingly, "take the Queen's place."

Still the woman hung back, speechless.

"I was born an Austrian," Marie Antoinette went on, "and would have been happy living in my homeland. But you brought me to France and you made me the wife of the man who became your King. I bore him children. I loved him. I loved you, too, when I first came here. I think you loved me. Have you children of your own? A son, perhaps, the same age as mine? Would he be brave, standing here among a horde of shrieking women?"

An unexpected silence had fallen. With her hands pressed down on the table she tried to steady her shaking legs. What she had said had come to her instinctively. Her throat was parched now; her whole body quivered with the beating of her heart. She had reached the end. Let them do as they wished; she could protect herself no further.

She looked at the woman who still faced her in silence. She was rubbing her eyes, which were amazingly full of tears.

"I never gave it a thought before," the woman said. "You're just a mother, same as me."

"No," Marie Antoinette said, making a great effort to speak. "Not the same. You are free. *I* am a prisoner."

The woman leaned across the table and snatched the red cap from the Dauphin's head.

"It's too hot in here to wear a cap."

A few men had pushed their way into the Council Chamber. One of them shouted for attention.

"Listen, all of you. He's dead, the big fat pig. Long live the Republic!"

Marie Antoinette felt her throat constrict. Her son whimpered and buried his face in her gown. Her daughter gave a little moan but continued to hold her head high.

More guards had entered too, and were pushing their way through the women.

"A lie!" one of them cried. "Not a finger's been laid on the King."

The man who had made the announcement laughed brutally. "All I wanted was to see the Queen's face."

Marie Antoinette made a supreme effort. "Step forward then, get a closer view. Come, Monsieur, what are you afraid of? Not a helpless woman, surely!"

The women seized him and hustled him towards the table.

Marie Antoinette pointed a finger at him. "Am I to judge all Frenchmen by *you?*"

He shook himself free of the women and shouldered his way to the door. There he turned and raised a clenched fist.

"A clever tongue, the bitch has. Perhaps we've failed this time, but we'll be back, by Christ we will!"

"He calls on Christ," Marie Antoinette cried, "this man who wants a godless France!"

A young girl sprang on the table. She was barefooted. Her skirt hung about her legs in tatters. Her bare breasts, small and pointed, were ringed with dirt.

"Long live the Queen!" she cried.

The cry rang dimly in Marie Antoinette's ears. The red-capped mob danced before her eyes; her heart throbbed suffocatingly in her throat. She gripped the edge of the table, fighting, fighting.

"Here, take a swig of this," said a distant voice.

She was conscious of the young girl's face close to her own; she felt the bottle pressed against her lips. The wine was harsh, like vinegar, and bit her throat as she swallowed a gulp.

Faint still but fighting all the time, she remained standing at the table, her daughter on one side, her son on the other. Not conscious of the passing of time, she grew slowly aware that the room had darkened. She knew that more women had crowded in, stared at her, then given way to others. She knew that lamps had been lighted, that torches had flared in her face. She knew, much later, that she was lying back in a chair, that all was quiet. The room seemed to have shrunk in size, and was empty now of all but one man.

"Marie, my dear . . ."

"Louis."

"You were magnificent, Marie."

"Where am I? Where are the children?"

"You are in your own apartments. You walked here steadily from the Council Chamber. You refused all help."

"The children, the children!"

"In bed, my dear. All is quiet now. The people have gone. I knew I was right. No defense, no protection. Just passive resistance. This is a real triumph. My first real victory."

"You are . . . quite unharmed?"

"Quite. I remained calm. I talked with the people. When they cursed me I laughed. I remembered an English expression I have always liked. I told them their bark was worse than their bite. I admit there were times when I expected a bayonet in my chest, but the turning point came when I said I was thirsty and asked for a glass of water. Someone thrust a filthy bottle under my nose. I drank the horrible cheap wine and I apologized for having asked for water. I said I had forgotten for the moment that I was a Frenchman."

"I think they made me drink wine too." She touched her brow numbly. "Yes, wine. How long did the ordeal last, Louis?"

"Seven hours."

She laughed weakly. "Neither more nor less? Come, my little clockmaker, you always know the precise time."

"Seven hours exactly," Louis said, and laughed too.

"And now all is quiet. You withdrew the vetoes, of course?"

"By heaven I did not!"

"Yet they went quietly."

"I tell you, my first real victory."

"Brunswick. You are forgetting the war, Louis."

"Brunswick will fail."

Brunswick . . .

The name stayed in her mind all night through the fitful hours of sleep. She heard it spoken repeatedly by the man who had shouted that the big fat pig was dead. She woke at dawn, panting. A voice was crying that Brunswick would never reach Paris in time. The voice, she realized, was her own. She was screaming it aloud till the room echoed with it.

355

In the days that followed it seemed that her mind could hold only one thought. *Brunswick, Brunswick* . . . Was there really such a man? Was he marching now on Paris to snatch her from this prison, or had she only dreamed it?

"Brunswick," Louis announced one morning, "has issued a manifesto. He has even sent a copy to the Assembly. They are debating it now."

"How indignant you sound, Louis."

"Passive resistance would have won the day. Brunswick has wrecked all my hopes of settling my personal affairs myself, in my own way. Yet in another sense he has made certain another hope. The whole of France will now rise. Even women will march against him. He will never reach Paris! Never!"

"Tell me about the manifesto."

"Arrest for the Assembly, imprisonment, trial . . . any soldier in Paris taken bearing arms to be declared a rebel . . . any citizen daring to defend himself, immediate death . . . if you and I, the children, my sister, are as much as touched, destruction of the whole city."

"It should make us feel safe, Louis."

"I care nothing for that! If France were a nation capable of intimidation, perhaps we might feel safe. But France is proud, proud, I tell you! Brunswick will never march into Paris." Louis bared his teeth in a sneer. "He claims he will march into Paris on October tenth. Why that date in particular? The soulless precision of these Germans!"

Louis was right. The whole nation rose. She listened to the marching feet, she watched the ragged battalions—yes, women marching with the men, as Louis had said—she wrote feverishly to Axel that Brunswick must hurry, hurry! October tenth. When was that? A whole lifetime away.

"Stubborn resistance, and more to come," Louis said. "French blood means nothing to Frenchmen now."

Still she listened to the marching feet. It was July now, a torrid, breathless month, the weather in keeping with the mood of Paris. The marching and the singing, her head reeled with the sound of it all. July tenth, three more months to go. Fantastic! Brunswick was a figment of imagination, his declared date a voice in the nightmare of her existence. If only she could think clearly. Impossible to know these days whether she was alive or dead.

356

August now, the tenth, and a change in the tempo of the marching. A new song too, quite a stirring tune. The "Marseillaise," she thought it was called. They were singing it in the Cour des Princes as they marched outside her window. Of course it was a different tempo! She remembered the storming of the Bastille, the attack on Versailles, the invasion of the Tuileries.

"Marie . . ."

She swung round from the window. Louis was standing behind her.

"Louis, this song, this 'Marseillaise' . . ."

"The people of Marseille, remember? They sang it when they marched on Paris."

She remembered. They had come, those people of the south, or so they claimed, to remove the royal family, to do the job the people of Paris had shirked.

"But Louis, here in the Cour des Princes!"

Louis stared beyond her, out of the window.

"I am shortsighted, I can see nothing. I am deaf, I can hear nothing."

The singing swelled. *Allons, enfants de la patrie . . .*

She listened intently. *Le jour de gloire est arrivé!*

"Dear heaven, Louis, the day of glory!"

Louis came to her and took her in his arms. "Perhaps even for us, if we keep our heads high."

"Passive resistance will gain us nothing this time."

"Nothing."

Afterwards she tried to remember what had happened. Not an immediate attack, but the mob holding back, gathering its forces during a sleepless night . . . Louis reluctantly issuing the order for defensive action, then growing more helpless and bewildered than she had ever known him, a man moving in a dream, already dead.

Safer for the royal family with the Assembly in the Riding School, somebody suggested. Very well, to the riding school, there to wait with the quaking deputies, there to listen dumbly to the din echoing across from the Tuileries. Screams of rage, screams of agony. All hell let loose.

A deputy standing before her. She thought at first he was Barnave.

"Barnave?" she said uncertainly.

"No, Madame, Barnave has left Paris."

The man continued to speak in a hoarse, unreal voice. "The massacre is dreadful. Women dancing on the naked bodies, the corridors running with blood, the Quay des Tuileries stacked high with corpses. Heads kicked about the street, tossed in the river. May God forgive us, Madame!"

SEVEN

"My dearest axel . . ."

With one part of her mind she was able to convince herself that she really was writing to Axel, that the pen was firmly gripped in her fingers; with another part she knew that the letter was being written in imagination only. Of course it was! They had refused to give her writing materials, and in any case it would be impossible to get a letter out to him.

The phrases began to form in her mind.

"They have shut us up in the Temple, this grim dark fortress of olden times. Crueller times, you might think, but I doubt it. For seventeen hours we sheltered in the Riding School. Louis assures me that the time was seventeen hours, neither more nor less. Let us by all means laugh at something!

"I think they gave us soup. The deputies put a very brave face on things. They debated this and that while the terror went on outside. I seem to remember a decree depriving Louis of all royal authority and declaring his wife and family hostages. A new name for us, too. Capet. A remotely old family name.

"We are in the Little Tower of the Temple. It took them two hours and a half to bring us here through the shrieking crowds in the streets. That is the correct time. Louis told me. He always remembers to wind up our watches. The Great Tower, which is more like a dungeon, is being got ready for us."

Absently she sat in her chair, arms folded, her mind a blank again.

"Your Majesty . . ."

She looked up. "Why, Louise. You are here also." She had forgotten Louise de Lamballe. "Are the sleeping arrangements satisfactory? We must make ourselves as comfortable as possible this first night. Tomorrow they will murder us."

Louise de Lamballe said gently, "We have been here for some time. The sleeping arrangements are still the same. Yourself and Madame Royale in one room, Madame de Tourzel and the Dauphin in another, Madame Elizabeth and two waiting women in the kitchen."

"And Louis?"

"A small room to himself, with two valets at the door. The others—"

"Enough, Louise. You may withdraw. I must finish my letter to Axel."

The next day—it might well have been the next week for all she knew—she began another imaginary letter to Axel von Fersen.

"Louise de Lamballe and Madame de Tourzel have been taken to a prison called La Force. We are alone, except for two valets. Louis and I, the children, Elizabeth. The guards come daily to look at us and make sure God has not cheated the revolution by taking us in our sleep.

"The guards sometimes speak of what is happening outside, but they may be taunting us with lies. They say a republic has been declared. They speak of a National Convention. A Minister of Justice now, not a King. One guard told me that my 'dear friend' Antoine Barnave had been denounced and would be brought to trial. Another said sulkily that Brunswick was still advancing . . ."

She looked up. Louis was standing before her. To her surprise her daughter was sitting at her side, holding her hand, while her son was lying at her feet.

"You hear the noise?" Louis said.

She listened. Drums. Marching feet. Brunswick at last, Brunswick to the rescue?

"What is the date?"

"September the 2nd."

"Ah, not the methodical Brunswick. He said October 10th."

She heard the familiar cries then, the baying of the pack stressed rhythmically by the drum-beat. A guard had entered the room and was stepping obsequiously aside. Officious-looking men—municipal officers, Louis whispered—crowded about her.

"Go to the window and look out of it," she was ordered.

She rose obediently. Louis tried to press her back into the chair but she moved steadily to the window. She saw the hate-filled faces below, and there on a pike a still-bleeding head. She saw something white, the headless naked body. Louis turned her quickly away.

"That was Louise," she sobbed.

"Brunswick is at Verdun," one of the municipal officers said harshly. "That is our answer to Brunswick. She's not the first, she'll not be the last."

The room was quiet again, unbearably quiet. She knew, as all feeling flooded back, that she had fainted and was now lying on the bed. Louis was bending over her, stroking her brow.

"Louise, no one so gentle and innocent as Louise. Why not *my* head on that pike?"

"I think they still fear Brunswick."

"And Brunswick is still advancing."

"They spoke of Verdun. He must be."

"But not afraid of him. All they want to do is torture us."

"Marie, my dear—" Louis was still stroking her brow—"you must stir yourself a little. We are prisoners, expecting death at any moment, but we are together. A little family group. Shall we remember that and forget all else?"

She stirred herself. She played with the children each morning and again each afternoon. She sat with Louis in the evening while he read the books allowed him. She tried to talk calmly with Elizabeth, and both did needlework. A harmless, quite genteel routine!

But every day she asked, "Brunswick is still advancing?"

"Still advancing."

So often did she ask this question and so often did Louis make the same reply that one day when he said, "No, he has suffered a defeat," she scarcely took in the meaning of his words.

"Defeat?"

"The guards say he is in flight."

"Are you pleased, Louis?"

"It is the only thing left to be pleased about."

"Will they murder us now, waste no further time?"

Louis smiled faintly. "We are something of an embarrassment to them. I think they have delayed too long. They are holding us here, safe from the mob. Can the guards murder us in cold blood?" He touched her shoulder gently. "Let us forget it. Will you help me give the children a geography lesson?"

But the geography lesson was never given.

A number of guards clumped into the room.

"They're ready, the new quarters in the Great Tower. Get a move on."

Louis inclined his head. "We are at your service, Monsieur."

361

"It's you we want, Citizen, no one else."

Louis looked steadily at Marie Antoinette. "Separation. It is not unexpected." He dropped his voice to a whisper. "Say nothing to the children. Not immediately." He turned to the spokesman of the guards. "I may visit the Queen on occasion?"

"What Queen, Citizen? France is a republic."

"Are you a married man?" Louis asked. "If so, you may understand this better. I may visit my *wife* on occasion?"

The man's face softened momentarily. "There's nothing against it that I know of."

"I may take a valet with me?"

"There's nothing against that either."

Again Louis looked steadily at Marie Antoinette. "Put your faith in God. Lift up your eyes to heaven."

For four weeks the family was allowed to dine together in Louis' room in the Great Tower, then Marie Antoinette, the children and Madame Elizabeth were given accommodation there. How splendid to be completely together again! That was her first thought, but how could they ever really be together when guards sat in all the rooms during the day, and outside, with the doors open, during the night? Private conversation was impossible, even in whispers. The slightest whisper and out rasped a voice, "Speak up or hold your tongues!"

Yet a simple family routine was established, and under Louis' never-failing cheerfulness they achieved a sort of happiness. They were together as they had never been together before. Life at Versailles, even at the Tuileries, had not been a family life; now they were a simple small family, united, even strong. The day of glory? In a way, yes.

Pretense, of course, was necessary. They even pretended they had a court hairdresser again. He was Clery, Louis' valet, who came after breakfast to dress their hair. For the rest of the morning Louis gave his young son lessons, even made the hated Latin an amusing game, and Marie Antoinette helped her daughter with embroidery. At midday they walked in a walled-in garden, damp, airless, sunless, but they ignored the conditions and played vigorously with a ball. They dined at two o'clock, and after supper at nine Marie Antoinette and Louis put the children to bed, kneeling at their bedsides to say prayers with them. Yes, a sort of happiness, that not even the iron bars at the windows, the dampness of their

362

cell-like rooms, the watching and listening of the guards, could quite dispel.

"They want to forget us," Louis said. "No doubt we shall spend the rest of our lives together like this, a real family to the end."

To the end . . . An unhappy choice of words, that.

And Louis was wrong. A few days later—it was winter and bitterly cold—the Dauphin burst into the room, glanced uncertainly at the guard who sat in a corner smoking his pipe, and rushed to his mother's side.

Marie Antoinette signed to Clery, who was dressing her hair, to stand back.

"Yes, darling, what is it?"

The boy flung his arms round her neck and kissed her. "Papa said to kiss you for him. He said I must be brave."

She kept her voice steady. "Darling . . ."

Her daughter and her sister-in-law gathered about her.

"Papa has gone," the Dauphin said, his lips trembling. "We were having a history lesson. They came in, a lot of men wearing red caps. They called Papa Louis Capet. Then they said something about the bar of the National Convention. What is that, Mama?"

Marie Antoinette was conscious that her sister-in-law and her daughter had stiffened and gasped almost inaudibly.

She said quietly, "It is a place where Papa will stand, and be as brave as he expects you to be." As he expects us all to be, she added, to herself. She glanced at the guard. He was staring at her curiously. She wanted to ask if they would see Louis again, but instead she said, "What is the date, Monsieur?"

"December 11th," he said, without removing his pipe.

"Thank you." She kissed her son and smiled at Clery who was standing as if frozen. "Come, Clery, you must dress Madame Elizabeth's hair now."

December 11th, she thought. I must make an effort to remember that tomorrow is the 12th, the next day the 13th. I must keep count, remember, keep count. It seemed in that moment the most important thing in life.

Louis returned to the Temple that night. She could hear his heavy tread in the room above. Clery went to him but was not allowed to return with messages. Each morning, as the days went by, she repeated yesterday's date, today's and tomorrow's. Once, the absolute quiet in the room above filled her with horror, but the heavy tread began again in the evening. Unable to contain herself she spoke briefly to the guard.

"Does the King go to the Convention each day?"

"There is no King."

"But I can hear him up there! Or—dear heaven, am I dreaming!"

"The man up there is Louis Capet."

She heard, comprehended, but was thinking wonderingly, yesterday was Christmas Day. None of us remembered. She had kept count, but the days had become numbers only, and as numbers they continued. Yesterday was January 1st, today is the 2nd . . . Yesterday, the 5th; today the 6th . . . Today, the 20th . . .

"Mama . . ."

It was her daughter, looking at her intently.

"Yes, darling?"

"They want to speak to you."

She looked beyond Madame Royale's shoulder. A group of men, stiff, solemn-faced, perhaps a little hesitant.

"What is the date, gentlemen?"

"January 20th."

"Ah, I have kept count accurately. What do you want of me?"

"You and your family may visit the prisoner, Louis Capet, tonight in a room downstairs."

"Thank you."

"Four guards will be present."

"That is understood. You may withdraw."

She waited with amazing patience for the evening.

"All is in readiness," a guard announced, and led the way down the narrow winding stairs. Her son clung to her hand with a fierce hot grip. Her daughter and Madame Elizabeth, stumbling in the darkness, followed close on her heels.

Louis was standing in the center of the dimly lit dining room. All four flung themselves upon him. He kissed and embraced them gently. She saw through her tears that he looked surprisingly calm. His dress was neat, his hair tied back and powdered. Clery had looked after him well.

"Tell me the time, Louis."

"Half-past eight, my dear."

She glanced about the room, looking for the four guards. She saw the glass partition. Yes, there had always been a glass partition. The guards were behind it, able to keep a strict watch but unable to hear.

364

"A special concession," Louis told her. "Come, sit down. Let us make ourselves as comfortable as possible."

They seated themselves about him. A tense little silence fell. So many questions to be asked, yet if only for the children's sake, questions one dared not ask.

"Louis—" she began, and fell silent again.

Speaking in rapid German, Louis said, "It makes me happy to know there is no uncertainty now. Yes, speak in German. The children won't understand if we do so quickly."

Marie Antoinette spoke in German. "What is there to say when I know in my heart the meaning of your words."

Nevertheless, Louis told her briefly what had happened. The charge, conspiracy against the nation; the sentence, death by decapitation. So many other accusations, but only one that really hurt him.

"Responsibility for the shedding of French blood. My responsibility, mine alone. I think I wept then. I think a few honest men in the Convention wept too. Had I been selfish enough years ago to shed French blood I would not be here now."

She brushed this aside.

"When, Louis?"

"Tomorrow."

"You will go to it bravely."

"I shall face the ordeal more bravely than I have lived. That is my tragedy."

He took his son on his knees and playfully tweaked his nose. Marie Antoinette heard a sob. Torn from her own throat, or from Elizabeth's? Or from her daughter's? Both were weeping openly now. What use to have spoken in rapid German? The children knew.

"We will have a little lesson," Louis was saying gently. "When I have gone away, I want you, my son, to think with compassion on those who have taken me away. I want you to be strong enough to grant them pardon. Oh, a hard thing to ask, but I beg you to obey me."

The boy slipped from his father's knee, stood between his legs and buried his face in the broad, still powerful chest.

"Come, child, give me your word."

"I give it, Papa," the boy sobbed.

"Try always to put your faith in God, lift up your eyes to heaven. I have been much alone these days, and alone I have learned what I always knew. God will give you comfort." Louis looked at Marie Antoinette, at his sister; he drew his daughter into a fierce embrace. "I can say no more." His face was broken, tears were rolling down his cheeks. "Not weakness, Marie, only love."

No further words were spoken by any of them. They remained in a silent, close little group, embracing each other. Presently Louis freed himself gently and rose. He made a great show of looking at his watch, and spoke with a forced briskness.

"As usual, I know the exact time. It is ten o'clock. The children should be in bed." He gave his sister a little push. "What are you thinking of, you great idiot!"

Clutching the children close, Madame Elizabeth stumbled from the room. Marie Antoinette hung back for a moment.

"Louis, forgive me."

"For what, dearest Marie? The great happiness you have given me?"

"I— Louis, you will see me again tomorrow?"

"Naturally. In the morning. Immediately after breakfast, in your room. Permission has been granted."

She embraced him lingeringly. "Till tomorrow, then."

"Till tomorrow, my dear. May God bless you forever. And remember, faith in God, lift up your eyes to heaven."

She knew then that he was saying goodbye, that in spite of his words she would never see him again. She knew it in the morning, after a sleepless night. She knew it as she listened to the footsteps clattering up and down the stairs, and in the distance the steady ever-rising beat of drums.

She sat on the bed, her son on one side, her daughter on the other, both leaning against her. Madame Elizabeth was standing motionless at the window, a window so constructed that only the sky could be seen. She noticed that not one guard but two sat in the room. They sat near the door, arms folded, eyes averted, pipes in their mouths but unlit.

"I think the thaw has started," Elizabeth remarked.

"Of course. I had forgotten. It was snowing yesterday, the day before."

"I hate it when the thaw starts."

"So do I. Such a grand and noble world, covered in snow. Then horrible desolation and ruin."

She rose and went to the door.

366

The two guards looked at her.

"It is not permitted," one said gruffly.

"I want to go to my husband."

"It is not permitted," he repeated. "The King himself ordered it."

"The King? You forget your oath to the republic, Monsieur!"

He flushed. "A slip of the tongue."

She heard a carriage drive up and stop. She heard more footsteps on the stairs. She heard the carriage start again, listened to the muffled hoofbeats till the sound was lost in the blast of trumpets and the roll of drums.

"Fog now," said Elizabeth, from her place at the window.

Marie Antoinette joined her and stared unseeingly at the swirling fog above the bars of the window. All was quiet now, no drums, no trumpets. The silence hurt so much she pressed her hands against her ears. And then, the reverberations echoing in her heart, she heard the first cannon, the second, the third . . .

She turned and threw herself on her knees at her son's feet and spoke the few stilted words which seemed imperative.

"Your Majesty, let me be the first to kiss your hand."

EIGHT

WAKING SUDDENLY SHE THOUGHT, LOUIS SAID HE WOULD SEE ME THIS morning.

She opened her eyes and stared uncomprehendingly about her. The dawn, a faint diffusion of gray light, was drifting through the barred window. She saw the bulky seated shadow of the guard. The smell of his pipe turned her stomach. With a sickening plunge of her heart she remembered where she was. Not at the Temple any more, but in this damp evil-smelling cell at the Conciergerie. Louis had spoken those words on the night of January 20th, 1793; today was October 16th. Memory was excellent now, clear, cold, exact.

She rose slowly from the bed. The guard made no sign of moving but she knew his eyes were following her as she went quietly to the window. The last few hours of life . . . Tears filled her eyes; her body shook, not with grief or self-pity, but a sudden spasm of fury. She felt anger against everybody, everything; those who had sentenced her, the guard, the broken armchair, the small rough table on which two candles stood, burning still, the iron bedstead, the straw palliasse.

The anger spent, she shuddered and went back to the bed. She lay there rigid, her eyes closed. Memory, beyond control now, drifted back over the timeless months. What a mockery to remember that friends had appeared after Louis' death, there in the Temple itself. The kitchen-hand, for instance, who brought up the meals, he had smuggled in messages written on tiny scraps of paper wrapped round the stoppers of the wine bottles. Thus she had learned how Louis had died, calmly and with great courage, and thus she had learned that Axel was planning a daring rescue, a dash into Paris with light cavalry. Another friend, one of the four commissioners set to watch over her, had hatched a scheme, but nothing had come of it, while yet another had planned an escape, even here in the Conciergerie, but he for his pains had gone to the guillotine.

She began in her mind to write a last letter to Axel.

368

"Dearest Axel, the agony of waiting is nearly at an end. I know now Brunswick will never come. I even know that my own Austria cares not whether I live or die . . ."

She assembled two dates in her mind.

"They came to the Temple, Axel, on the night of July 3rd and took my son from me. I cursed them and left the marks of my nails on their faces. In the interests of public safety, they said, he was to be removed from my polluting influence. I still cursed and fought, but I must have done so in desperate silence, for my son remained sleeping and undisturbed. While four men held me a fifth carried him away. They put him in another part of the Temple. I never spoke to him again. They gave him a tutor, a former shoemaker. He is to be brought up as a good republican. He is only eight. They will teach him to forget me. Once, with an air of triumph, they allowed me a distant glimpse of him. He was playing in the courtyard and looked quite happy . . .

"They came again on the night of August 2nd. I was in bed. The Widow Capet, they said, must get up. They made me dress in the widow's weeds they had given me earlier. They allowed me to see my daughter and my sister-in-law. No words were spoken. We embraced in silence, we parted in silence. They brought me to this prison, the Conciergerie. The first cell was larger, with a partition between me and the guard."

She remembered another date, October 12th.

"That was only four days ago, Axel. I sat between two guards while the public prosecutor and the president of the Revolutionary Tribunal asked me questions. They addressed me, of course, as the Widow Capet. Well, why not? Marie Antoinette of France was said to be beautiful, gay, imperious, haughty. The Widow Capet —I have seen her many times in my mirror—has a white mask of a face framed in white hair, and on her head a white bonnet covered with shabby black lace. She is the same age as the beautiful Queen who died so long ago. She is thirty-eight. The questions were accusations. They said the Widow Capet had forced Louis Capet to deceive the people and shed their blood. I remember that in her answers the Widow Capet, if no longer beautiful like the dead Queen, was just as haughty."

There was another date.

"October 14th, Axel, the beginning of the trial of the Widow Capet, the charge, high treason. The trial went on all day and was renewed the next day, which was yesterday. So many accusations,

Axel, and one which went beyond the vilest infamy. They showed her a document to which her son had put a pathetic scrawl of a signature, and with a frozen horror she read the words they had put into his mouth, words which described how she had taught him abominable practices. The pattern set so long ago by Provence and Madame Adelaide had been repeated to the end with even grosser lies.

"The sentence of death, decided so long ago by so many, was pronounced at four o'clock this morning. The Widow Capet was brought back to her cell. They gave her a pen, ink and paper. She wrote a letter to Madame Elizabeth. Then she slept for a short time, and when she woke she remembered she had once been Queen of France.

"I can say no more, Axel, except that I love you dearly. I have Louis to thank for that early, brief splendor, unreal as it seems now; and you to thank for that brief, full happiness."

She saw as she lay waiting that more daylight had filled the cell with a paler grayness. The two candles, burning low on the table, shone like stars through a mist of cloud. The door opened and the kitchen-maid was allowed to offer her a bowl of soup. She refused it at first, then to please the girl, who had always been kind and was weeping now, she took a little.

With her eyes fixed on the candles she began to dress. Only by staring at the candles was she able to ignore the guard who refused her privacy for this last toilette.

He raised his voice once. "No widow's weeds, Citizeness."

She remembered the order, issued on her return to the cell. Widow's weeds on the scaffold might cause a sudden rising of the unpredictable French emotion. So, to the guillotine in what was no more than a long white shift. For her shoulders a white *fichu*, for her head the white bonnet without the shabby black lace.

A priest stood before her.

She looked at him stonily. "You have of course taken the civil oath?"

"Of course. It was expedient."

"So, it seems, is my death. I have no need of you."

"Nevertheless, my orders are to remain at your side."

"As you wish. A godless priest must obey a godless republic."

She sat on the bed, clasped her hands in her lap and waited. After a few moments, remembering Louis' words, she knelt and tried to pray. She was still kneeling when she heard the tramp of feet outside the cell. She rose to her feet and faced the men who entered. There were five of them, the four judges and the recorder. She noticed incuriously that the recorder's voice trembled as he read the sentence. When he had finished she pointed a finger at the five of them.

"Citizens, you forget yourselves. You have taken off your hats."

They shuffled their feet and fingered their hats.

A tall young man strode into the room.

"Are you the executioner?" she asked.

"Yes."

"It was you who attended his Majesty the King?"

"That was my father." The young man's eyes wavered. "He died three months ago."

"I can only wish his successor, in what must be an honored trade these days, a longer life."

The executioner flinched, stepped closer and prepared himself for his task. Marie Antoinette glanced back at the table. The candles had gone out. The acrid smell filled her nostrils. Was this the smell of death? She looked at the young man again.

"Make all the haste you can."

She had the strangest feeling that all this had happened before. She grew more convinced of it as the executioner tied her hands and clipped off her hair, as she drove through the crowded streets, as she reached the Place de la Revolution. She knew she had heard the laughter before, the gay light-hearted laughter of a young girl dressed in white, a girl with red-gold hair, a pretty face with a promise of beauty in it, and so much haughtiness. She searched the scaffold. Surely such a girl had been dancing there. A delusion, no more. But she could see Louis, his cheeks tear-stained, his lips mouthing the words, *Faith in God, lift up your eyes to heaven.* And Axel too, waving at the end of a corridor.

Hands reached out roughly. She found herself lying face down on a plank. She heard the voice of the priest whose services she had refused.

"Courage, courage . . ."

"Courage!" she echoed indignantly. "I need it no longer. Have courage yourself. It is life that calls for courage, not death."